3

The Kabbalist: a cinematic novel

Published by ARI Publishers
www.ariresearch.org hq@ariresearch.org
1057 Steeles Avenue West, Suite 532, Toronto, ON, M2R 3X1, Canada
2009 85th Street #51, Brooklyn, New York, 11214, USA

Printed in Canada

ISBN: 978-1-897448-75-5

Library of Congress Control Number: 2012936447

Translation: Avraham Cohen, Yana Balyasny
Associate Editors: Leah Goldberg, Gianni Conti, Mary Miesem
Copy Editor: Claire Gerus
Design: Alexander Mochin
Layout: Baruch Khovov
Executive Editor: Chaim Ratz
Printing and Post Production: Uri Laitman

FIRST EDITION: JANUARY 2013
First printing

the K

2

This novel is about Baal HaSulam, one of the greatest Kabbalists of all time.

Baal HaSulam climbed all 125 levels of spiritual attainment.

He obtained a complete connection with the power that governs the world.

He lived in the 20th century and foresaw all that has happened.

He passionately desired to save humankind from future disasters and affliction.

That is why he wrote for us a complete interpretation of *The Book of Zohar*.

We can observe the actions of a Kabbalist, but it is practically impossible to penetrate his inner world.

This story is an attempt to understand the inner man and to show that there are no miracles besides that of a person transforming himself.

the Kabbalist

1

A CINEMATIC NOVEL

LAITMAN
KABBALAH
PUBLISHERS

To Michael Laitman-
the teacher of our generation

by Semion Vinokur

the Kabbalist

... A story about the most mysterious personality of the 20th century...

Warsaw – end of the 19th century – night.
A lone street light illuminates the empty street.
Wind and rain blow along the deserted streets.
Suddenly, a man screams. A woman's voice responds immediately:

-Simcha, what happened?!

Rain pours over a two-story building; inside, a window on the second floor is dimly lit.

A woman's voice: Don't scare me! What did you dream about?

Simcha's voice: You will give birth to a son.

A woman's voice: You dreamed about our boy?! Speak!

Room. Night. An open book is lying on the table.

Simcha's voice: Six letters came out of this book and formed one word.

A woman's voice (*exhausted*): It's all because we keep this book in our home. Rabbi Feldman asked you to take it as far away as possible... as far as you can....

A woman's hand reaches for the book, but a man's hand touches it and stops hers from reaching it.

Simcha's voice: The Creator will shake this boy's hand.

Just as he utters these words, there is a loud knock on the window.
Now it's the woman who screams.
A white bird is resting on the windowsill.
It takes off, soars over a bench, and disappears into the darkness of the night.

A man dressed in a black coat is sitting outside on the bench in the pouring rain. Water is pouring down his hat onto an open book in his hands. The man lifts his head and looks up at the window on the second floor. He looks like Baal HaSulam in his later years.

***

On September 5,1886, a son is born into Simcha Halevi Ashlag's family.
A woman's hands lift up a tiny wrinkled baby boy.
The baby cries out silently, as if sighing,
then stops and grows quiet.

A woman's voice: Look at him, he's not crying. Shake him!

Whirling white walls… white ceiling… windows…
blurred faces of women.

A woman's voice: What are you looking at?! What is he looking at? What does he see on that wall?

A second woman's voice *(quietly)*: Or maybe behind it?

The newborn is silently lying in the cradle looking at the ceiling with wise, adult eyes.

***

A synagogue – daytime.
Rabbi Feldman bends over the child.
A circumcision knife glitters briefly in his hand.
A moment later he throws the foreskin onto the sand.
He looks at the baby with bewilderment. The infant is not crying.
Rabbi Feldman lifts him and hands him over to his father, concluding the service with the words:

- … Let him be known in Israel as… *(looks at Simcha)*

Simcha: Yehuda Leib.

Rabbi Feldman: Yehuda Leib, son of Halevi Ashlag *(and adds)* - the child who doesn't cry.

***

Ashlag family home. Morning.
Three-year-old Yehuda is sitting at the table.
His father is watching him from a distance.
Yehuda's small finger moves along the lines of an open book.
Yehuda's voice is heard:

- "These gates have one lock and a narrow opening to insert the key. It is said about that secret: 'in the beginning, God created…'"

***

Yehuda and his father are walking down the street.
Yehuda is holding his father's hand.

Yehuda's voice echoes while fading into the distance:

- "The key is a master of six gates; it locks and it unlocks six gates. 'In the beginning God created the heaven and the earth.'"

They walk into the synagogue past a long line of old books, and approach Rabbi Feldman, who is watching them closely.

Simcha: I need your advice, honorable Rabbi. Yehuda, you can go and browse the books.

Yehuda walks toward the books.
While he is walking we hear his father whispering:

- We are very worried about him. Sometimes we have a feeling that he is older than we are.

Yehuda is walking along the bookshelves, examining the black book covers. Rabbi Feldman's gaze is fixed on him.
Suddenly Yehuda stops next to an old tattered book.
Rabbi Feldman jumps up and quickly walks over to the boy, stopping behind him. He mutters:

-*The Book of Zohar*... I see.

He turns and quickly walks back.
He stops next to a window and calls Simcha.

Rabbi Feldman: Do you confirm that you have *The Book of Zohar* in your home?

Simcha (*under Rabbi Feldman's piercing stare)*: Yes, I do. It's a gift from my wife's father.

Rabbi Feldman: Unfortunate soul! Hide it, and as far away as possible.

Rabbi Feldman brings his face very, very close to Simcha's and whispers:

I want your son to be a Jew, and this book will lead him away from the path of Torah. He doesn't understand what is written there, does he? He doesn't understand, right?

Simcha: I have a feeling he does.

Rabbi Feldman glances back at Yehuda.
Yehuda is struggling to hold the heavy book in his hands, opened to the first pages.
He reads it, syllable by syllable, moving his lips:

- "Every day the voice calls upon all the people in the world: 'it depends on you. Separate a part from what's yours to the Creator...'"

Rabbi Feldman: Nonsense. If grownups can't master it, what can this child understand? How old is he?

Simcha: Three years old.

Rabbi Feldman sees Yehuda turning the page and hears his voice:

- "There are fire, water, and air, the first three days of creation."

Rabbi Feldman *(sighs)*: Hide the book, as quickly as possible! Now!

Ashlag family home. Yehuda's room.
Simcha is standing on a chair pushing the book into the far end of the uppermost shelf. Then he looks over his shoulder, jumps from the chair, and walks out of the room.

***

Heider.[1] Morning.
Shmuel, the teacher, is walking along the aisle between rows of long desks with little children sitting behind them. Their feet dangle above the floor, and their eyes are following the teacher's pointer stick.

Monotonously repeating after him, the children recite a quote from the weekly Torah portion:

- "Terah lived seventy years and became the father of Abram, Nahor, and Haran. Now these are the records of the generations of Terah. Terah became the father of Abram, Nahor, and Haran. Haran became the father of Lot..."

Secretly, Yehuda takes an apple out of his pocket. The teacher's long pointer stick hits his hand immediately.
Yehuda screams as the apple rolls on the floor.
The teacher brings the pointer next to Yehuda's lips.

1 A *Heider* (Hebrew: A room) is a small classroom, the orthodox Jews' equivalent of elementary school.

The teacher: Find the strength to kiss the stick that beats you, Yehuda.

Yehuda turns away.

The teacher *(firmly)*: In that case, Yehuda, you will have to ask the Creator for the strength to kiss it.

The pointer lingers before Yehuda's eyes.
Yehuda bows his head, but the teacher does not concede.
The end of the pointer touches Yehuda's lips again.

The teacher (*insisting*): Well, do it!

Yehuda gives in.
He kisses the pointer, and it immediately flies over the children's heads. The teacher walks away.
The children monotonously recite:

- "Terah lived seventy years, and became the father of Abram, Nahor, and Haran..."

Yehuda's friend, Yankele,[2] sits at his side.
As soon as the teacher turns away, Yankele picks up the apple and puts it back in Yehuda's pocket.

***

Warsaw. The Jewish quarter. Yehuda and Yankele are walking down the street taking turns biting the apple.
Yehuda drags Yankele around the corner, and after a few steps they wind up at the entrance to an odd-looking shop.
Books line the walls from floor to ceiling in the dimly lit store.
Yehuda dives inside, walks past an old man sleeping against the wall, and sits down at a large wooden table in front of a pile of books.
He flips through the pages as if photographing them.
Yankele observes him with a mixture of awe and fear.

Yankele: God gave you such powers, Yehuda.

The pile of books in front of Yehuda is quickly disappearing. One last book remains.

-I don't know who gave them to me, Yehuda mumbles.

2 "Le" is a common suffix to a person's name used as a term of endearment.

Yankele: The Creator wants you to become a great rabbi so that you will teach others.

Yehuda (*putting down the book*): What do I have to teach them?

Yankele: To love God, to observe his commandments, to pray wholeheartedly, and to be a Jew.

Yehuda: Who told you all that?

Yankele: It's written in all our books.

Yehuda (*irritably*): I don't know. I don't know what's written in these books!

An old raspy voice comes from behind Yehuda:

- Old Solomon prepared you a good portion.

Old Solomon approaches the kids, shuffling along in his shabby old slippers.

Solomon (*in awe*): What, you have read them all already?!

Yehuda: Solomon, where is...

Solomon (spreads his hands): Old Solomon does not have this book. Solomon searched everywhere; he looked into places he had never looked before.

He points his finger up.

Up there, on the shakiest shelf Solomon found the letters of Ramak.[3] And over there (he turns sharply), in the spider's corner, he found the great Ramchal.[4]

Solomon stops in front of Yehuda and spreads his hands.

-But he couldn't find *The Zohar* anywhere.

Solomon turns around abruptly and starts walking along the bookshelves.
He appears to be talking to himself.

---

3 Ramak – Rav Moshe Kordovero (1522-1570), a great Kabbalist. Lived and taught in Safed (a Kabbalists' town in Northern Israel). The title Rav, as opposed to Rabbi, will be used throughout the book to indicate one's being not just an ordained rabbi, but also a Kabbalist.

4 Ramchal – Rav Moshe Chaim Luzzatto (1707-1747), a great Kabbalist. Lived and taught in Italy and Holland.

-But it was here, I can swear! Old Berele brought it to Solomon.

He sits at the table and slams his hand onto it.

-Berele told Solomon: "Save this book for little Yehudale."

Solomon's voice grows softer.

-So where is it, I'm asking you, Solomon, you old fool?!

Solomon grows silent.
Yankele looks back.
The old man is sleeping in his place.

Yehuda is lost in the book.
Everything disappears for him.

Yankele: I have all kinds of thoughts about God, too, Yehuda. I, too, have an opinion.

Yehuda doesn't answer. Yankele continues:

Don't think that there aren't others like you.

Yehuda is silent.
His mind is somewhere else.
Yankele walks out of the store.

***

The Jewish quarter. Daytime.
After taking just a few steps, Yankele hears Simcha's voice calling him from across the street.

Simcha: Where is Yehuda? Do you know where he is, Yankele?

Yankele steps up his pace as he walks away pretending not to hear him.
Simcha chases him, crossing the street.

-"Where is Yehuda?"- He asks. "He didn't come back from school."

-"Your Yehuda is sitting in a bookstore with an old man who mumbles to himself and is reading forbidden books."- Yankele answers abruptly and angrily.

***

The bookstore.
A shadow appears over Yehuda, who is lost in a book.

Simcha's voice: Come, Yehuda. That's enough.

Yehuda looks up at his father.

Simcha: Your mother and I are worried about our boy!

Solomon's voice is heard from the corner:

-Spare him your foolish care. He has been under the Creator's care for a long time already.

Simcha grabs hold of Yehuda's hand and sharply Yanks him. They walk past Solomon.
Solomon stealthily reaches out to touch Yehuda's clothes … and then kisses his hand.

***

Heider. The morning sun's rays seem to be dancing on the tables.
Yehuda is surrounded by a crowd of children. He is blindfolded.

A child's voice: Page nine, row thirteen from the top.

Without a moment's hesitation, Yehuda recites by heart a text from the Torah:

- "And God saw that the wickedness of man was great in the earth..."

A child's finger moves along the line of text.
Someone says with admiration: Yes!
They flip a few pages forward and another child continues:

-Page fifteen, third line from the bottom.

Yehuda *(instantly)*: - "And they said, come, let us build ourselves a city, and a tower, whose top may reach unto heaven..."

The children (*in awe*): Wooooow!

Suddenly, Yankele raises a long needle and smashes it into the book – precisely into the letter kaf. The needle penetrates the book, page after page.

Yankele: Take off the blindfold!

Yehuda takes off the blindfold and looks at the letter *kaf*.

Yankele: Well?!

Yehuda: *Samekh.*

Yankele turns the page.
The letter "*samekh*" is pierced through by the needle.
An admiring whisper: Right.

The children *(in unison)*: Wooooow!

Yankele: Next!

Yehuda: *Het.*

Yankele turns over the next page… and everyone sees: The needle has gone through the letter "*het.*"

- "Wooooow! More!" Urge the children.

Yankele: Next!

Yehuda: *Peh.*

He turns another page.
He's right, it's "*peh.*"

The children (*shouting unrestrained*): Woooooooow!

Yehuda continues:

-*Mem, dalet, aleph, bet…*

Suddenly the voice of Shmuel, the teacher, is heard.

-Well done, Yehuda!

The teacher stands at the door looking down at Yehuda.

The teacher: Many great *Hassidim*[5] knew the Torah so well that it appeared to them in their dreams, word for word, letter by letter. You will become a great *hassid*, Yehuda, if you bring your big "I" under control.

The teacher approaches Yehuda and strokes his head.

-The Creator guides us the same way, Yehuda. One day you get the stick, the next day – a candy.

5 *Hassidim* (pl. for *Hassid*) – pious followers.

The teacher takes out a lollipop covered with tobacco crumbs from his pocket and gives it to Yehuda.
The children's eyes are all fixed on this treat, which appears to them as the most delicious thing in the world.

The teacher: Everything he does is because he loves us.

The teacher looks at the class: Learn to love Him, children, and you'll see that our God is always with you whether you are good or bad.

Yehuda sees the eyes of the other children burning with envy and puts the candy on the table, away from him.

The teacher: No, no, no, Yehuda. Eat it. You deserve it. And all the others have earned the privilege of watching you eat it. Maybe their envy will make them know the Torah as well as you.

Yehuda: Why know it like that?

The teacher: What do you mean?

Yehuda: I know it by heart, every line, each word. So what?

The teacher: We-ell, Yehuda, it's strange to hear such a question from you.

(Suspiciously) Are you doing it on purpose? I have a feeling that you want to check my knowledge, Yehuda? Don't.

Yehuda (*very clearly*): I really don't get it. Why do I have to know this book by heart?

The teacher: To observe the laws and commandments, one should learn them by heart.

Yehuda: Why observe them?

The children turn their eyes from the teacher to Yehuda, then from Yehuda back to the teacher. They are scared.

The teacher (*firmly*): So as to be the chosen people (*he quotes, lifting the pointer stick above his head*): "You will be unto Me a kingdom of priests and a holy nation" (Exodus, 19:6). This is what is written, "And all the people answered with one voice and said, 'All the words which the Lord has spoken we will do'" (Exodus 24:3). Do you remember?

Yehuda: Yes, I do.

Yehuda is pale but doesn't look away from the teacher.

The teacher: What is it that you don't understand, Yehuda?

Yehuda *(quietly)*: I don't understand... why I was born.

A silent pause. The teacher Shmuel looks at Yehuda.

The teacher: You were born to observe the laws of God almighty.

Yehuda: I don't understand who He is. What is God?

The teacher: I don't understand your question.

Yehuda: I have never seen him, what He is like.

The teacher: Your forefathers and Moses saw him on Mount Sinai.

He quotes again, waving with the pointer:

"Moses then went up, along with Aaron, Nadav, and Avihu, and seventy of the elders of Israel" (Exodus, 24:1). "And they saw the God of Israel" (Exodus, 24:10).

The teacher suddenly points his finger at Yehuda:

-Continue!

Yehuda: "and they saw God, and they ate and drank" (Exodus, 24: 11).

The teacher: Well, you know everything. Why are you asking questions then?!

Yehuda: I don't know anything. I don't want to know. I want to...

He falls silent. His breath grows fast and shallow.

The teacher *(impatiently)*: Well?

Yehuda: I want to ...feel. I want to ... meet Him. See Him! I want to know who He is - our God, if He exists. I want to know what stands behind all these words.

The teacher watches Yehuda with his mouth open.
All the children are stunned.

The teacher *(barely coming to his senses, very slowly):* I think, Yehuda, that you'd better leave the classroom.
(And suddenly screams) Out! Get out!

***

Warsaw. A street in the Jewish quarter.
Yehuda walks along the street. He doesn't notice street merchants laying out their goods or the old beggar sleeping in a puddle or the mad violinist playing on one string. Yehuda is immersed in his thoughts. He crosses the road and suddenly hears a scream:

-Whoa! Whoa!

A horse's head hovers above him; the face of a redheaded coachman appears behind it.

Coachman: Are you tired of this life?!

Yehuda turns around, startled, and runs down the street. Store signs flash by, people's eyes follow him. He turns around the corner and bumps into Yankele. They both fall on the ground. Without getting up, whispers to Yehuda:

-Don't go home. The teacher is there.

Yehuda jumps to his feet, Yankele follows him.
Yehuda tries to walk around him.
Yankele grabs the sleeve of Yehuda's shirt:

-I know a place not far from here. We can wait there.

Yehuda pulls free and heads home.
Yankele runs after him.
He looks around and whispers, pressing himself to Yehuda:

-There is no God. I am with you, Yehuda.

***

Ashlag family home.
Yehuda opens the door.
In the far end of the room, his parents and Shmuel, the teacher, are sitting together.
The teacher is waving his hands.
His hands stop in mid-air when he sees Yehuda.
Yehuda walks past them into his room, separated by a thin partition.
He sits on his bed and hears the teacher's hushed words:

-Yes, I am blaming you. Who else should I blame?

Yehuda lies down and covers his face with a pillow.
There is silence. He looks at a pillow feather that sways back and forth to the rhythm of his breath.
He hears light footsteps.
Someone is sitting on the bed next to him. Someone's hand removes the pillow from his face.
Yehuda sees his father with his mother standing nearby.
His father tucks in his blanket.
His mother leans down and kisses him.
Yehuda desperately pleads with his eyes and whispers almost inaudibly:

-I don't know what I am living for.

His father looks at him, terrified:

-You are our son. You are only five, Yehuda! You are forever our little beloved son. Nobody thinks about such things at your age!

Yehuda sits up restlessly, leans forward to Simcha, and whispers, looking straight into his eyes:

-I don't want to live.

Simcha glances back at his wife, who is covering her mouth with her hand. Simcha turns back to look at his son.

-There is no greater sin, my poor, poor boy. It's not easy living in this world, especially for us Jews. But such is the world the Creator has given us. Children are meant to be happy in this world... (with anguish) Why are you robbed of your childhood? Why are you so mature? Why?!

His mother leaves the room. We can hear the sound of her muffled sobs.

Simcha: We will go to Rabbi Feldman tomorrow and you will tell him everything. Get some sleep now. Sleep and don't think about anything but the Creator. He is always with you.

Simcha stands up.
The door closes behind him, and only the moon casts a faint light on the windowsill, the table, and the white linen.
Yehuda's hands rest on the blanket.

Yehuda observes the cold crescent of the moon peering into the room, then turns his eyes to the ceiling.
The ceiling is covered with circles of accumulated moisture.
A black point sticks out in the middle of the circles.

Yehuda *(counting the circles)*: One, two, three, four...

He closes his eyes.
Suddenly he hits the wall, moaning with despair.
The thin wall shudders from the blow.
The bookshelves hanging above the bed shake, and slowly a book comes tumbling down from above.
The book falls on Yehuda, its pages flapping like a huge bird with white wings.

The book falls down on him in slow motion and covers his face entirely.
Darkness falls.
Yehuda sighs with relief. His face becomes lit with joy for the first time in a long time.
We can hear only the boy's breathing.

Yehuda's face is under the book.
He sees letters very close up.
They float out of focus and seem very large.

Yehuda carefully lifts up the book.
He holds it with his arms stretched out.
His lips are moving and we hear him whispering:

-"...And he said: "for the one who wishes to come unto me, let it be the first gates on his way to me. Who enters these gates, enters..."

The boy is reading.
The darkness of the night is chased away by the dawn's light outside the window.

***

Early morning.
Street cleaners are cleaning the streets.

A candle is burning in the second floor window of the old house.
It is the candle in Yehuda's room.

Morning sounds permeate the room: The creak of a trolley, the yell of a coachman, the rustle of brooms on the pavement.
But Yehuda does not hear them.
He is sitting up in bed avidly reading the book.
The door opens and his father enters the room.

Yehuda slowly looks up. He is silent.
Simcha sits next to his son and hugs him.
He sees the name of the book that lies on his son's knees.

Simcha: So you've found it?

Yehuda: Yes.

Simcha: Have you read it?

Yehuda: Yes.

Simcha: All of it?

Yehuda: Yes.

Simcha: Did you understand anything?

Yehuda: I understood that it contains everything.

His father shifts his glance to the book, then back to Yehuda. He sighs.

-I heard that you can go insane by reading it, and that you can't read it until you fill yourself with all the wisdom of the holy Torah, and that you can't come close to it before you turn forty. People say a lot of things. I've never tried to read it. You've read it and even understood something. You opened it when you were three. I was ordered to hide it, so I did. But you found it again. Well, I suppose that is how it's meant to be.

***

Morning. Synagogue.
Simcha and Yehuda stand before Rabbi Feldman.

Rabbi Feldman: So he's found it after all, and even understood something?

Yehuda: It fell on me from the top shelf. I've read it and understood only that it is my book. It was written for me.

Rabbi Feldman stares at Yehuda for a long time, then gestures at two empty chairs next to his table.
Yehuda sits down closer to Rabbi Feldman; Simcha sits down behind him.

Rabbi Feldman: I want to tell you, Simcha, that there are people whom you can't restrain by force. You can't hide anything from them, either. They say that such people have a "point in the heart."[6] The Creator treats these people in a special way. They, too, have a special attitude toward the Creator.

Rabbi Feldman shifts his glance to Yehuda.

Rabbi Feldman: How they come into this world and how this great book finds them is beyond our understanding.

Rabbi Feldman is lost in thought. His unfocused gaze wandering somewhere behind Yehuda and Simcha.

Rabbi Feldman: I saw only one such a man in my life. His name was Mehachem Mendel of Kotzk.[7]

Rabbi Feldman shakes his head. His eyes suddenly well up with tears and his voice is full of longing:

-A *truly* great soul burned within him. He strove to reach the Creator, casting aside anything that stood in his way. And everybody. His disciples followed him but fell along the way, unable to withstand that unbearable burning. He had no mercy, neither for himself nor for them. He wanted only the Creator.

Yehuda watches Rabbi Feldman keenly.
Rabbi Feldman shakes his head:

---

6 A point in the heart is a special kind of emptiness and lack of satisfaction that appears in a person's heart, compelling that person to search for answers to the questions about the meaning of life. This is how the Creator leads someone towards Him.

7 Rabbi Menachem Mendel of Kotzk (1788 – 1859), a great Kabbalist who formed one of the most famous Kabbalah groups.

Rabbi Feldman: No, Yehuda, he is not with us anymore. People say that he never left his room during the last twenty years of his life. What went on in there no one knows. He died without saying a word, not even to his closest students.

Rabbi Feldman falls silent. He looks at Yehuda, then at Simcha:

Rabbi Feldman: I know one of them.

Yehuda eagerly leans forward.

Rabbi Feldman: Relax, Yehuda, I doubt he would take you. He is a strange man, and my word means nothing to him. But before we decide anything, I want your poor father to know that he is choosing a life of hardship for you. Let your father know it and then decide.

Yehuda looks pleadingly at his father. His father stares at Rabbi Feldman.
Rabbi Feldman stands up and walks in the direction of the books.
He pretends to browse them, observing the father and son out of the corner of his eye.

Simcha is silent for a long time.
Yehuda is also silent.
A minute, two, three pass by.
Finally, Simcha looks up at Rabbi Feldman.

Simcha: What is his name?

Rabbi Feldman: Baruch.

Simcha: How can we find this Baruch?

***

Simcha and Yehuda are walking along a narrow country road between a field and a forest.
It is spring time; birds are singing in the sky.
The road leads to a small village.
Its little wooden houses, blackened by rain water, appear in the distance.

A lone house stands at the edge of the forest.
It seems deserted. The windows are boarded shut.
Simcha walks up to the door, knocks, but no one answers.
Simcha walks around the house, returns to Yehuda.
Yehuda is staring, eyes wide open, at the boarded window.

Simcha looks intently at the same place and suddenly sees through the cracks in the planks a pair of strikingly blue eyes following him, studying him closely.
Simcha opens his mouth slightly, bewildered; he wants to say something, but before he can, a high-pitched, squeaky voice of a stranger says:

-I will take a dozen eggs, two tomatoes, and half a loaf of bread. The door opens. Let the little Jew in, and you stay there.

Simcha *(indignant)*: No, I'll come in with him.

The voice: Then nobody will come in. Go back where you came from!

Yehuda squeezes his father's hand and looks at him pleadingly.

Simcha *(in doubt)*: Well, how can I... let you go in there alone?

He falls silent after seeing Yehuda's eyes.
Yehuda takes a step forward, opens the door, and disappears inside.

Simcha presses himself against the boarded window.
Through the cracks he can make out a squalid room and a large, crudely made table standing at its center.
Simcha sees Yehuda at the table and the disheveled old man, Baruch, across from him.

Simcha can hear the high-pitched voice of the old man.

-Believe no one. Test everything yourself. Everything that they call faith out there is nonsense.

Simcha shakes his head in anguish.

Baruch: They told you the Creator exists. Don't believe it!

Simcha strains to see into the room through the cracks and his eyes fill with tears of hopelessness and fear.

Simcha sees Baruch leaning over Yehuda.

Baruch: Find Him yourself. Faith is a knowledge of the heart. Feel Him yourself! Got it?

Yehuda: Yes.

Simcha covers his ears with his hands, turns, and quickly walks away from the house.

In the room, Baruch stands up and starts walking in circles around Yehuda, then suddenly stops in front of Yehuda.

Baruch: Have you ever seen a man turn into a bird?

Yehuda: No, I haven't.

Baruch: Do you believe it can happen?

Yehuda: No, I don't.

Baruch: You don't believe in miracles, huh? Very well. Right you are. Don't.

Baruch's face is very close to Yehuda's.
All of a sudden he turns sharply and walks up to the wall and stops.
Yehuda is watching him intently.
He sees the right shoulder of Baruch begin to shiver.
There is the sound of cloth being torn. Before Yehuda's eyes, the old man's tattered shirt rips apart.
Suddenly, a white wing lashes out and starts to flutter, as if trying to lift Baruch off the floor.

Yehuda freezes. He is barely breathing, terrified.

Then, a second wing tears through the shirt, shivering, as if in agony. Then both wings viciously pound the air, stirring powerful gusts of wind. The gusts tear away the cobwebs in the corners and raise the age-old dust from the floor; an empty bucket clangs somewhere.

Baruch turns to face Yehuda. Stunned, Yehuda sees a long beak where Baruch's nose used to be, piercing button-like eyes and a yellow-red tuft of feathers sticking up on the top of his head.

Yehuda's back freezes in fear.

He sees Baruch's legs turn into the strong, muscular legs of a large bird. Bird-Baruch screams and gushes past Yehuda into the sealed window. The boards covering the window shatter into tiny splinters.

Yehuda sees how a large white bird tears away from the house and, slowly beating its powerful wings, climbs toward the setting sun.
It rockets past Simcha, who is walking in the field.
Barely touching the tips of the trees, bird-Baruch flies past the forest toward the sunset.

Yehuda cannot move.

***

All is chaos in the house.
In the corner, a spider hangs by the thread of a cobweb.
All is absolute stillness.

Suddenly, everything becomes blurry in Yehuda's eyes, and when the scene comes back into focus, Yehuda sees Baruch's face, still close to his.

Baruch: Have you seen it?

Yehuda (*whispering*): Yes, I have.

Baruch: Do you believe it now?

Yehuda (*trying to swallow a lump stuck in his throat*): Y-yes, I do.

Baruch: What do you believe in, *(Baruch leans lower)* this nonsense?!

Yehuda *(stuttering)*: But I…I saw…

Baruch: What did you see?

Yehuda: A bird.

Baruch: What bird?

Yehuda: A huge… bird.

Baruch: What if I tell you that nothing happened, you foolish little Jew?

Yehuda: But I … saw it … myself. You turned into…

Baruch: What if I tell you that what you saw was a trick?!

Yehuda: A trick?!

Baruch: Yes! A simple hocus pocus! A cheap trick!

Yehuda: A trick?!

Baruch: That was enough to lead you away from the Creator.

Yehuda's hands begin to shake.

Baruch *(as if not noticing his condition)*: You were weak. You fell for a cheap trick and gave it a great definition: Faith.

Now Yehuda's lips tremble.

-Never do this again, you hear me! - Baruch suddenly yells at him. – Remember! You have to become strong! And understand - there are no miracles in this world! All the miracles in this world are nothing more than cheap tricks!

Baruch towers over Yehuda.

-Tricks! You hear me?

Yehuda's face is frozen in fear.
His eyes look at Baruch pleadingly.

All of a sudden, Baruch goes limp and sits down at the table wearily.
He looks into Yehuda's eyes.

-I used to know many such tricks, – he says. - I could manipulate people as I wished. And I did. Those fools, they were mesmerized and followed me anywhere I would lead them. I became famous. I made a fortune.

He pauses.
Suddenly he starts speaking clearly so Yehuda can hear every word:

Baruch: But the more I was sinking into this lie, the more I discovered an abyss between myself and the Creator. He was leaving me. Do you hear me, Yehuda? Do you hear me?

Yehuda (whispering): Yes.

Baruch: Faith is when the Creator appears to you. And you truly feel him, the way you feel me. He will appear to you only when you stop believing in all that nonsense: That some miracle can actually happen here in this world, on this earth. It can't.

Baruch stops talking. He rocks in his chair and looks at Yehuda.

Baruch: Why did you come to me? Because life treated you hard?

Yehuda: I was desperate.

Baruch: How so?

Yehuda: I didn't know what I was living for.

Baruch: Do you know now?

Yehuda: Yes, I do.

Baruch: Well... tell me. What is it you are living for?

Yehuda (*in doubt*): I want... I want... *(stops talking)*

Baruch: Well?

Yehuda: I want...

Baruch *(impatiently)*: Well, what do you want?

Yehuda *(exhales)*: I want to meet Him.

Baruch stops rocking in his chair and asks:

-What?

Yehuda: I want to meet Him.

Baruch *(quietly)*: You want to meet Him?

Yehuda: Yes.

Baruch *(louder)*: Him?

Yehuda: Yes.

Baruch (*in disdain)*: You-u-u-u... want to meet the King of the Universe?

Yehuda *(mutters)*: Yes.

Baruch *(crushingly)*: You sorry bug, you-u-u-u-u... Little drop of filth that believes in all the scum of this world?!

Baruch's face twists into a grimace. His mouth opens to swallow the air in big gulps.

-You want to meet Him?! Do you know what it means to meet Him?! Do you?!

Yehuda is silent, either out of fear or because he doesn't know what to say.

Baruch (*hisses*): It means to become worthy of this meeting.
Wor-thy!

He bears down on Yehuda again and asks him straight to his face:

-And what does it mean to become worthy of such a meeting?! The greatest, the wisest have failed! The best of the best!
Do you know that?

And without waiting for an answer, he exhales:

-The greatest, the wisest... those who gave up their lives for it...
He didn't accept them!

Baruch suddenly falls silent.
He again sees Yehuda's terrified face and his childish hands raised as if in defense.
Baruch silently gets up, towering over the boy.
A mouse is scurrying in the corner.
It's unusually quiet outside.

-Are you scared? – Asks Baruch.

-Yes, – Yehuda answers almost inaudibly.

-Good. The first commandment is fear. But you shouldn't fear me. Who am i? I am nothing. Fear Him!

Baruch sits down and turns his eyes from Yehuda to the soiled table top in front of him.
He forces himself to speak:

-You should be afraid... of disappointing Him.

Baruch's hands wrapped in a web of swollen veins are resting powerlessly on his knees. He sighs:

-You can't imagine how right you are, Yehuda. You discovered His plan. More than anything else, He wants that all of us would say what you just said: "we want to meet You; we can't live without You, and having said that, would do anything to make it happen!"

Through the cracks in the window one can see Simcha walking back toward the house. He approaches it and peers inside.
He sees Yehuda and Baruch sitting peacefully facing each other, and he too sits down onto a stack of firewood beneath the window.

He rocks silently as if in prayer.
The sun is setting behind the forest.

Inside the house, Baruch, silent and old, reaches below the table and takes out an old book in a tattered cover. He puts it on the table and covers it with his hand.

Baruch: Do you know this book?

Yehuda: This is *The Book of Zohar.*

Baruch: Have you read it?

Yehuda: Yes, I have.

Baruch: Did you understand it?

Yehuda: No.

Baruch: Did you feel it?

Yehuda: Yes, I did.

Baruch: What did you feel?

Yehuda: Warmth.

Baruch: This is good.... Warmth is very good. *The Book of Zohar* is humanity's greatest book, although people still don't realize it. (*Baruch is being restrained and soft now. He wants Yehuda to hear and to understand him.*) All of the holy books, Yehuda, were written by kabbalists. Kabbalists live in the spiritual worlds, while you, Yehuda, are here. They are writing to you personally, little Yehuda, from up there. Up there is the light, and here it is darkness. They describe to you, Yehuda, the path toward the light.

Baruch brings his face close to Yehuda's and whispers loudly:

-Yearn to come close to Him all the time. Do you hear me, Yehuda? Realize that if you do not succeed, nothing else is worth living for.

Baruch suddenly spreads out his arms and pronounces mysteriously:

-"2Nd century CE. Judea is under Roman rule. Like dogs, the Romans are searching everywhere, sniffing each trail, prowling every road, stopping every passerby."

***

Suddenly, a picture appears.
2[Nd] century Judea. Romans are running with their armor clanking.
Here they walk in the forest, lifting every bush.
Here they are pressing two old Jews against the wall, their spears pressing deeper and deeper into their flesh.

Baruch's voice: What are these dogs looking for? They are hunting for Rabbi Shimon bar Yochai,[8] the foremost student of the great Rabbi Akiva.[9]

Yehuda is watching Baruch, captivated.
Baruch, the great actor, impersonates every character in his story.

Baruch (*changing his voice*): Rabbi Akiva was executed horridly, publicly tortured to death. Now it's the turn of his prime disciple, Rabbi Shimon. "Exxxxx-ecute him! Execute him before the crowd!" - Scream the simpletons. "Skin him alive and let everybody see how their great sage moans, pleading for mercy! Their grea-a-a-a-t sage!"

A trail snakes up the side of a hill, dodging trees, through the forest and climbing up stony creeks, squeezing through winding passages, higher and higher.

Baruch's voice: Of course! Someone told the romans that the great one is none other than Rabbi Shimon. That he, together with his great son, Elazar, are undermining the roman rule. These roman dogs, tin heads, just can't figure out how two pitiful Jews could subvert the roman behemoth, the empire, the power! They can't grasp it, but they feel it!

The path is lost in the tall grass and suddenly reappears before the mouth of a cave.

- But their fears are justified. At that very moment, in a cramped, damp cave in the north of the land of Israel, a mighty force is being unleashed against all the evil that is and ever will be on the face of the earth.

A candle burns deep in the cave, barely lighting the bearded faces of the men sitting inside.

8 Rabbi Shimon bar Yochai (a.k.a. Rashbi) wrote with his nine students *The Book of Zohar*.
9 Rabbi Shimon's teacher and the greatest sage of his time. He coined the maxim, "Love your friend as yourself."

Yehuda hears Baruch's voice:

-Do you see the cave?

Yehuda: I do.

Baruch's voice: Is there anyone inside?

Yehuda: Yes. There are ten men. I see them.

Baruch's voice: What do you think they are doing there?

Yehuda: They are hiding from Romans.

Baruch's voice: Correct. And why is that?

Yehuda: I don't know.

Baruch voice: They are writing the great *Book of Zohar*, that's why they are there. (*Baruch's voice is calm and confident.*) They are writing the book that describes how the entire world and every single person in it can exit the filth of this world, exit the hatred toward each other, and learn how to truly, not for his own sake, Yehuda, but truly love.

Baruch nods his head and tries to animate his explanation with gestures.

-Love your neighbor, love the whoooooool e world, love everybody... love! And know, Yehuda, that love is not just a word. Love is not thinking of yourself, but only of others! It is living not for your own sake, but for the sake of others! This is love.

Baruch's eyes are burning; he is breathless with exhilaration.

-Do you understand, Yehuda, how sublime it is? It is so very high, my son! It makes my head spin! Just imagine, it all happened in the 2nd century, when the world was drowning in blood, when people were mowed down by epidemics like blades of grass. It was a time when power, fame, and wealth were the principal values in the world. Yet, at such a rotten time, ten scrawny, starving men were writing a book about love, about what they had attained. They were writing a book about your connection with the Creator, Yehuda.

Baruch is in front of him, shaking his head, as if amazed by his own words:

-What will you say to that, son?!

Yehuda is silent. What could one possibly say to that?!
He is looking at Baruch in admiration, and Baruch goes on:

-What are all these romans so afraid of? It's only a book, only a book about love. But they felt it, Yehuda, they felt that a tremendous force was being put into it, a force capable of transforming this filthy, unjust world entirely.

Baruch moves closer to Yehuda:

-And now answer me, Yehuda. How can this book possess such a power?

Yehuda *(quietly)*: Because they are not writing it alone.

Baruch *(pointing a finger at Yehuda)*: Well done!

Yehuda: It's because... the Creator is writing the book with them.

Baruch is looking at Yehuda.
From the window, Simcha is looking at Yehuda, too.
Baruch mutters:

-The lesson is over. Take him away.

***

A country road.
Yehuda and Simcha are following it toward a faraway forest.
Simcha is constantly leaning towards Yehuda and probing him with questions. Yehuda responds briefly, lost in his own thoughts.

It's cold. Simcha takes off his black frock coat and covers his son's thin shoulders. Yehuda doesn't resist.
The coat's flaps drag in the damp road.

Baruch's eyes are following them from behind the boarded window.

Yehuda turns back and sees Baruch's house swaying, its old wood squeaking in the wind.

***

The Ashlag family home.
Yehuda is resting in bed. Simcha covers him with a blanket.
As soon as the door closes behind Simcha, Yehuda slips out of bed and runs barefoot up to the table to pick up the book.
The door swings open immediately.

Simcha is standing at the doorstep.
Yehuda's mother is craning her neck from behind his back.

Simcha: We have agreed that you are going to sleep, haven't we, Yehuda?

Yehuda leaves the book on the table and returns to his bed without saying a word.

Simcha: Your mother and I can't bear it if you go insane.

Yehuda closes his eyes and sees…

***

2nd century. Judea. Cave.
A man's face is lit by a candle.
It is hard to tell his age because of his beard.
He is dictating something to another man who is obviously much younger than him.

Baruch's voice: Rabbi Shimon was dictating, and Rabbi Abba was writing. It's because only he, Rabbi Abba, could encrypt the words of Rabbi Shimon. You are asking why he was doing it. He was doing it so that no corrupt men would be able to misuse it. The book contained mighty powers. Tremendous! And yet, immediately following its completion, the book vanished for centuries.

***

Morning, in front of Baruch's home.
Simcha sits on the stack of firewood below the window. He can hear everything that's happening inside the house.

The Book of Zohar is resting on the table between Baruch and Yehuda. Yehuda sits, motionless, with his mouth half open, listening to Baruch.

Baruch: Is it interesting for you?

Yehuda: Yes, very much so.

Baruch: No, that's not the right word. Absolutely not! "Interesting," what kind of word is that? (*He mimics himself.*) "In-te-res-ting!" It is life for you, Yehuda! Here, Yehuda, it is written how you should live. How you, Yehuda, can reach the Creator, come to Him and tell Him: "I, Yehuda, have come to You! And the great *Book of Zohar* has led me to You."

***

10Th century CE. A colorful oriental bazaar.
The high-pitched calls of market vendors fill the air.
The crowd moves lazily about the market.

Baruch's voice: The book disappeared for centuries. People forgot that it ever existed. It showed up again only when there was a real need for it.

***

Suddenly the crowd in the marketplace parts.
A barefoot boy rushes through the market.
A breathless, screaming merchant is chasing him.
He shouts, gasping for air:

-Stop him, stop him!

Someone trips the boy, and he rolls into the dust.
The merchant crashes down on him then picks him up.
Pages of parchment fall from under the boy's clothes.

Baruch's voice: It emerged in the 10th century CE at the Safed marketplace. A boy was selling pages of the manuscript to merchants, who used the pages to wrap the spices they were selling. Many pages were lost this way until one sage recognized in these parchments the most precious thing on earth.

***

Baruch's home.

Baruch: That's right, Yehuda, *The Book of Zohar (raises his finger)* was used to wrap figs and candy. *(With excitement)* Huh?! A fine example of human life, Yehuda: Superficial and false to the core. Beauty conceals emptiness. Dirt hides wisdom, poverty masks a precious soul. Don't be misled by beauty, Yehuda, don't get carried off by flattery. Search for the inner meaning behind all things. Learn to live like that.

Baruch does not let Yehuda ponder it even for a second.

He opens the book in front of Yehuda.
It's tattered, even torn in a few places.
He gently caresses it.

Baruch *(gently)*: Many tried to solve its mystery. The smartest people in the world racked their brains over it until one day, 400 years ago, a boy was born. He became known as the Holy Ari.[10]

Baruch grows silent and fixes his eyes on Yehuda.
A minute passes.
Baruch keeps looking silently at the boy.

Yehuda: Why are you looking at me like that?

Baruch: He was the one who turned everything around. That boy.

***

15Th century. An old synagogue in Cairo, Egypt.
A 15-year-old boy, dressed in a long white robe, is praying.
Ten other people are praying inside.
One of them, a strange old man dressed in rags, stands by the window.
He is rocking, hunched over a book.

Baruch's voice: The Ari was three years old when he came to Egypt with his mother. When he was 15, he saw a strange-looking pauper in a synagogue. He was young and very curious.

The Ari approaches the pauper, stands behind him, and looks over his shoulder at the book the pauper is reading.
He notices that the pauper is holding the book upside down. It is neither a prayer book nor the Torah, but some other book in aramaic.[11]

The pauper turns to look at the Ari.
The Ari steps back in horror.
Two scars, instead of two eyes, are looking at him.

---

10 The ARI, an acronym for *Eloki* (Godly) Rabbi Itzhak (1534-1572), was born as Isaac Luria. He was born in Jerusalem, moved to Egypt, but worked and taught in Safed during the last 18 months of his short life. He founded what is now known as Lurianic Kabbalah, approaching Kabbalah from a scientific perspective. Like Rashbi, his books were not written by him, but by his prime disciple, Rav Chaim Vital.

11 *The Book of Zohar* was written in Aramaic. In his Sulam (Ladder) commentary, Yehuda Ashlag translated the book into Hebrew, as well as interpreted the meaning of the words for today's readers.

***

Baruch's home.

Baruch: Thus *The Zohar* came into the Ari's possession - from the hands of a marano,[12] made blind by the Spanish inquisition. He brought it with him to the Ari through all of Europe and Africa, enduring thirst, hunger, and exhaustion just to pass it on to the Ari. Truth be told, he was bound to bring it. In this world, Yehuda, everything is predetermined.

***

15th century Cairo. A synagogue.
The Ari opens the book and starts to read it avidly.
The blind pauper is sleeping on the bench next to him, finally at rest.
After many sleepless nights, he is smiling in his dream.

Baruch's voice: When did you discover *The Book of Zohar*?

Yehuda's voice: It fell on me when I was five.

Baruch's voice: It "fell" on the Ari when he was fifteen.

***

Baruch's home.
Baruch is gazing into Yehuda's face once again.

Yehuda: Why are you looking at me like that?

Baruch: I'm thinking of something.

Yehuda: What?

Baruch: Maybe I will tell you later... or maybe you will understand it yourself.

***

15th century. Cairo.
The Ari is walking down the street with the book open in his hands.
Oblivious to his surroundings, he can't stop reading.
He walks through the entire city without stopping, and into the forest.

Baruch's voice: The Ari became the greatest kabbalist, the greatest

12 Maranos—Jews of Spanish origin who were forced to accept Christianity during the Spanish Inquisition, but secretly continued to observe the Jewish tradition.

of them all! He knew everything about us, Yehuda, about our entire sorry world. He knew that new times were coming, that lowly souls were beginning to descend into the world, and that by our time, all the human ugliness would surface. He prepared a medicine for us, a system of refinement: The Ari's Kabbalah. He "brewed" this medicine within the pages of this book, *The Zohar*.

***

Baruch's home.
Baruch gently caresses the book.

-It won't disappear any more, no. Its time has come – the time of despair. No one can ever mistake man for anything but the self-indulgent animal that he is!

Baruch shakes his head. He looks at Yehuda.

-Yes, yes! We all live only for our own sake, Yehuda, and only because of that, do you understand, Yehuda? Only because of our selfishness are wars being waged, to be followed by far more terrible ones. Illnesses will not be cured, and doctors will cry in defeat; the suffering will be unbearable, and people will cry for help!

Baruch sits up and spreads his hands.

-But help won't come.

Baruch spreads his hands. He gets up, walks up to the wall, and raises his head to the ceiling. He watches the spider methodically weaving its web. He points his finger at the spider.

Baruch: This spider is as old as I am. I call him Baruch.

He turns to Yehuda. Their eyes meet.
He understands that he has to come back to their conversation.

-You want to know how to help them?

Yehuda nods his head.

-When they stop believing in themselves, Yehuda, only then will they beg for help.

He taps his finger on the table and points at the book.

-And they will find it in here.

Again, he watches Yehuda closely.

-Our wise fathers sent it for us a long time ago. They saw it all, they knew everything. They knew that this book would find you, Yehuda.

Another long pause and total silence.
Even Baruch, the spider, stands still in its web under the ceiling.
Simcha is sitting under the window, mesmerized by the heavy silence inside the house. He is straining to listen. Then he stands up and tries to look inside through the cracks between the boards.
He looks closer but he does not see anyone. In panic, he rushes to the door and hurls it open. There is no one in the house.

-Yehuda!

Simcha darts into the house, running to and fro, looking in every corner.

-Yehuda, son!

And suddenly he hears Baruch's calm voice behind him:

-What's all the fuss about, Simcha?

Simcha turns around.
Baruch and Yehuda are sitting at the table against each other as before.

-What's happened, father? – Yehuda asks as if nothing had happened.

-I... I was looking for you, I was knocking... - Simcha mumbles – nobody was here. It was silent. I got scared.

Baruch: Don't be afraid, Simcha. There's nothing you can do now. Step outside, sit down for a while. I want to ask your son a very important question.

Simcha: But there was no one here.

Baruch: You think so? And in your opinion, does this entire world exist?

Simcha (*irritated*): I don't want to listen to your nonsense!

He walks over to Yehuda and takes his hand:

-Yehuda, it's late already. Let's go!

Baruch *(sharply)*: Leave!

Simcha drops Yehuda's hand, turns around, and obediently walks to the door. He opens it and steps outside.

Simcha sits back at his place under the window and hears Baruch speaking:

-So, Yehuda, answer me, do you know the burden you are placing on your shoulders?

Simcha is rooted to the logs.
He can hear everything but is unable to move.

Baruch: You will assume a huge responsibility, not for yourself – who are you after all?! – but for the entire world. And you will suffer not for yourself, but for the entire world. Have you considered that, Yehuda? You are making a far-reaching, radical decision here. Better think a hundred times before you make up your mind.

Simcha tries to stand up but can't.
Wriggling, he pulls himself to the windowsill with his hands.
He wants to scream to his son: "Wait! Think it over! Don't rush!"
But it's too late.

-I've thought about it. I want it. – He hears Yehuda's answer.

Exhausted, Simcha slides from the logs onto the wet grass.

In the house, Baruch is fixing Yehuda with a hard stare.

Baruch (*ruthlessly*): If so, here is your first assignment. Take the Ari's poem. It is not a simple poem. It is about the beginning of all beginnings. Here it is.

Baruch, without looking, opens the book at the right place.

Baruch: Penetrate it. Submerge yourself in it. Try to hear the teacher, the great Ari. Follow him.

Baruch raises his hand. Yehuda follows it with his eyes. Slowly and gracefully Baruch moves his hand before him, as if drawing circles in the air.

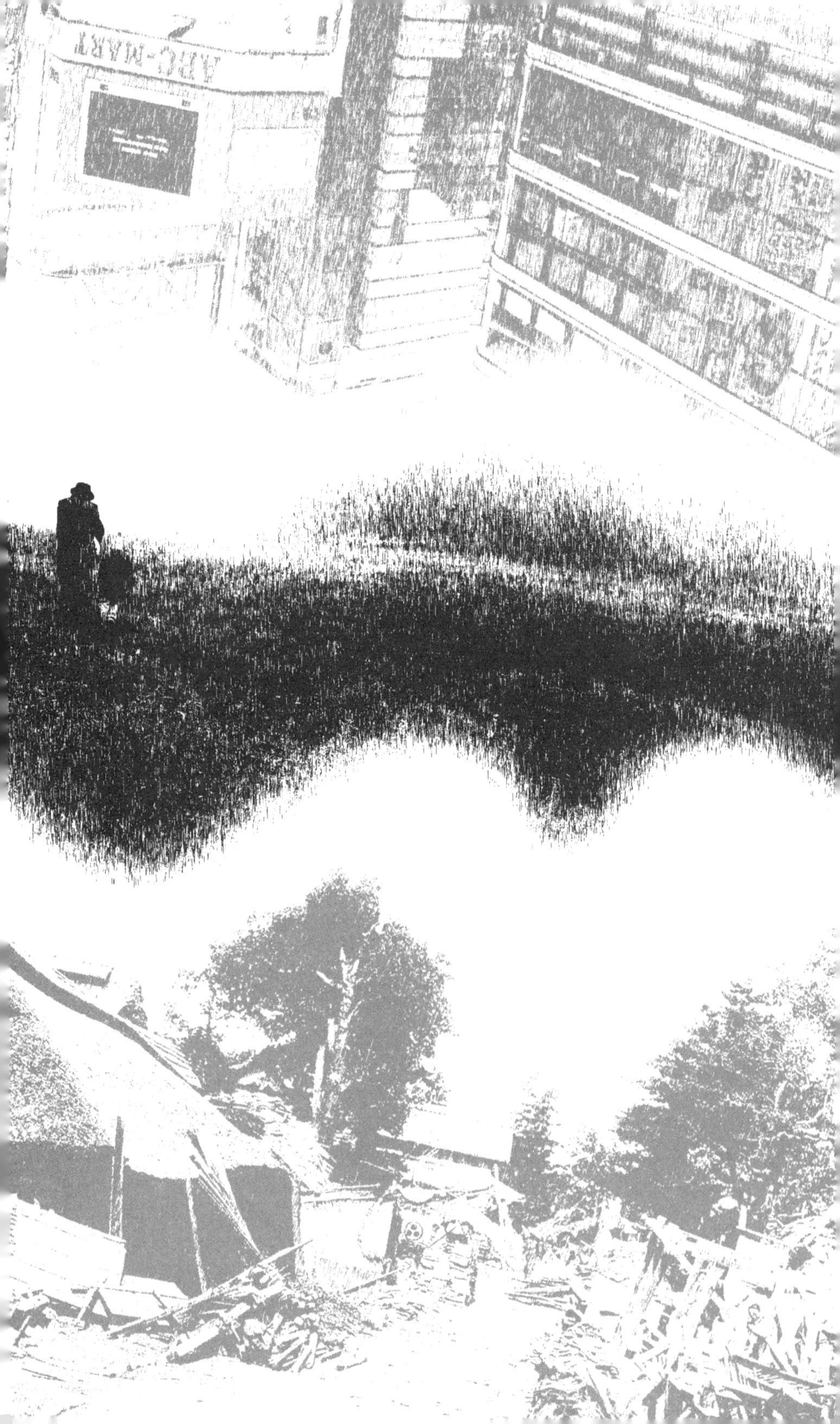
ABC-MART

Baruch *(rhythmically, as if singing)*: "Behold, that before the emanations were emanated and the creatures were created, the simple upper light had filled the whole of existence. And there was no vacancy, but all was filled with a simple, boundless light."

***

Simcha and Yehuda are walking silently by the side of a lake.
The sun has already set.
Warsaw appears up ahead.
We can hear the Yehuda's childish voice, continuing:

- "And when upon His simple will came the desire to create the worlds and emanate the emanations, to bring to light the perfection of His deeds, His names, His appellations, which was the cause of the creation of the worlds, He then restricted Himself, in the middle, precisely at the center. He restricted the light. And the light drew far off to the sides around that middle point."

***

Ashlag family home. Night.
Yehuda is sleeping in his bed.
His father, watching him from the doorstep, approaches and listens to Yehuda's breath. He adjusts the blanket and quietly leaves the room.

As soon as the door closes behind him, Yehuda opens his eyes. He quickly stands up, picks a book from the shelf and a lamp from the windowsill, and ducks under the table, covered by a long tablecloth that reaches all the way down to the floor.

The lamp burns under the table.
Yehuda is reading the book. We can hear his voice:

- "And the restriction had been uniform around the empty central point, so that the space was evenly circled around it.

There, after the restriction, having formed a vacuum and a space precisely in the middle of the endless light, a place was formed, where the emanated and the created might reside."

In the window, the moonlight wanes, dissolving in the light of the new day. The sweepers go out to the streets.

A milkman rides past the house, his bottles rattling.
We hear a sharp rooster's call.

Yehuda's eyes are fixed on the lines in the book:

- "Then from the endless light, a single beam came down, lowered down into that space. And through that beam, He emanated, created, formed, and made, all the worlds."

***

A heider (classroom). Children are sitting in rows, leaning over their books. The morning sunlight struggles through the tiny windows, playing with the dust as if it were gold dust.

Yehuda seems to be reading the Torah, just like the others.
But he is not.
Shmuel, the teacher, silently approaches Yehuda from behind.
He notices pages from another book concealed inside Yehuda's Torah book.
It is the poem of the Ari, rewritten neatly in a child's handwriting.

Yehuda is immersed in reading and doesn't hear anything.
He whispers to himself:

- "And through this beam the light came down unto the worlds, each and every circle from all the worlds, that are within the void, and each circle that is closer to the light of infinity is higher and superior to the other, and this worldly, material world is the middle point within the circles, inside the empty space."

Suddenly a hand flashes in front of Yehuda's face and the pages disappear.
Yehuda looks up.
The pages tremble in the teacher's hands.
He brings the pages closer to his near-sighted eyes and reads suspiciously.

- "It is so removed from the infinite, more so than all the other worlds, which is why it is so lowly and material in its base corporeality since it resides in the midst all of the circles."

The teacher: The Ari's poem. I see, I see.

Yehuda stands up.

The teacher: Can you explain it?

Yehuda is silent.

The teacher: Who gave it to you?

Yehuda is silent.
The entire class is silent, too, frozen in anticipation of a punishment.

The teacher *(loudly)*: I don't want these texts to go around the class. You are lost, your parents surrendered, but my goal is to save the rest. Go, Yehuda *(waves his hand)*. Get out!

The teacher turns his back to Yehuda and hears the boy's voice:

-Give me back those pages.

The teacher is transfixed, he looks around the class and utters, without turning back:

The teacher: Are you talking to me?

Yehuda: To you.

The teacher: What?

He turns around suddenly and his pointer abuts on Yehuda's nose.

The teacher: What did you say?!

Yehuda *(stubbornly)*: The pages!

The teacher (suspiciously): Is this a request or an order?

The entire class holds its breath in sheer dread.

Yehuda: Give me back the pages. Those are my pages.

Again a pause and a long silence.

The teacher: I warned your parents – people go mad from it. Well, it happened. They will cry their eyes out, your parents, when you are foaming at the mouth, fear and anguish living in your eyes forever! When this world becomes your hell.

Yehuda extends his hand toward the teacher.
The teacher becomes silent.

Yehuda takes the pages out of his hand, turns around, and quickly exits the classroom.

***

Baruch's home.
Baruch is pacing back and forth.
Yehuda is watching him.
The light of dusk permeates the house through the cracks in the boarded window.

Baruch's voice: Five worlds, one hundred twenty-five degrees, separate you from Him. He is calling you from up there. His appeal comes from the world of *Atzilut*[13]: "come back, son! Break through! Break through the doubts, the pain, the downs and the ups. I am waiting for you! I love you! Hear Me, I am pleading!" But His call fades, growing weaker and weaker. Man's pride stands in the way. Only a person with a broken heart can hear His voice.

Baruch is standing with his back to Yehuda, looking at the setting sun through the cracks in the window.

Baruch's voice: Why is it broken? Because the Creator is absent in our world. He has locked us up in the world of lowly desires. We suffer in anguish, our blood spills onto this dirty earth for centuries. Why did He make it so? Where was His love for us?! Where was His compassion for these lowly, ignorant creatures?!

Baruch turns to face Yehuda.

Yehuda: He loves us.

Baruch: Who told you that?

Yehuda: I can feel it.

Baruch: What can you feel, you drop of filth?

Yehuda: I can feel that I am a drop of filth. And He... He is the light, He is love! He is everything.

Baruch: But how could the light have created darkness? How could love have created hatred? How could He... He have created a drop of filth?! So many of these drops?! This base humanity? Where were His eyes? Tell me! Can you justify Him, Yehuda?

13 The word, *Atzilut,* is derived from the Hebrew word *Etzlo* (at His place). *Atzilut* is the world that we reach when we are corrected and discover the Creator to the fullest.

Yehuda is thinking and we can see that he is struggling with these questions.

Yehuda: I don't know. I don't know yet because I haven't met Him yet. I can only feel it.

Baruch sits in front of Yehuda.

Baruch: You don't know?

Yehuda: No, I don't.

Baruch *(with great urgency):* You really don't know?!

Yehuda: I don't know.

Baruch: You are correct. He – the purest of all - couldn't have made filth. Just as a lion can't give birth to a mouse, perfection can't give rise to imperfection.

Baruch is silent, watching Yehuda.
He is expecting Yehuda to ask a question, but Yehuda is not asking.

Baruch: Well, ask! Ask me, why did He create all of this?

Yehuda: Why?

Baruch: Simply because... come on, you've already answered this question. Well?!

Yehuda: I don't know.

Baruch: So that you, Yehuda, yes you, of your own free will, would decide, would realize that it's unbearable to exist in all this filth; that you cannot stand to be so far away from Him, so that you would then plead from the very bottom of your heart. He heeds only such a prayer. He wants you to come to Him on your own, of your own free will. And then you will tell Him: "Here I am, I have come to You through my own efforts because I want to be Your friend." And you will do it all on your own. Of your own free will, Yehuda!

Yehuda: What do I have to do to be able to say that?

Baruch speaks clearly, dryly and distinctly.

Baruch: If you haven't made contact with the Creator in this life, you are nothing.

Yehuda: How can I achieve that? This is why I have come to you.

Yehuda suddenly gets up, towering over Baruch, as if they have exchanged roles. Now little Yehuda is speaking angrily and authoritatively.

Yehuda: I am sick and tired of this empty talking. I don't have time for this.

Baruch looks at him with awe.

Baruch: Oh, how you remind me of someone! But he wasn't eight years old; he was forty-eight!

Yehuda: I don't need all these stories. You must lead me to him!

Baruch *(laughing and pointing his finger at Yehuda)*: Yep, Mendel from Kotzk was just like that: Unyielding, uncompromising.

And suddenly he stops laughing, seeing that Yehuda is past laughter.

Baruch: We led a peaceful life. We believed in God. We were told that He exists and we believed it. We followed His laws, studied the Torah. Mendel came and ripped our peaceful life apart. He made us abandon this world and demand another. He yelled at us, threw his fists at us, and cursed us. But nothing came out of us. We remained the beasts we were. *(He sighs and orders sharply:)* Sit, Yehuda.

Yehuda sits down.

Baruch: Open!

Yehuda opens the book.
Baruch puts his hand on the first page and taps his finger on the first line.

Baruch: The cure is here, Yehuda! Only here! This is where life is. Do you get it?

Yehuda: Yes.

Baruch: Well, if you do, then start. Start looking for it within you, son.

Yehuda begins to read slowly.
The child's finger traces the lines of the book.

Yehuda's voice: "A river stretches out from Eden..." what is "river?"

Baruch: "River" stands for your readiness to bestow everything to others–every single thing you've got...

Yehuda: What is the Garden of Eden? *(Smiles)* It must be something very, very good.

Baruch: Right you are, son! The Garden of Eden is a collection of your best desires. The best! Friendship, love, bestowal... these desires are planted in you, son, like trees in the ground. They are called "the Garden of Eden," and they yield the tastiest fruit.

Night falls behind the window. The old house creaks in the wind. The candle on the table lights the faces of Yehuda and Baruch.

Yehuda's voice: "That river swells and flows, it enters the lower garden and irrigates it with waters from above, satiating it, bringing forth fruit and seeds."

Shadows dance in the corners of the room.
Baruch's hands are clenched in gnarled fists. Yehuda's finger travels along the lines of the book.

***

Seven years pass. Seven years of studying, searching, and waiting for an answer.

Old Baruch and the fifteen-year-old Yehuda are sitting at the same table, in the same positions.
Yehuda is reading, moving his finger along the lines of the book, Baruch is listening and nodding his head every once in a while.
Snow is falling outside the window, engulfing Baruch's old house.

***

Black and white documentary sequences show 1900 New Year's celebrations. Big Christmas trees line the streets of St. Petersburg, Paris, New York, and Warsaw. Store windows shine like jewels in the big cities. Happy people loaded with shopping bags are walking through the streets.

Holding each other's hands, a boy and a girl are skating on the ice, laughing. Above the skating rink, the number 1900 is twinkling in bright colors.

A new century is starting. Nobody knows yet how many tragedies it holds.

***

An old cart is moving along a bumpy country road, its wheels creaking. It is drizzling.
A skinny horse barely moves, its feet sinking deep into the autumn mud. The coachman is asleep.

Fifteen-year-old Yehuda sits barefoot on the edge of a cart, his head covered with a tattered rag. He is holding a book in his hands. His wet boots are next to him on the dirty straw.

Yehuda raises his eyes and sees raindrops trickle down the wet leaves of the forest trees. Here and there, a mushroom peeps out from under the foliage. Ripe raspberries, heavy with rain droplets, weigh down the stalks of raspberry bushes.

Yehuda smiles. He continues his ride, smiling as he approaches Baruch's house.
Yehuda jumps off the cart, picks up his shoes, and runs to the house. Baruch is sitting with his back to the entrance and does not turn around as the door squeaks open. Yehuda walks up to the table. Baruch still doesn't notice him.
Yehuda sits at the table facing Baruch. Baruch's eyes seem to be focusing at a point far behind Yehuda.

Yehuda *(whispers)*: It's me, Baruch, me.

Baruch touches Yehuda's hand.

-It's me, Yehuda. Don't you recognize me?

-Yehuda, - repeats Baruch.

Baruch comes back to his senses.

-A-a-a-ah, you're here.

Yehuda *(concerned)*: Are you well, Baruch?

Baruch *(quietly)*: Of course. What could happen to me?

Yehuda *(rising unexpectedly)*: You probably want to be alone.

Baruch: Sit.

Yehuda sits down.

Baruch: Today I miss my teacher, Mendel from Kotzk. Sit, share my longing.

Baruch quietly shakes his head.

-He wanted to ascend in one lifetime past all the degrees separating us from the King so as to never come back into this filthy swamp.

Baruch spreads his hands.

-We believed in him. We followed him, dedicating ourselves to our mendel, our commune, our Kotzk!

***

Kotzk.[14] Evening.
A rain-blackened wooden house. The light of an oil lamp flickers through the window.
The lamp is standing on a long table surrounded by thin, poorly dressed hassidic students with burning eyes.
All eyes are fixed on their 40-year-old teacher, Menachem Mendel.
The collar of his stained shirt is torn, his hair is tousled, bread crumbs dot his disheveled beard.
He is speaking passionately, just like Baruch, waving his hands.
They look very similar.

Baruch's voice: We decided to take the Creator by storm. For long, hungry evenings, we stood frozen before our teacher, and he before the Creator.

We see young Baruch behind the table.
Just like the others, his eyes never leave mendel.

Baruch's voice: A bottle of vodka, three onions, a few loaves of bread, and the Creator – the great and true one! Right here! Right next to us! See Him! Feel Him!

The Hassidim[15] grasp their dirty glasses filled with a murky liquid, raise them passionately, then down their drinks in unison.

---

14 Kotzk – a small town in Poland, where the Kabbalah group of Rabbi Menachem Mendel was founded.
15 Plural of Hassid—a devout student. The *Hassidut* movement circulated the wisdom of Kabbalah among Jews throughout Eastern Europe.

Baruch's voice: We were trembling with cold and happiness, we were waiting for Him to be revealed to us. He was testing our perseverance. How long could it possibly continue?! We were holding on with our last bit of strength.

Close-ups of the famished, exhausted Hassidim.
Mendel is saying something to them, and suddenly begins to rhythmically pound his fist on the table.

Baruch's voice: I remember that evening. It was so cold that birds froze solid in mid-flight. Mendel said: "We have a chance to break through. Prepare to attack."

Following Mendel's rhythm, everyone began to pound their fists on the table in unison. The blows were like a single blow, drumming in rhythm, as one beat!

Looking from the street through the dimly lit windows, we can see the fists of the Hassidim rising and falling in unison. We can hear blows like peals of thunder, and the dilapidated house shakes with each thud.

***

Baruch's house.
Baruch empties the bottle in one long gulp.
Yehuda looks on as Baruch's scrawny adam's apple jumps up and down.

Baruch: He shouldn't have said those things to us, our Mendel. We failed the trial. Suddenly we became homesick. We wanted to go back to warmth, to our wives, to our snot-covered kids, to our ordinary lives devoid of great deeds and heroic attacks. We caved in. We failed by a margin of a single assault. One last push!

Tearfully, Baruch raises his eyes to Yehuda.
His face is tormented. He can barely summon the strength to speak:

-We failed to arrive at a single thought! One thought–that we are together, that we are a single whole. That these dirty, worn-out bodies simply do not exist, that there is just one common soul (*weeping*). One soul... Aimed at the Creator!

Baruch's eyes begin to scan the wall, going up to the ceiling, then down, then back to the table.

Baruch (*in tears*): We are standing before you pleading: "Give us strength! Help us! Accept us!"

***

The house in Kotzk.
Everyone around the table is pounding it with passion.
The table rocks with the blows.
Suddenly the table's legs cave in and it collapses to one side, taking down the Hassidim with it.
The house turns silent.

***

Baruch's house.
Pause. Silence.
Yehuda watches Baruch, mesmerized.
Baruch shakes his head from side to side.

-We failed. We did. *(Closes his eyes)* Ohhh, if only you could hear how mendel mocked us! How he teased us!

***

Kotzk.
Mendel is towering above everyone.
He laughs, pointing his finger at them.

Baruch's voice: He told us: "You are nobodies, unfit for his revelation. Leave, go back to your homes, hide under your wives' skirts, wipe the snot off your children's noses, forget about eternity. For you, there is no eternity.

***

Baruch's house.
Baruch is weeping loudly, paying no attention to Yehuda.
A minute passes.
He wipes off the tears, smearing dirt over his face.

Baruch: Our great teacher, Mehachem Mendel, disappeared behind the locked door of his room. He stayed in it for twenty years.

***

Kotzk.
Mendel turns on his heels sharply and walks to his room.

Everybody stares at his suddenly stooping back. He disappears behind his door and slams it shut.

Baruch's voice: His attack was triumphant. Ours wasn't.

Kotzk.
The light wavers in an oil lamp.
It goes off.
Complete darkness falls.

***

Baruch's house.
It's getting dark. Baruch puts his hand over Yehuda's hand and says in a surprisingly soft tone:

-There are guards watching the path to Him, Yehudale. They force back all those who approach his palace. They beat you with their sticks until you bleed. But you must keep on walking! This is how He tests you, how He can tell if you really want, more than anything else in the world, to meet Him or if you have simply taken a wrong turn somewhere. Have you burned all the bridges behind you or not? If you really desire it, if you truly burned them all, they will let you through. But if you haven't, you are better off not setting foot on this path.

Yehuda: Why are you telling me all this?

Baruch: I have a feeling that soon you will find the story helpful.

Yehuda: I've burned my bridges. Nothing in this life interests me. Only Him.

Suddenly Yehuda freezes.
He is sitting upright, looking in the direction of the boarded window.
Then he suddenly stands up and walks up to the wall.
He sees the crude boards that make up the wall, a rusty head of a nail.
Yehuda is standing with his back to Baruch.

Baruch's voice comes from behind him, calm, sober, and even:

-I believe that it can happen any time.

Yehuda is silent. He stares at the wall. His breath disturbs the cobweb hanging from the boards.

Baruch: You will be great, Yehuda. Yehuda Leib Ashlag.

Yehuda remains silent.

Baruch: It's Him. Don't be afraid.

Yehuda is silent.

Baruch: This field has five circles. His entire thought is contained here.

Yehuda closes his eyes.
Baruch walks up to him.

Baruch: Can you hear me?

Yehuda starts to walk slowly along the wall.

Baruch: Not a thought about yourself, you hear me?! Not a thought.

Yehuda is walking along the wall.
Baruch is following him.

-Get ready, - *(Baruch whispers.)* You are on your way to Him. He is holding your hand. He's guiding you. You are leaving your body.[16]

Suddenly the wall disappears.
Baruch's voice recedes into the distance.

-It's all within you, my son ... Within you![17]

***

A burst of light.
Yehuda sees a white, endless space.
Silhouettes of trees begin to appear, as if out of a fog.
A garden[18] in bloom spreads out into infinity.

Baruch's voice: What, what do you feel?

Yehuda's voice: Peace.

Baruch's voice: It's Him, Yehuda.

---

16 "Leaving the body" means leaving the egoistic desires in favor of altruistic (spiritual) ones. In Kabbalah, the "body" is not the biological body, but the desire to receive pleasure.
17 All the worlds are within us. Kabbalah teaches that one perceives the whole of reality within. When the desires change from egoistic to altruistic, a person begins to feel the unity and love—the Creator—within.
18 The garden within—the quality of bestowal and of loving others.

Yehuda's voice: Warmth.

Baruch's voice: It's Him, Yehuda, it's Him.

Yehuda's voice: I feel... love.

***

Baruch's house.
Yehuda is walking along the wall.
Baruch is watching him.

Suddenly he begins to sing a melody.
Then stops, as if testing Yehuda.
He is waiting.
Yehuda picks up the melody.
His voice is deep and sensuous.

Baruch *(excited)*: Yehuda...

Yehuda is still there, in the same sensation. He continues to sing. He does not hear Baruch.

***

A garden in bloom.
A valley filled with translucent air.
A gentle tune is playing in the background.

-I feel so good, - utters Yehuda.

Immediately, his heart clenches with fear.
It's as if a snake is approaching.

The wind blows high, bending the tree tops.
Suddenly the head of a giant snake[19] appears in the grass.

-What are you thinking about?! – Baruch's voice can be heard.

The snake slithers fast toward Yehuda.

-What are you thinking about?! – Baruch's voice becomes louder.

Two red eyes are staring at Yehuda.

---

19 A snake is an egoistic thought that has suddenly infiltrated into a pure and altruistic desire.

The snake's forked tongue lashes forward.
It swiftly closes the distance to Yehuda.

-What are you thinking about?! – *(Baruch screams)* Anything but yourself!

The snake approaches swiftly.
Only a few feet separate them... now a few inches.
It's impossible to prevent the strike.
The snake's poisonous tongue is about to touch Yehuda's face...

***

For a moment, we are back in Baruch's house.
Baruch sees Yehuda burying his face in his palms.

***

The snake rockets past Yehuda without slowing down.
Its head smashes into a tree, breaking up into numerous small black snakes that vanish in the grass.

***

Baruch's house.
Yehuda is silent.

-This was the boundary. – *(Baruch's voice is calm and even.)* You were afraid, but you didn't run away. Good for you, Yehuda!

Yehuda leans against the wall to avoid falling down.

Baruch: It took me years to do what you did. But you He marked from the beginning.

Yehuda *(he is still there)*: This is indescribable.

Baruch: There is no need to.

Yehuda turns his face to Baruch.

Baruch: You needn't tell this to anyone.

Yehuda moves towards Baruch.

-I felt him... the way I feel you.

Baruch is silent for a moment.
He sees Yehuda's eyes full of yearning and delight.

Baruch (quietly)**:** Well, I told you, son! You see!

All of a sudden, Baruch's eyes well up with tears.

Baruch: It was Him, son!

Yehuda: He engulfed me, like a mother engulfs her baby.

Baruch is crying, completely unashamed of his tears. He is crying without wiping them away, and repeats in admiration:

-Yes, yes! He is like that, Yehuda. He is like that!

- I was engulfed with His love! – Exclaims Yehuda.

-Engulfed! – Repeats Baruch still with tears in his eyes. Precisely, son! Engulfed with love! Because He is love, son! He is all the good there is. He gives everything to us and wants nothing in return.

Suddenly Yehuda starts crying along with Baruch. He smears his tears all over his face, attempts to say something, but can't.
He mumbles and suddenly moans:

-But w......h......y! Why did I leave Him? Whyyy?

***

A black flash.
The snake's head appears in the grass.
The snakes hurtles toward Yehuda.

Baruch's voice: You thought of yourself.

-But why, why did I think of myself?!

-You couldn't have done otherwise, calm down.

-But why, why! I knew that I shouldn't!

Baruch carefully places his hand on Yehuda's bony shoulder.

-Who told you it was easy - to peek into yourself? – He asks.

-But... He let me pass. - Yehuda mumbles.

-He tested you.

Yehuda raises his eyes to look at Baruch.

-And did I pass the test?!

-You did!

-But He... disappeared.

-No, He is with you. He is always with you. You are the one who stopped feeling Him. He is here. Constantly...

Yehuda looks around.

-Where is He?

Baruch: Here.

Yehuda: Where? Why can't I feel Him? Why?!

Baruch: You will continue to work on yourself. And one day He will not disappear. It's because you will become like Him.

Baruch glances at Yehuda's face:

-Bestowing and loving. You really want it, don't you?

Yehuda *(exhales)*: Very much!

Baruch: And you won't back down?

Yehuda: Not a single step!

Baruch is silent. He shakes his head.

-You're going to be great, Yehuda - he finally utters – I can see it. But always remember your own conclusion, it is very precise: You are always engulfed in His love like an embryo in its mother. Do you hear me?

Yehuda: Yes, I do.

Baruch: An embryo does not think of itself. Do the same. Not thinking of yourself, son – this is the main thing!

Baruch stares at Yehuda.
And suddenly sighs loudly:

-Oh, how I would love a drink right now! Oh, I would get drunk. I would dance for you, I would sing!

Yehuda: What tune were you humming? I heard a tune. And I knew it.

Baruch: Oh, it's a great melody, "Mordechai Yosef."[20] Starving and freezing, we used to sing it in Kotzk.

---

20 Mordechai Yosef – a melody that the great Kabbalist Rabbi Mendel of Kotzk heard during the spiritual ascent.

Yehuda tries to recall it but fails.

Yehuda: I knew it, but now I forgot.

Baruch starts to sing and Yehuda tentatively joins in.

Now both their voices soar in a duet above the village, above the forest, above the country road, above Yehuda, walking along the edge of the forest, above Warsaw, above the Jewish quarter.

***

Warsaw. The Jewish quarter. – Day.
Many faces of people on the street, walking on the rain-drenched sidewalk.
Older and more wrinkled, the mad violinist is still playing his single-stringed instrument.
The same shopkeeper is selling sausages, lazily fending off the flies...
Nothing changes in the Jewish quarter.
Nothing foretells the coming trouble.

Yehuda appears from around the corner.
He is walking, looking down, yet not seeing that he is stepping in puddles and mud.
He hears the same melody, but it ceases.
Yehuda turns to a side street.

Suddenly someone's hand stops him.
Yehuda looks up.
A young, secular guy is standing in front of him.

-Do you recognize me? – He asks.

Yehuda (looking closely): Yankele?

Yankele: In the flesh. But not Yankele, no, Yan. Yan Terletsky – a free citizen of the great Poland, liberated from any religion.

Yehuda (smiling): Hello there, free citizen of Poland.

Yan: I recognize you, still smart, still sarcastic (examines Yehuda). Just the kind we need... *(embracing Yehuda's shoulders.)* Yehuda, I'm asking for an hour of your time.

Yehuda *(hastily)*: I don't have it. I need to write something down. Urgently!

Yan: Half an hour, then.

Yehuda: I am sorry; I have to go.

He is trying to leave, but Yan blocks his way.

Yan: Even for the sake of an old friendship?

Yehuda: Even for the sake of friendship.

Yan *(gently holding Yehuda with his hand)*: Then I will tell you quickly and simply. We, the Social Democratic Party of Poland, invite you to join us. Equality of all people on earth is our principle!

Suddenly Yehuda looks at Yan with interest.

Yan: We are a party of young, passionate people. There are neither Jews nor Poles among us. We are united above any narrow national interests by the great purpose of uniting the world. What do you think?

Yehuda: It is an exalted idea.

Yan: I knew you would say that. I've always felt you very close.

Yehuda *(suddenly getting excited)*: This is a great idea because it stems from a great root, Yankele.

Yan: Of course! Love and equality will unite us all! *(Happily.)* I knew you would be with us! I am so happy! *(He hugs Yehuda.)*

Yehuda: It's precisely because the Creator, Yankele, *is* equality and freedom!

Yan (brusquely): Let's leave this subject aside.

Yehuda *(even more excitedly)*: But this is truly so, Yankele. Trust me! And it's the most important thing of all!

Yan: This is the least important thing! *(Raising his voice.)* Leave all your fantasies behind. He – your God – is just an invention, the psychological trickery of our crafty ancestors! Everything is in the hands of man, Yehuda. There is no God!

Yehuda: Yan, listen to me...

Yan: No, you listen to me. You know why I came to you? Because I remembered the moment when that rogue thought came to my mind. You provoked it! Do you remember how you asked the teacher in the classroom: "Where is He?" Do you remember when you said: "If I can't feel Him, it means that He does not exist." Do you?

Yehuda: Yes, I do. We really do need to feel Him, and it can be done. It can and must be done!

Yan: Wait, let me finish. It was you who crushed my tiny Jewish world. I'm grateful to you for that. That's precisely why I came to you with this proposal to join us.

Yehuda: But listen...!

Yan: That's it. I don't want to hear it. Are you with us or not?

Yehuda is silent.

Yan: Say something. I'm waiting for an answer.

Yehuda: You will fail.

Yan: So you say.

Yehuda: Without the Creator, Yankele, it cannot work.

Yan *(pauses, sighs, looks at Yehuda)*: It's a shame. Such a shame. I thought that you would understand.*(Resolutely)* I'm sorry, now it's me who has to go.

Yan turns sharply and begins to walk away.
Yehuda is looking at him.
Suddenly he starts to run after him, catches up with him, and tries to explain something to him, but we can't make out his words.
Yehuda is waving his hands, talking passionately.

Yan keeps on walking resolutely toward the main street.
Yehuda lags behind.
Yan dissolves in the bustling crowd.

***

Yehuda's room. Night.
A candle is burning on the table.
Yehuda is sitting in front of an open book.
He gets up and approaches the window.
A few lit windows are scattered in the dark.

Yehuda's father quietly comes in, sits down in the corner.

Simcha: Do you mind?

Yehuda turns around to face him.

Simcha: You have grown up, Yehuda, especially in the last few weeks.

Yehuda looks at his father without responding, walks up to his desk, sits down, and starts to write something briskly.

Simcha: That's it, Yehuda. You have grown and became more distant from us. Do you hear me, Yehuda?

Yehuda *(continues to write)*: I'm sorry, father, I don't have much time.

Simcha: Yehuda, we're still your family, and I wanted to tell you...

Yehuda *(quickly raising his head)*: Father, you can't even imagine how unimportant is everything that you are going to say. Every moment of this night can save or destroy many lives.

Simcha: Rabbi Feldman warned us that this would happen. You stopped being our son. You stopped being a Jew.

Yehuda reluctantly stops writing and turns to face his father.

Yehuda: To the Creator we are all equal.

Simcha: I won't let you go to your Baruch tomorrow.

Yehuda: There is nothing you can do now, father.

Simcha rises fatefully and leaves the room.
The door slams.
The thin plywood partition is shaking.
Yehuda follows him with his eyes.

***

All of a sudden he finds himself in the blooming garden.
Just for one moment. For one brief instant he can hear Baruch's quiet voice.

-It's within you, this garden! Do you realize it, son? It is the garden of your desires.

Branches are swaying. Flower petals flutter.

-And they are all striving for the Creator.

Yehuda is enveloped with peace.
He has never experienced anything like this before.

***

Yehuda is sitting in his room, the oil lamp is flickering, the book is open in front of him, and the evening light is penetrating the open window.

***

Morning.
Yehuda walks up the country road leading to Baruch's house.
Yehuda sees his teacher sitting alone on the doorstep of his house.

Baruch squints at the rising sun, he looks older and somehow more peaceful.
Yehuda takes a seat next to him.

-Why don't you ever come outside into the light?

-You call this light? - Baruch answers. - What kind of light is that? The light for us is the night, when all the fools of this world are asleep and no one disturbs you when you are thinking about the light. *That's* when the light comes out.

Baruch tries to stand up but can't.
His skinny legs quiver under his weight.

Baruch: Still, it's better inside my den, after all. Give me a hand.

Yehuda carefully helps Baruch, propping him under his arm.

Instead of going inside, they walk slowly toward the forest.
They walk under tall, arching pine trees and heavy silence engulfs them. It is filled with nothing but the low rustle of grass, the greeting trill of a bird, a little beetle climbing up a blade of grass. A tiny flea is hanging by a drop of morning dew, a mushroom is popping its head from under the fallen pine needles.

Baruch *(looking around and sighing)*: I wish I could live like them, without hatred.

Yehuda: It's good here.

Baruch *(unexpectedly sharply)*: What did you say?! Good?! It's good when you feel bad! Only then you scream to Him! When you feel good, you don't need the Creator.

Yehuda *(reflectively)*: How can I explain that to those who feel bad? That bad is good?

Baruch: You can't. They will think that you are mad.

Yehuda: How do you explain that we feel bad only because we've lost the connection with the Creator?

Baruch *(scornfully)*: What? What did you say?! You want to explain this to them, to those two-legged beasts?! They won't even hear you *(taps his ear)*. They don't have anything to hear you with! They live according to a different law! Their law – the human one – is to seize! And you're telling them about some Creator, about His law?! To *give?* No. Noooo, Yehuda. Only blows will teach them that they have to live differently. One cannot avoid the suffering, Yehuda.

Yehuda: Yes, you can.

Baruch: And I say, "You can't!"

Yehuda: And I say, "Yes, you can!"

Baruch *(louder)*: And I say, "You can't!"

Yehuda *(even louder)*: And I say, "You can!" You can do without the suffering. You can! We can explain to them that He is waiting for us there, in dizzying happiness; that He is leading us to pure happiness. Yes, we can!

Baruch doesn't answer. He looks at Yehuda wearily.

Yehuda: Listen *(pacing back and forth in front of Baruch)*, we can explain to them, quite simply, that there is only one force in the world, one law – His law – love of others, that this is the greatest fortune we can obtain, that a great evil – the human ego - stands in the way to this fortune, provoking all misfortunes, and that it can be corrected, bringing all misfortunes to an end.

Baruch (*wearily*): They won't listen! All my attempts...

Yehuda *(stops in front of him)*: We should try again and again.

Baruch: They can't hear.

Baruch is rocking back and forth on his thin, old legs shaking his big head:

-He doesn't care about the bodies, Yehuda! Don't you get it?! The Creator converses with the soul, and *only* with the soul. He couldn't care less about your body and its vain desires. You want to be a great rabbi, know the Torah by heart, become famous, make money, gorge yourself on rich foods, and sleep well! We live for our sake, whereas He lives for the sake of everybody else. We love only ourselves, and He – only others. *(Wearily and painfully)* Do you understand that there is no connection between us *(throws up his arms)*, none whatsoever?

Yehuda: When will it appear, this connection?! It does appear, doesn't it?

Baruch *(very quietly, very wearily)*: When we realize that it does not and cannot exist. It is then that it appears.

Baruch sighs and spreads his arms.

-When we become desperate, when we flood our hearts with tears and plead, truly plead for this connection to materialize (*squirms*) – at least for a tiny bit, at least for a split second - when we plead with all the strength that we have left because without it there is nothing to live for.

Baruch pauses, completely worn out, and looks at Yehuda.

-It is then that a prayer emerges - *(sighs)* from the bottom of the heart. In response to this prayer the gates of tears open and you begin to feel Him. Then, finally, you understand the meaning of it all. And you cry and cry, but this time they are tears of joy. And everything falls beautifully into place.

Yehuda *(beaming with exhilaration)*: *This* is what I will tell them! And they will understand. I know they will. I am sure. After all, nobody likes to suffer.

Baruch is looking at Yehuda. Suddenly, his legs buckle under him but Yehuda manages to catch him and Baruch wearily descends onto a tree stump.

Yehuda *(frightened)*: Are you okay? Should I take you home?

Baruch: No. I feel good.

Yehuda squats next to Baruch. He strokes Baruch's back as if he were a child.

Baruch: Yehuda...

Yehuda: Yes, Baruch.

Baruch: I will agree on one condition. *(Watches him attentively)* If you tell me now that you have spoken with Him about it. Have you?

Yehuda: Yes, I have.

Baruch (*lights up with a sudden smile*): And He gave you His blessing?

Yehuda: Yes. Tonight.

> The second Yehuda utters these words, he feels the blossoming garden again.
> The garden extends far into the horizon to the distant hills.

-Here He is! – Yehuda whispers.

> He is standing still, afraid to move.

-Do you remember the rule? – He suddenly hears Baruch's voice.

-Yes, – he whispers in response.

-Good for you! – The old man's voice is calm. – No one here thinks of themselves.

-Neither do I.

> A ray of light plays on the trunk of a huge tree[21] to Yehuda's right.

> Something attracts Yehuda's attention. He gazes attentively at the foliage.

-Don't... - Baruch's voice comes.

> But Yehuda has already taken a step toward the tree.

-Yehuda...

> Something among the leaves glitters and catches his attention. He reaches with his hand to touch the tree trunk.

-You are not listening to me, son.

> Yehuda places one foot on the lower branch of the tree.

-There is nothing I can do. - Baruch's voice comes from far away. – Evidently, you have to go through it all by yourself. Yourself.

---

21 A tree is the quality of love and bestowal in a person. When this quality is used for the sake of others, one is regarded as being in the Garden of Eden. But when used for one's own sake, the laws of the Garden of Eden break and a person is "expelled" from it.

The wind glides above the grass, bending its blades down. Yehuda climbs up the tree using its branches as a ladder.
The wind blows harder. Yehuda tries to reach the glittering object hidden in the foliage.
The wind turns into a storm. The birds take off abruptly. Clouds rapidly cover the sky.
Yehuda, unable to hold on to the branch, falls down onto the grass.

A flash of light.
Yehuda is running in a field.
The roar of the gale and of approaching water is coming from behind.
Yehuda turns his head back, still running, and sees columns of water sweeping the flourishing garden away.
He notices a crack between two rocks up ahead.
The rain turns into a full-blown deluge.[22]

***

A forest near Baruch's house.
Yehuda is walking quickly in circles among the pine trees.
Now he is running.
Baruch is watching him closely.

-Hold on, son! Hold on! - He repeats.

A flash of light!
The swell of water uproots the ancient tree that was standing in the middle of the garden. It throws it spinning into the air and tosses it after Yehuda.
At the very last moment Yehuda leaps head first into the narrow burrow between the rocks.
He hears Baruch's voice trembling with exhilaration.

-You are being born!

The wave comes crashing onto the rocks and into the tunnel, picking Yehuda up and carrying him ahead. The powerful current lifts him up, turning him upside down, and slams him against the stones as it carries him forward.

---

22 The rain is the quality of bestowal in a person, the quality of the Creator. The rain turns into a flood when a person wishes to use it for self-gratification rather than for gratification of others.

***

Back in the forest.

Yehuda is running across the forest, caressing tree trunks with the tips of his fingers.

Baruch watches him and continues to whisper to himself:

-You are being born, son, you are being born.

***

A flash of light.

Yehuda goes underwater.

A tree trunk rushes toward him, its pointy top aimed at Yehuda.

Yehuda closes his eyes in terror.

The tree tips over, revealing a black hollow in the middle of the trunk, wide enough to fit a tall man.

It swallows Yehuda.

***

The forest.

Yehuda suddenly stops running. He is motionless.

Baruch raises his hand, but he is unable to utter a word.

***

A flash of light!

Another tree emerges in the vortex of water. Its top wedges into the cavernous hollow in the first tree trunk, sealing it shut.

Silence falls. Darkness.

***

The forest.

Yehuda is standing, his face buried in the hollow of an ancient oak.

A squirrel, further up the trunk, is looking out of its hole.

Baruch is by Yehuda's side. He pats him on the back as if he is a little child.

Both are silent for a long time.

Yehuda cannot come back to his senses.

-I know, son, you can do it! – Baruch finally says with a calm voice.

-I will try,- answers Yehuda.

-You won't try, you will make it!

Baruch looks into Yehuda's eyes.
Yehuda is still heavy with emotion from the experience.

-You will fall and rise[23] again, it's part of the process. It is necessary! – Says Baruch. – There can be no light[24] without darkness; no day without a night.

-I understand. But it's very hard, - answers Yehuda.

-The first stage is over. It is the most important stage. –Baruch says. - Now, begins the process of cleansing your dirt.[25] You understand that it is absolutely necessary, son.

-Yes.

-You realize that you can't live for yourself, son, when He "lives" only for everyone else.

Baruch smiles and looks into Yehuda's eyes.

-Living for yourself is so filthy.

-I understand, Baruch, – answers Yehuda. – I do.

-We have to purify ourselves of it, son.

Yehuda (*sighs*): If I could only... rip it out of myself all at once!

Baruch: You can't do it all at once. The sunrise doesn't happen immediately, but bit by bit. You will make it.

Yehuda: And how long will it...

Baruch: Take? Until you are like Him. He doesn't think of Himself. You already know it. And you will be the same. You will make it, son, you will!

Yehuda (*resolutely*): I will make it, Baruch.

---

23 A "fall" or "descent" is when a person who aspires to spirituality senses an egoistic desire that is beyond one's ability to restrain, causing one to "fall" into it and live for oneself. An "ascent" is when one corrects that egoistic desire and rises above it.

24 "Darkness" is the ego's rule over a person, a rule that hides the Creator and the spiritual world from a person. "Light" is the revelation of the quality of bestowal and love in a person, allowing one to rediscover the spiritual world, the Creator.

25 "Cleansing" means cleaning the dirt—working on correcting the egoistic desires, receiving with the aim to delight others, i.e. the Creator.

Baruch smiles.

-Well done! Don't dare say anything else! Thousands upon thousands of the greatest, the greatest sages, Yehuda, are watching you with love and hope. They were willing to be torn to pieces, cut into bits, only to feel what you have felt! And He chose you and not them. Go to Him, son, go, yearn, pray, break, scream, just don't stop!

Yehuda: I am going to Him, Baruch. I am flying to Him.

***

A flash of light.
The water is gushing on, tossing the sealed trunk of the giant tree like a monster toothpick, with Yehuda inside.

-You've entered the ark.[26] (*Baruch's voice is heard through the roar of water*) The ark that is inside of you!

Another tree trunk, perpendicularly wedged into the hollow like a mast, rushes along in the narrow ravine.

-Hold on, son! Keep us in your thoughts, all of us.

***

And again the forest rustles. Grass sways in the light breeze.
Baruch is silent, he squints as he looks away from Yehuda into the thicket. He gazes at a bee flying from flower to flower.

Baruch: It's so peaceful here, clean. You should look for another teacher, Yehuda.

Yehuda looks up at him. He does not answer.

Baruch: I have nothing more to teach you. Your soul will guide you from here on.

Yehuda: Where will I find another teacher?

Baruch: Keep looking. Ask. If you ask, it will be revealed to you. The Creator will not leave you now. He has some big plans for you. New times are coming, not suited for old timers like me.

Yehuda: Should I take you home?

---

26 The "ark" is a closed system of desires that aim only toward bestowal and love. A person seemingly rises above the ego and temporarily "drowns" the rest of the desires, meaning avoids using them. Thus, one "sails" in the ark, protected within one's pure thoughts.

Baruch: No, I will sit here on this stump, and listen to the silence. I might learn a thing or two.

Yehuda stands up.

Yehuda: I have to go.

Baruch: Go.

Yehuda turns around and starts quickly down the road.
Baruch follows him with his gaze, as he calls his name.

-Yehuda!...

Yehuda can't hear him.

Baruch: Don't come back here anymore, Yehuda! You mustn't return here.

Yehuda increases his pace, almost runs.

-But I will be waiting for you, Baruch whispers, my great student... and teacher.

***

Warsaw. Main street.
Yehuda is walking quickly, barely minding his steps. Immersed in his thoughts, he is responding to nothing and no one.

***

Documentary footage:
Chronicle of the beginning of the 20th century.
A majestic costume ball at the winter palace in St. Petersburg.
The first Tour de France race.
America acknowledges the independence of Panama.
First communist demonstrations in Poland.
The Wright brothers make their first flight.
Cars are the new "it" thing.

***

Warsaw. Main street.
A growing hum of a crowd is nearing from somewhere.
Yehuda looks up.
He finds himself in the middle of the road; a crowd is Marching toward him.

Red flags are waving over people's heads. The international (communist anthem) is playing in the background.
Yehuda finds himself in the middle of the crowd, walking with them in the front rows.
Flags fly above his head.
Young men and women are Marching next to him.

Someone grabs him by the elbow.
Yan's face appears from the crowd.

Yan *(shouting over the crowd):* I knew you wouldn't sit on the sidelines.

Someone pushes the red flag into Yehuda's hand.

The crowd: Brotherhood! Equality! Freedom!

Yehuda begins to shout along with them.

People on the sidewalks are staring with amazement at an orthodox religious Jew carrying a red flag, shouting communist slogans together with everyone.

A pretty woman takes Yehuda's hand, Yan is holding his other hand.
Yehuda is smiling.
Everyone's faces are lit up with happiness and inspiration.

Suddenly a unit detachment of mounted police attacks the crowd from two side streets.

The police: Shut up, scum!

The baton-wielding policemen charge the crowd, their batons descending on people's heads.
The crowd stirs, then collapses.

The crowd: What are you doing, you sons of bitches!

People fall on the pavement, holding their heads, blood trickling between their fingers.
A baton rises above Yehuda.
A distorted face of a policeman:

-Aaaah, you dirty Jew, so you want equality?!

ENNIK POLSKI
THE POLISH DAILY NEWS.
Detroit, Mich., Piatek 2-go Stycznia, 1920.
Single Copy 2 cents.
Preliminarya pokojo- we rzadu sowietów z Estonia.
Papież wstawia się za 200,000 jeńców
PIĘDZIESIĘCIO
LEUSZ

Immediately a strong arm pushes the policeman away, grabs the lapels of Yehuda's coat, and throws him aside.
Yehuda is pressed against the wall of the house.
Yan is standing next to him.
He pushes Yehuda into a doorway.

Yan: Are you alive?! Then call to your God!

Through the half-open door we can see people running.
Policemen are chasing them on horseback, hitting them with their batons.

Yan: There is no one to call, hah?! No one! Because he can't exist! Just look what he, your God, is doing!

Yehuda tries to say something, but Yan jumps at him, pressing his hand against Yehuda's mouth, stifling his words.

Yan: He doesn't exist! He doesn't! And if he does exist, no one needs such a God because he is covered with our blood!

Two policemen are clobbering a young boy.
The boy is sobbing:

-I won't do it anymore. I won't...

Another policeman is dragging the pretty girl who Marched at Yehuda's side by the hair.

Yan *(whispering)*: You won't be able to explain this to me, you won't!

He tears away Yehuda's hat and throws it on the ground.
Then he runs out into the street, hurls himself in front of the policeman's horse, jumps up, and drags the policeman down by his jacket. He grabs the woman's hand and runs with her, disappearing around the corner.

***

Evening. The Jewish quarter in Warsaw.
An elderly couple walks past Yehuda, who is sitting on the steps of the house.

His coat is dirty; his hands are bleeding.

A woman: Are you all right?

Yehuda *(raising his head)*: No, not at all.

A woman: Can I help you?

Yehuda: I don't know.

He stands up and walks down the street.
Yehuda turns into his alley. Slowly, he climbs up the stairs to his apartment and opens the door. Once inside, he goes straight to his room.
His mother rushes toward him, looking at him with alarm.

Yehuda: I fell. Nothing serious.

Mother: There, in your room...

She doesn't finish, Yehuda opens the door to his room and stops at the doorstep.

Rabbi Feldman and teacher Shmuel are sitting at the table. His father is standing by the wall on the other side of the room.

Yehuda *(immediately)*: Don't worry, father, I merely slipped. *(Turns to the guests)* Hello, Rabbi Shmuel. Something happened?

Rabbi Feldman *(examining him)*: Don't be surprised, Yehuda. Your father, Simcha, invited us here. Please, take a seat.

Yehuda looks at his father, keeps standing.

Rabbi Feldman: You are studying Kabbalah, and we can't stop it now.

The teacher *(harshly)*: Forbid him to study Kabbalah! I said it many times, and I will say it again!

Rabbi Feldman: Well, it's not that simple anymore.

The teacher *(addresses Yehuda)*: You've broken every boundary. And what your father, Simcha, has told us...

Simcha tries not to look at Yehuda.

The teacher: Simcha is saying that you consider gentiles equal to Jews.

Yehuda: The most important thing is whether a person aspires to the Creator.

The teacher: And it's not important whether he is a gentile or a Jew, right?

Yehuda: Correct. It's irrelevant.

The teacher quickly looks at everyone:

The teacher: Well, I think the case is clear. We must stop this completely, right away! *(Pointing his finger at Yehuda)* This man came to destroy everything that has held us together for centuries. He is deadly to us. Yehuda, we forbid you to study Kabbalah *(seething)*. This madman, Baruch, this scoundrel and idiot!

Rabbi Feldman: Shmuel, please, I ask you...

The teacher: But look what he does to my students. *(Turning to Yehuda)* I repeat, we forbid you to study Kabbalah.

Yehuda: I cannot listen to you, Rabbi Shmuel. What you are telling me is to stop breathing, stop living. I cannot do that.

The teacher *(addressing Rabbi Feldman)*: We must ban all Jews in Poland from speaking to him. All Jews in Poland.

Rabbi Feldman: I recall that you applied for ordination as a rabbi?

Yehuda: Yes, I would like to take exams for ordination as a rabbi and to begin teaching.

The teacher: Whaaaat?! Do you think that after all we heard now it is possible?

Yehuda: I am asking for a minute of your patience; I can explain everything to you.

The teacher: Why should we listen to you?!

Rabbi Feldman: Wait a minute, Shmuel. We are listening to you, Yehuda.

Yehuda: We must introduce, as soon as possible, the study of *The Book of Zohar* into all our educational institutions. We must begin compulsory Kabbalah studies from the earliest age possible. By this, we will bring the light into the world and put an end to suffering. I can create the syllabus. I can begin teaching...

The teacher: A gentile can't teach Jews. And you are a gentile!

A pause. The teacher looks at Yehuda, Rabbi Feldman, then at Simcha, and back at Yehuda.

The teacher *(firmly)*: I, as a member of the council, will do everything in my power to make sure you fail the exam. You will not be a rabbi! I can't allow this plague that you have picked up to contaminate and destroy our people.

> He stands up abruptly and leaves the room. The door slams shut behind him.
> Rabbi Feldman shakes his head, watching him leave.

Rabbi Feldman: Why do you have to create confrontations with everyone, Yehuda? Why?

> Yehuda sits down, looks at Rabbi Feldman, then at his father.
> Simcha does not know where to put his eyes. He turns away.

Rabbi Feldman *(addresses Yehuda)*: Tell me, why on earth can't you, with your brilliant mind, keep silent when it's needed, keep certain things unsaid? You are so clever! You want to become a rabbi, don't you?

Yehuda: Yes.

Rabbi Feldman: Do you want to teach people?

Yehuda: This is the only reason why I want to become a rabbi.

Rabbi Feldman: Well, play it smart! Look at what you've done with the teacher! He starts shaking at the mere sight of you. He almost had a stroke just now. What is he to blame for? He was taught that way, he isn't to blame. You need to explain everything to him from an entirely different perspective.

> Yehuda is silent, looking at the floor.

Yehuda: I'm trying, but I'm not succeeding.

Rabbi Feldman: Well, realization is already a sign of progress. Well done. And now, *(sitting back comfortably)* tell me what you haven't told him.

> Yehuda is watching Rabbi Feldman suspiciously.

Yehuda: Everything?

Rabbi Feldman: Well, go ahead, tell me as it is. We Jews are bad, aren't we?

Yehuda is ill at ease.

Rabbi Feldman: I told you not to be afraid, so don't be afraid, speak up!

Yehuda *(makes up his mind)***:** The eyes of the whole world are fixed on us.

Rabbi Feldman: So it's always been.

Yehuda: Now it will be more than ever. There will be no leniency.

Rabbi Feldman: Why? Why now in particular?

Yehuda: A terrible century is dawning, a century of horrific suffering, terrible hatred, and unprecedented selfishness. And we Jews will be to blame for the suffering of the entire world.

Rabbi Feldman: Is that what the gentiles think?

Yehuda: It is what Kabbalah thinks, *The Book of Zohar*, it is what the Creator thinks.

Feldman is silent, conflicting thoughts racing within him.

Yehuda *(passionately)*: We are the ones who are stopping the Creator from being revealed in the world.

Rabbi Feldman: We are the people of the Creator; we observe the Torah and the commandments.

Yehuda: We shouldn't boast, fill ourselves with knowledge, and become arrogant, priding ourselves with scrupulous observance of the commandments. No!

Simcha: Yehuda, stop!

Rabbi Feldman: Let him speak!

Yehuda: We need to observe everything only in order to reveal the Creator, the light, love, to the entire world. To become the bearers of the light, instead of darkness.

Simcha watches his son with wonder and awe.

Rabbi Feldman: If you're going to talk like that, nobody will understand you. You are much too straightforward, too blunt.

Yehuda: You asked me to tell you the whole truth.

Rabbi Feldman: This is way too much.

Yehuda: I will try my best to make myself clear. I will search for ways to express it better so they can understand. I will make every effort. Why was I given this life if not for that? Otherwise, all of us, the whole world will experience unprecedented anguish.

Rabbi Feldman: How do you know that?

Yehuda: I do.

Rabbi Feldman: How?

Yehuda: I see it.

Rabbi Feldman stares at him in silence.
Silence hangs in the air. Raindrops fall behind the window.

Rabbi Feldman: I suppose you know that you have to submit three recommendation letters to be admitted to the exam.

Yehuda: Yes, I do.

Rabbi Feldman: Do you know anyone who will recommend you?

Yehuda is silent.
Rabbi Feldman stands up and walks to the door. He stops at the doorstep.

Rabbi Feldman: I will give you my recommendation. I will also ask Rabbi Zilber and Rabbi Epstein to vouch for you. They love you for your diligence and deep knowledge. Certainly, I won't tell them what I heard from you today.

Yehuda: I am grateful to you, honorable Rabbi.

***

Rabbinate.[27] A long corridor.
Jews in black capotas (traditional frock coat) and shtreimels (a typical fur hat) are sitting along the walls, crowded next to a closed door.
Two students press their ears against the keyhole, trying to hear what is happening inside, reporting what they hear to others in low tones.

Student #1: He responds at once!

Student #2 *(in admiration)*: He didn't even pause to think!

---

27 Rabbinate, from the Hebrew word *Rabanut,* is a religious establishment run by rabbis who test students' knowledge and ordain them as rabbis. The Rabbinate also judges, rules, marries, and divorces couples within the orthodox Jewry.

Student #1: Oh, what an answer!

Someone from the crowd: It's been more than three hours now.

Student #1: They are silent.

Student #2: They are silent.

Someone else from the crowd: Welllll?

Student #1: Well, they are still silent! Not a word.

Student #2: Hush, Rabbi Zilber is speaking. Congratulates him, he has passed. Excellent knowledge. Hopes that...

> The door opens, the two Jews almost get knocked down.
> The teacher goes out, makes a few steps along the corridor.
> Rabbi Feldman and other members of the commission are following him. They are talking to each other and nodding their heads.
> The teacher stops abruptly, waits for Rabbi Feldman.
> He whispers to him, but loud enough so everyone can hear.

The teacher: You are making a terrible mistake.

> Rabbi Feldman walks past him.

The teacher *(approaches an elderly rabbi who is walking behind Rabbi Feldman)*: Rabbi Zilber, we have to stop him. *(Turns to another elderly rabbi)* Rabbi Epstein!

Rabbi Epstein: I have done my best to stop him, you saw it for yourself. But it is impossible.

Rabbi Zilber: I can't recall anyone with such phenomenal knowledge... *(lingers)* and feeling.

> The rabbis walk on, talking to each other.
> Yehuda comes out of the room.
> Simcha jumps at Yehuda, his joy making him look like a child.
> Jews surround them, shaking Yehuda's hand.
> The teacher Shmuel is standing at a distance, at the end of the corridor, watching the scene.

***

> The Jewish quarter in Warsaw.
> A bright morning.
> Simcha and Yehuda are walking down the street.

Simcha can't stop talking, unable to contain his joy.
Two 16-year-old girls walk in their direction.
One of them raises her eyes and smiles timidly at Simcha.
Simcha smiles back.
The girls walk past them.
Yehuda looks back.

Yehuda: Who was that girl, father?

Simcha: Rivka, a distant relative.

Yehuda: How old is she?

Simcha: Sixteen.

Yehuda: I would like her to be my wife.

Simcha looks at Yehuda. Yehuda nods.

Yehuda: A kabbalist must be married.

***

A foot in a black shoe breaks a glass, wrapped in paper.
Immediately, brisk Jewish music starts playing; we are at a hassidic wedding.
Yehuda, the groom, is thrown up to the ceiling in the chair. Hassidic hats are tossed in the air, cheerful Hassidim jump up and down in a traditional dance. A kleizmer band is playing, twisting in tune to the music.
The wedding is joyous, a time to forget all the troubles!
It seems as though the Hassidim (pl. Of Hassid) are gliding in the air.

Baruch is watching the festivities from a corner.
A crowd of children surrounds him.
An almost empty bottle of vodka is in front of him.
Baruch is following Yehuda with his eyes.
Yehuda, in the midst of a dance, meets his gaze.
Baruch nods to him, raises his glass, drinks, and suddenly the glass disappears from his hand.
Baruch smiles and carefully picks up a glass full of vodka from the sleeve of his greasy frock coat.
The children around him laugh.
Yehuda laughs.
What lies ahead for Yehuda?

***

Right after the wedding, newlyweds Yehuda and Rivka move out from Warsaw to the small town of Pursov.
They rent an apartment directly across from Rivka's parents.

***

Midnight. Silence.
The small Polish town is asleep. The moon is gliding in the star-filled skies.
Beneath it, an old wooden home, its windows all dark.
A flickering, dim light appears in one of the windows.

Suddenly the silence is broken by the sound of cracking ice.
A pair of bare feet break through an icy crust and plunge into a small basin full of ice water.
A half-lit room.
Yehuda shakes his head and brings the book closer to his face. His feet are submerged in the ice water.
His young wife, Rivka, is watching him from behind a curtain.
She seems frightened.

***

From the street we can see Yehuda's silhouette in the dimly lit window.
A woman is looking at it from the house across the street. It is Dvora, Rivka's mother.
She turns her head from the window into the room and says something. Her husband's sleepy face appears in the window next to her. Both of them look out the window. They are watching Yehuda's sharp profile, still as a picture and deep in concentration.

***

Yehuda's and Rivka's apartment. Dawn.
Yehuda is leaning over the book.
The flame in the lamp dies out in a plume of smoke.
The clock shows five in the morning.
Rivka is already up, cooking breakfast.
Only now we can see that she is pregnant.

A quiet knock on the door.

Rivka answers it.
Her parents are standing at the doorstep.
They come inside.
Yehuda greets her father.
The father is wearing a white tallit.[28] He is full of self-respect in anticipation of the morning prayer.
Dvora kisses Rivka.

***

A synagogue in a small town.
Rivka's father and Yehuda are standing next to one another, praying.
The room is white with tallits, covering the prayers' heads.

***

Yehuda's and Rivka's apartment.
Rivka's father and Yehuda are sitting at the table.
Rivka and Dvora are busy serving them a simple breakfast.

Father *(addresses Yehuda)*: You look tired. Are you getting enough sleep?

Yehuda: Yes, I'm fine.

Father: How many hours of sleep do you get?

Yehuda: Three hours are enough for me.

Father: Nonsense!

Yehuda: I think that even that is too much.

Father: I see... Yehuda, you have a young wife.

Rivka: Father, please...

Father: There is no money in the house.

Rivka: We will repay you the debt next month.

Father *(firmly)*: And you are doing who knows what ... why do you wake up at 1 a.m.?

Yehuda: The night is given to me for my studies.

Father: No, the night is for you to be with your wife (to Rivka: Keep quiet, Rivka!) so that you may rest and then greet each day refreshed, with a prayer, and last but not the least, in search of the daily bread. You have a family to feed.

28 *Tallit*—a thin white prayer shawl that Jews wear during service.

Dvora moves behind her husband.

Father: We gave you Rivka thinking you were serious about building a family.

Rivka: Father, stop! You are interfering with our lives!

Dvora: No, this is wrong. We can't stand to watch him leaving you alone every night... doing only Lord knows what!

Rivka: Yehuda knows what he is doing!

Dvora: I think he's doing nothing. He hasn't brought home a single penny!

Rivka: Mother!

Dvora: Start listening to elders. Both of you. We want you to have a normal family. His Kabbalah interferes with your lives.

Rivka *(stands up)*: My husband is a great scholar. We earnestly ask you to stop interfering with our lives! Besides, he still has a little bit of time left to get some sleep, and you are distracting him with your senseless conversations.

Father: Whaaat?! Senseless?!

Dvora: In other words, you are asking us to leave?

Rivka: I want you to understand that I have a husband, whom I love, and we have a life together. I wish you would stay out of it.

Father: Stay out of it?

Rivka: Please.

The father stands up and walks toward the door. Dvora hurries after him.

Father *(from the door)*: Well, don't cry when you have nothing to feed your kids, and he – your great scholar – is too busy studying to find a job and care for you. Don't come to us crying then! Let's go, Dvora!

They leave. Yehuda looks at Rivka.

Yehuda: They won't come back here anymore.

Rivka: I've made my choice. I have you.

Yehuda comes up to her and hugs her.
Rivka puts her hand to her belly and says, smiling:

-He's so strong, he just can't keep still in there. He doesn't stop kicking.

She looks up at Yehuda and puts her head on his shoulder.

Rivka: I think we have to move away from here. They won't leave us alone. What do you think?

Yehuda: As you say.

***

Morning. A skinny horse is pulling a wagon. Yehuda and Rivka are sitting inside. Their entire belongings consist of two sacks – one full of clothes, the other full of books.
The coachman gently urges his horse as he recites verses from Psalms.

- "Happy is the man who has not walked in the counsel of the wicked, nor stood in the way of sinners..."

He raises one crooked finger up.

- "...Nor sat in the seat of the scornful."

He shakes his head, almost singing.

- "And he shall be like a tree planted by streams of water, that brings forth its fruit in its season, and whose leaf does not wither; and in whatsoever he does he shall prosper."

The coachman turns to Yehuda and Rivka and winks to them.

-I can see that you are a rabbi, an educated man – he says,- and your wife is a beautiful woman. I, on the other hand, have been working since I was seven years old, I can't read or write anymore - I don't need it. I just memorize everything my son is reading, and I cry. ...It's just so beautiful. It's a wonder anyone could write like that.

Yehuda looks at him and smiles.
The coachman urges his horse and cocks his finger up again.

The coachman: "Though a host should encamp against me, my heart shall not fear; though war should rise up against me, even then will I be confident."

The coachman shakes his hand and clicks his tongue loudly.

The coachman: Ahhh! How sweet, how beautiful, ay! My son reads it so beautifully. He sits and ponders over it, then explains it all to an old fool like me. He says that I love only myself, but that the Creator loves everybody.

Yehuda: Does he say that?

The coachman: Yes, he does! He's so clever, my boy!

Yehuda: What's your son's name?

The coachman: Moshe. He is only ten. He always says, "Father, just look how kind is our Creator." - Yes, I say, sure, He is kind.

He shakes his head, then turns back, and urges his horse.

The coachman: Well, hurry up, you old jade!

Suddenly his voice changes. We can see him wiping tears with his sleeve.

The coachman: E-hhh! Sure, He is kind. If He is so kind, then why did He take my son's legs?

Turns back to Yehuda, his eyes sparkling with tears.

The coachman: Huh? He's such a golden boy, my son, esteemed Rabbi, he knows everything, but his legs don't work since birth. Of course, I'm not complaining, the Lord knows best. But can you just tell me, Rabbi, why He took my son's legs?

Yehuda is silent.
Rivka, holding her belly with one hand, is looking at her husband.

Yehuda: How far do you live from here?

The coachman: Not that close. About two hours ride with my jade, if she doesn't drop dead on the way.

Yehuda: I want to talk to your son. Will you let me?

The coachman: O-o-h my esteemed Rabbi! He will be so happy! He saw a rabbi only twice in his life, one of which was on his *brith*.[29] (*Glances at Rivka*) But the road is very bad, your wife is almost ready to...

Rivka: No, I am feeling just fine. (*Looks at Yehuda.*) Let's go.

29 *Brith* (circumcision): A Jewish custom in which the foreskin of a newborn male is removed from the penis 8 days after birth.

Yehuda *(to the coachman)*: Let's go.

The coachman tugs at the reins vigorously.

The coachman: Come now, you old hag, don't you linger! Whoa! Little Moshe is in for a big surprise!

The old horse looks at its driver out of the corner of its eye and starts trotting a little faster.
The wagon is riding along an uneven road, swinging from side to side.
The coachman recites in his raspy voice:

- "The words of the preacher, son of David, king of Jerusalem: 'vanity of vanities,' says the preacher; 'vanity of vanities, all is vanity.'"

The coachman recites aloud from Ecclesiastes:

-How right he is! "One generation goes, and another generation comes; but the earth remains forever."

The wagon drives on.
Yehuda covers Rivka with his coat.
She presses herself against him.
A great gray wilderness stretches before them: Fields, a far away forest, a lonely pine tree on a faraway hill.
The coachman's voice:

- "That which has been is that which shall be; and that which has been done is that which shall be done: And there is nothing new under the sun."

The sun is setting.
The wagon tosses from side to side on the rugged road.
Rivka is sitting, pressing herself against Yehuda, holding her belly anxiously.
A moment later she steps off the wagon and walks behind it, her legs knee-deep in mud. She is holding Yehuda's hand.

The wagon enters a small, poor village.
It veers from the main road and a few turns later the coachman points toward a low black wooden house.
A child's pale face is looking out the window.

The coachman: Here is my little boy.

> They enter the house.
> Simple, scant furniture.
> A child, Moshe, is sitting on a wooden chair, made especially for him.
> A book lies open before him on the window sill.
> His legs, like shoelaces, dangle lifelessly from the chair.
> Moshe smiles to the guests.
>
> The coachman spreads his arms in joy and effortlessly lifts Moshe from his chair.
> Moshe hugs his father and kisses his stubbly cheek.

The coachman: Well, honorable Rabbi, here is my little boy, my Moshe, the joy of my life.

> Yehuda looks fixedly at Moshe, who stares back at him.
> Yehuda extends his arms and takes Moshe from his father's lap.
> The boy hugs him by the neck and pulls himself close to him.
> Rivka sits at the door and quietly looks at them.

Moshe (*addresses Yehuda*): How are you?

Yehuda: I am always thinking about Him, every day of my life.

Moshe: There is none else besides Him. He cares and thinks about us...

The coachman (*grumbles*): Why did He do this to you, if He cares?

> Moshe smiles and touches Yehuda's hand.
> Yehuda sits down.

Moshe: Don't listen to him. He simply loves me so much, he just can't get that everything that comes from the Creator is absolute good.

The coachman (*sighs*): O-o-o-oww!

Moshe: He is doing all this intentionally, to confuse us, so that we may rise above all our thoughts and suffering and say, "All that exists is You! You are the greatest good, our beloved father who loves all, all of us."

> Yehuda looks at the boy in admiration.
> Moshe slaps his hands on his motionless thighs.

Moshe: As for the body, it will always go on moaning. The body loves only itself. (*Secretively and with a smile Moshe goes on*) But there is a little part of Him in us, really small, like that (*he shows his little finger*). No, even smaller (*he brings his thumb to the last phalange of his pinky*), that small, a little tiny point. It is called "a soul." He gave it to us. He talks only with it. The soul, not the body, speaks to the Creator. Do I have it right, dear Rabbi?

Yehuda (*with admiration*): Your every single word is truth.

Moshe: I don't want to be my body's companion, I want to cling to my soul. Let the body suffer; I don't want to deal with it. I am with my soul and my soul is singing.

The coachman (*excitedly*): Such is my little beloved boy, esteemed Rabbi, so strange, so adorable. Silly me – I don't get what he says; I just want to sing on Sabbath[30] and drink some vodka. And to earn some money to support us and to buy him books. He has thumbed this one down to its threads; he knows it word for word. Just ask him! Well, ask him! Come, Moshe, let our esteemed Rabbi hear you recite something the way you recite to me.

> Suddenly everybody can see that Moshe is not there. That is, he is there but his gaze is fixed on something far away, outside the window. A silent, peaceful gaze.
> Yehuda is watching Moshe, afraid to distract him.
> How similar they are at this moment!

The coachman (*whispering*): It often happens like this. He will sit and read for hours on end and then he will lift his eyes and look. At what? Our mare? The road outside?

Yehuda (*whispering*): Can't you see with whom he is conversing?

> The coachman strains to look out the window in the direction of Moshe's gaze.

The coachman: Is it our old horse he's taking to?

Yehuda: Your son is right, you are silly. Beyond this window there is light. And your boy is a great and happy man. He can see this light.

---

30 Sabbath (Saturday), the holy day for the Jews

Moshe shifts his gaze to Yehuda and suddenly says in an adult voice:

-You have to tell all of them about this so they understand. Know that the Creator has chosen you for a reason. He wants you to explain everything to them. They are blind; they can't be blamed. You, however, have to find the right words for them.

Yehuda: I'm doing my best, I am thinking a lot about how to do this.

Moshe: You will succeed.

Yehuda: I don't know...

Moshe: But I do.

Yehuda (*looks at him*): Wait, just a second.

Suddenly Yehuda stands up and leaves the house.
He returns with a bag, unties it on the table, and takes out *The Book of Zohar*.

Yehuda: I want to leave this book with you.

Moshe examines its cover with awe.

Moshe: *The Zohar*... I must finish it in time. It would be a shame if I didn't.

He opens the book and is immediately lost in it. He dives into the book, and the room and the people in it disappear for him. His eyes swallow the text, drinking in its lines.
Everyone is looking at Moshe.

The coachman: That's it, now he'll be gone till the morning. He doesn't eat, doesn't drink, just asks to feed the kerosene in the lamp. I need to buy more; what's left won't last for more than two nights. Thank you so much for the book, honorable Rabbi– it's such a great gift for my boy. I will take you home free of charge.

They silently come out into the yard and climb into the wagon.
The coachman tugs on the reins and the old mare starts moving.
Yehuda looks at the window of the lonely house where the little boy can be seen reading his book.
The kerosene lamp is already lit.
Night falls.

Yehuda turns to Rivka.

Yehuda: So it happens, a messenger[31] has come to me and put everything in its right place. (*Thoughtfully*) I must explain all of this to them..., so they will understand. I must!

***

Documentary footage rolls slowly, in silence: Russia–Japan war, the battle of Tsushima. The defeat of the Russian fleet. Cheerful Theodore Roosevelt waving his hand after being elected for the second term. Sailors revolt on the "Potiomkin" ironclad. The English football club "Chelsea" is founded. The onset of the first Russian Revolution – police fire at peaceful demonstrators.

***

A Warsaw street.
Rav[32] Yehuda Ashlag stops abruptly in the middle of the street.
Terrified and astounded, he watches as people are shot.
He looks closer. The revolutionary sailors of 1917 emerge from the fog and drizzle. They run in Yehuda's direction, their rifles spewing out fire.

Yehuda lifts up the collar of his coat. He walks down a misty street, shivering from cold.

Suddenly he spots Lenin marching next to him.
Yehuda follows him with his eyes and sees wagons full of prisoners disappear into the mist.

Yehuda continues down the street.

German storm troopers pass him by. The young Hitler salutes them with an outstretched arm.

Now he is walking through the Jewish quarter.

A nuclear mushroom cloud rises above the houses.

---

31 A messenger – the Creator manifests to a person through any phenomenon, book, or person. One only needs to be ready to accept His message.

32 In Hebrew, both "Rav" and "Rabbi" can be used as a title before someone's name. But since the term "Rabbi" has a more orthodox connotation than "Rav," the latter will be used here to denote rabbis who are also known as Kabbalists. Exceptions are Kabbalists who are already known as rabbis, such as Rabbi Shimon bar Yochai and Rabbi Akiva.

RADIATION HAZ
TOUCHING or REMOVING
SCRAP OBJECTS IS
PROHIBITED
THIS INCLUDES BLASTED DEBRIS, FUSED SILICA
METAL FRAGMENTS etc. LOCATED North of this POINT

Yehuda enters a building.

Ben-Gurion proclaims the establishment of The State of Israel.
A plane crashes into a skyscraper.

***

Rav Yehuda Ashlag enters a classroom.
Sitting among the students, whose age ranges from twenty to sixty, is Rabbi Feldman.
Rav Ashlag starts talking the moment he walks through the door.

Rav Ashlag: There is one unified soul. (*He draws a circle in the air with his hands.*) In it, all of our souls are linked closely together. They are bonded with the force of love, the only law that exists.

Rav Ashlag scans the faces of his students.
Rabbi Feldman is sitting in one corner, listening attentively.

Rav Ashlag: The Creator broke this one unified soul, and now we have to restore that union by ourselves. That is, we have to rise above our egos, up to the degree of love.

Chaim (*a young student*): Love between all.

Rav Ashlag: Love between all.

Chaim: All Jews.

Rav Ashlag: The entire world.

Chaim: ...which hates us.

Rav Ashlag: The whole world will rise from hatred to love.

Aaron (*another young student with a nervous face and feverishly burning eyes*):

Why did the Creator have to break this unified soul?! What for?! He wants us to be happy, doesn't He? We were all happy, united, so why, then?!

Rav Ashlag: What for?

Aaron: Yes-yes-yes! Why did He cast us into this crazy world, separated into nations, races, rich and poor, Jews and non-Jews, what for?!

Rav Ashlag (*stopping in front of Aaron*): He wanted us to become His equals.

Aaron: I don't understand.

Rav Ashlag: Not His slaves, but His equals.

Aaron (*frantically*): I still don't get it!

Rav Ashlag: When you bathe in the light, when you are completely filled with it, what else do you desire?

Aaron: To be inside the light all the time. What's wrong with that?

Rav Ashlag: He doesn't want to turn us into slaves of the light. He wants us to become free, to be truly equal to Him. What good are we to Him as mindless beings He can bend as He wishes? He wants free humans by His side, who voluntarily decide to be by His side, to become equals, friends, rather than slaves. Equals! How can this be done?!

> Rav Ashlag stops and looks around the classroom.
> Everyone is waiting for him to continue.

Rav Ashlag: There is just one way: To break the unified soul into small, individual pieces, clothe them in bodies of this world, plunge them into all that egoism, that hatred, make them His opposites so that from this reality they would return to Him by themselves. Independently! They need to wish to rise up from this blackness back to Him by themselves and willingly live according to His law.

> Silence.

Chaim: How can this be accomplished?

***

> Rav Ashlag's home. Night.
> Rav Ashlag is writing.
> Neat lines appear on the paper.
> We can hear Rav Ashlag whispering:

- "How can this be accomplished?! How can we live according to His law if we are born as wild beasts, absolutely opposite to Him? He is the light of the world, and we, on the other hand, are at the lowest, grimiest point, living only for ourselves! How can we rise toward the Creator?"

> A quiet knock on the door. Everybody is asleep. Yehuda answers the door.
> The coachman is standing outside holding *The Book of Zohar* in his

hands.

Yehuda looks at him and asks without hesitation:

-When?

The coachman: Tonight, an hour ago. The last thing he said to me was to give this to you right away, my esteemed rav.

He hands over *The Book of Zohar* and a note.

The coachman (*in haste*): Well, I must be on my way; I don't want to leave him all alone. He became so tiny all of a sudden...

Suddenly the coachman's face contorts and he begins to sob like a little boy. He wipes his eyes with a muddy glove, smearing dirt across his face.

The coachman: He seemed so much bigger when he was alive. It appears that you, dear Rav, added a few days to his life. (*Then, almost cheerfully*) He died peacefully. He was smiling when he passed away.

He stops, ruffles the gloves in his hands, and lowers his gaze.

The coachman: What will I do now, without him? All by myself...

The coachman turns away and wearily walks down the stairs.

Rav Ashlag opens the note.

His eyes run along the lines. He reads:

- "The Creator is taking me to Him now. But before He does, He gave me a precious gift, a chance to read such a great book! It's a book about my soul, about the whole world, about the path to Him, which everyone will have to walk. He is inviting us to come to His feast. He has fixed a table for us, but we didn't show up. Tell them about it. Be patient with them, as with little children. Tell them what bliss the Creator has in store for us. I am grateful to you for staying here to accomplish this task. I have faith in you, our beloved Rav Yehuda. We had to meet, and I had to tell you what I did. My poor, poor father doesn't know how magnificent the Creator truly is!"

A pair of hands wraps a duvet around Rav Ashlag's shoulders.

He turns around. Rivka is standing behind him.

Rivka: You can't afford to get sick.

He looks at her with gratitude.

Rivka: I have a feeling that it wasn't a boy at all.

Yehuda: Who then?

Rivka: It was Him...

***

Rav Ashlag's home. That same night.
Rav Ashlag is sitting at the table, covered with the duvet.
The Book of Zohar that the coachman returned is opened in front of him.
A dried blade of grass sticks out from between the pages.

Rav Ashlag opens the book where the blade is placed.
His gaze falls at once on a few lines of text scribbled by a child's hand.
He can make out only the first line: "find Him in yourself..."
The letters rush toward him, and he senses...

***

A dusty road unfolds like a carpet before Rav Ashlag.
Behind him lies the exit of the tunnel and a great tree – "the ark" – with its dark hollow facing up.

***

For a moment, he is back in his room.
Rav Ashlag looks out the window.
He plunges his quill into the blue black ink, then a straight line appears under his quill:

"Time to leave the ark.[33]"

***

A burst of light.
A bright day after a heavy storm.
A dusty road curves among blue mountains.
Shaded forests rise up.

---

33 A person leaves the ark when the pure thoughts with which he has lived thus far prepare him for birth, after nine months and one day. This does not refer to physical time, but to a spiritual state: A person contemplates bestowal and love, lives in these thoughts like a fetus in the womb, and grows stronger. When the initial structure of one's soul is designed, it is time to leave the ark and work (receive) with the egoistic desires, which have thus far been put aside.

- "The ark protected you from... yourself. Now that you are stronger, you have to leave it."

Rav Ashlag is walking through fields of flowers in bloom, contemplating the endless beauty.
But his quill is producing lines of a different nature:

-"Expect the descents,[34] and be ready for them."***

Back in the room, Rav Ashlag gazes out the window.

-"You are letting your 'self' into yourself" – he whispers - "and it is dark, very dark there."

***

Suddenly the ground splits open under him and he falls into a deep, black pit. Scratching himself on the sharp edges of the hole, he keeps falling on and on, and the echo multiplies his screams:

-Aaaaah!

He lands flat on a stone floor inside a dimly lit hall.
Immediately, an unseen force lifts him up, turns him on his heels, and pushes him forward. He makes a few automatic steps.

Another line appears on the paper:

-"You have no idea who you really are!"

Torches are burning on all four sides of the hall.
Suddenly Rav Ashlag sees a golden throne right in front of him and a man sitting on it, his face cloaked in darkness. Rav Ashlag grabs one of the torches and raises it above his head. Pharaoh[35] is sitting on the throne.
Pharaoh has Rav Ashlag's face.

***

Rav Ashlag's room.
The Book of Zohar is open to the portion "in the end," precisely on the line that reads, "and he faced the Pharaoh of Egypt."

---

34 A descent is a loss of contact with spirituality. It happens when a new portion of egoism is added to a person, which must now be dealt with and corrected. Our mission is to shorten the duration of these descents as much as possible, but they cannot be avoided altogether.
35 Pharaoh is the egoistic force of self-love that governs a person.

He can read a few words in a child's handwriting:

-"Face him and defeat him."[36]

***

The next day. Rav Ashlag's classroom.
Again, all eyes are fixed on him. Rabbi Feldman is sitting in the corner.
Rav Ashlag stops before Chaim.

Rav Ashlag: You asked how can we return to the Creator?

Chaim: Yes. I couldn't sleep. I thought about it all night.

Rav Ashlag: Do you feel that your state is unbearable?

Chaim: Yes, I do.

Rav Ashlag: Why?

Chaim: I feel that there is no end to these sufferings.

Rav Ashlag: Do you know why you are suffering?

Chaim: I don't know. Everything is so empty, tasteless, that nothing brings me joy.

Rav Ashlag (*sharply*): You are to blame for all of this!

Chaim (*in astonishment*): Me?!

Rav Ashlag: Yes, you, who else? It's you who won't let him manifest!

Chaim: But I love the Creator!

Rav Ashlag: You love yourself, not the Creator.

Chaim: That's not my experience.

Rav Ashlag (*pointing his finger at him sharply*): This is the first stage that we have to go through. (*He takes a step back and surveys the class*) We need to understand that we are not righteous at all, we are liars and thieves who love no one but ourselves.

***

A flash of light. Pharaoh's chamber.
Pharaoh with the face of Rav Ashlag is staring at the rav from his golden throne under the light of torches.

36 A person who sees Pharaoh is one who feels that force within, and oneself as a servant of that force. Defeating Pharaoh means aiming one's internal forces toward bestowal and love, rather than toward self-gratification. When that happens, the Creator will take Pharaoh's place within that person.

Rav Ashlag's voice:

-It's not given to just anyone. Nobody enters there by chance. Only those whose heart is broken enter there, those who can't bear to live without an answer to the question about what they are living for. The truth can be revealed only to such people. Only they can endure it. Only they will be allowed to descend into the abyss, the place where no one ever dared look: Into the self, into the pitch darkness of egoism. And what do they see there?

***

A flash of light.
A Pharaoh with the face of Rav Ashlag is sitting on the throne.

Rav Ashlag's voice:

-The awful grin of your master.

Pharaoh smiles.
He points at a golden chair next to his throne.
An unseen force pulls Rav Ashlag forward and an instant later, he's sitting next to Pharaoh.
He tries to stand up but golden shackles bind his hands and feet to the chair.

Rav Ashlag's voice:

-Pharaoh is our essence. We work all our lives to satisfy no one but him. He rules us. He is our nature, our "I."

Pharaoh on the throne is laughing.
He removes a golden ring from one finger and offers it to Rav Ashlag.
It attaches itself to his finger as if glued by a powerful force.

***

Classroom.

Aaron: But isn't Pharaoh a man? It says in the Torah...

Rav Ashlag: The Torah doesn't speak of people.

Aaron: I don't get it. Was there no Abraham, no Moses, the story of the Egyptian exile?

Rav Ashlag: If you read the Torah like that, you are killing it and yourself. There is not a single word there about this world. There are no people. The Torah speaks about forces that can guide you back to the Creator. It is a secret instruction for the revelation of the Creator. *The Book of Zohar* is the key to that instruction.

Aaron: So Pharaoh is a force?

Rav Ashlag: And an enormous force at that.

Aaron: Is this force within me?

Rav Ashlag: Pharaoh lives within each of us.

Aaron: We are slaves to this force, aren't we?

Rav Ashlag: It rules us. It is our every thought and action; it is our life. If we realize this, if we feel that it's unbearable, it will mean that we do not agree with its dominion over us. It will mean that we have chosen the Creator. By hating our ego we take the first step toward the Creator.

He looks around the class again. Pauses.

Chaim (*very distinctly, almost syllable by syllable*): How can I go to Pharaoh? How can I come to hate my ego? How?!

The classroom door opens and an old Jew obsequiously approaches Rav Ashlag:

-The prayer is about to start, the revered Rav Ashlag.

Rav Ashlag (*to his students*): Go, pray and consider what we talked about.

The students leave the class.
Rav Ashlag sits down and stares fixedly at his hands; they are shaking.

***

Synagogue.
Rav Ashlag enters.
The parishioners whisper to each other excitedly when they see him.
An old Jew reverently offers him his seat.
Rav Ashlag walks on.
His students, Chaim and Aaron, stand up to greet him.
He walks past them without stopping.
He is ushered toward the cabinet where the books of Torah are kept.
People make room for him right in front of it, but he turns away and walks to the window.

They don't leave him alone even there.

The elder of the community comes up to him and shakes his hand.

The elder: Honorable Rav, your students tell me that you are a great teacher. I would like to ask you to give us, old men, a few lessons. You can choose any topic you wish.

Everyone is watching him, waiting for his reply.

He is silent.

The elder *(addressing everyone)*: The honorable Rav Ashlag will be leading the service today.

Rav Ashlag remains motionless.

The elder: Well, Rav Ashlag, everyone is waiting for you.

Rav Ashlag *(unexpectedly loudly and clearly)*: Do you need someone to bow to?

The congregation quiets down abruptly and everybody turns to face him.

The elder: I don't understand...

Rav Ashlag: Isn't the Creator good enough for you?! *(Looks around)* Well, of course, He is somewhere up there! You need someone close at hand, someone you can hold in your pocket, see, peek into his mouth, offer him your chair, kiss his hand! You need someone to honor here, on this earth, in this synagogue!

A loud whisper. Someone yelps in the back, the crowd stirs, surprise and fear show up on people's faces.

Rav Ashlag: But know this – it will not be me.

Chaim: Are you feeling well, teacher?

Rav Ashlag: I feel great, Chaim.

The elder: Are you sure?

Rav Ashlag: Yes, I am sure.

Heavy silence hangs in the air.

The elder *(looking around with a light smirk)*: And this man has taken upon himself to teach us something?!

A voice: Throw him out!

An old Jew *(who attended Rav Ashlag's lesson)*: Such arrogance! Just moments ago he had sung such sweet sermons to us! Oh, how he condemned the ego! You could have easily believed that a righteous man was standing before you, but now we see his true face!

A voice: Out!

Voices: Ouuuut!

Rav Ashlag walks through the crowd.
People step back to let him through.
Chaim and Aaron try to follow him but the elder stops them.

The elder *(loudly)*: If you leave now, you can forget the way back.

Immediately, a few men surround Chaim and Aaron, firmly blocking their way out.
Aaron takes his seat at once.
Chaim remains standing, surrounded by the men, watching with anguish and pain as Rav Ashlag leaves.
The door closes behind Rav Ashlag.

***

Outside, in front of the synagogue.
Rav Ashlag comes out of the synagogue.
Rabbi Feldman follows him out.

Rabbi Feldman: Wait.

Rav Ashlag stops.

Rabbi Feldman: If only I could continue to be your student...

The elder looks out of the synagogue, behind him are a few other Jews and Chaim among them.

The elder *(firmly)*: Rabbi Feldman, the prayer has begun. Leave him alone, he won't understand anyway. *(Now firmly, almost like an order.)* Come inside now, honorable Rabbi, we are waiting for you.

Rabbi Feldman makes a gesture to shake Rav Ashlag's hand, but his hand stops in mid-air. He turns around, lowers his head, and quickly walks back to the synagogue.

Chaim, standing alone at the door to the synagogue, watches Rav Ashlag leave. A hand appears from the shadows behind him and pulls him inside by the shoulder. He doesn't resist.

***

Rav Ashlag's room. Night.
Bare feet stand on a bed of sharp stones.
Rav Ashlag is leaning over a book.

Rivka sits in the dark, a little baby in her arms.
Eight-day-old Baruch Shalom[37] is sleeping, having nestled next to her.
She is rocking the baby and looking at her husband.

Rivka: They are asking us to leave this place as soon as possible. The landlord refuses to wait another day.

Rav Ashlag *(meeting her eyes)*: Can't you see I am studying?

Rivka: Forgive me, I just wanted to tell you that I will have to disturb you in the morning. I must pack. I have found a new place. The coachman will be here in the morning to take us.

Rav Ashlag *(looking at her for a long time)*: I am sorry I'm making it so hard on you.

Rav Ashlag stands up, and suddenly...

***

A flash of light. The dimly lit chamber of Pharaoh.
The golden shackles that cuff Rav Ashlag's hands and feet suddenly turn to dust. He tries to stand up, but he can't move.

***

Rav Ashlag's room.
He takes a step toward Rivka and suddenly collapses on the floor before Rivka can catch him.

***

37 Rav Baruch Shalom, the Rabash, Rav Yehuda Ashlag's firstborn son and successor. The Rabash was authorized to pass on the tenets of the spiritual work—which was thus far conveyed only orally—by way of personal letters. The Kabbalah group, Bnei Baruch (sons of Baruch), is named after him.

A flash of light.
Pharaoh's laughing face is inches from his.

***

Back in the room.
Rav Ashlag collapses on the floor. He tries to stand up but fails.
Rivka bends down, holding his head in her hands.

-What's happening to you? – She screams frightened.

***

A flash of light.
Pharaoh touches Rav Ashlag with his finger and the rav is hurled back in his chair, crashing against the far wall.
Pharaoh raises one hand, and to his horror, Rav Ashlag sees his own hand going up as well. He takes a step toward the rav and the rav takes a step toward Pharaoh. He is helpless.

***

The room.
Rav Ashlag cannot get on his feet.

-What is it? Is it your heart?! – Rivka's big eyes are now full of worry.

-The first lines... - he mumbles - the first words are...

Rav Ashlag wrinkles his face, trying to remember them.[38]
His mind is blank... complete emptiness...

-"Behold, that before..."

He falls silent.

... "The emanations..."- Rivka continues in apprehension.

He looks at her.

-Don't scare me, dear, she says, "the emanations were emanated and the creatures were created..." please, repeat after me, "the emanations were emanated and the creatures were created..."

38 Descents, where the Kabbalist completely forgets everything, are sometimes given preceding a great ascent.

Rav Ashlag *(faintly repeating after her)*: ... "The emanations were emanated... *(wrinkles his forehead)* and the creatures were created...

Rivka: ... "the upper simple light..."

Rav Ashlag mumbles as he tries to pronounce the words.

Rivka *(gently)*: Don't rush! Calm down...

Rav Ashlag: "the upper simple light..."

Rivka: "had filled the whole existence..."

Rav Ashlag: "had filled the whole existence..."

Rivka holds his head. She looks into his eyes and talks to him as if to a child:

Rivka: "and there was no..." *(repeats)* "there was no..."

Rav Ashlag: "and there was no..."

Rivka: "...vacancy..."

Rav Ashlag: "...vacancy..." *(in despair)* I can't remember!

Rivka: Yes, you can! You remember everything! "But all was filled with simple... simple...?!"

Rav Ashlag *(wearily, almost whispering)*: "But all was filled with that simple... *(making an effort to recall)* simple...

Rivka: Now on your own... remember, please try to remember, my love! What's next?

Rav Ashlag *(with the last ounce of willpower)*: "But all was filled with that simple ..."

Rivka: Yes!

Rav Ashlag *(with effort)*: "Boundless..."

Rivka: Yes, yes!

Rav Ashlag: "light."

Rivka: Well done!

Rav Ashlag *(exhales, and repeats after her)*: Well done.

Rav Ashlag is rocking back and forth on a chair.
Rivka pats him on his head and repeats:

-See, everything is all right! You remembered everything. A few more minutes and it will go away.

He pulls the book closer to him. The lines seem blurred.

Rav Ashlag *(to Rivka)*: Go... go. I will be fine.

His finger moves along the lines of the book; his lips move, forming words out of letters, but he cannot say them out loud.
His hand drops. Rav Ashlag is asleep.

Daybreak.
The kerosene lamp is out. Pale plumes of smoke rise from its blackened coil.
Rav Ashlag opens his eyes.
He is lying on a bed, alone in the room.
He gets up with effort, opens the window, and frosty winter air flushes his face. He inhales deeply.

***

Morning. A wagon is jogging down the uneven brick road.
The coachman is reciting lines from "Ecclesiastes."

The coachman: "The words of the preacher, the son of David, king of Jerusalem: Vanity of vanities, says the preacher, vanity of vanities; all is vanity. What profit has a man from all his labor which he does under the sun?"

Rav Ashlag is sitting atop sacks full of his family's meager belongings.
His gaunt face reveals that he had lost a lot of weight that night.
Sitting next to him are his eight-year-old son, Baruch Shalom, and Rivka, with a baby in her arms.
The streets of Warsaw are drifting by.

The coachman's voice: "One generation goes and another generation comes, but the earth abides forever..."

Suddenly the paved road slips out of focus, and Rav Ashlag's vision becomes blurry.
He sees four silhouettes of forest trees sway against the gray background of the autumn skies.
Passersby are looking at him.

The coachman's voice comes from a distance:

"That which has been is that which shall be; and that which has been done is that which shall be done: And there is nothing new under the sun."

-I wish... - Rav Ashlag whispers. – I need... - he barely utters the words, - to see old Baruch.

-Good! – Rivka understands what he mumbles. – Turn around! – She orders the coachman. - I know the way.

***

Evening. Country road.

The cart approaches Baruch's old house with its familiar tilt.

-Stop here. Wait for me here.- Rav Ashlag mumbles faintly.

The wagon stops. Rav Ashlag climbs down and walks to the house. The house with its boarded windows, black from the rain, is getting closer. Baruch's baby blue eyes are watching Rav Ashlag through the cracks.

Rav Ashlag *(his tongue heavy)*: Let me in.

Baruch *(curtly)*: What are you doing here? There's nothing I can give you!

Rav Ashlag: I am tired-d-d....

Baruch: Did I ever say it would be easy?

Rav Ashlag: A little rest...

Baruch: Nonsense! Get away from here! Turn around, you hear me?

Rav Ashlag: I can't see anything! He will never let me go.

Baruch: Crybaby! How could He have possibly chosen you, such a weakling. Is He blind? Can't He see who is standing before him?! *(Yelling sharply.)* Scram!

Rav Ashlag turns around as if in a dream.

Baruch *(much softer)*: Didn't I tell you that I am not your teacher anymore, Yehuda?

Rav Ashlag sits down wearily on the stack of firewood, his back pressed against the side of the house, he shuts his eyes in exhaustion.

That instant, dirty water splashes across his face. An older, wearier-looking Baruch is standing next to him, an empty bucket in hand.

Baruch: I told you to keep walking and to not sit down! Go, keep on walking! I've shown you the way!

Rivka is running toward them from the nearby standing wagon. She leans over the drenched Rav Ashlag.

Rivka: What is he doing to you?! *(Turning to Baruch.)* This is my husband! What are you doing?!

Baruch *(casually)*: Take him away!

Rivka helps Rav Ashlag up.

Rivka: Everything's going to be all right, my dear. It will be over soon.

Suddenly Baruch leaps at Rav Ashlag, tearing him away from Rivka, and whispers in his ear, venomously:

-Before each ascent there will come a descent. Haven't I told you that?! There is no ascent without an abyss!

Rav Ashlag *(his lips barely moving)*: He won't... let me go.

Baruch: You are not demanding hard enough. There is just one force. Demand it!

Rav Ashlag: I... am...

Baruch: Then demand harder!

Rav Ashlag: I'm dem...anding... that the Creator ... will help... me.

Rav Ashlag goes limp in Baruch's hands.
Rivka supports him.

Rivka: Can you help him?

Baruch *(shaking his head)***:** I can't help him anymore.

Rav Ashlag *(mumbles to himself)*: I am howling... but He doesn't hear. He has forsaken me... Pharaoh has... found me... instead.

Rivka: What is he talking about?

Baruch: He is all right. It's just that he is at such a high degree. Truly great! My head is spinning from these heights. Take him. Everything is going to be fine, woman!

Rivka helps Rav Ashlag to his feet.
He is leaning on her, his legs barely moving.

Baruch *(from behind)*: See, God has rewarded you, and me as well - in my old age - to have such a miracle grow in our hands.

He watches Rivka drag Rav Ashlag away, and shakes his head.

***

Five long years go by in persistent search of a teacher. Rav Ashlag combs Poland east to west and north to south.
He comes across knowledgeable people, sages, and famous ravs.
Sometimes he needs a few hours, other times only several minutes to figure out that he is far ahead of them.
Time and again they send him away saying:

-What more can I give you, Rav Ashlag? I don't think there is someone who can become your teacher. Ask the Creator. There is nothing else you can do.

Rav Ashlag keeps asking, but a teacher doesn't show up.

***

Documentary footage from the years 1912-1914.
Chinese soldiers lead captured monks at gunpoint. Tibet is proclaimed a Chinese territory.
A crowd of sobbing people in the streets of London mourns the death of their relatives on the Titanic.
Woodrow wilson becomes President of America.
Charlie Chaplin shoots his first film, *Caught in the Rain*.
A Serbian terrorist kills prince Franz Ferdinand of Austria.
World War I breaks out.
Soldiers run into barbed wire.
A young, short German corporal is running towards the camera and stops abruptly in front of it with a grin on his face. It is the young, and as yet anonymous, Adolph Hitler.

***

The streets of Warsaw.
Rav Ashlag shuffles wearily on the street.

He has a feeling that someone is watching him.
He's right.
An old man of unremarkable appearance is watching him.

Narrator's voice: This letter was discovered only after Rav Ashlag's death.

***

A stained old letter, its sides torn, appears slowly.
The camera moves along the neat lines of dense handwriting.

Narrator's voice: It was written by him and he ordered it be destroyed right after his death along with many other letters and essays that he wrote. Miraculously, it survived.

***

Rav Ashlag turns into a small alley.
The man is following him.
Another turn.
The old man stays close behind.

Rav Ashlag's voice: On Friday morning, the 12th of *Cheshvan*,[39] a man came to me.

***

A knock on the door.
Rav Ashlag, his face pale with exhaustion, opens the door.
We cannot see the man's face.
Rav Ashlag looks at the man, and the man steps through the door.

Rav Ashlag's voice: He revealed himself to me as a great sage well versed in Kabbalah.

The man enters Rav Ashlag's room.
Rav Ashlag takes a few steps back.
We still can't see the man's face.

Rav Ashlag's voice: And as soon as he started to speak, I could feel that his words were full of divine wisdom. Everything he said was like a gushing waterfall in its greatness.

39 The 2nd month in the Hebrew calendar, usually between October and November.

***

Warsaw. Night.
Inside the teacher's small room with a table, two chairs, empty walls, and a mattress on the floor.
Rav Ashlag and his teacher are sitting at a large table.
The teacher is sitting with his back to us.
Rav Ashlag is listening attentively, absorbing his every word.

The teacher's voice *(soft, colorless)*: The escape[40] takes place at night, in a state of absolute exhaustion.

***

A flash of light.
Flickering torches along shadowy chamber.
An exhausted Rav Ashlag is sitting on a chair.
His head droops on his chest.

The teacher's voice: He will come at midnight. Don't miss his arrival. He is small, but strong; he is sharp and therefore precise. He is the answer to your prayer. He is Moshe (Moses).[41]

Rav Ashlag raises his head.
He sees Pharaoh. Pharaoh is watching him intently.

The teacher's voice: "Moshe" is your great desire to break free from Pharaoh.

***

Warsaw. Night. The teacher's room.
Rav Ashlag and his teacher sit at the table facing each other.
The teacher's finger floats out of the darkness and retracts back into it.
Rav Ashlag's eyes are burning.

Rav Ashlag's voice: I have studied with him at his home for three months, night after night, from midnight till dawn. Each time he revealed a new secret to me.

---

40 Escaping at night: When one realizes that one is completely under the rule of egoism, that sensation is called "night." The desire to run, along with the inability to do it, produce a prayer, a litany, a demand for help. When that happens, the prayer is answered and the person receives the strength to escape.

41 Moses (Moshe) comes from the word Limshoch (to pull out). In Kabbalah, Moses is the force that pulls one out of the reign of egoism.

The face of the teacher can be seen just outside the circle of light thrown by the kerosene lamp.
Rav Ashlag shifts his weight slightly in an attempt to see him.
But we can suddenly see that there's no one sitting in the chair in front of him. The teacher is sitting alone with his back against the wall, in darkness, in concealment.
We can hear the teacher's soft, colorless voice:

-The prayer consists of two parts.

A hand holding a pencil draws a rectangle and divides it in two.
The pencil's tip points at the lower part.

The teacher's voice: The first thought...

The pencil draws an arrow above the lower rectangle, pointing upward.

The teacher's voice: The first thought makes "Father and Mother[42]" turn to face each other.

In the upper rectangle, the pencil quickly draws two semicircles facing one another.
It writes "Father" in the upper semicircle, and "Mother" in the semicircle below it.

The teacher's voice: The second causes their union.[43] They both hear your prayer for help!

The two semicircles merge into one circle before Rav Ashlag's eyes.

The teacher's voice: The state of "conception" begins instantaneously. The upper waters break and Moshe is born. This is the force that you have merited.

The pencil's tip marks a dot on the meeting point between the two semicircles, then sharply extends a downward line.

The teacher's voice: Moshe will put the force of evil to sleep. But only for a short while.

---

42 "Father and Mother" are the force of bestowal and love within a person. Only a prayer can activate that force.
43 A *Zivug* (coupling, union) is an answer to a prayer. Out of that Zivug, the force of Moses is born, after which Moses will pull one out of the hateful egoistic state one is in.

***

A flash of light.

Rav Ashlag looks into the eyes of Pharaoh, who is sitting opposite him.

Suddenly Pharaoh closes his eyes.

The teacher's voice *(very low)*: Don't miss Moshe. He is here only for a moment.

A flash of light.

A ray of light zips through the chamber over the floor tiles, past Rav Ashlag's feet, and points at the door.

The teacher's voice *(sharply)*: Follow it!

Rav Ashlag darts from his seat and runs through the dimly lit hall after the ray.

At that very moment, Pharaoh opens his eyes.

Rav Ashlag reaches the door.

Pharaoh opens his mouth in a roar:

-Sto-o-op!

Rav Ashlag freezes, his arm outstretched.

The ray of light flashes and shines at Pharaoh's eyes, blinding him.

Rav Ashlag makes a desperate dive toward the door and throws his weight against it.

The door falls.

A long dark corridor stretches ahead.

Rav Ashlag runs along it, his eyes fixed on the ray of light zigzagging just ahead of him.

***

Warsaw. The teacher's room.

We can see the teacher's half-lit face, the lamp reflecting in his eyes.

His lips are moving:

-And all of this is within you.

***

A flash of light.
Rav Ashlag is running along the narrow corridor, approaching a door. He bursts through it to find himself on a dark street. The houses are standing one next to the other.
He looks back.
The glare of torch lights is rapidly approaching him.
At the forefront we can see Pharaoh's furious face illuminated by the torch he is carrying.

The teacher's voice: Don't stop, don't think, don't be afraid!

Rav Ashlag turns around and begins to run.
A vile howl pierces the darkness behind him:

-Sto-o-op!

***

Warsaw.
Rav Ashlag is walking along a dark empty street. It's pouring.
Rav Ashlag is soaked.
He looks up and the rain streams down his face.
He is smiling.

***

The even lines of the letter scroll up.

Rav Ashlag's voice: Once, after repeated pleading, my teacher had revealed one secret to me. My joy was endless.

***

Warsaw. Rav Ashlag is running down the street, his feet stomping in the puddles, splashing water everywhere.

Rav Ashlag's voice: From that moment on I started to gain my independence.

***

A flash of light.
Rav Ashlag is running down the narrow streets of the lifeless city. His chasers are not far behind.
One street blurs into another. Twisting and turning, Rav Ashlag follows the ray of light until he suddenly sees the sea in front of him.

Rav Ashlag runs out onto the shore and stops.
The ray of light dives into the sea, and only now Rav Ashlag realizes that it is a sea of molten lava.
It's impossible to even stand near it.
The inferno forces Rav Ashlag to take a few steps back.

-Your reason[44] won't let you go that easily, - he hears the teacher's voice. – It serves Pharaoh.

Now the light of a thousand torches appears from the darkness behind him.
His enemies are approaching.

-It's not easy to escape! – The teacher's voice says.

The ray of light points at the lava persistently.

-It's not easy!

Rav Ashlag shields his face with his hands against the scorching heat.
He takes a step forward, but then retreats.

-We are Pharaoh's slaves! – The teacher's voice grows louder.

Pharaoh approaches.
Now he is stepping onto the shore leisurely.
He can see that his prey has nowhere to run.

-He is our whole life!

Pharaoh smiles.

-Spent in vain!

Pharaoh opens his arms and approaches Rav Ashlag.

***

Suddenly we are back in Warsaw again.
Night. The teacher's house.
Rav Ashlag walks quickly up the stairs to the second floor and knocks on the door. No one answers.
He listens.
Nothing.

44 Our corporeal mind, or reason, always serves the egoistic desire, searching for ways for the egoism to be satisfied. This is all that it does. The intellect is a product of the egoism.

***

The lines of the letter are rushing past.

Rav Ashlag's voice: As my "I" grew larger, my teacher distanced himself from me, but I could not feel it.

***

Warsaw. Rav Ashlag pushes the door.
It opens with a squeak.
He enters the teacher's room and looks around.
The room is empty.

Rav Ashlag's voice: ...Until one day I did not find him at home.

A gust of wind blows the thin curtains and tosses around a piece of paper with some drawing.

Rav Ashlag's voice: I looked for him everywhere but he was nowhere to be found.

Rav Ashlag is sitting alone in the teacher's home.

***

A flash of light.
Seashore.
Pharaoh embraces Rav Ashlag.

***

Warsaw. Rav Ashlag is walking the streets alone.
He looks into the faces of passersby.
It's not the first time that he leaves the house in the morning and returns late at night.
He is looking for his teacher.
All his regular work grinds to a halt: Writing at night, teaching.
He is barely eating; he cannot sleep.

Three weeks go by.

One day, while walking down the street, completely worn out, a familiar sensation overcomes Rav Ashlag: He can feel that someone is watching him. He turns sharply to gaze at the other end of the street where a man was standing just a moment ago.

But there is no one.

***

Night. Rav Ashlag opens the window in his room and again sees a lone silhouette of a man standing on the other side of the street.

This time the man does not disappear but turns around and starts to walk away.

***

Rav Ashlag runs out into the street. He looks around but there is no one to be found. He begins to run through the dark streets of Warsaw, the heels of his shoes echoing loudly on the empty cobblestones. A lonely passerby presses himself against the wall in alarm as he dashes past him.

Rav Ashlag stops only near the house of his teacher.
He sees a light in the window on the second floor.
He flies up the stairs and flings himself through the door.

***

The teacher is sitting at the table; only his hands are lit.

Rav Ashlag's voice: On the ninth of Nissan,[45] I found my teacher at his home. I apologized, deeply, and tried to make amends for the past.

Rav Ashlag is standing before the teacher, crying.

Rav Ashlag's voice: He relented, as before, and had revealed a great secret of faith to me. My joy was immeasurable.

Rav Ashlag's face.
The teacher's hand is drawing circles on a piece of paper.

The teacher's voice: The circle of faith above reason.

***

A flash of light.
Seashore.
Rav Ashlag pushes Pharaoh away and turns to approach the sweltering lava.

---

45 *Nissan*—the seventh month in the Hebrew calendar.

The teacher's voice: Faith above reason![46]

Rav Ashlag closes his eyes and jumps into the fire.

The teacher's voice: You have heard me, Rav Ashlag.

Rav Ashlag's body slowly sinks into water.
He is swimming in shimmering water.
Pharaoh points his hand at him and hundreds of dark shadows obediently jump in after Rav Ashlag, only to burn in the lava.

***

Warsaw. The teacher's room.
A pale arm hangs down from the bedside.
A small vial with medicine is lying on a small stool.
The teacher's head is resting, motionless, on the pillow.
His face is shaded.

Rav Ashlag's voice: But my great teacher appeared to be losing his strength. I wouldn't leave his side, and the next day, on the tenth of *Nissan*, his time in this world had ended.

The teacher's body is lying in bed.
Opposite him, rocking back and forth, sits Rav Ashlag.

***

A yellow page of the letter; the lines grow blurry.

Rav Ashlag's voice: It's impossible to describe my grief and my anguish. My heart had been filled with hope of meriting supreme wisdom.

***

A flash of light. The sea.
Rav Ashlag is swimming.
A tiny dot in an endless ocean.

---

46 Faith above reason: In the wisdom of Kabbalah, faith is the sensation of contact with the Creator, the quality of bestowal and love that appears in a person. The reason symbolizes the quality of reception for oneself. Faith above reason is not blind faith. Rather, it is a state in which one activates one's mind, contemplates, examines the situation, and only then assumes the faith—bestowal and love. By increasing the importance of faith above reason, one becomes wiser.

–But instead here I am, alone and naked, without any attainment...

The lonely swimmer is losing strength and hope as he swims slower and slower.

-Even the knowledge that I'd received from him temporarily evaporated from my mind because of my deep grief.

His body grows heavier and heavier.
His hands and legs grow numb.
Rav Ashlag begins to sink into the blue water. But his voice is heard:

-My eyes sought hungrily the vision of heaven, in great anticipation and hope.

Rav Ashlag manages to look ahead one last time.
Through blurry eyes, he suddenly catches a glimpse of the shoreline.

-I didn't allow myself a moment of respite until I found favor in the eyes of the Creator.

***

Warsaw. Rav Ashlag is walking briskly down the street.
A strong wind is blowing up the skirts of his coat.

***

Documentary footage from around 1917: Russia, the February Revolution. Kerensky and members of the provisional government smile to the camera.

America. The slick-haired president of the "Victrola" record label presents the first gramophone recording of the original Dixieland jazz band to a cheering crowd.

Berlin. Train station. A few people jump onto a freight train wagon right before its doors close. And before it closes, we catch a glimpse of the face of young Lenin among the passengers.

***

A street in Warsaw.
Rav Ashlag stops in the middle of the street and gazes at a dark gray cloud shaped like an island and hanging low above the city.
A man is running across the street.

Российская
Социальдемократическая
Рабочая Партія

EN AVANT

ВПЕРЕДЪ

Пролетаріи всѣхъ странъ соединяйтесь!

№ 4.

ЖЕНЕВА, 31 (18) ЯНВАРЯ

1905 г.

НАЧАЛО РЕВОЛЮЦІИ ВЪ РОССІИ

Первые шаги.

Suddenly he slows down to a walk and finally stops. He looks at Rav Ashlag but does not come closer.
The wind blows Rav Ashlag's hat off his head and rolls it across the street. He tries to catch it but misses.
The man on the other side catches it and extends it to Rav Ashlag, who comes running up to him.
It's Yan.

Yan: I couldn't make up my mind whether I should approach you or leave you alone with your God, but then your God tore your hat off your head and resolved my dilemma. Lenin is coming to town. Have you heard about him?

Rav Ashlag: I even read a few of his works.

Yan: Well...?

Rav Ashlag: He is a clever man.

Yan *(smiling)*: Clever?! He is a genius! Have you heard of what's happening in Russia?

Rav Ashlag: A revolution.

Yan: A fire is starting there. It is starting in Russia, and then it will spread throughout the world. Do you want me to arrange a meeting with Lenin for you? Right now? Mind you, it's your only chance. Say "yes."

Rav Ashlag: Yes.

Yan and Rav Ashlag turn into a nearby side street. They walk up to the entrance of a small unassuming house.
Immediately they are surrounded by four grim men.

Yan: He's with me.

One of the men starts frisking Rav Ashlag as if he didn't hear Yan.
When he's done, he steps aside keeping his dour expression.

The man: Come on in.

***

A safe house.
Lenin is sitting behind a table.
He is very emotional and open, radiating tremendous charisma.

All those gathered in the room, most of whom are fairly young, are watching him admiringly.
Rav Ashlag stands out in his religious Jewish garb.

Lenin: People want actions from us, not empty talk. We should throw down the rotten bourgeois government and hoist the banner of justice – create the first national state of workers and peasants in the world! This is our mission, comrades!

Everyone applauds.

Yan: Comrades, please keep it down. Don't forget we are not yet in communist Poland, but in a country ruled by a bourgeois government. Police agents are trying to sniff out Comrade Lenin all over Warsaw.

Lenin: Generation after generation of oppressed people have dreamed of such a state. Control over factories, plants, and land will be turned over to the workers and peasants. We will create our own people's police and the people's red army. Our party will be called The Communist Party of Workers and Peasants, and it will lead the noble fight for freedom, equality, and independence for all the oppressed around the world.

A low moan of admiration rolls over the crowd.
Rav Ashlag raises his hand.

Lenin: Yes, the comrade in the religious attire...

Rav Ashlag: I find your ideas very appealing.

Lenin *(addressing everybody)*: Usually both our bishops and your rabbis are opposed to my ideas!

Rav Ashlag: You are talking about equality, brotherhood, and love – there is nothing more exalted than that.

Lenin *(addressing everybody)*: It appears there are some progressive rabbis as well. I am listening, ask your question.

Rav Ashlag: My question is: Who is going to build this just society?

Lenin: The oppressed, the have-nots, the ones who know firsthand what injustice means.

Rav Ashlag: What will happen to the bourgeoisie?

Lenin: They will have to yield and work for the benefit of the young state; otherwise we will have to exercise force. What's the matter? Something about this scenario is bothering you?

Rav Ashlag: Only the fact that it's going to lead to more bloodshed and even worse injustice.

Lenin: Well, I have heard that many times and I call that cowardice and empty speculation.

Yan *(whispers to Rav Ashlag)*: Shut up!

Rav Ashlag: Sooner or later, your workers and peasants will begin to steal, kill, and hate. Not right away, but everything will inevitably come to that.

Lenin: Nonsense! We shall erect a new education system, based on communist values, and examples of equality and justice.

Rav Ashlag: There is none, nor can there be justice on this earth.

Lenin: Is that so?

Rav Ashlag: Man is selfish by his nature. Interference of another kind of force is needed in order to transform him.

Lenin: Is it God?

Rav Ashlag: You can call it God if you like. I prefer to call it the Upper Law of Justice. Or the Law of Supreme Love. It exists. We are surrounded by it. It is the fundamental law of the entire creation. You just need to know how to call upon it, that's all.

Lenin: How do you know this?

Rav Ashlag: I know.

Lenin: Have you read about it somewhere?

Rav Ashlag: There is a book that talks about this very concept – *The Book of Zohar*.

Lenin: Give it to us, we want to read it.

Rav Ashlag: It requires preliminary preparation.

Lenin: A long one?

Rav Ashlag: A few years.

Lenin: I have a good education, my dear, and I will try to understand.

Rav Ashlag: It's impossible, the mind is not the instrument that can attain it.

Lenin: Then what's the instrument?

Rav Ashlag: The heart. You have to prepare your heart for reading this book. The same way you need to prepare your heart to run a government.

Lenin: What will I have to do?

Rav Ashlag: Correct your heart, make it unselfish and loving. A person cannot do it on his own, but there is a method by which one can evoke other forces that will perform the correction.

Lenin: Well, I suppose we have to move on. *(Turns to Yan)* Yes?

Yan: Yes, it's time, Comrade Lenin.

Lenin *(stands up and addresses Rav Ashlag)*: My dear Rabbi, I am a sworn atheist and do not believe in any upper force or any upper law. We will raise the new man on our own - without your upper force.

Rav Ashlag: You will fail.

Lenin *(picking up his cap from the table)*: My dear, visit us in ten years time and you will see.

Rav Ashlag: You will spill a lot of blood, and this great idea will be devalued for a long time. Please listen!

> Lenin looks around, no longer listening to him.
> Rav Ashlag stands up, trying to hold Lenin's attention for just a little while.

Rav Ashlag: It is going to be a terrible experiment!

Lenin: Unfortunately, I am in a hurry. Goodbye. Please leave your details with Yan so we might have a chance to talk again... perhaps... some day...

> He shakes Rav Ashlag's hand and they bid each other farewell. Immediately a group of people surrounds Lenin. One of them hides his face under a toothache bandage.
>
> Lenin waves his hand to everybody and walks out of the apartment followed by a group of men.
>
> Yan approaches Rav Ashlag.

Yan: Such a shame. You had a chance to listen to the greatest man of our time.

Rav Ashlag: It's a shame he didn't listen to me.

Yan: You have an over-inflated self-esteem. I think that this has been our last meeting.

Rav Ashlag: It's a pity he couldn't hear what I was saying. I didn't have time to explain. I wanted to tell him so much.

Yan: He doesn't need your sermons!

Rav Ashlag: One mustn't pick an unripe fruit, Yankele, you must let it mature! People need to have a desire for change and then everything will be possible.

Yan *(harshly)***:** The revolution cannot wait! That's one thing. And also, I'm not Yankele, I am Yan. Remember that. I think you can find the way out by yourself. I am staying. Farewell, you pitiful victim of religion. Perhaps one day we shall meet again. *(Turns away without shaking Rav Ashlag's hand.)*

***

A stream of documentary footage cuts in.

The Russian revolution of 1917. Storming of the winter palace. Lenin giving a speech before a huge gathering of people. Trotsky is riding a white stallion in front of cheering troops. The beginning of the civil war. The execution of the tsar, his wife, and five children. More executions in the public squares of the main cities of Russia. A terrible famine in Ukraine. The silent stare of Lenin right into the camera. Behind his back, a young Stalin stands upright.

***

Warsaw. Rav Ashlag's room.

Rav Ashlag *(turning around from the table)*: Rivka!

Rivka walks in and we can see that the Ashlag family is expecting another child.

Rav Ashlag: Rivka, start packing. We are leaving for the land of Israel.

Rivka *(confused)*: But...

Rav Ashlag: I want us to leave as soon as possible.

Rivka: Are you going to leave your students?

Rav Ashlag: They will go with me.

Rivka: With families, kids, wives?

Rav Ashlag: I will explain to them why they have to leave, and they will understand.

Rivka: I am in my seventh month, Yehuda.

Rav Ashlag: I know that you can handle it.

Rivka *(a pause, an attempt to grasp what is happening)*: Can this wait?

Rav Ashlag: It cannot wait. Are you coming with me?

Rivka: They won't let you go. You are their arbitrator. You are their teacher.

Rav Ashlag: They are not the ones who decide whether I should leave. I have important work to do in the land of Israel.

Rivka: Yehuda...

Rav Ashlag *(interrupting her)*: If I don't go, I will die.

Rivka *(irritated)*: You are saying this to me on purpose!

Rav Ashlag: I have done everything I could here. Will you come with me?!

Rivka: What about the children?

Rav Ashlag: We will take them with us.

Rivka: No, we can't. The journey is hard.

Rav Ashlag: As you say.

Rivka: Yehuda, we just started to put down roots and I thought...

Rav Ashlag *(interrupting her)*: How much time do you need to get ready?

Rivka is silent.

Rav Ashlag: Rivka?

Rivka *(lifts her head and looks straight in her husband's eyes)*: I am ready. I will leave the children with my parents. Only Baruch Shalom will come with us.

***

The Rabbinical court.
Ten rabbis are sitting opposite Rav Ashlag at a long table.
Shmuel, the teacher, is among them.
They are quietly talking among themselves.

Rav Epstein: We received reports that 300 families have agreed to leave with you.

Rav Ashlag: That is correct.

Rav Epstein: And that you have chartered a ship in Sweden to carry all of you to the land of Israel.

Rav Ashlag: Yes, everything is ready. All that is needed is your decision.

Rav Epstein *(consults again with the rabbis sitting next to him, finally he turns to Rav Ashlag)*: Honorable Rav Yehuda Leib Halevi Ashlag, we have decided to tell you one thing: An arbitrator, a teacher, can't leave his community to migrate freely to the land of Israel. You are to stay here. It is the verdict of the rabbinical court, and I advise you to heed it and retract your decision.

Rav Ashlag: I cannot do that because I am not my own master. I must leave here and I must warn you that I will do everything I can to take as many people with me as possible. Were it in my power, I would take with me every last one of you.

Shmuel, the teacher, stands up and looks around at the people in the room.

Teacher Shmuel: You are facing the demolisher of our community. I have told you that a hundred times.

Rav Ashlag: The Jews need to leave Europe as soon as possible. If they don't, they will perish and bring unspeakable suffering to everyone.

Rav Zilber: Our community is stronger than it's ever been. There are three million of us Jews; we are a force to be reckoned with!

Rav Epstein: Why must you always swim against the tide?! Who needs all these endless conflicts? Can't you subdue this pride of yours that brings you nothing but destruction?!

Rav Ashlag: How can I explain this to you?!

Teacher Shmuel: What?! Explain what?! Your hatred toward us, toward our laws, toward our holy Torah?!

Rav Ashlag: We Jews are concealing the light from the world. The world will not let us continue living as we do.

Rav Ashlag falls silent. He looks at them all, one at a time.
In the silence, we can hear the voice of Shmuel.

Teacher Shmuel: Do you need any more proof? A criminal is standing before us who should be brought to justice.

Rav Zilber: Rav Ashlag, please wait in the corridor for our final decision. We need to ponder what you have said.

***

Rav Ashlag walks out.
He finds himself alone in the long empty corridor.
A murmur of voices comes from behind the closed doors.
Rav Ashlag walks away from the door. Pacing slowly, he begins to talk to himself. He is walking and waving his hands in the air.
The doors open and Shmuel, Rabbi Zilber, Rabbi Epstein, and the others are standing at the entrance, watching him.
Rav Ashlag turns around and sees them looking at him.

Rav Zilber: Come on in, Rav Ashlag.

***

Rabbinical court room.
Rav Ashlag is facing the rabbis.

Rav Ashlag: I would like you to hear what I have to say, so I wanted to add to what I have said...

Rav Zilber: No need. By the decision of the rabbinical court you are hereby excommunicated. From this moment on, no one is allowed to talk to you. Tomorrow we will collect the signatures of all ninety members of the council, and the decision will be sent all around Poland. You may leave.

Rav Ashlag: You are sentencing countless people to terrible suffering. You are taking upon yourselves the responsibility for what is going to happen.

Teacher Shmuel: Why should we listen to you? You were told you may leave, so leave! Out!

***

The streets of Warsaw.
People are passing by Rav Ashlag.
He looks into their eyes as if wanting to tell them something or to bid them farewell.

He walks toward a house.
Rivka's parents come out the door.
Rivka's father is holding two little children by the hand. They are Rav Ashlag's son and daughter - David and Bracha.
Rivka's mother is sobbing quietly into a handkerchief.
They walk past him in silence.
Rav Ashlag follows them with his eyes.
Suddenly, Rivka's father stops at a distance and turns to yell at Rav Ashlag:

-You have destroyed her life! You don't care about your own children! You are not a Jew; you are a monster! We are erasing you from our memories. We didn't have a daughter and you never even existed for us. That's it!

Rivka's mother is wailing now.
Rivka's father orders her to follow him.
Rivka's mother manages to say:

-Please have pity on her... if only a little.

***

Rav Ashlag enters his home.
Empty walls, empty room.
In the center of the room there is a small pile of their few remaining belongings; the older son, Baruch, is sleeping on top of it.
Rivka gets up to greet her husband.

Rivka: I've managed to sell everything. For pennies, of course, but still... we are ready now. *(She looks into Yehuda's face.)* You look strange.

Rav Ashlag: I couldn't explain anything to them.

Rivka: David and Bracha will stay with my parents for now. They wanted to join us so badly, but how could we take them?!

Rav Ashlag: Don't worry. We will send for them later, once we settle down.

Rivka: Still, they really wanted to come with us!

Rav Ashlag *(wrapped in his thoughts)*: I can't explain anything to anyone – neither to my friends, nor to my enemies, nor to the teachers. No one!

Rivka: I can't stand to leave the children here.

Rav Ashlag: They don't hear me. How can I explain it to them?

Rivka: I have a bad feeling about them, Yehuda.

Rav Ashlag: They don't believe me. It's as if I hit a wall.

Rivka looks at him in silence.

Rav Ashlag: How can I explain it to them? How?!

Rivka steps closer to him.
She tries to meet his eyes.
She sighs and quietly says:

-You have explained everything. It was they who didn't hear you.

Rav Ashlag sees Rivka's face.
She nods and tries to comfort him.

-I met your parents at the entrance,- he suddenly says.

-They are simple people, don't be angry with them, – answers Rivka.

-I am not. I understand them.

He takes a few more steps into the room and looks around at the empty walls.
Rivka leans over their small bundles to tighten a few knots.
She notices a small tattered thread doll on the floor. She picks it up and examines it.
Suddenly she straightens up and says:

-You are saying that they didn't hear you. They couldn't have heard you.

Rav Ashlag turns to look at Rivka.

-You have to understand them. They are living in this world, they have the small, simple desires of this world: To work, to pray, to have a family, children, grandchildren, to hold on to one another as they have done for centuries, as the Creator has commanded us. And you want to take that away from them.

Rivka's eyes well up.

-They are right that they don't want to surrender to you the only thing they've got. I am sorry. Sorry for saying this to you, but they are small, ordinary people, and you are a giant compared to them. They will never understand you; they can't understand your words. It's impossible to unite with the Creator, Yehuda. Let them be. I am sorry for not siding with you on this.

> Silence hangs in the room.
> We can only hear Rivka's labored breathing.
> She is barely holding herself back from bursting into tears.

Rav Ashlag: Are you sorry that you married me?

Rivka: I will never, ever be sorry for that.

> Rav Ashlag takes a step toward her, hugs her, and so they stand in the middle of the empty room.
> A quiet evening behind the open window.
> Rivka calms down in the arms of her husband and presses herself tightly against him.
>
> A knock on the door.
> Rav Ashlag's students, young and elderly Jews alike, cautiously enter the room. Rivka steps aside.
> The students stand there trying to avoid Rav Ashlag's glance.
> At the back of the pack hide Chaim and Aaron.

Elderly student: We have come to tell you that we can't leave with you... to the land of Israel.

> Rav Ashlag watches them silently.

Elderly student: We believe you, and you are a great teacher, but we can't go against the decision of the community.

> Rav Ashlag shakes his head. He remains silent for a long while.

Voices: Forgive us.

Rav Ashlag: I can't force you to leave. If I could, I would get on my knees and beg you to leave with me. But I know you won't hear me. The Creator has sealed your ears with wax. *(Silent.)* All of us will have to suffer terribly! Do you hear me?!

Voices: Yes, we hear you.

Rav Ashlag: And you don't believe me, do you?

Voices: We do.

OF GENTS
CLOTHING
ACIL
TAILOR
23

Rav Ashlag: And yet you are not going?

Elderly student: How can we leave? Our relatives are here, we are too tied up with one another. You know how it is with us Jews.

Rav Ashlag: Yes, Jews, unfortunate Jews... *(to Aaron and Chaim)* why are you two hiding behind their backs?

> Aaron and Chaim are standing tongue-tied, not daring to meet Rav Ashlag's eyes.
> Suddenly Chaim shakes his head decisively.

Chaim: I am going!

> Everybody turns to look at him.
> He clenches his hand into a fist and waves it in the air, shouting:

Yes, I'm going! I'm leaving this place! I am leaving with our great teacher, and you can stay here if you want! *(He looks at everybody)* I am going! Yes, I'm going!

> He pulls Aaron by the sleeve.

Chaim: Aaron! Let's go!

Elderly Jew: Aaron is not going anywhere.

Chaim: Aaron, don't listen to anybody!

Elderly Jew: Aaron, you are staying. One word out of you and you know what will happen; you won't see a penny from your uncle's fortune. We will give it all away to the town's beggars. You understand?

Chaim: Aaron, we are going!

Elderly Jew: No, Aaron, you are staying.

Chaim: You will regret it, Aaron!

Aaron *(sighing heavily)*: I can't.

Chaim: You will become a millionaire, Aaron, but the most unhappy millionaire of all because you didn't join Rav Ashlag.

Rav Ashlag: Chaim, run home to pack, I'll be expecting you in two hours. (*He looks at everyone*) Just don't curse the Creator when He comes for you.

***

Evening. An unpaved road in Warsaw.
A slow-moving wagon carries Rav Ashlag and Rivka, their son Baruch, and a carefree Chaim with a bottle of vodka in his hand.
Once in a while, Chaim takes a sip, winces, and chases it down with some bread and onions.
People are looking at them. Someone stops, another points a finger at them, someone moves away.
The coachman is silent.

Chaim: Farewell, Warsaw, farewell forever! We are going to the land of Israel!

Rav Ashlag takes the bottle from him, takes a swig, and passes it to his son. Baruch drinks, too, with a grimace, and passes the bottle to the coachman. The coachman gulps down the last sip and grunts with pleasure.
Rivka is watching them with a smile.

Rav Ashlag *(to the coachman)*: How come you're so silent today?

The coachman: I don't know what to recite for such an occasion.

Rav Ashlag: There can be no place for sorrow if you are connected to the Creator. Remember the words of your son, Moshe: "the Creator - He is one, unique, and unified. Only good extends from Him."

The coachman: I feel good when I'm with you.

Chaim *(his speech slurred)*: Well, come with us then!

The coachman: I can't. I can't leave my Moshe behind. I have secured a place next to him. He is cold lying there all alone.

The coachman tugs at the reigns and cheerfully yells at the horse. Suddenly he begins to recite.

- "He who watches the wind will not sow, and he who looks at the clouds will not reap..."

Rav Ashlag joins him and now they are both reciting the words of Ecclesiastes melodically, waving their hands in rhythm:

- "Sow your seed in the morning and do not be idle in the evening..."

Chaim joins them. He jumps off the slow moving wagon and trots next to it, watching Rav Ashlag's mouth as he forms each syllable.
All three are repeating with exhilaration.

- "The light is pleasant and it is good for the eyes to see the sun. Indeed, if a man should live many years, let him rejoice in them all, and let him remember the days of darkness, for they will be many. Everything that is to come will be futility."

On a bumpy road, the wagon rocks and rolls past a forest.
Rav Ashlag's long arms are resting on its rim, and a wide smile adorns the coachman's face.

Chaim prances around the wagon in a hassidic dance; one moment he is running ahead, in the next he is trailing behind.
Now he parades next to Rav Ashlag.
Suddenly, the coachman pulls sharply on the reins.

The coachman: Whoa!

A short man comes out of the forest and stops in the middle of the road, holding a tight little bundle wrapped in cloth.
Rav Ashlag strains to see the stranger's face, jumps off the wagon, and walks up to him.
It is old Baruch.
Rav Ashlag approaches him.
Baruch is watching Rav Ashlag crossly.

Baruch: Take it with you.

He hands the bundle over to Rav Ashlag.

Rav Ashlag: What is this?

Baruch: It is *The Book of Zohar*. It is almost three hundred years old. It is a book that belonged to my teacher the Rabbi of Kotzk. It's priceless. You can sell it if times get rough.

Rav Ashlag: Thank you, teacher.

Baruch: We won't see each other again.

He turns around and disappears in the forest.

***

Documentary footage of the 1920's.
An old, overcrowded ship is rocking on the waves of the Mediterranean, heading for the land of Israel.

***

Night. The stars are twinkling in the dark waves.
The Ashlags and Chaim are huddled together on the crammed deck.
Rav Ashlag is lying down and watching them, his arms under his head.
Suddenly Rivka's hand touches him.

Rivka *(whispers)*: It's starting.

Rav Ashlag wakes up Baruch and Chaim.

Rav Ashlag: Look for a doctor or a paramedic – quick!

Baruch Shalom runs to the captain's bridge; Chaim runs to the lower decks.
We can see Baruch gesturing emphatically to the navigation officer, but the man shakes his head negatively.

Rivka looks at her husband.
Her face is a mask of pain and resilience.
Rav Ashlag hugs her, pressing her against him. She is moaning quietly.
Baruch and Chaim come running back almost at the same time.

Baruch: There is no doctor on board!

Chaim: There's no one who can help!

Rivka pushes everyone away sharply and looks down.

Rivka *(through the pain)*: Get them out of here, Yehuda! Now!

Chaim's clothes fly through the air and land on the deck.
The Ashlags' bundles are emptied.
In no time, Chaim and Baruch construct a tent around Rav Ashlag and Rivka made of sheets, shirts, skirts, and trousers.
Rav Ashlag sticks his head out for a moment.

Rav Ashlag: Hot water, quickly!

Baruch runs out to get it.

Chaim: But how... you've never done this before.

Rav Ashlag *(calmly)*: To receive life is not so difficult a task. To live, now that's where you need real skill.

Rivka is moaning inside the tent.
Baruch sprints back with a bucket of hot water.
Rav Ashlag folds his sleeves back.

Rav Ashlag: That's it, boys; take a walk you two. Soon our daughter will be born.

He dives into the tent.
Rivka's face is pale.
Her eyes follow her husband's every move.
Large beads of sweat condense on her forehead.
Rav Ashlag tenderly wipes her forehead with a towel.

Outside, Chaim and Baruch are walking in circles under the starlit skies.

Inside the tent, Rivka is biting on a folded towel to stifle the screams, her eyes filled with pain.

The waves thunder and crash against the sides of the old ship.
A full moon hangs above the water.

Suddenly we hear the cry of a newborn.
Rivka is weeping with pain and joy.

Rav Ashlag *(cradling the newborn in his arms)*: Well, hello there, Bat Sheva!

Rivka *(quietly, with love)*: Bat Sheva.

***

The ship rocks on the waves.
Tied to the mast, a makeshift cradle made of rags, is swaying from side to side.
Rivka is sleeping nearby.
Rav Ashlag is sitting a few feet away.
Opposite them – Chaim and Baruch.

Rav Ashlag *(explaining to Baruch)*: The name, Israel, is made of two words – *yashar* (directly) and *el* (God), meaning directly toward the Creator. Only those who yearn to meet the Creator live in this land.

Baruch: And the ones who don't?

Rav Ashlag: They simply cannot live in it.

Baruch: But there are lots of people living there.

Rav Ashlag: No, there aren't.

Baruch: I don't understand, all kinds of people live there right now.

Rav Ashlag: Baruch, let me give you an example. Let's take two people who are walking on the same street. For one of them, it is a street of stones, a pavement filled with dirty puddles, with a pauper begging on one corner. But for another, it is a road leading to the Creator. Well, tell me, are they walking on the same street or not?

Baruch: Clearly they're not. The one who is looking for the Creator sees before him the most beautiful, light-filled street in the world.

Rav Ashlag: Such is this land. It is very beautiful, full of light, blooming, and bountiful. The land of Israel is a desire to be by the Creator's side – it's a land within us.

Rivka opens her eyes and smiles at her husband.
She's never seen him so inspired.

Baruch: Is the land of Israel inside me as well?

Rav Ashlag: Each person contains this land within him.

Baruch: So this land is for everybody?

Rav Ashlag: Yes, it is.

Baruch: For each and every one?

Rav Ashlag: For all people.

Baruch: And not just for Jews?

Rav Ashlag: For Jews and non-Jews, blacks, whites, yellow, and red. It is for everyone.

Baruch: So, one day the whole world will become the land of Israel?

Rav Ashlag: Precisely. Each and every person who wishes to meet the Creator will live in this country.

Baruch: Then why are we going there, if this land is inside every one of us?

Rav Ashlag: It's because we are running out of time. We can't wait. We have been marked by the Creator, and we can't help it. We want to find the spiritual land of Israel while living in the geographical point called "the land of Israel." It will give us additional strength, it will!

Baruch: I wish it would happen already.

***

Documentary footage.
The ship is rocking on the waves. Passengers are standing on deck.
Everyone is anxiously waiting for land to appear.

Our heroes are standing with them as well: Rivka with the newly born Bat Sheva, Chaim, Baruch, and Rav Ashlag.

***

Port of Jaffa.[47]
People are coming down the ship's gangway.
A British patrol is scanning the newcomers' faces intently.
Rav Ashlag comes out of the port gates.
Rivka with Bat Sheva, Baruch, and Chaim can barely keep up with him.
He turns to them:

Rav Ashlag: Quick!

Rivka: Where are we going?

Rav Ashlag: To Jerusalem.

***

Documentary footage of Jerusalem in the 1920s.
Streets busy with people of various nationalities: Turks, British, Armenians, Arabs, Bedouins, and Jews.
Lazy merchants sit by mounds of goods in dizzying colors.
A flamboYant Turk smokes a hookah.
Two orthodox Jews argue in the shade of a house.

***

Rav Ashlag, Chaim, and Baruch are walking down the street.
They stop before a modest sign that reads: Kabbalistic yeshiva[48] *Ganey Hochma* (Gardens of Wisdom).
They walk up stone steps worn down with time.

47 Port of Jaffa – the arrival place of many immigrant ships to Israel until the early 50s.
48 A Jewish seminary

They arrive at a large open hall on the second floor filled with students of various ages.
Some are conversing, others are reading, someone is pacing around engaged in deep thought, another is dozing off, his head resting on the pages of an open book.

Rav Ashlag stands still at the entrance.

Rav Ashlag *(excitedly)*: Just look at that! They are studying Kabbalah!

Suddenly someone's hand touches Rav Ashlag's shoulder. He turns around to see an old sephardic[49] Jew.

Sephardic Jew *(looking at them)*: Where do you come from, kabbalists?

Rav Ashlag *(happily)*: From Warsaw.

Sephardic Jew *(with a welcoming smile)*: Come with me.

They walk along a long corridor.
Through the windows on their right, the Western Wall[50] flashes by.
Many people are standing next to it, praying.

***

Inside the room of the sephardic Jew.

Sephardic Jew: I am Rav Hadad, head of this yeshiva. *(He points at a small old man sitting in the corner in front of a gigantic book.)* This is Rav Levi, my teacher. Tell us about yourselves.

Rav Ashlag: We have come to study.

Rav Hadad: What do you know about us?

Rav Ashlag: That you are a great kabbalistic yeshiva dating back two hundred years.

Suddenly, a coarse voice comes from the corner.

Rav Levi: Genesis 2:22, "And the Lord God constructed the rib..." *(Looks up from the book at Rav Ashlag)* Continue!

Rav Hadad: He's just arrived, teacher...

---

49 Sephardic – A Jew of Spanish and/or Portuguese origin.

50 "The Western Wall," also known as "The Wailing Wall," is part of the outer wall of the Second Temple that remained after its ruin in 70 CE. It is the most sacred place to religious Jews and is always crowded with worshippers.

Rav Ashlag *(without thinking)*: "Here it points to the meaning of the levirate marriage..."

Rav Levi: Take him.

Standing in the doorway, Chaim and Baruch shift their eyes from Rav Levi to Rav Ashlag and back.

Rav Hadad: You memorized the entire *Book of Zohar, Ashkenazi*.[51] Good for you!

Rav Ashlag: I didn't intend to.

Rav Hadad: You sound apologetic, and yet this is the very essence of our work – to memorize these texts. Rav Levi, my teacher, can recite the entire *Zohar* by heart, as well as all the writings of the Holy Ari. That is what makes him a great kabbalist.

Rav Ashlag: I don't think that Rav Levi is a great sage because he has a good memory.

Rav Hadad: Certainly, he studies the holy texts every day, reciting the holy words! *(Emphatically)* That's why he knows them by heart and that's why he is such a great teacher of Kabbalah!

Pause.
Rav Ashlag looks at Rav Levi.

Rav Ashlag *(dryly)*: Is that what we have to do?

Rav Hadad: This is what we have to do.

Rav Ashlag: But we do this while trying to penetrate the inner meaning of these words, right?!

Rav Hadad: These words don't have any inner meaning. The words themselves are holy, that's it. By pronouncing them, we hasten the coming of the Messiah.[52]

Rav Ashlag (*sardonically*): And who, may I ask, told you that?

Rav Hadad: I don't understand your question.

Chaim takes a step back and his back now presses against the door.

---

51 *Ashkenazi* – a Jew of European descent.

52 In Kabbalah, the Messiah is the revelation of Light of Wisdom for a person (Messiah Son of Joseph) or for the whole of humanity (Messiah Son of David).

Rav Levi *(from the corner)*: We believe in it, and that's enough for us.

Rav Ashlag *(turning to face him)*: You can believe only when you attain.[53] When you feel it with your heart, when you see it for yourself, only then do you believe.

Rav Levi: Nonsense! What can you possibly see, you pitiful creature! What can you feel? You have to believe and that's that. Blindly! *(Staring intently into Rav Ashlag's eyes)* You will learn how to do it still, *Ashkenazi*![54]

Rav Ashlag *(without turning his eyes away, steadily, almost by syllables)*: You can only study from someone (*pause*) who teaches how to attain, how to see.

Rav Levi: And I say, put it out of your mind. I say it's nonsense!

Rav Ashlag *(persistently)*: Only one who has attained the inner meaning can teach!

Rav Levi *(slowly getting up and raising his voice)*: Gibberish! There is no inner meaning here. There is no inner attainment, only the literal meaning of what is written and nothing more, God forbid!

***

All of a sudden, the room disappears in a flash of light.
Rav Ashlag sees a beautiful, peaceful, sunlit country stretching before him. Then the earth begins to quake.

***

The kabbalistic yeshiva.
Rav Ashlag is looking silently at Rav Levi, who is piercing Rav Ashlag with his gaze.

Rav Levi: Where were you just now?!

Chaim and Baruch are standing at the door, afraid to breathe.

Rav Ashlag: In the land of Israel, the great country that lives within each and every one of us!

Rav Levi: You are resisting me, *Ashkenazi*!

Rav Ashlag: I must have come to the wrong place.

Rav Levi: You are an arrogant man!

53 Attainment—the highest level of understanding, an absolute vision of all that is happening, from the thought of creation to the end of correction.
54 *Ashkenazi*—Here the term *Ashkenazi* is said in a derogatory manner.

Rav Ashlag: When I was in Warsaw, I imagined you all to be so great.

Rav Hadad: You are insulting the authentic Kabbalah!

Rav Ashlag: You have nothing to do with authentic Kabbalah.

Rav Ashlag pauses again and watches Rav Levi seethe with anger.

Rav Ashlag: This is a place of charlatans, not kabbalists!

He turns around and leaves the room.
Chaim and Baruch quickly follow him.
Rav Hadad is looking at Rav Levi.

Rav Levi: You have to keep an eye on him, Rav Hadad. He can get us into a lot of trouble.

Rav Ashlag, Chaim, and Baruch are walking down the corridor.
A young man in his twenties catches up with them.
He is devouring Rav Ashlag with his eyes.

Young man: I heard your entire conversation.

Rav Ashlag: Were you eavesdropping?

Young man: I couldn't help it.

Rav Ashlag: What's your name?

Young man: Shimon. I've been studying here for a year already. I don't know what I should do.

Baruch: Come with us!

Shimon: But...

Rav Ashlag: There is no coercion in spirituality, Shimon. A man must reach his own decisions.

They exit the yeshiva.
Rav Hadad and Rav Levi are watching them from the second floor window.

***

Jerusalem. A small inner courtyard.
Rivka is looking out the window on the commotion outside.
Rav Ashlag, Chaim, and Baruch are prying open large wooden crates and taking out various metal parts, vises, presses, and pieces of hide.

They arrange all this on the grass.

Rav Ashlag looks up.
Two young Jews are watching him from behind the low fence.
One of them is Shimon.

Shimon: This is my friend, Moshe. We want to study with you.

Rav Ashlag: Do you wish to become tanners? You should know it is a stinking business.

Shimon: We want to study Kabbalah and the craft of a tanner together with you.

Chaim smiles broadly at the two of them from behind Rav Ashlag's back.

Shimon: We won't leave until you accept us.

Baruch is overwhelmed with excitement.
He is doing a little dance.

Rav Ashlag *(without turning back)*: Baruch, you've already lost a wrench, you'd better think how you're going to assemble this machine. *(To Shimon and Moshe)* Are you prepared to scrape a living in the most grimy work there is?

All together: We are.

Rav Ashlag: To study at night?

All together: We are ready. We are!

Rav Ashlag: To get three hours of sleep, no more?

All together: Yes, we are ready! We are!

Rav Ashlag: Have you thought this out carefully?

They, together: We have.

Rav Ashlag: Then come on in. You will help us assemble the machines. We are holding the first lesson tonight.

In an emotional outburst, Chaim and Baruch run up to Shimon and Moshe, hug them, and drag them inside.

***

Night in Jerusalem.

Empty streets.
Jackals howling beyond the city walls.
Narrow streets snake between dark houses.
A single, dimly lit window.
Inside, a small room was converted into a classroom.
Rav Ashlag's four students, Shimon, Moshe, Chaim, and Baruch, are sitting around him.
He points at *The Book of Zohar* on the table in front of him.

Rav Ashlag: This is the holy *Book of Zohar.*

Moshe *(excitedly)*: I've been studying it for three years.

Rav Ashlag: It's impossible to study it. You can only feel it.

Moshe: I'm trying.

Rav Ashlag: Nonsense. Drop it.

Moshe: But...

Rav Ashlag: If you don't place yourself inside it, this book is nothing but an empty space, a stack of pages stained with ink.

Shimon: What do we have to do to feel it?

Rav Ashlag places his hand on the book.

Rav Ashlag: Here, behind these pages, there are one hundred and twenty five degrees of spiritual ascent. One hundred and twenty five degrees of descent into your self, into your "I." The picture that is waiting for you down there is not a pretty one.

Rav Ashlag is silent.
Everybody's eyes are fixed on him.

Shimon: What's down there? Inside of me?

Rav Ashlag: A disease.

Shimon: A disease?

Rav Ashlag: It's been eating away at you for a long time. *The Zohar* can detect it for you.

Everyone turns their eyes to Shimon.

Rav Ashlag *(without turning his eyes away from him)*: You are full of hatred toward the whole world. You live only for yourself. It is a terrible disease.

Shimon: How can I see that?

Rav Ashlag: The light. A small ray of light penetrates you. On each degree there is more light. That's how the Creator reveals Himself to you.

Shimon: Will I see him?

Rav Ashlag: He is behind every word.

> Rav Ashlag turns to the first page of the book and points his finger on the first line.

Rav Ashlag: There he is.

> Everybody leans over the book.

Rav Ashlag: Can you see him?

Chaim: No, I can't.

Shimon *(whispers)*: Is he here?

Rav Ashlag: Yes.

Moshe: Are you making fun of us?

Rav Ashlag: This matter is too serious to waste our time on jokes. He is here. All the time. *(Looks at the book closely)* There he is. This is His world.

> Everyone keeps staring at the book.
> Then they turn their gaze to Rav Ashlag.

Shimon: Why can't we see him?

Moshe: Yes, why?!

Rav Ashlag: You cannot see a world that operates according to the laws of absolute love.

Moshe: Why?!

Rav Ashlag: Because you are not like it.

Shimon: When will I see him?

Rav Ashlag: When the light cleanses you.

Shimon: When?!

Rav Ashlag: When you become similar to Him. It's impossible to do it all at once. That's why the degrees have been created. Each degree has its own light. First a weak light, then stronger and stronger. And on each degree there are ascents and descents. One has to withstand them.

Shimon: Will I be able to endure it?

Rav Ashlag: You? No.

Shimon: How then?

Rav Ashlag: Together.

Shimon: What does He want?

Rav Ashlag: He wants us to unite.

Rav Ashlag points to the first lines.

-There He is, behind these lines. Read, Shimon!

Shimon *(looks at the lines, then whispers)*: "It is written, 'as a rose among the thorns.'" What is a rose? It is the assembly of Israel...

Rav Ashlag: *Isra* (pronounced *yashar*) – straight, *el* (God) – to the Creator. We, Israel, are one heart with one desire... to meet Him! *(Stares at the lines in the book)* He is here right now as well. He is waiting.

A pause. Rav Ashlag is silent.

Shimon: Lead us there. To Him.

Rav Ashlag is still silent.

Moshe: We will follow your every step.

Chaim: We all want it, badly.

Baruch: It's what we live for.

Rav Ashlag leans over the table, closer to them.

Rav Ashlag: Stay together. Don't think of yourselves. Ask for strength. Not for yourselves. For the whole unfortunate world. Demand the strength to unite. Do you hear me?

Shimon: Yes!

Moshe: Yes!

Chaim: Yes!

Baruch: Yes!

All of them lean over the book.

***

Rav Ashlag's room. Morning.
Rivka enters the room.
It's empty.
She approaches the table.
A note is lying on *The Book of Zohar*.
Her husband's neat handwriting reads: "I will be back in three days. Don't worry about me. Yehuda."

***

Germany. Munich of the 1920's.
A figure drifts slowly along busy streets, past people walking, shop windows, antique houses.
The figure stops outside a beer house.
The sign above the door reads "Burger Broikeller."
The figure glides inside.

Hitler is standing on one of the wooden tables dressed in Polished boots and surrounded by a crowd of storm troopers.
They are hitting their iron cups on the tables.
The crowd chants in German: "kill the pigs!" "Away with the government of traitors!" "Germany – for the Germans!"
Hitler's hand rises and falls in tune.
Hitler turns his head sharply to the right.

He looks in that direction for a long moment.
Finally, he jumps off the table and walks to the corner of the beer house.
In the corner sits Rav Ashlag holding a large beer mug, dressed in traditional Jewish orthodox clothes.
Surprisingly, no one is paying attention to him.
Hitler walks up to him.

Hitler: Can no one see you or have I become schizophrenic?!

Rav Ashlag: They can't.

Hitler *(looking around)*: They can't see you. Amazing! Who are you?!

Rav Ashlag: My name is Rav Ashlag.

Hitler: How did you get here?

Rav Ashlag: It's not important. *(Looking into Hitler's eyes.)* You can be completely open with me.

Hitler *(suddenly sits down)*: I have to tell you something... *(he leans closer.)* I can't explain this logically but somewhere deep inside me, in my subconscious... *(he points to his chest)* I feel untamed hatred to your kind! Profound loathing!

Rav Ashlag: I know. Sit closer, I can't hear through all the yelling.

Hitler *(shifts his chair closer and glances back at the chanting crowd)*: One other thing... I have a feeling that it's not me, that I was chosen, shaped, and thrown into this fire. I, a mere corporal, suddenly turned into a king. Can you explain this to me?!

Rav Ashlag: "The hearts of ministers and kings are in the hand of the Creator." The Creator is moving you.

Hitler: He hates the Jews?

Rav Ashlag: He is absolute love, how can he hate anyone? This attribute does not exist in him. He loves everyone. We all are one to him.

Hitler: Then why am I so full of hatred? Explain this to me. *(His voice drops to a whisper)* I will ruin half the world if I am not stopped, won't i? Well, try to explain this to me, maybe after your explanation I will come to my senses, and you will save millions. You have a rare chance. Try me, Jew! Please try, I am pleading with you!

Rav Ashlag pushes the beer mug aside and doesn't say a word.

Hitler: Well, why aren't you speaking?

Rav Ashlag: The tragedy of the situation is that it's not you that I should be explaining everything to. If not you, then somebody else will take your place. You really don't have any free choice... indeed, you were simply chosen, molded, and thrown into this inferno.

Hitler *(bleakly)*: I am a puppet.

Rav Ashlag: You are. I can't explain anything to a puppet, and I shouldn't. You won't understand it anyway. I have to explain it to other people. But I can't. They just can't hear me. They have turned a deaf ear to me. They don't want to listen; they just won't!

Rav Ashlag slams his beer mug against the table in frustration and turns to face the wall.

Hitler: Why did you come here anyway?

Rav Ashlag: I wanted to see everything with my own eyes. To be able to feel... in order to scream!

Rav Ashlag stands up and starts walking toward the door.

Hitler: I will let you go this time. But don't come back here. Bad times are coming for you Jews.

***

Warsaw. Rabbinical court.
Shmuel, the teacher, is waving a few wrinkled pieces of paper in the air.
Rabbi Feldman, Rabbi Epstein, and Rabbi Zilber are sitting in front of him in silence.

Teacher Shmuel: That scoundrel! He doesn't let up his attempts to undermine our community even from Palestine. This open letter is challenging our authority! It is being copied and spread around. Listen to this: "You are in terrible danger. Your teachers and your leaders must hear me, and if not, then heed my calling you, my dear brothers and sisters. You must leave Europe at once. As comfortable as it may seem to you now, leave everything and come to the land of Israel. The time of exile is over. We have been charged with a great calling – to bring the light into the world. As long as we do not assume this task, we will continue to turn the entire world against us. Your leaders do not understand this and so condemn us all to a terrible fate. It's all of you, however, who are going to suffer first! But not all is lost if you leave Europe as soon as possible!

The teacher stops reading and looks around the room. He throws the pages on the ground in contempt and proceeds to trample them.

Teacher Shmuel: I demand to put an end to this! We have people everywhere! (Screams) We need to find him and teach him a lesson! He should not feel safe, neither here nor there nor anywhere.

***

Morning. Jerusalem. Rav Ashlag's room.
His head is resting on the table.

Next to him, an overturned cup with dried coffee leftovers and an ashtray full of stubs.

Suddenly the windowpane shatters with a terrible din and a large stone rolls onto the floor next to Rav Ashlag.
Shouting women can be heard through the broken window.

Rav Ashlag jerks up. A scared Rivka runs into the room.
Rav Ashlag walks over to the window and sees a remarkable sight.

A crowd of yelling women surrounded by Jewish men is clamoring in front of the house.

Young woman: I don't want my husband to lose his mind. What have you done to him?!

Elderly woman: Look at him, how he stands there, watching us! You can't scare us! Our children are righteous Jews, and we won't let you take them away from us!

A man's voice comes from the crowd.
We can't see his face.

Man's voice: We demand that you to leave our sacred city. You defile it with your presence. Get out of here!

Elderly woman: Or we will poke your eyes out! Yours and your wife's. We will burn down your disease-infested house!

Rav Ashlag *(calmly)***:** You are full of hatred. That's not good.

The elderly woman turns to the crowd.

-Are you men or children?! Bring this house down!

A few more rocks, cast by skilled hands, break the windows next to Rav Ashlag.
His face is showered with shards of broken glass.
Rivka grabs his sleeve and tries to Yank him away from the window.

Rivka *(yelling)*: What are you doing?! Shame on you! Are you not Jews?

Another stone whizzes above her head.
Suddenly, Rav Ashlag's calm voice overtakes the din of the mob.

-Do you know that I am studying the secret wisdom?

The crowd freezes in silence, as if on command.

Rav Ashlag: You can break down all the glass in my house. But I can mend it all with a single word.

The crowd is silent.

-And then the whole world will witness my great power and what happens to those who oppose it.

A woman shrieks.

Man's voice: What are you afraid of?! He can't do anything to you!

Rav Ashlag: You have come here and broken the windows of the house of a kabbalist, who knows the secret of life and death.

The crowd begins to move with discomfort.
The women in the first row begin to disperse silently, walking away from the house. They cast scared glances behind their shoulders. The men start retreating after them.
Rav Ashlag looks at them from above.
Rivka, shuddering, is standing close to her husband.
The square in front of the house quickly becomes deserted.

Rivka *(whispering)*: Is it true what you said? Can you fix everything with a single word?

Rav Ashlag: Yes, it is. *(Turning to look at her)* Do you doubt it? I can fix everything with a single word.

Rivka: What is that word?

Rav Ashlag: One word to Amikam, the glassmaker who lives two blocks down, and he will be up here in no time to fix all our windows.

Rivka smiles.
Her smile broadens and grows into laughter.
And now they are both laughing together.
Rav Ashlag picks up his daughter in his arms and begins to dance with her.
Rivka and Baruch are clapping their hands in joy.

***

Jerusalem. Night.

A makeshift classroom inside Rav Ashlag's home.

Rav Ashlag is seated behind the table.

His students are sitting opposite him.

The lesson is about to start.

Moshe *(ill at ease)*: Teacher, it was my wife who came screaming at you today. She told me that an old rabbi gathered all the women in the synagogue this morning, literally set them up against you. She said his name was...

Rav Ashlag *(cuts him off)*: You are wasting valuable time. You should leave everything that doesn't concern the lesson out there. *(Points at the door)*

Suddenly the door opens and a tall, elderly Jew steps in.

He is wearing a large, expensive fur hat.

At the sight of him Shimon rises and all the students follow suit.

Elderly Jew: Please allow me to be present in your lesson, honorable Rav Ashlag.

Rav Ashlag: I teach only my students.

Shimon *(whispering)*: But this is Avraham Kook, the Chief Rabbi of Israel.

Rav Ashlag *(ignoring him)*: This is a time for studying, not interrogation.

Rav Kook: I didn't come here to interrogate you, I came for your lesson.

Rav Ashlag: Then I must warn you that I was excommunicated by the Warsaw community leaders and your visit here may be misconstrued by other rabbis. You are asking for trouble; you are a public figure.

Rav Kook: I know. I received stern warnings from here and from Warsaw. You have many enemies.

Rav Ashlag: Clearly. Besides, I have firm opinions on every matter.

Rav Kook: I am aware of that, too.

Rav Ashlag: I teach Kabbalah and only Kabbalah.

Rav Kook: I know all that; no need to detail all your virtues. Rav Hadad is standing right outside demanding that I stop you.

Rav Hadad's pale face appears in the window for a brief moment.

Rav Ashlag *(ignoring Rav Hadad)*: It's impossible.

Rav Kook: This, too, I know very well. I've asked to be admitted to your Kabbalah lesson. If you have no objection, I will stay.

Rav Ashlag *(after a pause)*: You may stay.

Rav Kook: Thank you.

Rav Ashlag turns to his students.

Rav Ashlag: Kabbalah is not a religion. Kabbalah is a science.

All the students look furtively at the guest.
He is staring at Rav Ashlag, unblinking.

Rav Ashlag: Religion is based on faith in what somebody else said. Kabbalah is based on fact, on results of first-hand experiments. I believe only after having attained for myself.

Rav Ashlag starts pacing around the room, paying no attention to anyone or anything.
Rav Hadad's head bobs up and down in the window.
He is looking at Rav Kook, as if trying to understand why he is not intervening.

Rav Ashlag: Religion pacifies. Kabbalah, on the other hand, demands constant inner combustion. It's only for those who are consumed by the question: "Why was I born?"

The students' eyes are fixed on their teacher, pacing from wall to wall.
It is evident that they are proud of him.

Rav Ashlag: There is a crucial distinction between Kabbalah and religion.

Rav Hadad gestures anxiously to Rav Kook.
Rav Kook doesn't respond.

Rav Ashlag: Religion says, "Ask of the Creator, and He will help, He will forgive, He will have mercy. Ask, and He will change His attitude toward you." But Kabbalah says that the Creator is unchanging.

He stops by the window and looks at them all.

Rav Ashlag *(articulately)*: He is unchanging! It's we who must change in relation to Him. Only one request can come from us to Him – for Him to correct us.

Rav Ashlag leans on the windowsill.

Rav Ashlag: I have moved closer to the window on purpose, so that Rav Hadad can hear my every word. All of our holy books were written by kabbalists and explain only one thing: How we can rise above the angel of death - our egoism. One hundred and twenty-five degrees of the revelation of love – this is the wisdom of Kabbalah.

It emerged long before any religion did, and for one purpose only: To bring the world to unity. To fortify it with love. What can be more exalted than this?!

The door flies open and Rav Hadad bursts in.
He is breathless with fury.
He looks only at Rav Kook and yells.

Rav Hadad: You are the chief religious leader of Israel, and you calmly listen to this?! To a man who, before your very eyes, undermines the foundations of our religion! How can you keep silent?!

Rav Kook *(calmly)*: I don't hear any contradiction in his words.

Rav Hadad: What?! Kabbalah is a science? Religion is psychology? Kabbalah is for everyone? The Creator is a companion?

Rav Kook: I agree with every word the honorable Rav Ashlag is saying.

Rav Hadad pipes down as if thunderstruck.
Rav Kook gets up and walks to the door. He stops before it.

Rav Kook *(addressing Rav Ashlag)*: If you only knew how I much I would love to stay with you and study Kabbalah. Alas, I can't. My duty is elsewhere. What a shame, a real shame.

Rav Kook leaves.
Rav Hadad follows him with his eyes.

Shimon: Rav Hadad, perhaps you would like to stay?

Rav Hadad *(to Rav Ashlag)*: Mark my words, we will make life unbearable for you here.

***

Jerusalem. Daytime.
A massive iron shed. Instead of windows, it has perforated wooden boards.
People walk around it, clutching their noses.
We can see through the cracks as a man is standing amidst a cloud of lime dust and repeats the same monotonous motions. The man is Rav Ashlag.
Sweat pours down his face. The veins on his forearms are swollen.
He is using a wooden scraper fastened with a sharp metal tooth to dry-scrape a piece of hide.
Baruch is standing a little farther off, working on a primitive leather processing machine. He sends the leather through two wooden rollers covered with emery paper.
Chaim is stretching the leather on a special frame using wooden pincers.
Moshe, wincing, is scraping off pieces of meat from a stretch of wet leather.
Shimon is hammering frozen hides with a small mallet, prying pieces apart and throwing them into a tub of water.
Rav Ashlag occasionally hits the metal frame with his scraper.
The chime resonates dully inside the shed.

***

Everyone is sitting by a long table in the corner of the shed.
Baruch takes food out of a basket and lays it on the table: bread, eggs, onions, and water.
Rav Ashlag recites a blessing over the bread and begins to eat.
Suddenly Moshe groans, tries to stand up, but can't do it in time. He throws up on the table.
Shimon takes him to the side.
Moshe continues to vomit, nonstop.
Baruch quietly wipes off the table.
Rav Ashlag eats as if nothing had happened.
Shimon and Moshe return to the table.
Moshe sits down and closes his eyes in exhaustion.

Moshe: Why do we have to work so hard in all this filth? Do we really have to?

Rav Ashlag: I warned you that it wouldn't be easy.

Moshe: But we could have found something cleaner because...

Rav Ashlag: This is the cleanest job there is.

Chaim: How come - I always wanted to ask you – how come the Torah is inscribed on leather – dirty, stinking, leather?

Rav Ashlag pushes away the empty plate and straightens his back.

-Because the Torah exists only for correction.

He looks at Chaim.

-Do you understand it?! (*And without letting him answer, he continues*): If you want to be purified, scrape away all the evil in which you live. Only then will you be ready to unlock the Torah. It is a guide on how to purify your self, a cleansing guide. By no means is it a book of stories. It is a path from you to the Creator.

Rav Ashlag looks around.

-This path goes through all this filth, he concludes.[55]

Everyone is silent.
The sound of water dripping somewhere.
Beyond the windows - life goes on.
Inside, all is quiet.
Rav Ashlag closes his eyes and suddenly starts to sing.
It is the same melody that was sung in Baruch's house and in Kotzk – "Mordechai Yosef."
Quietly, everyone joins in on the singing, their arms embracing each other's shoulders.
They are all together, in perfect unity, at that moment.

Passersby peek through the holes in the windows.
They see a group of Jews, huddled together, hugging, rocking silently with eyes closed.

The door to the shed opens carefully.
A short man with a postman's bag slung around his shoulder enters the workshop.

55 The sages say that a person has to "write the Torah in his heart." It means that he has to correct his egoistic heart into bestowal and love. This will signify that he has written the Torah. In Hebrew, the word "Torah" [Horaa] means the instruction on correction.

He stands there, unsure if he should disturb the moment.
The song slowly and gently comes to an end.
For a few more moments, everyone is sitting with their eyes closed.

Finally the postman lets out a shy cough.

Postman: Sorry to interrupt, but the matter is quite urgent.

All turn to him.

Postman *(to Rav Ashlag)*: Are you Rav Ashlag?

Rav Ashlag: I'm listening.

Postman: Great, I've been searching for you since morning. I was at your place and your wife sent me here. Lenin is looking for you. Can this be?

Rav Ashlag: It's possible.

Postman: I was convinced someone was pulling my leg. They said: "Lenin is on the line." *(He walks inside the workshop, speaking briskly, with excitement, addressing everyone.)* Well, I know who Lenin is. All my relatives are there. I speak Russian and write it, of course, and so I replied in Russian: "Listen, this machine was not made for practical jokes, you know. It is very expensive. This is the post office you're speaking with."

Rav Ashlag *(interrupting him)*: What did they say?

Postman: That Lenin is going to call you *(looks at his watch)* in half an hour.

Rav Ashlag stands up promptly and walks toward the door.
The postman patters after him in small steps.

Postman: They set up the device only yesterday, and suddenly... Lenin.

***

A bright day in a lively Jerusalem street.
Rav Ashlag is Marching along with the postman.
Baruch, Moshe, Chaim and Shimon are having a hard time keeping up.
They approach the post office.

***

Post office.

Rav Ashlag is standing in front of a shiny new telegraph machine.

The postman looks at his watch.

-They said they are going to call at two in the afternoon sharp, but you know, it's not as if they are calling from Tel Aviv. There, it's two o'clock exactly.

The hands of the clock show two o'clock exactly.

A second later the telegraph starts spewing lines on a ribbon.

Rav Ashlag reads: "I need to speak to Ashlag. Lenin."

Rav Ashlag nods to the postman:

-Please write: "Good afternoon, Lenin. This is Ashlag."

The postman quickly types and whispers in disbelief:

-I can't believe it. It's Lenin himself!

-"Finally, I tracked you down," – Lenin responds.

-"How are you feeling?" – dictates Rav Ashlag.

-"I am dying. But believe me, it's not the worst that could happen."

Gorki, 10km south of Moscow, Russia.

A large window overlooking snowcapped fir trees.

Behind them, a white forest.

A blue cobweb of veins covers a pale skinny hand on an armrest.

Lenin is sitting in his rocking chair with a duvet across his legs.

Sunk above his hollow cheeks, his eyes are foggy and feverish.

He dictates in a weak voice.

A young telegraph puncher promptly types.

- "You were right. I don't know what else to do now."

-"You cannot change anything now," - replies Rav Ashlag - "terror is afoot."

***

Jerusalem.

-"Is it really going to be so terrible there?" – asks the postman anxiously.

-"Just type!" – responds Rav Ashlag.

The postman types quickly.

-"Lenin, you missed the main point. Man cannot change his nature on his own. It's impossible. A man is born and dies an egoist."

***

Gorki.
Lenin suddenly stiffens in his chair.
His thin hand trembles.

-"I wanted to build a new, better world." – His voice grows louder. – "Doesn't your Creator want people to be happy?"

-"He wants just that. But why did you want to build such a world?"

Lenin, with tears in his eyes, screams at the top of his weak lungs:

-"So that everyone would be equal! So there would be no more rich and poor! A just and pure world! Why didn't he let me do that?!"

- "Egoists can't build a just world. They can only build an unjust world - for themselves."

The telegraph puncher is looking at Lenin, waiting for his response.
Lenin says quietly:

-"What will happen to me now, Ashlag? To all of us? To everything that we have done here?"

She types.

***

Jerusalem. The telegraph ribbon snakes through Rav Ashlag's hands.
The postman looks at Rav Ashlag.
His students are watching him intently.

-"Everything will be fine," – he says. – "Humanity will go through dead ends, pain, and suffering. And in the end it will build a just world, a world of love, without hatred."

Rav Ashlag stops talking.
The postman's fingers stop.

-"Unfortunately, it will involve much suffering."

He walks to the window.

-"The world doesn't listen. *(He is talking to himself, but the postman still types his words.)* People can't understand that there is a path of light," - says Rav Ashlag. –"They aren't hearing me... yet."

Moshe, Chaim, Baruch, and Shimon exchange glances.
Rav Ashlag is standing quietly near the window.
It's a sunny day in Jerusalem.

***

Gorki.
The telegraph ribbon dies away on the table.
Lenin sinks back into his rocking chair, exhausted.

-Yes, I understand... and still, I'm afraid to die, Ashlag.

Snow is falling outside.
Lenin closes his eyes.

-Farewell...

Jerusalem.
The wriggling of the telegraph ribbon comes to a halt.
Rav Ashlag dictates the last two words:

"Farewell... Lenin."

-Rav Ashlag, - the postman breaks the silence. - All my relatives are there.

-Tell them to get out of there any way they can and come here. - Rav Ashlag replies.

***

Night.
Rav Ashlag's room.
Neat narrow lines flow out of the tip of a quill.
Rav Ashlag is whispering.

Rav Ashlag's voice:

"...But for a single grave sin that could not be forgiven unto them, namely that the precious work they undertook of coming to love thy neighbor as thyself should have been for the sake of merging with the Creator in the name of that exalted law of love, which envelops us as a womb envelopes an embryo. Instead, they did it for their own egoistic ends."

His hand keeps writing.
We hear Rav Ashlag's voice:

-"But had the Creator himself been the purpose, then without a doubt they would have risen in just a few short years above all the other nations of the world put together and would have revealed the great land of love, the land of the Creator."

The dawn is breaking.
The quill is resting on a densely filled sheet of paper.
Its title reads, "The Peace."
Rav Ashlag is asleep, his head resting on his arms.

Baruch's voice: Father!

Rav Ashlag raises his head.
He sees his son, Baruch, leaning over him.

Rav Ashlag: Why did you let me sleep?

Baruch: We felt sorry for you. You've been up all night, and we have to get to work in less than an hour...

Rav Ashlag *(sternly)*: This is none of your business. I ordered you not to let me fall asleep!

***

The tannery.
Rav Ashlag is scraping rawhide with an iron scraper.
Droplets of sweat rain down on his grime-covered hands.
Everyone is working silently and in unison.
The dust-filled air is diffusing the rays of the morning sun, coming in through the holes in the window.

***

Jerusalem. A bitter cold wind blows in the faces of Rav Ashlag, Baruch, Chaim, Moshe, and Shimon as they walk along the city walls. They are bundled helplessly under their thin coats that do little to fend off the biting chill.
Moshe and Shimon break off, turning into one of the alleys.

***

Rav Ashlag and Baruch enter their house.
Rivka is standing facing the window and doesn't turn to greet them.
Bat Sheva is sitting quietly behind a curtain.
An unusual, deafening silence hangs in the air.

Rav Ashlag notices an open letter in Rivka's hand.
He takes it and reads it quickly.
His eyes stop on the last line of the letter:

"We couldn't do anything to help them. The doctors were powerless. They died quietly, one after the other... without you."

His hand begins to shake.
Rav Ashlag looks up at Rivka.
They stand there in silence for long while.
Baruch comes up to his father's side.

Baruch: What happened?!

Rav Ashlag *(to Rivka)*: You are blaming me for this, aren't you?

Rivka *(quietly)*: Yes, I am.

Rav Ashlag: Do you think we could have taken them with us?

Rivka: No...

She turns around to look at her husband.

Rivka *(a quiet moan arises from deep within her)*: I felt that something terrible was going to happen. What can I do with this feeling now? Huh? Tell me! You are so wise, you know everything, you are in contact with Him. Ask Him, why He had to take our babies away!?

Baruch *(exclaims)*: What?!

Rivka starts to cry.
Rav Ashlag remains next to her and doesn't attempt to soothe her.
Outside the window, two birds are perched on a tree branch.

Rivka *(rocking from side to side, her voice breaking down)*: David was begging me to take him with us, and Bracha... I will never forget her eyes when we were leaving. I knew that something was going to happen, and still... I left them there.

Baruch slumps down on a wooden stool.

He is weeping soundlessly.
Rav Ashlag is quiet.

Rivka: I always repeated: "There is none else besides Him," but now, when disaster strikes, I can't justify Him. How come, Yehuda?

Rav Ashlag holds her.
His hand is gently stroking her shoulder.

Rav Ashlag: It's because you can't see the joy of the soul. You can see the death of the body, but can't see the soul that is moving ever closer to the Creator. With each life cycle, it comes closer and closer. When the body comes into the world or leaves it, those are His calculations. And trust him, they are always accurate.

Baruch wipes his tears with a dirty sleeve and looks at his father.
Rav Ashlag is looking out the window.
The two birds take off from the branch in unison.
He follows them with his gaze as they glide across the street, over the heads of a boy and girl who are walking along.
The girl is holding the boy's hand tightly.

They both turn to look at Rav Ashlag.
They smile and wave their hands at him.
Rav Ashlag nods to them.

Rivka glances up at him, her eyes full of tears, then she turns to look out through the window.

Rivka: What do you see out there?

Rav Ashlag: Life... going on. *(Turning to her)* You are strong. You are the strongest woman in the whole world! Just trust Him.

She rests her head on his chest.
He caresses her in silence.
They stand there together for a long, long time.
Baruch is sitting quietly by the wall.

The wind intensifies.
The glass in the window shakes and trembles.
It is getting darker behind the window.
They continue to stand together.

Night falls.
They are still standing there, pressed against each other.
He doesn't let go of her.
She, too, is afraid to let go of him.

Rivka watches the clock hand moving.
It is midnight.
She pulls back from her husband, wipes her tears, and looks into his eyes.

Rivka: Please forgive me. You have to be up for lesson in an hour and you didn't get any sleep. Forgive me, Yehuda. I can cope with this. Eventually I will, but not all at once. Will you bear with me?

Rav Ashlag: It's not easy for us, but we will persevere. We will carry on, Rivka, because we are together.

She moves away from her husband to the corner of the room and returns with a small plate of simple food.
She puts it on the table.

Rivka: Sit down and eat, you are tired.

***

The nightly lesson.
Rav Ashlag is sitting in front of his four students in silence.
The students are exchanging glances.
Baruch comes up to his father, whispers something in his ear, and waits for an answer.

Rav Ashlag *(loud and clear)*: There is only one reason, Baruch, why the lesson can be canceled... *(stands up)* only in case of the death of the body.

Rav Ashlag is pacing from one wall to the other, taking big steps as usual.

Rav Ashlag: Bodies come and go. The soul remains the same. The same souls come into different bodies over thousands of life cycles.

The students follow him with their eyes as he paces from wall to wall.
It feels as if he is telling this to someone other than them.
Shimon dares to raise his hand.
Rav Ashlag stops and looks at him.

Shimon: What's the point of this endless exchange of bodies?

Rav Ashlag: To purify the will to receive of self-love and fully arrive at love for your neighbor.

All are looking at Rav Ashlag.
He turns to the window.

Rav Ashlag: I'm leaving with my family to Givat Shaul[56] tomorrow.

Moshe: But what about our lessons?!

Rav Ashlag: The lessons continue as usual.

Moshe: But from here to Givat Shaul it's...

Rav Ashlag: An hour's walk.

Moshe: People say that it's impossible to make it alive at night from here to Givat Shaul. (*Looks at his friends*)

Rav Ashlag: Unless you walk together.

Everybody looks at their teacher.

Rav Ashlag: Lesson starts at 1 a.m. Sharp.

***

Early morning. Jerusalem.
A wagon is riding along a deserted road.
It's pulled by a donkey.
Rivka and the children are sitting in the wagon in silence.
Rav Ashlag and his four students are following the wagon on foot.

***

Givat Shaul.
Baby in hand, Rivka is standing in the middle of the empty apartment.
The paint on the walls is peeling, the floor is dirty, and the windows overlook a rocky, semi-arid land.
The wind is howling under the beams of the roof.
Rav Ashlag is looking out the window.
He watches his students plodding back on the narrow trail.

***

56 A neighborhood outside the old city of Jerusalem.

Givat Shaul. Night.
Rav Ashlag's house is silhouetted against the dark starry skyline.
A kerosene lamp stands lit in the window.

***

Rav Ashlag's room.
A hand pours a large cup of coffee.
A cigarette is burning in an ashtray full of stubs.
Under the table, Rav Ashlag's feet sit in a washbasin of ice water.
Rows of neat lines flow out from his quill.

***

Night. Jerusalem.
The outskirts of the old city.
A dark open stretch of wilderness separates the last row of houses from the neighborhood of Givat Shaul.
Moshe and Shimon are standing on a narrow path past the last house.
The path disappears in the darkness ahead of them.

Moshe: How much longer can we wait for him?!

Shimon: Just a few more minutes.

Moshe: He won't come. We have to go.

Shimon: And what if he does? How will he get there alone?

Silence.
They wait.
Suddenly a jackal howl shatters the silence. It is coming from nearby.
Moshe and Shimon sprint back toward the houses.

Moshe's voice: To hell with him! I saw yesterday how his hands were shaking. He is not here, and it means that he doesn't want to come to the lesson. That's it. Let's go.

Moshe and Shimon amble slowly along the city walls.
We can hear the patter of their feet.
They freeze. They press their backs to the wall and stand there, afraid to breathe.
Somewhere a nocturnal predator is tearing apart its prey in the darkness.

We can hear its ferocious growls.
Moshe and Shimon are unable to move.

Finally Shimon takes the first step forward and immediately a raspy voice commands them to stop.
A British patrol appears from the darkness.
The two British soldiers look closely at the Jews.

British soldier #1 *(in English)*: Where are you heading?

Shimon: Givat Shaul.

British soldier #1: Why at this time?

Shimon: Our teacher holds his lessons at night.

British soldier #1: How come?

Shimon: We work during the day.

British soldier #2 *(shaking his head, addressing the first one)*: A lesson at night... – I can't figure those Jews out... *(to Chaim.)* You have to be in your warm bed at night, next to your warm wife... o-o-oh well, best not to think about it...

British soldier #1 *(handing back the papers)*: Well, on you go.

Moshe and Shimon continue past the patrol and disappear into the night.
From further down we hear the voice of British soldier **#1**:

-What are you studying?

Shimon's voice from the dark (*in Hebrew*): The wisdom of Kabbalah.

Voice of British soldier #1: What's that?

Moshe's voice: It's about how to see the Creator.

British soldier #1: Ah...ha...

Voice of British soldier #2: You better watch your backs. We are the last patrol. Abu Khalif and his gang are out tonight. If they catch you, they will send you to meet your Creator.

The soldiers laugh.

***

Open wilderness.
Two silhouettes are moving through the night.
All is quiet but their soft footsteps.
A barely visible narrow path unfolds beneath them, leading them toward a dark cluster of houses.

Suddenly, a hyena laughs just a few feet ahead.
Moshe and Shimon freeze in mid-step.
The dark outline of the hyena can be seen crossing their path, only its red eyes shine back at them through the darkness.

They walk on.
Now they start to run.
We can hear someone chasing them.
A gruff voice commands them to stop, but they can already see the houses clearly and press onward.

***

Rav Ashlag's home.
Shimon and Moshe rush inside, scared to death.
Rav Ashlag is sitting at his table, writing as always.
He doesn't even turn to greet them.

They sit down on their chairs, struggling to catch their breath.

Rav Ashlag: Where is Chaim?

Moshe: We waited for him, but he didn't show up.

Rav Ashlag stops writing and stares at Moshe.

Moshe *(unable to bear his stare)*: Why are you looking at me like this?! He didn't come! Shimon, you tell him!

Shimon *(hesitantly)*: Yes.

A gunshot rings through the night outside.
They all turn their heads sharply to the window.

***

Night. On the edge of the neighborhood.
A knife's blade glistens for a second in the light of a distant lamp, before lashing out to meet Chaim's throat.

His adam's apple is trembling.
From the complete darkness comes a threatening Arabic voice:

-Your money, Jew!

Chaim: I have nothing, not even a penny!

The voice: We'll see about that.

A hand feels through Chaim's clothes, shaking him this way and that.
A rough face with a huge ugly scar across the right cheek appears from the darkness.

The Arab: What the f... *(he brings his face close to Chaim's.)* I know all you rich, fat, sly Jews can pretend to be naïve little sheep. But there's a wolf hiding underneath there. You cannot lie to Abu Khalif!

Chaim *(pleadingly)*: Please let me go.

Abu Khalif *(harshly)*: Take off your clothes. Quickly!

Chaim: I beg of you, please don't kill me!

The knife presses harder on Chaim's throat.
Chaim quickly undresses.

Abu Khalif: Now pray, Jew!

Chaim looks into the cold eyes of the Arab robber.

Abu Khalif: Say your Jewish prayer for the last time!

Chaim closes his eyes. His lips utter a prayer.

***

Rav Ashlag's home.
Rav Ashlag still hasn't started the lesson.
The clock shows quarter past one.
Suddenly the sound of running feet come from the outside.
The door opens and Chaim, wearing nothing but his socks and underpants, runs in.
He is shuddering from cold and from fear, his knees buckle, and he falls onto the closest chair.

Rav Ashlag stands up, walks up to him, takes off his coat, and puts it on his quivering shoulders. He then takes off his wool hat and puts it on Chaim's head.

Rav Ashlag: Were you scared?

Chaim *(faltering)*: He made me take off my clothes, put his knife to my throat, and told me to pray. *(His voice quivers and he looks up at Rav Ashlag)* I wanted so much to be with all of you in the lesson. I prayed for that. I opened my eyes and he was gone.

Rav Ashlag *(looking at all of them)*: We shall have a meal now. *(Turns to Baruch standing by the wall)* Set the table.

***

The table is set. The meal consists of a plate with sliced onions, half a bottle of unrefined olive oil, half a loaf of pumpernickel bread, and a bottle of vodka.

In front of each man is a heavy vodka glass filled to the rim.

Rav Ashlag: I promised to reveal to you the secret of how to unite with the Creator, how to enter His land.

His students are watching him, their eyes red with exhaustion.

Rav Ashlag raises his glass of vodka.

He is silent for a brief moment, then he looks straight at Shimon.

Shimon lowers his eyes.

Rav Ashlag: You will get there on one condition only.

Chaim *(mumbles)*: I wanted so much to be at the lesson today...

Rav Ashlag: If you unite your hearts into one. *(Looks at Shimon)* I will not tire of repeating this to you. This is the only condition!

Shimon can barely hold back his tears.

His lips are trembling.

Rav Ashlag: If you dissolve into each other. *(He rests his gaze on each of his students)* If you establish mutual guarantee among you.

Shimon covers his face with his hands.

Rav Ashlag: If you can see beyond your friend's wretched body, and into the huge desire burning within him, only then will your "I" surrender and you will unite.

Chaim: Can we do it?!

Baruch: We can!

Rav Ashlag: Can you do it?

Moshe *(clearly)*: We will!

Only Shimon does not answer. He is silent, staring at the floor.
Everyone turns to him.
Suddenly he jumps up from his seat, screaming:

Shimon: We will never be able to do it! We can't! Why are we lying to ourselves! We are weak! We are miserable! We cannot become brothers because we cannot overcome our fear and envy, because we are so... so full of shit - scum, living just for ourselves! (*He is gasping, looking around*) We're not cut out for this! No...! We can't enter that place where we aspire. We... *(whispering)* we are such...

Shimon sits down and covers his head with his hands.
Everyone is watching Rav Ashlag.
He is sipping vodka slowly from his glass.
Everyone is watching him, waiting to see what he will say.
He puts his glass down.

Rav Ashlag: The lesson starts now.

He picks up the book and opens it.

Chaim *(to Rav Ashlag)*: Won't you answer Shimon?

Moshe *(through his teeth)*: Weakling!

Shimon *(lifting his head, his eyes are full of tears)*: Forgive me...

Moshe: If not for people like you... be a man!

Chaim: Hang in there, Shimon!

Shimon: Forgive me, I will try. *(Looks at Rav Ashlag)* Just don't send me away.

Rav Ashlag: We begin our lesson. *The Zohar* will lead you to the Creator.

He looks at Shimon and utters loudly so that everyone can hear him:

-I envy you.

He then looks at each of them.

-I am warning you: Not a single thought about yourselves. We are speaking of the most precious thing one can have, and that's why your responsibility is so heavy.

They look at him, hanging on every word that comes out of his mouth.

-You won't be let in easily. The main condition is - not a single thought about yourselves! Not even one! If you succeed, you'll break through.

Their eyes are aflame.
Each word penetrates like a spear.

-Each of you has to tell himself: "we are connecting into one great desire."

Rav Ashlag looks at the wall in front of him.

-And we won't leave you, - he says.

He stops talking.
They wait motionless.

-Great sages – they hear Rav Ashlag's voice, - connected into a single spiritual pyramid and then wrote *The Book of Zohar*. If we unite, we'll break through.

***

Suddenly, the classroom disappears.
Rav Ashlag is walking along a path.
His students are following him, holding their breath,[57] looking around them in disbelief.

-All of this is inside of us, - they hear Rav Ashlag's voice.

Endless rows of vineyards stretch out to the horizon.
Clusters of ripe grapes bask in the sun.

---

57 There are states when the teacher "takes" the desires of his students into himself and neutralizes their egoism with his influence. He as if transfers them from one world to another, like a bird carrying its nestlings on its back, and that's why this action is called "Knafaim" (Hebrew: "wings"). It happens when the teacher decides that the students need his support.

Ahead, translucent mountains rise majestically behind a forest; clear rivers cut through their sides and meet at a crystal clear lake.
Peace and silence everywhere.

Rav Ashlag's voice *(warm and fatherly)*: Hang tight! Not a shadow of a thought about yourselves. You should be ready to give everything to each other.

Rav Ashlag is walking a step ahead of them.

-Not a single thought about yourselves, - he repeats.

They stop and observe this magical world with awe and excitement.
Moshe leans down to touch a flower.

Rav Ashlag's voice: No-o!

Frightened, Moshe straightens up, takes a step forward, and bumps into an invisible wall.
They all make a step forward and hit the wall as well.

They see how ahead of them, Rav Ashlag keeps walking toward the trees.

They punch the invisible wall in vain.

Rav Ashlag walks away.

Screaming, they try to shatter the invisible wall with their fists.
Their fists begin to bleed but the wall doesn't give in.
They hurl themselves against the wall smearing their blood all over it.
Their muffled screams cannot be heard.

Rav Ashlag is already far off, about to enter the forest.

Moshe grabs a rock and starts hitting it madly against the invisible wall.
The rock scatters and sharp chips pierce their faces.

***

Back in Jerusalem. A classroom.
Rav Ashlag is sitting in his place.
Moshe looks around at everybody.

Moshe: What just happened?!

Chaim *(stuttering)*: I've never felt anything like that in my life!

Moshe: Was this...?! *(Looks at his hands, his friends, then turns his eyes to Rav Ashlag)* We didn't cross?

Rav Ashlag: You are unable to cross.

Moshe: So it was real!

Rav Ashlag: You saw yourselves as you truly are.

Moshe: You left us!

Rav Ashlag: I couldn't help you.

Moshe: You did it on purpose!

Rav Ashlag: Nothing there is done on purpose.

Chaim: We were calling you, and you just walked away from us!

Rav Ashlag: Over there – you either cross or you don't.

Moshe: But why, why, why didn't we cross?

Rav Ashlag: Don't you get it?

Moshe: No-o-o!

Chaim: We tried really hard. It was such a... such a great world. We tried our hardest.

Moshe: When we were bleeding, we called you, and you were just walking away, but you heard us?! You did, didn't you?!

Rav Ashlag: Yes, I did.

Moshe: And yet you kept on walking!

Rav Ashlag: It was you who were moving away from me.

Moshe moans in helplessness.

Baruch: What should we do?

Rav Ashlag: Conquer Pharaoh.

Baruch: How?!

Rav Ashlag: By realizing that it's impossible to conquer him.

Silence. Everybody is looking at Rav Ashlag.

Rav Ashlag: Only he with a broken heart arrives at a prayer and ultimately crosses.

Shimon begins to sob.
Moshe stands up and goes to the window.
He stands there with his back turned to everybody.
His shoulders begin to quiver.

***

Suddenly, a flash of light.
They see the beautiful country again.
The path is running across green hills.
Rav Ashlag is walking down the path.

In front of him lies the White City.[58]
We can hear children's laughter, soft voices, and gentle music coming from somewhere up ahead, while from behind come screams of agony.
Rav Ashlag stops and hears his own voice.

Rav Ashlag's voice: Don't turn around – keep walking!

He remains standing.
The White City is just in front of him.

Behind him, his bleeding students are thrashing against the invisible wall.
A deer's head appears from the shrubbery.

Rav Ashlag hears his own voice: Don't turn around!

The deer emerges from the bushes and strolls toward Rav Ashlag.

-The barriers you've put up are too high, says Rav Ashlag. They won't make it through.

In the distance, his students are still beating against the wall, shrieking.
The deer walks past Rav Ashlag, then turns his head toward him.

The voice: Leave them.

Rav Ashlag: I can't.

58 White symbolizes a state of enlightenment, complete cleansing from the ego. The White City symbolizes man's final, corrected desire, which was egoistic and ignoble and has become the most exalted, white. In the city occurs the complete unification with the Creator.

A bird lands on a tree branch above his head.

The voice: Leave them.

Rav Ashlag: What is my purpose then?

A butterfly flutters by.

The voice: You want them to make it across?

Rav Ashlag: You created this world for them. Isn't that so?

The butterfly lands on a flower.

The voice: Turn around and watch!

Rav Ashlag turns around and sees the invisible barrier is no longer holding his students back.
Shimon is the first to burst through.
He tumbles to the ground, lifts his head, and jumps to his feet.
Baruch, then Chaim, then Moshe follow him.

Rav Ashlag *(whispering)*: Careful, friends, not a single thought about yourselves. Let each support the others.

***

For a moment, we are back in the classroom in Jerusalem.
Shimon is leaning over the book. He is focused intently.

Shimon *(mumbles)*: Not one thought about yourself... no... we are one whole.[59]

Baruch: Not one thought about yourself.

Chaim: Not a thought.

***

A flash of light.
They get up from the ground and look around, taking their first steps.

Rav Ashlag: Can I come closer to them?

Rav Ashlag sees the flower nodding at him with its blue petals.

59 The sensation that we are part of one collective soul replaces the sensation of the individual self. From the perspective of the Creator, we are one unified whole. Therefore, for Him to hear us, we must also be so—united.

He can hear his own voice: Wait. Look!

Suddenly Rav Ashlag sees Moshe ignite like a torch.
He bursts into fire before he has time to scream, and the blaze incinerates him in an instant.
Chaim takes a step back and is incinerated too.
Shimon and Baruch turn around, but don't make it either - they disappear in flames.
Four smoldering piles of ashes remain on the ground where they were standing a moment ago.

Immediately, we are back in the classroom in Jerusalem.
The students, as if thunderstruck, are unable to move.
Rav Ashlag covers his eyes with his hand.

Shimon: We won't make it?

Baruch: Help us... Father.

***

A flash of light.
Rav Ashlag is standing on a path, surrounded by emerald green fields, dotted with flowers in dazzling colors.
The White City lies behind him.
The wind blows the ashes off the path, caressing the sea of tall grass, creating ripples and waves.

Rav Ashlag can hear his own voice:

-Have you seen it?

Rav Ashlag: Yes, I have.

The voice: Do you still want it?

Rav Ashlag *(looking at the ripples of green grass)*: You have made your world for them, so give me a chance to open it before them, even a little bit. Help them take the first step.

The wind dies out.

The voice: Well, you may try.

Rav Ashlag: Do I have your permission?!

-You do.

***

Jerusalem. Classroom.
Rav Ashlag stands up and walks to the door.
He leaves the classroom.

***

Documentary footage from all over the world: 1926. French fashion shows; Soviet Russia military parades; Eugene O'neill's *The Great God Brown* opens at the Greenwich Theatre; astronomers jubilant at the discovery of the Comas Sola comet; a coup d'état in portugal installs the Ditadura Nacional (National Dictatorship); the Warner Brothers' Vitaphone system premieres with the movie, Don Juan, starring John Barrymore; Agatha Christie disappears from her home in Surrey; she is found at the Harrogate Hotel.

***

All these scenes blend into the Jerusalem night.
The light is on in Rav Ashlag's room.
We can see him pacing from wall to wall.
Suddenly he stops, sits down at his desk, and begins to write.

***

Again, documentary footage:
Dance marathons in the United States; grand openings of new restaurants; Hollywood stars enjoying themselves; the public's squeals as it greets Rudolph Valentino; elephants are mercilessly hunted in Africa; Sigmund Freud starts his experiments; boxers in a ring exchange blows before a wild cheering audience; Hitler is drinking with his friends; Mussolini is elected in Italy.

***

Jerusalem. Rav Ashlag's room. Night.
His hand brings the manuscript to the kerosene lamp.
The paper burns with a crackle as the fire eats away at rows of letters.
We see its reflection in Rav Ashlag's eyes.

Baruch screams: Father, what are you doing?!

Rav Ashlag: It's not good. No one will understand it.

***

Rav Ashlag's home. A living room.
A rough wooden table, Rav Ashlag at its head.
Rivka is sitting by his side, pregnant with another baby.
Seven kids sit around the table, eating silently.
On each plate is but one potato, half an onion, and a little piece of bread.
Rivka passes her potato to her three-year-old daughter.
The girl eats it eagerly.

Suddenly, Rav Ashlag stands up and walks to the window.

He sees a man standing in the street, watching him closely.
The man wears an expensive double-breasted suit.
He stands out in this poor neighborhood.
The man gestures to Rav Ashlag with his hand.
Rav Ashlag opens the window.

The man: Don't you recognize me, teacher?

Rav Ashlag *(taking a closer look)*: Aaron?!

Aaron *(smiling)*: Yes. Will you let me in?

Rav Ashlag: What are you doing here?

Aaron: I've become rich and came to ask for your forgiveness.

Rav Ashlag: Come on up.

Rav Ashlag's home. Rav Ashlag and Aaron are sitting at the table.
Aaron's face is a pale yellow, with dark circles around his eyes.
Rivka is watching from the side.

Aaron: You left and I stayed behind, cursing myself for being such a coward. I couldn't shake off the feeling that I had betrayed you. Oh, if only you knew how many nights I cried because of it. Finally, I decided to leave everything and travel to you, to ask for forgiveness, and to stay by your side forever. And then it happened. I received my inheritance. I knew it would happen, I just didn't expect it to happen so soon. My rich uncle had died in England and left everything he had to me on the condition that I move to England. Suddenly, I realized what a great mission the Creator had charged me with. I understood that all my previous decisions had been correct. It wasn't I who had made them! *(Pause)* and now I am here.

Rav Ashlag: Why?

Aaron: I know that you don't have enough money to publish your books *(looking at Rivka)* and barely enough to support your family.

Rav Ashlag *(cutting him off)*: One needs to be satisfied with but the necessary.

Aaron: How much money do you need?

Rav Ashlag: Enough to provide modest food for my household, and for ink and paper.

Aaron: How much is that?

Rivka: A little. He has been writing on paper scraps for a while now, and the children haven't had a proper meal for a long time.

> Aaron takes out a stack of bank notes from his side pocket and lays it on the table.

Aaron: I want you to write such a book that everyone could understand, even idiots like myself. Is it possible?

Rav Ashlag: I have to try.

Aaron: I am leaving you enough money to live on and to write. Here. *(He pushes the money closer to Rav Ashlag.)*

Rav Ashlag: Do you have a place in London?

Aaron: Yes, a big three-story house. *(He takes out a vial with pills and pops one in his mouth.)*

Rav Ashlag: I will do my writing there.

Aaron *(surprised, looks at Rivka and at Rav Ashlag)*: I didn't think it possible. It's a great honor.

Rav Ashlag: I will leave this money to my family.

Rivka *(quickly)*: But it's way too much.

Aaron: Nonsense! I will leave more. But... *(looks at Rivka)* your wife is pregnant.

> Rav Ashlag turns to look at Rivka.

Rivka *(to him)*: Don't worry. I will be fine.

Rav Ashlag: I must go.

Rivka: You will be able to write quietly over there.

Rav Ashlag: I need some quiet.

Rivka: Go, we will pray for you from here.

***

Israel, port of Jaffa.[60]
A white ship is getting ready to set sail.

Rav Ashlag and his students are standing by the ship's gangway.
All are called aboard.
Rav Ashlag hugs everyone.
He hugs Baruch and whispers:

-I'll be waiting for your letters.

He hugs Chaim, Moshe, and Shimon.

Shimon: You are leaving on purpose. You could've written here.

Rav Ashlag turns around and starts to walk up the ladder.

Shimon: It will be hard for us without you.

Rav Ashlag walks without turning back.

Shimon: Impossibly hard!

Moshe *(interrupts him)*: Let the rav go! Stop whining! *(To Rav Ashlag)* Don't worry, we will be fine.

Rav Ashlag has already boarded.
He is standing next to Aaron, who is leaning on the handrail.
The ship sets sail.
Shimon is the first to turn around and leave.

***

The ship cuts through the waves.
Rav Ashlag is sitting on deck wrapped in a duvet.

60 Jaffa—An ancient city by the shores of the Mediterranean, mentioned in the Bible (Joshua, 19:46, and Jonah, 1:3). Today it is adjacent to Tel Aviv.

***

Documentary footage:
1926 England… pretty, flourishing.
A celebration in honor of the queen.
A former British Prime Minister, Lloyd George, meets with Winston Churchill. They are feeding seagulls by the seaside.
The birth of future queen of England, Elizabeth II.

***

A three-story house on a quiet London street.
The window on the second floor is open.

***

Rav Ashlag's room.
Rav Ashlag is sitting by his desk.
Smoke rises from an ashtray full of cigarette butts.
He is writing fast.

A door opens and closes behind Rav Ashlag's back.
Aaron enters the room quietly and sits down on a chair by the door.
Rav Ashlag doesn't notice him and continues to write.
Aaron swallows a pill. He coughs, intentionally.

Aaron: Did you get any sleep?

Rav Ashlag *(excitedly)*: It seems to me that I've found the right style of explanation. *The Zohar* is simple, you know, if you only remember that it speaks of what is within you. I have found a way to explain it.

Aaron holds a heavy manuscript in Rav Ashlag's handwriting.

Aaron: I've read it.

Rav Ashlag: Did you understand any of it?

Aaron: No. (*In hurry*) But maybe it's because I'm so dumb. I was a terrible student at school, as well.

Rav Ashlag stands up, brashly pushing his chair back.

Rav Ashlag *(irritably)*: I don't know how to make it simpler.

Aaron: Don't worry, it will come! Clearly, to write something simple, for simple-minded fools like me who want nothing more than their simple earthly lives is, well, not that simple.

Rav Ashlag *(reading out loud what he had written)*: "The Creator doesn't see our bodies; He sees one common soul. It is the union of all our souls. Our souls are bonded by the force of love. A single thought governs them, the thought of the Creator."

Aaron: What thought?!

Rav Ashlag: Love. Nothing else exists besides that. Complete, absolute bestowal.

Aaron: Where is it, this love?

Rav Ashlag: It permeates everything.

Aaron *(suddenly irritated)*: But where is it? Show it to me, let me touch it, feel it, just a little bit! *(Stops all of a sudden. Pause.)* I'm sorry.

Rav Ashlag *(spreads his arms)*: I am trying to explain it better.

Aaron *(pointing to the pages in his hand)*: I gave this to my friend to read, he is a well known publisher, a Jew.

Rav Ashlag: I can't write any simpler than that.

Aaron: He stopped on the fifth line and started to laugh at everything that's written here.

Rav Ashlag: Isn't it clear?

Aaron: No, it's clear. It's also clear that we are all egoists and that none of us possesses the same simple, sublime thought that the Creator has. We don't love anyone but ourselves. *(He shifts his gaze to the window)* But why does His love cause so much suffering, so much bloodshed? *(Pause)* It hurts so much... and I desperately don't want to die.

Rav Ashlag turns to the table, paying no more attention to Aaron.
The door closes quietly behind Aaron.
Rav Ashlag resumes his writing:

"The body suffers. It is born to die and to be buried. The body is a desire to live for one's own sake. Life for the sake of ourselves exhausts us."

For a moment he looks up.
Aaron is not there.

He desperately wants to share with him what he has just written.
He quickly continues:

"Only when we desire to bestow to each other, will the troubles and suffering of this world disappear."

An unusually warm wind blows through the windows.
The stars are clearly visible in the cloudless night sky.
Rav Ashlag gets up and leaves the house.

Nighttime. London. Empty streets.
Rav Ashlag is walking through the city.
Suddenly we can hear Baruch's voice, reading the first lines of his letter to his father:

Baruch's voice: "As soon as you left, we broke down. We are showing a brave face, but inside we are about to explode. I can feel it... there is no one here who can guide us, no one who can stop this insanity. I am prepared to let go. Energy is seeping out."

London. Rav Ashlag's room.
An open letter is lying on the table.
A wind coming from the half-open shutters is shuffling the pages.
The lines of the letter can be read clearly.

We hear Baruch's voice:

"We can't do it without you. Father, what should we do?"

Rav Ashlag takes a quill, the plume dives into the ink.
He is writing and reading it out loud:

Rav Ashlag's voice: "My beloved brothers! I know you are desperate, full of doubts and trepidation. And this is good! Despair is the beginning of ascent. Again and again, through descents and ascents, beyond your miserable bodies, try to distinguish those sparks of love that pulsate within each of you. Always remember that if you do not unite, this will be your burial place..."

Rav Ashlag's hand stops for a moment, then he adds something:

"...And you'll discover that you do not have the strength to unite!"

Another pause.
Again, Rav Ashlag's gaze examines what he wrote, and he continues:

BATAVIA-C
22. 10. 34. 20.
AUSTRALIE
Rotterdam

- "You were eager to unite. The Creator rewarded you with hatred. You thought that you were able to love each other, but it turned out that you are unable to achieve anything!"

***

Jerusalem. The classroom.
Baruch is reading from the letter:

Baruch: "You stand today before Mount Sinai.[61] It is a mountain of hatred that exists within each and every one of you."

Shimon shakes his head.

Baruch *(reading)*: "How can we rise above it? Where do we obtain the strength?!"

Chaim is listening acutely.
Moshe is hiding a tiny smirk.

Baruch *(reading, his voice trembling)*: "You are asking, where can you find strength?! Only the Creator can grant you that. It is He who revealed to you the truth about yourselves. He is waiting for you to turn to Him. Do it! Demand that He give you strength to love each other. How?"

Shimon *(whispers)*: How should we demand it, how?

Baruch *(reading the last line)*: "How? You have *The Book of Zohar*. Let *The Zohar* enter you."

***

London. Night.
Rav Ashlag is writing incessantly.
Neat rows of letters are flowing from his quill.
He is writing cleanly, not stopping once to make a single revision.
He reaches the end of the page and lays it on a hefty stack of other pages by the edge of the table.

The window is open. The night is warm and quiet.

---

61 The word *Har* [mountain] comes from the word *Hirhurim* [thoughts/reflections]. The name Sinai comes from the word *Sinaa* [hatred]. A man must arrive at Mount Sinai, that is, to crave to unite with the others and to suddenly feel that it's impossible. One must feel a "mountain of hatred" toward others, which is impossible to conquer alone. This comes in order to induce a collective request for help from Above. This is a real descent for the sake of an ascent.

Suddenly Rav Ashlag hears a strange groan.
He raises his head, then stands up and walks to the window.
The moaning is coming from downstairs.
It is getting louder and louder, by now it sounds more like a scream.
Rav Ashlag leans out the window and looks down.

He notices an open window on the first floor with light coming from it.
He walks down the old wooden stairway to the first floor.
Rav Ashlag approaches the door to Aaron's room.
Beneath it, a sliver of light spills into the corridor.
Rav Ashlag opens the door.
He sees Aaron, lying face down on the floor of his bedroom.
His deathly pale face is writhing in pain.

Rav Ashlag kneels by him.
Aaron is trying to whisper something but all that comes out is another groan.

Rav Ashlag forces Aaron on his back and opens his shirt.
He puts his hand on Aaron's stomach and looks into his eyes.
Suddenly Aaron's body jerks in a spasm and grows still on the floor.
Aaron looks into Rav Ashlag's eyes.

Rav Ashlag: How often do you have these fits?

Aaron *(weakly)*: Such strong ones once every two months... when the pills... don't work. I used to have them once every six months. Now they are more and more frequent.

Rav Ashlag: Diagnosis?

Aaron: Liver cancer.

Rav Ashlag: Since when?

Aaron: It started back in Poland, I think.

Rav Ashlag: You thought I could cure you?

Aaron *(silent for a long time)*: I am exhausted. I've tried everything. *(He looks into Rav Ashlag's eyes)* I was hoping.

Rav Ashlag: You don't need me, you need a doctor.

Aaron struggles to sit up straight.

Aaron: They gave me a year to live, at most. Is there nothing that can be done?

Rav Ashlag: Kabbalah doesn't heal the body.

Aaron makes an attempt to stand up, but gives in and remains seated on the floor instead.

Aaron *(looking at Rav Ashlag)*: I am ready to do whatever it takes to make these pains go away. *(His eyes are full of tears)* There must be something, an incantation, a prayer, or a charm. Something!

Rav Ashlag *(bluntly)*: No, there are no such things.

Aaron *(winces, fighting his pain)*: But you yourself are saying that Kabbalah is the path to happiness. Cure me, and I will give you everything.

Rav Ashlag: If one could read a line out of *The Zohar* and heal, everyone would rush to Kabbalah. No, it doesn't work like that.

Kabbalah cures the soul, not the body. It's for those who are asking, "What am I living for?" And not for those who are asking how to cure cancer.

Aaron finally manages to stand up.

Rav Ashlag: Lie down and rest. You will sleep well tonight.

***

Documentary footage.
London. Morning.
Big Ben strikes on the hour.
On their way to work, people fill the streets, two-storey buses, and the railway stations.
Traffic wardens wearing bobby hats are dancing in the middle of busy intersections, their whistles competing with car honks and shouts.
A new workday begins.

The façade of Aaron's house.

***

Inside Aaron's home.

A maid is carefully resting a breakfast tray in front of Rav Ashlag's room and picks up a similar tray she had put there earlier, it's untouched.
She listens.
The sound of even footsteps comes from behind the closed door.

***

Rav Ashlag's room.
The manuscripts are lying on the table.
Rav Ashlag is pacing around the table, his head down.
He stops, presses his forehead against the wall.
He stands like that for a very long time.

***

A flash of light.
He is walking along a path.
Clear blue vastness all around.
Green valleys full of flowers to his right; the welcoming shade of tall ancient trees to his left.
The White City gleams on the hilltop up ahead.
From the depth of the blue vastness comes an enchanting melody, as lucid as water, barely touching Rav Ashlag…

***

Rav Ashlag's room. Rav Ashlag takes a step back from the wall.
He strains his ears to listen.
The melody is not there.

***

A street in Jerusalem. Night.
Moshe and Chaim are walking through the city.
A British patrol comes out of the darkness and waves to them.
They walk on.
Two shadows cross their path and stop for a moment.
A rifle is loaded loudly somewhere.
The shadows disappear into the night.
Moshe and Chaim walk across the open expanse and arrive at a lit window.

***

They enter the classroom.
Baruch is holding a new letter from Rav Ashlag.

Baruch *(reading out loud)*: "Where is it, the constant thought about unity? Where is the inner scream: 'Give us the strength to love one another!'"

Baruch lifts his eyes from the letter.
They are full of tears.

Chaim: Read on!

Baruch: "Think of ways to unite. Pray for his help! Don't give in. Break your hearts in search of love."

Baruch stops again.
He loses his breath and cannot talk.

Chaim *(pleadingly)*: Read!

Baruch: "Remember, the Creator heeds only the cry of a broken heart." *(Continues reading to himself)*

Moshe *(harshly)*: Well?!

Baruch *(continues reading)*: "But how can I forgive you when the ladder that was lowered down to earth is still standing empty? *(Lifts his eyes from the letter)* You are not climbing it."

Everybody is speechless. A long silence hangs in the air.
Baruch is crying.

Moshe *(suddenly, contemptuously)*: Wipe your snivel. *(Looks around)* What's going on with all of you?! One is sobbing like a girl, another won't even wake up for the lesson! *(Screams)* He gave up, this Shimon!

Baruch and Chaim are looking at Moshe.

Moshe: I think we should forget about him. He's been absent two nights in a row.

Baruch: We should wake him up and bring him to the lesson.

Moshe: There is no coercion in spirituality.

Baruch: He has simply grown weak.

Moshe: Do as you wish, I'm staying. It's just a waste of valuable study time.

Chaim (to Baruch): I am coming with you.

***

Night. A narrow street in Jerusalem.
Baruch and Chaim are moving slowly in pitch darkness.
They stop below the windows of a house. Baruch throws a little stone at the window. The stone clinks on the window, then falls on the ground. He throws another one. Silence.
Chaim leans against the wall. Baruch gets on his shoulders and pulls himself up to the window. He opens the latch and crawls inside, then pulls Chaim up into the house.

***

Inside Shimon's house.
They walk past the children's beds and come up to the parents' bed at the far end of the room.
They silently lean over Shimon, who is sleeping next to his wife.
They carefully remove the blanket and gently pick up Shimon in their hands.
Shimon opens his eyes, but before he can open his mouth, Chaim covers it with his hand.
The fear on Shimon's face gives way to indignation.
He makes an attempt to break loose, but can't.
Then he suddenly calms down.
Baruch picks up his clothes on the way out.
They silently disappear back out the window and then into the night outside.

***

London. Rav Ashlag's room.
Rav Ashlag is writing.
More perfect lines of text, devoid of corrections, appear fast on the page.
His hand puts page after page on the pile at the edge of the table.
We can hear a soft knock on the door.

Rav Ashlag (*without turning*): Come on in.

Aaron comes inside wearing a white robe.

He appears to have slept well.

Rav Ashlag: Sit down and read.

Aaron comes closer, takes a stack of papers from the table and drops down into a chair.
Immediately he is lost to the world, reading.
The light of dawn shines through the mist outside the window.
Aaron's eyes fly through the text, one line after another.

Rav Ashlag's hand holding the quill is moving swiftly, without stopping even for a second.

We can hear Aaron speak:

-It's going to be a great book.

The quill stops.
Rav Ashlag peers at Aaron from the corner of his eye.

Aaron *(in excitement)*: One can write such a book only if the Creator himself is dictating it to him. I don't understand a thing but I am trembling with the force that it contains.

***

Jerusalem. Early morning.
The four students are huddled around *The Zohar*, sitting closely next to each other.

Moshe *(reading out loud)*: "And then the common soul shattered into myriad fragments. And the pieces fell down into our world – the world of complete darkness."

Baruch *(whispering)*: Intention! Intention! Give us the strength to love one another!

Moshe *(continues reading)*: "The pieces inhabited the bodies of this world... and then came hatred."

Baruch *(whispering)*: Give us the strength to love one another! Give us strength to love one another!

Moshe puts down the book, irritated.

Moshe: What are you mumbling there all the time!

Baruch: Father wrote that...

Moshe: I don't care what your father is writing! You are mumbling and I can't understand what's written here for the life of me!

He jumps up, knocking his chair down.

Moshe: I've come to study Kabbalah – the great science, and instead we are being treated like little kids. Inte-e-ention! I came here to study the great books. I want your father to teach me that.

Shimon: Shut up, you fool!

Moshe*(approaching him)*: Wha-a-at?!

Shimon: Shut up! You are talking about our teacher!

Moshe pushes Shimon hard and he flies across the room.
Shimon tries to stand up.
Moshe approaches him with clenched fists.
Shimon jumps up, his face contorted with hatred.

Shimon (screaming): I will kill you, scum!

He lunges at Moshe, but Chaim is holding him.
Moshe swings his fist to hit him, but Baruch stops his arm midway.

Baruch: Brothers... brothers! What are we doing!

Moshe attempts to shake him off.

Baruch: Father is writing to us...

Moshe turns around and grabs Baruch's throat.

Moshe: What is he writing there, your father, huh?! He left us and now he is writing all kinds of nice words. He gathered us together and then left us—and not only us, but his family and his wife, who is about to give birth without him.

Shimon *(yelling)*: He is your teacher!

Moshe: Shut up, you weakling!

Chaim *(standing between them)*: That's it! We have to calm down.

Moshe shakes Baruch's hand off him and sits down behind the table.

Chaim: We must calm down.

Baruch: Let's read his letter again.

Moshe: No, let's open the book instead.

Shimon: How terribly wrong this is.

Baruch: We have a mountain of hatred between us. If we don't rise above it...

Moshe *(harshly)*: We are going to open the book in order to draw the great wisdom hidden within it. Listen to me *(with urgency in his voice)*. We shall open the book and we shall read from the great holy *Book of Zohar*.

***

London. Night time.
Rav Ashlag is strolling through the city.
He walks through wealthy quarters where store windows, laden with expensive goods, are brightly lit even at night, where expensive cars whiz by, white suede gloves, evening gowns, and fancy restaurants show off the good life.

He is traveling through other quarters as well, where the homeless warm themselves by barrel fires, and the streets bear the mark of poverty - dilapidated facades, grimy faces, and dirty pubs.

Suddenly a faint musical chord catches his attention amidst the bustling city… and instantly disappears in the noise of the bustling city.
Rav Ashlag stops.

***

A flash of light.
He is standing on the path.
The clear blue vastness is all around him.
He is motionless.
Heavenly music is wafting toward him from behind the walls of the White City.

***

London. Street.
The music can hardly be heard.

Rav Ashlag is standing frozen in the middle of the street.
A passerby turns to look at him…

***

Night. Aaron's house is dark.
Aaron's room.
Aaron wakes up to the sound of music coming from somewhere inside the house.
He gets out of bed, slips on his robe, and goes out of the room.
He goes up the stairs to the second floor.
He is walking along a long corridor as the sound of a piano is growing louder.
He reaches the living room on the second floor.

Aaron stops and opens the door carefully.

In the dim candlelight he can see Rav Ashlag sitting by the piano, his fingers hovering gently on the keys.

Aaron's face - stunned and fearful.

The divine music envelops the house as it rises up above the London skyline.

Aaron walks inside, cautiously…

Rav Ashlag doesn't pay attention to him; he is oblivious to everything.
Finally, his fingers stop their movement and hang in mid-air. The music stops.

Aaron's voice: It's divine... what a beautiful melody! I didn't know you could play the piano so well.

Rav Ashlag's fingers touch the keys again, and again music fills the air.
Aaron approaches the piano and watches in awe as Rav Ashlag plays.

Rav Ashlag: But I can't play.

Aaron: But you are playing the piano now!

Rav Ashlag: Nobody's ever taught me to play anything, but this is not important.

Aaron: What do you mean? Where is this coming from, then?!

Rav Ashlag: I can hear this music.

Aaron: Up there?

Rav Ashlag: Yes. There are no words there, just feelings. You can't share this experience with words. Music is the best way to convey it.

Aaron suddenly squats down before Rav Ashlag, trying to enter his field of vision.

Aaron: That's it! That is it! It's so simple, so clear! And so sensual! I want to hear it, just hear it forever, this divine music! Dear Rav, if only you could write just as clearly and simply as you play.

Rav Ashlag stops playing, his hands hang down.

Aaron: Play some more, please!

Night over London.

***

Night over Jerusalem.
The music played by Rav Ashlag is carried above the city.

***

Night at sea.
A ship is rocking on the waves, its lights flickering.
Rav Ashlag is standing on the deck.
The music is playing in the air.

Jerusalem. Rav Ashlag's home.
The table is set with simple food.
Rav Ashlag's family is gathered around the table, together with his students.
Everybody is eating silently.
Rav Ashlag raises his head.

Rav Ashlag: I want to hear about what stopped you from being together.

Chaim: When you left us...

Rav Ashlag: It's you who left me.

Chaim: We tried...

Shimon: But we had doubts.

Moshe: We decided to study the material better, deeper, in order to understand...

Rav Ashlag: Understand what? *(With pain)* What did you get from this study?

> Everyone except Moshe avoids Rav Ashlag's gaze.
> Moshe holds his ground with confidence.

Rav Ashlag *(in a booming voice)*: Which God were you praying to when I was there?

Moshe: We wanted to know more.

Rav Ashlag: Such knowledge is Pharaoh's greatest weapon!

Moshe: But knowledge gave us confidence!

Rav Ashlag: Too bad! I don't need those who know! I need those who are confused, sick, and unsure of anything! Those are the students I want!

> He looks around at everyone.
> Baruch and Shimon sit silently, their eyes lowered.

Rav Ashlag: I'm asking for the last time, why did you surrender?

Chaim: We failed.

Rav Ashlag: Why didn't you cry? Why didn't you pray?!

Chaim: We tried, but nothing came out of it... without you.

Moshe: No, you are being unfair! *(Turns to Chaim)* What are you mumbling about? We didn't give up, we were studying *The Book of Zohar*. What's wrong with that? We are now familiar with the system of the interaction of the worlds.

Rav Ashlag: I don't need students full of knowledge. I need students full of pain. You can leave – all of you.

Moshe: What do you mean - leave?!

Rav Ashlag: I don't want to see you anymore.

Moshe: How can you throw us out?! My heart has led me here!

Rav Ashlag: Your stinking pride has led you here.

Moshe: How can you say this to me? I gave up everything I had...

Rav Ashlag: Rivka, please show them the way out.

Moshe: You are not a teacher! We're leaving, never to return.

Moshe gets up and walks to the door first.
Chaim and Shimon follow him, they look crushed.
Baruch is standing by the wall.
Rav Ashlag stares at him sternly.

Rav Ashlag: This concerns everyone!

Rivka *(pleading)*: Yehuda?!

Rav Ashlag: Everyone!

Baruch nods and slowly leaves together with everyone.

Rivka *(moans)*: What are you doing?

Rav Ashlag: The only thing I can do for them.

Rivka *(almost crying)*: But they are gone. And Baruch has left with them.

Rav Ashlag gets up and approaches her.

-I brought back some money. Enough for a month.

Rivka: It is so hard for me to be with you, Yehuda. (*Rivka tries not to look at him*) So hard...

***

Night. Classroom.
Rav Ashlag is sitting alone in the empty room.
He glances at the clock and opens the book.
It's one o'clock in the morning.

Suddenly the door squeaks.
Rivka enters the room holding a book.
She sits down in front of Rav Ashlag and opens the book.
She waits in silence.

Rav Ashlag: You are here for the lesson?

Rivka: Yes.

He nods with understanding.

Rivka: I have come here to study. And why not...? I am your wife, after all.

He looks at her and smiles bitterly.

Rav Ashlag: You thought that nobody would come and so you came to console me. You think I won't have any more students?

Rivka *(sighs)*: You hurt them deeply, Yehuda. You threw them out.

Rav Ashlag: And you think they won't come back?

Rivka: But you practically kicked them out!

Rav Ashlag: If they don't return...

Rivka: What would make them come back, Yehuda?

Rav Ashlag doesn't answer.

Rivka suddenly stands up, walks around the little table, and sits down next to him.

-It feels so good to sit close to you,- she says sizing him up. May i?

He unbuttons his coat and wraps it around her.

-I'll read you an exquisite piece from *The Zohar*, - he says.

He turns a page.

-Listen: "Every day when the column of dawn rises, a bird wakes up on a tree in the Garden of Eden and calls three times. And its voice is heard clearly: 'See here, I propose to you: Choose life.'"

All of a sudden he interrupts his reading and asks:

-Do you think I am deprived of simple human emotions?

Rivka: Sometimes it seems like it.

Rav Ashlag: It hurts, believe me. It hurts very much.

Rivka: I believe you, my love. Forgive them! What have they done wrong? They are just children, and you are so great.

Rav Ashlag: If they don't come back, it will mean that I failed to explain the main principle to them.

Rivka: So you are to blame!

Rav Ashlag: Yes, I am. But I can't call them back. It's hard for me to explain this to you, *(looks into her eyes)* but try to understand me. It concerns their spiritual work.

Heavy rain begins to pour outside.

Rivka: Now they will surely not come. If you only knew how impossibly hard it is to be in your presence!

***

Night. Heavy rain.
A line of Jews, soaked to the skin, moves along a wall crowned with barbed wire. We recognize among them Baruch, Chaim, and Shimon.
Two armed British guards and an officer in long raincoats escort them.
The group walks through the main entrance of a prison.
The officer barks a loud command in English.
From all corners of the prison yard armed guards run to meet them.
Terrified, the Jews are lined up against the wall.
They are trembling with fear.
The officer walks in front of the line of Jews.
Baruch takes a step toward him.

Baruch: Excuse me, officer, sir...

The officer: I didn't tell you to speak!

Baruch: Officer, sir, we are late for our lesson.

The officer: This is precisely the matter.

Chaim: Sir, you don't have the right to hold us here.

The officer: Shut up and listen.

The officer turns to his soldiers.

The officer *(speaking English)*: Soldiers, do you see these Jews?

Soldiers: Yes sir, we do.

The officer: Do you know why I brought them here?

Elderly soldier: I guess you want us to throw them in jail or put them in front of a firing squad. Just give us the order.

The officer: No, George, you guessed wrong. *(Addressing everyone)* I've brought them here to show you that you can't hold a candle to these people.

The officer starts walking up and down the ranks of soaking wet soldiers.
The rain intensifies.

The officer: Yes, you maggots. Had you even an ounce of guts equal to these scrawny Jews here, we would have conquered this country without firing a single shot and without any bloodshed. And you know why? *(He doesn't wait for the answer)* Because every night, gripped with fear, they pass through our patrols, disappearing in the dense darkness. They cross the wilderness, risking death by wolves or by the blade of that dog, Abu Khalif. *(He stops and shakes his head)* Oh, Lord, how we could learn from them the meaning of dedication and sacrifice for a goal.

The officer stops at the end of the file between his solders and the Jews.

Raindrops bounce off the rim of his hat and the coats of the soldiers.

The officer: Atten...tion! Salute these Jews!

He turns sharply to the frightened Jews and salutes them.
All the soldiers obey him in disbelief and fear.

***

Rav Ashlag's classroom.
Rav Ashlag and Rivka are sitting side by side reading *The Zohar*.
Their feet are covered with a wool blanket.
Rav Ashlag is reading and Rivka is watching him with devotion.

Outside it's raining so hard, we can barely see the walls of the house next door.

The door opens.
First to enter is Baruch.
He is soaking wet.
Rivka runs to hug him.

Rivka: You are completely wet! Take off your clothes immediately!

Baruch: Mother, wait. *(Turns to his father.)* I came for the lesson, may I?

Rav Ashlag: Why did you come?

Baruch: I couldn't help it.

Rav Ashlag *(more gently)*: It's a torrent out there.

Baruch: But haven't you told us yourself that you can only miss a lesson if you're dead?

Rav Ashlag: In that case, sit down.

Baruch *(encouraged)*: But Father, wait... outside in the street... (he doesn't finish) One moment!

He pokes his head out the window and calls out.

Baruch's voice: Come in, quickly!

Shimon and Chaim timidly enter the room.

Rav Ashlag: Ah, yes, they sent you in first to soften me up, I see. Well... what brought you here?

Shimon: What else do we have in life?!

Chaim: Please don't send us away, teacher.

Rav Ashlag: Rivka, get them some dry clothes from my closet. We are starting the lesson.

***

Classroom. It's still pouring outside.
The students are sitting opposite Rav Ashlag, dressed in his oversized frock coats.
They listen intently.

Rav Ashlag: You have to attack[62] all the time. Keep the goal – our unity – in mind all the time and attack! Are you ready for this?

All together: Yes, we are.

Rav Ashlag: This is not an easy path.

All together: We know.

Rav Ashlag: An attack is when you do not rest for even a moment; when descents and ascents merge together into a single scream! *(Looks at them)* Are you ready?

62 A state within a person when he feels that together with his friends, he can rise above his egoism and unite with them into a common prayer. He feels there are all the conditions for it now, meaning that all sensations of failure and suffering have gathered together and there is only one thing left to do—attack the selfish desire!

All together *(confidently)*: We are ready.

Rav Ashlag: Then take your books and don't let go of the thought about your friends. Open *The Zohar*!

***

The rain pelts against the windows. It's pouring over Jerusalem. Water flows down roofs, gutters, and windowsills.

Only one window is lit in the heavy darkness.

Rav Ashlag's voice (*reading from The Zohar*)**:** "How good and how pleasant it is for brothers to sit together."[63]

Classroom.

Rav Ashlag recites from the text without looking in the book:

"...These are the friends, as they sit together inseparably."

The students' fingers follow the words.

Rav Ashlag's voice: "At first, they seem like people at war, wishing to kill one another."

Baruch *(mumbles)*: Together... toward you... together!

Rav Ashlag's voice: "Then they return to a state of brotherly love."

Rav Ashlag closes his eyes.

"The Creator, what does He say about them? 'How good and how pleasant it is for brothers to sit together.'...Moreover, the Creator listens to their words and He is pleased and content with them."

Baruch: Enter together... together.

Shimon: Give us the strength... together...

Rav Ashlag's voice: "And you, the friends who are here, as you were in fondness and love before, you will not part henceforth, until the Creator rejoices with you and summons peace upon you."

---

63 It refers to the desires called "brothers," meaning close desires. They are close in the sense that they have the same goal: To unite, to become similar to the Creator, to bestow and love. For this, they first have to sit together (to sit means to become equal). Afterwards, they have to undergo correction from hatred to love for one another. And then the Creator is pleased with them, connects with them, and says, "How good and pleasant it is for brothers to sit together." All of humanity is brothers. Unavoidably, they will have to undergo this path.

Rav Ashlag opens his eyes, looks at everybody for a long moment, and concludes:

"And by your merit there will be peace in the world."

And suddenly he pronounces loudly:

-Attack!

Chaim *(screams out)*: Hold o-o-n!

Rav Ashlag: Just don't think of yourselves!

Baruch's hand feels for Shimon's and grabs hold of it.
Shimon grasps Chaim's hand.

Baruch *(whispering)*: Together!

Rav Ashlag: Attack!

***

A flash of light.
The room disappears.
The path is winding through colorful flower beds, past the forest, toward the White City.
Rav Ashlag is walking first.
His students are following him, slowly, carefully, as if taking their first steps.

Rav Ashlag's voice: Hold o-o-o-on!

They are holding each other's hands like children.

Rav Ashlag's voice: We are incapable of loving, but that's the only thing we truly desire!

They approach the White City.
Its gates are slightly open.

Rav Ashlag's voice: There is no "me"... not a thought about myself, none!

They walk along a stream that runs toward the White City.

Rav Ashlag's voice: Hold on, my beloved brothers! This is the land of Israel – the land of those who are walking toward the Creator. Can you see now what he has in store for us?!

Baruch *(whispers)*: What... great... bliss...

Chaim: Give us the strength to... love!

Shimon: Our Lord, please help us... to love!

> The White City approaches.
> Through the slightly open gates we can see shaded alleyways
> And green terraces that ascend towards the windows of the houses.

Rav Ashlag's voice: Jerusalem, the city of the Creator.[64]

Baruch *(breathes out)*: Jerusalem!

Chaim: We are coming to you!

Shimon *(in admiration)*: The city of happiness!

***

> Night in Jerusalem. The classroom.
> It's still dark outside.
> The tenacious rain pours on.
> They lift their eyes from the book.
> Rav Ashlag is not in his place.
> Someone exhales heavily. It sounds like a moan.
> It is Shimon, he is rocking in his chair in despair.

Shimon *(moaning)*: Back he-e-ere! Once mo-o-re!

Baruch: But we almost made it.

Chaim: Where did we go wrong?!

Shimon (with tears in his voice): I felt you like one heart, my brothers!

Baruch: We shouldn't stop thinking about it. Even now!

Chaim: We are together! We are going to the White City together.

Shimon: But we are here and the rav is there, why?

---

64 The name Yerushalaim (Jerusalem) comes from the combination of two words: *Yirah Shlemh* (complete fear). In spiritually, this name describes a state of fear due to inability to give to the Creator to the same extent that He gives to a person. It is fear of not being able to love the Creator as much as the Creator loves the person. Only such a person can dwell in (the spiritual) Jerusalem.
Also, Jerusalem means *Ir Shalem* (a complete city), which is man's heart when it is devoid of self love.

Everyone turns to look at Rav Ashlag's empty chair.
Rav Ashlag is gone.
The rain is drumming on the window.

Rav Ashlag's voice: What are you whining about?!

They all swing around at the same time.
Rav Ashlag is leaning against the wall behind them staring at them intently.

Rav Ashlag: Are you crying about how good it felt there, under the wings of the Creator?!

Shimon: We were together and still we didn't make it! Why?

Rav Ashlag: A handful of individuals throughout human history have seen what you just saw, and you are complaining?!

Shimon: Why then? I just want to understand! Why did we come back?!

Rav Ashlag: You felt too good there.

Shimon *(moans)*: It's true, it was impossibly good.

Baruch: We were together, Father, and you were with us.... We left Pharaoh. It was an exquisite feeling!

Chaim: And the Creator, and that White City, and that sensation... the most exalted sensation of all!

Rav Ashlag: And what about those who were left here?

Pause.
Silence.
He glares at each of their faces in succession.
His anger is only mounting.

Rav Ashlag: I'm asking you!

Silence.

Rav Ashlag: Do you think you were chosen over everyone else only to feel good?! *(Evenly, very distinctly)* You want to so-a-r high up, and let this world go to hell? No. This world will scream within you until you extend your hand to every last soul here. You were chosen to bring the light to everyone, to the whole world. Until you do that, you will have no rest.

Silence.

Rav Ashlag: Are you ready?

Silence.

Rav Ashlag: You have discovered the secret of the main gates. You have to lead everyone through it. *(Suddenly whispering)* Hold tight! Hold t-i-gh-t!

Baruch: Hold on tight!

Chaim: We are all one man!

Shimon: With one heart!

Rav Ashlag: The whole world is one soul! We are all parts of one common soul. We feel the separation only in our egoistic senses. From the viewpoint of the Creator, we are all connected. Our task is to correct the sensation of separation that exists among us.

***

The room disappears once more.
A flash of light.
They can see the gates to the White City open wide.
They stand on their toes in expectation of a miracle.
Rav Ashlag approaches the gates.
They take a step forward.

Suddenly a great chasm splits the ground open. The dark crack approaches them with dizzying speed.

Rav Ashlag screams: Hold tight!

Baruch, Shimon, and Chaim press tightly against each other.
The crack is shooting toward them ripping the ground apart.

Baruch *(whispering)*: Hold o-o-o-n tight, brothers!

The land opens up and from it, hurtling up like a rocket, rises the peak of a mountain.
It ascends higher and higher, throwing dust and debris everywhere, obscuring the gates of the White City as it carries Rav Ashlag up with it.

***

Jerusalem. A pouring rain.

The students are sitting quietly, overwhelmed.
They are afraid to move a muscle.
Rav Ashlag looks at them.

-Once you decide to unite, you should be prepared for the worst, - he says, – prepare to abandon your own "I"[65]!

***

A flash of light.
The mountain is now protruding fully from the ground.
Chaim is pinned down by a large rock.

-Are you ready for that, my beloved brothers? – Comes Rav Ashlag's calm voice.

Baruch is pressed against the rocky wall, balancing himself on a narrow ledge.

-To give yourselves up, expect nothing in return?

Shimon is hanging against the face of a cliff, holding himself by the tips of his fingers.
His knuckles turn white from the effort.

Chaim *(moans)*: Shimon, hold on!

Shimon's hand begins to slip.
Baruch takes a step toward him, but Shimon lets go and plummets into the abyss.
Without hesitation, Baruch drops himself after him.
Chaim manages to roll the rock off his body and jumps down after his friends.

***

London. Central Hospital.
White room.
A few doctors are standing around Aaron.
An old professor feels Aaron, looks into his eyes, and asks him to open his mouth.
Then he exchanges glances with the other doctors.

---

65 Abandoning the "I" means to rise above one's egoistic desires, to "lose" oneself, to exit the sensation of one's singularity so as to learn to feel others.

He sits in the chair. Someone hands him a file with various documents. He reads through them attentively and exchanges more glances with the doctors.
Finally, he whispers something to the nurse who walks up to Aaron.

The nurse: Mr. Goldberg, could you wait outside, please? I will call you back in just a few moments.

Aaron walks out.

The professor *(shaking the file)*: Is this his diagnosis?

A doctor: Yes, it is.

The professor: Are you making fun of me? Who wrote this?

They pass over additional documents to him.
They are taking them out one at a time from a thick file.
The professor reviews them with great interest.

A doctor's voice: This is the conclusion of Professor Wilson. Here is another conclusion, by Dr. Greenberg. Here is a note from Dr. Atkins, and here is the conclusion of the medical board of her majesty's hospital. Note the royal seal.

The professor *(takes off his glasses)*: I don't understand any of this. *(Irritably)* I just don't get it!

***

Hospital corridor.
Aaron is sitting by the door.
The nurse's head pokes out and she invites him inside.

***

Hospital room.

The professor: I wish to tell you, dear Mr. Goldberg, that you have... a clean bill of health.

Aaron's legs unhinge.
He sits down.

The professor: You are as fit as a bull, my dear. They can send you to unload ships on the London docks! How can you explain this?

Aaron is silent.

The professor: Believe it or not, we are clueless as well! According to the documents *(shows the medical conclusion)*, you were sick. And yet now you are healthy. Tell us, please, how is it possible? Did you undergo some sort of alternative treatment?

Aaron suddenly gets up.

The professor: Where are you going?

Aaron *(walking to the door, picking up his pace)*: Please excuse me, but I have to leave immediately. I have a lot of unfinished work to attend to. I must leave right away.

***

London.
Printing house.
Workers are packing stacks of books into crates for shipment.
Aaron is leafing through one of the books. He inhales the smell of printed paper and smiles with satisfaction, then presses the book to his chest and laughs as tears run down his cheeks.

***

Documentary footage.
Orthodox Jews demonstrating in Jerusalem.
The streets are full of people yelling, waving their fists, picking up stones off the road.

The Chief Rabbi of Israel, Rav Kook, is walking among them. They surround him.

***

Jerusalem.
The office of the Chief Rabbi of Israel; Rav Kook is sitting at his desk.
Opposite him sits a delegation of rabbis headed by Rabbi Levi, with Rav Hadad at his side.
They are flanked by a few elderly rabbis.
Moshe is standing a little bit behind them.
Rav Hadad unfolds a letter and waves it in Rav Kook's face.

Rav Hadad: He is terrorizing the whole of Europe! Just look what he writes to them, incessantly, despite ours and theirs continued bans. He writes non-stop, like a madman.

Rabbi Levi *(ominously)*: He is mad!

Rav Kook: Please read it, Rav Hadad, don't be distracted.

Rav Hadad (reading): "Don't believe your rabbis!..." (To Rav Kook) how do you like that?!

Rav Levi *(addressing Rav Kook)*: I was told that you support him.

Rav Kook (to Rav Hadad): Go on!

Rav Hadad: "They can't see the impending doom that is converging over Europe. Heed my warning, I can see it and I am crying out to you." *(To Rav Kook)* He is crying out to them! *(Continues to read, panting)* "Leave your homes, leave everything and come to the land of Israel!" *(He shakes his forefinger)* Just listen to what he writes, listen! "Your teachers are blind. I cannot stop the looming disaster."

Rav Levi *(smirking)*: He cannot stop the looming disaster. Who does he think he is, the Messiah?

Somebody's voice: What an insolent fellow, huh?!

A commotion breaks out in the crowd.
They are all talking at once, interrupting each other.

Rav Hadad: I would like to add that this man—I don't want to mention his name—is nothing as a kabbalist. He is a charlatan, a self-proclaimed nobody, an upstart. *(Turning to Moshe)* Go on, tell the Chief Rabbi what he has been teaching you!

Rav Kook *(harshly to Moshe)*: Stop! Don't say a word (*looks at Moshe*) so you don't regret it later.

Everyone is looking at Rav Kook.

Rav Kook *(looking at his hands)*: Is that all you have to say?

Rav Levi: You have to make a difficult, painful decision.

Rav Kook *(looking around the room)*: I've made it.

Rav Levi: What is your decision, Chief Rabbi of Israel?

Rav Kook gets up from his chair.

He is taller than all of them.
He speaks slowly and clearly:

Rav Kook: As long as I'm alive, not a single hair will fall from the head of this great man.

Everyone is dumbfounded. They look at Rav Kook in bewilderment.

***

Jerusalem.
A small unassuming house on one of the streets of the old city.
Two guards are patrolling outside.
They eye with suspicion anyone who approaches.
A steady murmur of voices comes from the open windows.

***

A room inside the house.
Through clouds of cigarette smoke we can see people sitting on chairs.
One of them is Rav Ashlag, another is a small, energetic man with tufts of unruly white hair on his big head. It's Ben-Gurion.[66] The third, sitting in the corner, and sucking on a long cigarette holder, is the hardliner militant, Ze'ev Jabotinsky.[67]
Tense silence hangs in the air.

Rav Ashlag: Millions will die because of us.

Silence. They are all looking at him.

Rav Ashlag: You are being torn apart by self-interest. There's no love here, no unity. Simple egos won't even let you hear each other out.

Jabotinsky: Who are you?

Rav Ashlag: I am Rav Ashlag, a kabbalist. I've come here to make another attempt to stop the destruction of the world.

Jabotinsky: Spare us the high rhetoric. Destruction of the world... please - it sounds so lofty. Personally, I couldn't care less about the world if there is no place for the Jewish state in it.

66 David Ben-Gurion—One of the founders of the State of Israel and its first Prime Minister.
67 Ze'ev Jabotinsky—Leader of the right wing revisionist movement.

Ben-Gurion *(can't keep silent)*: But the world will determine if such a state can exist.

Jabotinsky: No, it depends only on us *(he stands up, begins to walk and make gestures)*, on whether the Jewish state is going to be powerful, decisive, with armed forces against which no Arab army can stand, and spread across both sides of the Jordan River.

Ben-Gurion: You are provoking hatred towards us!

Jabotinsky: And you don't want to see how...

> Rav Ashlag takes a glass from the table and throws it on the floor with full force.
>
> The glass shatters to bits.
>
> Ben-Gurion and Jabotinsky stop arguing at once and turn to Rav Ashlag.

Rav Ashlag: Even now, facing the deaths of our children, our families, and close relatives in Europe, you cannot stop fighting over power.

Ben-Gurion: We are debating essential issues.

Rav Ashlag: No. There is only one essential issue–to rise above your egos for the sake of one exalted goal. Right now, right here, all that's needed is just one thought about unity. Just a single thought! Forget about who is right and who is wrong in these debates and focus on attaining unity. Then a new state will arise, without blood or tears, an eternal state founded on spiritual laws, and the Creator will bless it.

Jabotinsky: Are you speaking on behalf of the Creator?

Rav Ashlag: Yes.

Jabotinsky: Did He authorize you?

Rav Ashlag: Yes.

Jabotinsky *(ironically)*: Are you holding discussions with Him?

Rav Ashlag: Yes, I do.

Jabotinsky: I see, and what does He tell you?

Rav Ashlag: He is saying that He gave us Jews the instructions for bringing all of humanity to happiness.

Ben-Gurion: And you know those instructions?

Rav Ashlag: I do. And I am calling upon you to hear me.

Jabotinsky: This is all delusions, every word you are saying, and it's strange to hear such words coming from a Jewish rabbi. Besides, I already told you, I don't care about humanity.

Jabotinsky gets up.
Ben-Gurion follows him.

Ben-Gurion: Unfortunately, what you are proposing is utopian.

Rav Ashlag *(takes out of his pocket a crumpled piece of paper)*: Here is my address. Hitler will come to power in Germany in three days. We can stop it.

Ben-Gurion quickly leaves the room.
Jabotinsky follows him.

***

Jerusalem. Night. Classroom.
The students are sitting opposite Rav Ashlag.
Their eyes are fixed on him.
He is standing before them.

Rav Ashlag: Start thinking about the whole world as if it were your child (*he stretches out his arms lovingly, looking at them*). Here it is, lying in your arms.

***

Documentary footage from 1933.
Demonstrations in Palestine.
Jabotinsky delivers a speech at the congress of the revisionist party.
Ben-Gurion is waving his fists aggressively at the labor party congress.
Stalin lights up his pipe.
Roosevelt smiles at journalists.

Hitler salutes a crowd of storm troopers. In three days he will become chancellor.

Suddenly Hitler turns his head. He is looking straight at us.

***

Jerusalem. Rav Ashlag's room.
The door opens and Rivka walks in.
The chair is empty, the bed is empty, the window is open.
She looks around the room and comes up to the table to find a note written in Rav Ashlag's meticulous handwriting: "I shall return in three days. Don't look for me. Don't worry. Yehuda."

***

Documentary footage.
A ride through Berlin.
Rav Ashlag is looking out from the bus window.
And here he is, walking in the street, approaching a crowd of shouting storm troopers, squeezing through them.
We can see Hitler, delivering a speech.
Suddenly Hitler stops, dumbfounded.
He turns his head and looks straight at Rav Ashlag.
Rav Ashlag is standing in the midst of the shouting crowd of storm troopers in his orthodox Jewish attire.
No one seems to notice him except Hitler.
He quickly walks toward Rav Ashlag.
He grabs his hand without slowing down and drags him into a niche in the wall of an old building.

Hitler: Why did you come here, Jew?

Rav Ashlag: To see everything with my own eyes... and maybe try to do something.

Hitler: There is nothing you can do now; the machine has been put into motion. Where have you been all this time?

Rav Ashlag: I was trying to prevent all this. I succeeded – partially. I already have a small group...

Hitler: And I have an army.

Rav Ashlag: We are trying to awaken people's hearts.

Hitler: You are trying, and I achieve it with one speech.

Rav Ashlag: I am writing a lot... and thinking.

Hitler: My book is a bedtime story for all Germans. They are not thinking. *(Pointing at the wild crowd)* They are acting.

Rav Ashlag *(silent for a long while)*: It's not simple to stop being a slave. I don't have enough money to buy paper, and I have so much to write.

Hitler: I'm flooded with money.

Rav Ashlag: Many people don't understand me.

Hitler: Everyone understands me. I am guaranteed to win the elections. No one can stop me now *(quietly, turning around)*. But I pleaded with you!

Rav Ashlag: I know that I don't have much time left, I know it. *(In despair)* I have to awaken people, to beg, to scare... to make them listen.

> Suddenly Hitler grabs his hand and drags him around the corner.
> They find themselves in a side alley where nobody can see them.
> Hitler takes out his gun from its holster and offers it to Rav Ashlag.

Hitler: You can stop everything right now. Well, do it! Generations of people will glorify your name forever.

> Rav Ashlag looks at the gun, then at Hitler.

Hitler: Well?! *(Tries to thrust the gun into Rav Ashlag's hand)*

Rav Ashlag: You've understood nothing, you poor thing. Don't you get that you are nothing? If not you, there will be another Fuehrer. The root of evil is not in you.

Hitler: Well, then... if you won't shoot me... very well.

> Hitler presses the gun against Rav Ashlag's belly.

Hitler: Farewell, Jew. You are either stupid or naïve, or you simply don't exist; you're just a figment of my imagination. Either way, farewell!

> Gunshot.
> Rav Ashlag's body slowly collapses on the pavement.
> Hitler is following it with his gaze.
> The dead eyes of Rav Ashlag are staring straight at him.
> Hitler turns around and quickly walks out of the alley.
> His security officers are already running up to him.

The first German security officer: Is everything all right, mein Fuehrer?!

Hitler: Take away this Jewish dog. Throw him in a ditch somewhere.

The officers disappear around the corner.
Hitler is walking fast toward the square where storm troopers are already greeting him.
Before he can reach it, the two security officers catch up with him, looking at Hitler in bewilderment.

The first German security officer: Is he a Jew?

Hitler *(leers)***:** Can't you see that for yourself?

The second German security officer: We checked him through and through, mein Fuehrer. He is of German blood as far back as at least ten generations.

Hitler *(stopping sharply)*: What?!

The second German security officer: Gunter, born in Austria to the family of...

Hitler: Which Gunter?

The first German security officer: Your adjutant, mein Fuehrer.

Hitler turns around and runs to the alley.
He stops over the dead body, lying in the very spot where Rav Ashlag fell.
But instead of Rav Ashlag, we see a dead German officer lying there, his glazed eyes fixed on Hitler...

Hitler *(whispering)*: Gunter... (leaning forward) it's impossible... (turning to his perplexed security officer)...it can't be!

The narrator's voice: On the 31st of January, 1933, Hitler came to power.

***

Documentary footage.
Hitler comes to power to the sound of a dazzling marsh.
He is surveying military parades.
Hundreds of thousands of men, women, and children greet him with fervent "heil Hitler" salutes.

***

Jerusalem. Night.
Rav Ashlag is walking down a narrow dark street.

Narrator's voice: On this day, the 31st of January, 1933, Rav Ashlag's most earnest and mysterious letter was written. It's one of the letters that were preserved by accident. It is the Creator's answer, the prophecy.

***

The yellow pages of a letter, written in Rav Ashlag's neat handwriting, its edges slightly charred.

Rav Ashlag's voice: "And it came to pass in the days of the war, the days of the dreadful carnage, that I was praying, crying bitterly all through the night."

***

Documentary footage.
We see all the 20th century's tragedies: The burning cities of the second world war, battles, concentration camps, executions, the deaths of millions and all the wars, great and small, that followed it; the famine in Africa, terror in the middle east, the crashing of the stock markets, the arms race.

The voice of Rav Ashlag is heard over it:

Rav Ashlag's voice (continuing the prophecy): "And behold, at the break of dawn, it seemed as though all the people in the world had gathered in a group before my mind's eye. And a man was hovering amongst them..."

***

Rav Ashlag is walking along the old city walls.
It's windy. The shadow of a storm cloud is moving ahead of him.

Rav Ashlag's voice: "I could not stride among the people who were vain and slandering the Creator and His creation, while I was satiated and praising, merrily walking, as though mocking those wretched ones. Matters have touched me to the bottom of my heart..."

Documentary footage of the 20th century continues to roll: A nuclear explosion decimating everything in its range, barren grounds with burnt trees, portraits of suffering people of every race and nationality.

Rav Ashlag's voice: "...And I resolved that come what may, even if I descended from my sublime degree, I must make a heartfelt plea to the Creator to grant me attainment and knowledge of the prophecy and wisdom, and to give me the words by which I could help the forlorn people of the world, to raise them to the same degree of wisdom and pleasantness as mine."

***

The yellow pages of the letter.
One line replaces another.

Rav Ashlag's voice: "Afterwards, the Lord spoke unto me in a vision, saying, 'Lie down on your right-hand side.' I lay down on the ground and he said unto me: 'What do you see?' I said, 'I see many peoples and nations, rising and falling...'"

***

Rav Ashlag is sitting in his room, silent.
His hand holding the quill is frozen above the table.
He is looking straight ahead.

Rav Ashlag's voice: "And the Lord said unto me: 'All my goals will be fulfilled through you.'"

Rav Ashlag's quill is writing briskly.

Rav Ashlag's voice: "All of us, the whole world, are one soul."

***

Storm troopers are running through the streets of Berlin.

Rav Ashlag's voice: "One unified soul, linked together by the law of unity - the law of love!"

The troopers are painting swastikas on Jewish store fronts.

Rav Ashlag's voice: "We are divided into bodies that loathe one another, yet we are one soul nonetheless."

Storm troopers are smashing store windows.

Rav Ashlag's voice: "And if we unite in mutual love, we will see You."

Jews displaying the yellow star on their clothes are running down the street.

Rav Ashlag's voice: So let us feel that we are one soul, that we are responsible for one another. Sooner or later we will have to do it."

Rav Ashlag's eyes.

Rav Ashlag's voice: "We must do it now, right now! Otherwise, great suffering will compel us to do it later."

Rav Ashlag's home. Night.
Rav Ashlag is sitting at his table, reading.
Baruch and Chaim are sitting in front of him.
The door opens and Shimon walks in.
A man of about thirty-five follows Shimon in.
They sit down silently on the side.
Rav Ashlag raises his eyes from the book and looks at Shimon.

Shimon: This is my uncle, Joseph. He understands nothing about Kabbalah and about our cause. Just as you requested.

Joseph is smiling timidly and makes a gesture of helplessness.
Rav Ashlag stands up and starts the lesson right away.

-The pyramid. *(He draws an imaginary pyramid in the air)* The entire world - the whole universe - is an integral system. It is built like a pyramid.

He appears to be addressing only Joseph.

-The light is coming to the world from above. The light has to pass through the apex.

Joseph nods.

-Here, at the top of the pyramid, are those who meet the light first.

He is talking very slowly now and very clearly.

-Those who have to make sure the light passes through them and isn't being blocked, are special souls chosen by the Creator. They have to be transparent, similar to the light.

Rav Ashlag moves closer to Joseph.

-What does that mean? It means that they have to be filled with love for one another and for the whole world. Otherwise the light won't pass through.

Joseph is listening attentively.

-We, and none other, happen to be up here at the top of the pyramid.

Rav Ashlag stops two steps away from Joseph and continues to speak even slower.

-When we let the light through, the world feels the light. Everyone is happy. There are no wars. There are only thoughts of the light, unity, and love, thoughts of spirituality. When we block the light, the whole world suffers.

For a moment, he stops talking and looks at Joseph.
Joseph is tense.

-If we don't let the light into this world, we become a redundant link in this chain, - says Rav Ashlag. Everyone begins to hate us, beat us up, and chase us out of every country... destroy us, because we are not true to our mission.

Joseph raises his hand.
Rav Ashlag nods, letting him ask a question.

Joseph: Excuse me, but you keep saying "we." Who are "we" exactly? Do you mean, you?

Rav Ashlag: An entire nation was chosen to tell the world how to arrive at happiness. It was given a special method that teaches how to do it, called the wisdom of Kabbalah.

Joseph: Why wasn't I told about it then? Am I not a member of this nation?

Rav Ashlag: Kabbalah is revealed only to a person who craves spirituality. It is said about such people that they have a point in the heart. Sooner or later that point will awaken inside of you as well.

Joseph: But for that to happen I need to at least know that such wisdom even exists!

Rav Ashlag: Correct.

Joseph: And that it speaks of light and love, rather than of some dark mystic secret or something.

Rav Ashlag *(smiling)*: Yes, very good, you've got it.

Joseph: Then why was it concealed for so long if it's so important?

Rav Ashlag: Because it is like a medicine. First, people have to realize that they are sick and that they need medication.

Joseph: Have they realized it?

Rav Ashlag: They are starting to feel their illness. We are living in the twentieth century – a century of sick people.

Joseph: What's wrong with them?

Rav Ashlag: They have no love for one another.

Joseph *(nods)*: That's true.

Rav Ashlag: Everyone lives for his or her own sake.

Joseph: Right you are!

Rav Ashlag: But slowly, people are starting to realize this.

Joseph: You bet!

Rav Ashlag: They are starting to see that the lack of love is the reason for all of their suffering. We are unable to agree with each other, to share equally, to unite...

Joseph (*sighs*): And how could we?

Rav Ashlag: This is what Kabbalah teaches. It tells us how to become equal, rise above our egos and unite.

Joseph: Is it even possible?

Rav Ashlag: We won't survive without it.

Joseph: Then how come our rabbis aren't telling us about Kabbalah?

Rav Ashlag: Because they themselves don't know about it!

Joseph: Why, then, don't they tell us that there are kabbalists, like you, and that we should listen to them?

Rav Ashlag: Because they don't feel that they are sick.

Joseph: Then we must make them feel it. Otherwise the whole world will suffer all the time and we will get beaten for it all the time.

Rav Ashlag: Correct.

Joseph: Who will make them listen?

Rav Ashlag: We will. We will test this medicine on ourselves and show the world how it works. We will disseminate it everywhere, announce it from rooftops. We won't stop, and the world won't let us rest now. People will gradually realize they are mortally ill and will demand the cure from us. Our time is coming.

Joseph is looking at them.
The students' faces are glowing.
They are looking at Joseph, waiting for his reaction.

Joseph: You are good people. I can sense that you are good people. I was afraid to come at first. I told Shimon: "Don't take me to these Kabbalists." *(Suddenly he starts to rummage in his pockets and takes out two one-pound notes.)* But Shimon paid me, gave me this money and said, "You just have to come and listen, that's all." He told me that you *(to Rav Ashlag)* had asked for someone off the street, a simpleton who doesn't understand a thing. So he brought me.

Joseph stands up and puts the money on the table.
He rummages through his pockets and adds another two notes.

Joseph: I would like you to use this money properly. Thank you. I've understood everything. (*Turns around, repeats his little gesture of awkward helplessness*) I can't study myself, but I can tell everyone about you. (*Turns to Rav Ashlag*) Everything you said was clear to me, I swear.

Rav Ashlag walks up to him and hugs him.
His students see, for the first time ever, his eyes becoming moist.
They all, as if on command, stand up and hug each other.

***

Jerusalem.
A graveyard on the Mount of Olives outside the walls of the old city.
A large crowd of people gathers around one of the plots.

A body, wrapped in a tallit, is laid in the grave.
We hear the chanting of a kaddish.[68]

Rav Levi is standing in front of the orthodox Jewish crowd.
Rav Hadad is at his side.
Rav Levi keeps looking to his right. Rav Hadad does the same.

---

68 *Kaddish* is a prayer recited in Aramaic as part of the Jewish prayer service. The central theme of the Kaddish is the magnification and sanctification of God's name.

Name
Vorname
Religion
Vorname des Vaters

To the right, Rav Ashlag is standing modestly, blending in with the crowd, surrounded by his students.
His face is tilted up to the sky.

The ceremony is concluded.

People disperse slowly.
Baruch, Shimon, and Chaim follow Rav Ashlag descending toward the main road.
After a few feet they are stopped by a soft whistle coming from one of the crumbling crypts to their side.
Moshe is poking his head from behind a ruined wall, gesturing for them to come closer.

Rav Ashlag, Baruch, Chaim and Shimon approach him.

Moshe *(whispers)*: I heard Rav Levi say to Rav Hadad: "now that Rav Kook is dead, there's no one to protect him." They are up to something.

Rav Ashlag turns around in silence and walks away as if it has nothing to do with him.

Moshe *(to the students)*: Don't let him out of your sight, even for a second.

Chaim: Thanks for the warning.

Moshe: And forgive me...

Baruch, Chaim, and Shimon run after Rav Ashlag.
They catch up with him and continue walking by his side.

Rav Ashlag (orders): Go home.

Shimon: No, we are staying with you.

Rav Ashlag *(stops)*: You are going home!

Chaim: We won't leave you.

Shimon *(stubbornly)*: Do whatever you want, but we won't leave you alone!

Out of the corner of his eye, Rav Ashlag sees a handful of students congregating around Rav Levi.
Rav Levi is telling them something.
They are listening.
He points in Rav Ashlag's direction and suddenly their eyes meet.

Rav Ashlag starts to walk in his direction.
Everybody around Rav Levi turns around to face him.
Shimon, Chaim, and Baruch are walking next to Rav Ashlag.

They feel the situation is getting tense, but they are prepared for it.

Rav Ashlag approaches Rav Levi.
Rav Levi looks around anxiously.
Rav Ashlag stops a step away from him.

Rav Ashlag: Why do you need this?

Rav Levi: I don't understand you.

Rav Ashlag: There's nothing you can do about me now. It's important for me that you understand it.

Rav Levi: Why are you telling me this at such a difficult time?

Rav Ashlag: So that you know that I have a mission and I will fulfill it in any case. Sooner or later... I will open *The Zohar* to everybody!

Rav Levi: That's impossible!

Rav Ashlag: Two days ago I thought the same.

Rav Levi *(looks at him fixedly)*: What has changed in these two days?

Rav Ashlag: Everything!

Rav Levi *(looking at him attentively)*: What do you mean, "Everything"?

Rav Ashlag: I mean that nobody can stop me now.

Rav Ashlag turns around to leave.
He takes a few steps, but his legs buckle suddenly and he collapses.
His students fail to catch him.
He lands in the dusty cemetery ground.
His alarmed students huddle over him.

Baruch *(whispers)*: Father!

He tries to awaken him, but Rav Ashlag doesn't respond.

Shimon: Rav...! Rav! *(Crawls in the dust by his teacher)*

Chaim *(screams hysterically and holds his head up)*: Someone, help!!

Rav Levi and Rav Hadad are standing close by.
Their students do not dare provide any assistance.

Shimon *(looking at Rav Levi)*: He is dying!

Rav Levi lowers his head.

Shimon: But he is dying! You can't leave him like that!

Rav Levi turns around slowly, but Shimon swiftly moves to block his way.

Shimon *(looking into his eyes)*: You won't forgive yourself, do you hear me?! If anything happens to him today, you'll never forgive yourself... and nobody will ever forgive you.

Rav Levi looks into Shimon's eyes.
Shimon is standing in the middle of the road, unwilling to budge.

Shimon *(whispers)*: I beg you!

Rav Levi turns around and slowly approaches the collapsed Rav Ashlag.

He looks into his lifeless face.
Rav Ashlag is lying still. He doesn't seem to be breathing.
Rav Levi pushes his students away and kneels down next to him.
He places his hands on both sides of Rav Ashlag's head and closes his eyes.
He is silent.
Everybody is watching him intently.
He applies more pressure to Rav Ashlag's temples.

Shimon *(almost mutely)*: Is he alive?

Rav Levi: Shut up!

Rav Hadad is standing behind Rav Levi.

Rav Hadad: Honorable Rav...

Rav Levi: You shut up as well!

He presses Rav Ashlag's temples harder.
Several minutes pass by.
All of a sudden Rav Ashlag's eyelashes begin to gently bat.

Shimon *(exhales)*: He's alive...!

Rav Ashlag opens his eyes slightly.
Rav Levi's face floats into his blurry field of vision.

Rav Levi: You work too much, Ashlag.

Baruch: He works 18 hours a day.

Shimon *(adds)*: He almost never sleeps.

Rav Levi: It's not good. He has to get some rest. You should rest more, Ashlag! (*He looks at Chaim*) What kind of students are you if you don't take care of your teacher?!

Chaim: It's impossible!

Rav Levi: Don't tell me this! Next time it could end much worse. This was just a warning. *(Looks at Baruch)* Tell your mother, Rivka, that he has to go to the seaside, (*Baruch doesn't have a chance to answer)* and don't argue with me, I know what I am saying.

Rav Levi gets up and wipes the dust off his knees.

Rav Levi: How cunning he is, Rav Kook... see how he had set us up to meet like this. *(Grins)* I knew that he was a great kabbalist!

He turns around and walks away.
His students follow him.
Rav Hadad walks in small steps next to him and glances at him.
He tries to say something, but Rav Levi is already deep in silent thought.

***

Jerusalem. Rav Ashlag's home.
Rav Ashlag is lying in bed. He is pale.
One week has passed since Rav Kook's passing.
All this time he hasn't been able to get up.
The doctors' diagnosis is strange – "acute exhaustion."
Only on the morning of the eighth day does he begin to feel better.
Rivka expected this exact moment:

-We are moving away from here tomorrow, - she says to him. -We are going to Jaffa. We will live by the sea and you will be able to think and write freely.

***

Documentary footage.
Jaffa of the 1930s.
Ships anchor at the docks.
Fish mongers; the smell of seaweed.
Narrow streets baked in the Mediterranean sun.

A small cart carrying Rav Ashlag, Rivka, their children, and their few belongings is moving along one of the narrow streets.

The Ashlag family walks down to the beach.
The children start playing in the sand, the elder kids watching over the little ones.
Rav Ashlag sits on the sand wearily.
The kids surround him.

Rav Ashlag: Do you want me to tell you a little story?

The kids: Ye-e-s!

They sit around their father.

Rav Ashlag: Two sailors go out to sea in a boat. They reach the open sea and can't see the shore anymore. Then, suddenly, one of them takes a drill and starts drilling a hole underneath him. The second one screams at him: "Stop! What are you doing?!" And the other one answers: "Why should you mind, I am drilling under my seat, not under yours!"

Bat Sheva *(13-year old girl, screams)*: What a fool!

Rav Ashlag: Why is he a fool?

Shimon *(a 5-year old)*: They are sailing in the same boat and they are both going to drown because of that hole.

Rav Ashlag: You are right, Shimon. *(Strokes his head)* Well done.

Rivka smiles.
She sits down on the sand.
She is holding Shmuel, their one-year-old son.

Rav Ashlag: Who can tell me what is the lesson here?

Bat Sheva: That we are all sailing in one boat.

Rav Ashlag: All who?

Shimon: All the Jews!

Bat Sheva: The whole world!

Rav Ashlag: So what?

Bat Sheva: Well, we don't understand that we are in one boat. And that we depend on one another...

Rav Ashlag: What a clever girl I have!

Shimon: Me, too, I know it, too!

Rav Ashlag: You are also clever, Shimon! So what should we do, then?

Shimon: Love one another.

Bat Sheva: We need to understand that we are sailing in the same boat.

Rav Ashlag hugs Shimon and Bat Sheva...
He holds them tightly.
Then his eyes switch to Rivka.
She is happy, proudly watching over the entire scene.

Suddenly Rav Ashlag stands up sharply, undresses to his underwear, and starts to march into the sea.
It's winter, the water is cold, but it does not seem to bother him.
He dives in and disappears underwater for a long time.

A minute goes by, then two.
Rivka squints her eyes, looking into the sea.
He is nowhere in sight.
She moves closer and closer to the water.
Her feet become wet. The small waves lap at her shins, wetting her skirt.
Another minute passes.
There is no trace of him.

Rivka *(whispers)*: Yehuda... *(suddenly screaming)* Yehuda-a-a-a!

Rav Ashlag emerges far away from the shore and begins to paddle in long, graceful strokes toward the ships standing anchored next to the far docks.
Rivka follows him with her gaze until he is a tiny dot in the distance.

Open sea. Rav Ashlag is floating on his back with his arms outstretched to both sides.

***

Documentary footage. 1933, 1934, 1935. Nazi Germany celebrates its achievements.

***

The sea. Rav Ashlag is staring at the skies, unblinking.

***

Documentary footage of Stalin's repressions.
All the previous footage is gathered together: Hitler's Nazi Germany, the multitudes who greet him with a Nazi salute, Mussolini's fascist Italy, Churchill's aristocratic England, Stalin's communist Russia, Roosevelt's capitalist America.

***

Rav Ashlag floats alone in the open sea.

***

Documentary footage of 1936.
Orthodox Jews demonstrating in the streets of Jerusalem, communist demonstrations in the streets of Tel Aviv, excerpts of speeches by leaders of different parties: Ben-Gurion, Jabotinsky, Weitzman, and others.

1936. Los Angeles, Hollywood.
The set of the movie *Modern Times*.
The scene is not working out.
An irritated Charlie Chaplin is screaming at everybody.

Chaplin: I will fire each and every one of you!

He throws his tattered gloves on the ground and walks aside.
None of the crew or cast dare approach him.
Suddenly Aaron appears from behind the painted scenery.

Aaron: Mr. Chaplin, I've been trying to get a hold of you for a week now.

Chaplin: Who the hell are you?!

Aaron: My name is Aaron; I have a very important matter to discuss with you.

Chaplin: How did you get in here?

Aaron: I climbed over that fence.

Chaplin: And now climb back.

Chaplin *(yells)*: Sidney, I told you not to let anyone near me! Get rid of that moron over there! *(Points at Aaron)*

Several robust production assistants come running.
They grab Aaron and drag him off the scene.
Aaron tries to resist to no avail.

***

Evening.
Chaplin walks out of the studios, looking very tired, and heads to his car.
Aaron is waiting for him there.

Chaplin: Don't you know that boxing is my favorite sport?

Aaron: You can hit me. I won't move.

Chaplin: Do you want to become an actor?

Aaron: No, no way!

Chaplin: Ah, of course, a director?!

Aaron: No, no.

Chaplin: Then you have written a brilliant script.

Aaron: I haven't. But the script is brilliant.

Chaplin: I've no time and I'm dead tired.

Aaron: Just give me ten minutes of your time.

Chaplin: No.

Chaplin gets in the car and closes the door.
The car starts moving.
Aaron begins to walk by it.

Aaron: I am rich. I will pay you for every minute of your time!

Chaplin: Wha-a-a-t?! *(Stops the car, opens the door)* You want to buy me?

Aaron: Yes, this matter is very important, and not just to me.

To the
Interamerican Aerotravel & Supplies, Inc.
for Mr
NEW-YORK
BROADWAY, 11
USA

Chaplin: How much are you willing to pay?

Aaron: Name your price.

Chaplin: Five thousand dollars a minute.

Aaron: Deal.

Chaplin: Seven...

Aaron: I agree.

Chaplin: Ten.

Aaron: I will pay you anything you want.

Chaplin: Well then, come on in.

Aaron jumps in the car.
Chaplin slams his foot on the accelerator.

Chaplin: Today I'm hosting a company of stars. Would you like them to listen as well?

Aaron: Certainly.

Chaplin: What is the script about?

Aaron: About love. About how we can love one another.

Chaplin: Are you homosexual?

***

Chaplin's house.
A lavish salon packed with a chic Hollywood crowd showing off their shiny jewelry and bright smiles.
Charlie Chaplin, with Aaron by his side, is walking through the crowd.
We hear his voice.

Chaplin's voice: Greta Garbo – charming, mystical, lonely.

Garbo puts on half a smile.

-Paul Muni – recently received an Oscar for his role as Emil Zola. A small town Jew, full of fears and neuroses.

Paul Muni flashes a bogus smile.

-Victor Fleming – director. Ironic, heartless, devilishly talented. He is shooting his new film, *Gone with the Wind*. I think it's going to be a hit.

Victor Fleming is wagging his finger at Chaplin.

-Vivien Leigh.

She offers a melancholic smile to Aaron.

-Lovable and... depressed.

-Clark Gable – dashing and married to a woman seventeen years older than him. And that says something, doesn't it?

Clark Gable squints at them and adjusts his hair.

-Rachmaninov, my close friend. A great pianist and an unhappy exile.

Rachmaninov follows them with his gaze.

-My beloved, my good luck charm, Paulette Goddard.

Paulette gives Chaplin a loving look.
Amiable waiters are walking around carrying trays laden with drinks and sandwiches.

Finally, the noise settles down and everyone finds a place on comfortable chairs and sofas.
Chaplin and Aaron remain standing in the middle of the room.

Chaplin: Aaron Goldberg is from England. He is a very wealthy man, ready to pay ten thousand dollars for a minute of our time.

Greta Garbo: Can you afford a beautiful woman?

Chaplin: Greta dear, with all due respect, we have something much more serious on our hands. Aaron intrigued me. He said he knows how to make us love one another. How do you like the idea?

Greta Garbo: Utopian.

Clark Gable: But interesting.

Chaplin: Aaron, please, the clock is running.

Aaron: It's not a secret that you have big egos.

Victor Fleming: No, it's not.

Paul Muni: Otherwise we wouldn't be here.

Rachmaninov: The worst place on the goddamn earth.

Aaron *(looking at Rachmaninov)*: You are just another proof of the fact that money can't buy happiness.

Rachmaninov: I'm miserable with it and miserable without it.

Chaplin *(to Aaron)*: I must warn you that you've already spent ten thousand dollars of your time.

Aaron: You may not believe me, Mr. Chaplin, but I truly don't care about the money.

Greta Garbo: But why?

Aaron *(addressing everybody)*: Because if I'm able to explain it to you so that you understand what I have to say, it'll be worth all my millions.

Vivien Leigh: Interesting. Well, speak on!

Aaron: I adore Charlie Chaplin. How come everyone loves him?

> Charlie Chaplin stands up and does his famous penguin walk. He picks up his cane on the way and propels it around his finger.

Aaron: He gives everything to people. He is a great altruist who doesn't think about himself.

Chaplin: Keep this up, Aaron, and I will give up part of the money you owe me.

Aaron *(to all)*: You can influence the world like no one can; that's why I came to you. You are Godlike! People listen to you. You have to tell the world that it needs to change.

Greta Garbo: Good God, are you a revolutionary?

Rachmaninov: He is a Commie.

Paul Muni: I can't stand Commies.

Aaron: You have to pass on to the world just one thought, and the world will change!

Chaplin: And that thought is...?

Aaron: That we are all one.

Greta Garbo: It will never happen. A Nazi will never love a Jew.

Aaron: Because he doesn't know to what extent he depends on him. He doesn't know that by hating someone else, he is killing himself. Just imagine that each of us is but a wheel in a machine.

Vivien Leigh: No, he is not a Communist, he is an idealist and I love it.

Aaron: I represent here the most pragmatic person alive today, my teacher, Rav Ashlag.

Paul Muni: A Jew. Of course. We can't keep our noses out of other people's business, and now we want to correct the whole world, do we?

Aaron: No, we want the world to understand – on its own, that it has to correct itself.

Victor Fleming: What's so wrong with our world?

Clark Gable: Yes, what's wrong with it?

Aaron: Everyone cares only for themselves.

Victor Fleming: We wouldn't survive otherwise.

Aaron: We won't survive if we *keep* living like this.

Rachmaninov: Do we have to divide all property evenly among the rich and the poor?

Aaron: No! We just have to understand that we are all united. We are one! We are like cells in a body, as my great teacher says. But we are cancerous cells.

Vivien Leigh *(with dread)*: Cancerous?!

Aaron: Each one of us lives only for himself and by so doing he's destroying the world.

Fleming: It's baloney. If not for our egos, there would be no art.

Aaron: Not this art, but we would have art that unites us with Nature!

Vivien Leigh: Is Nature altruistic?

Aaron: Absolutely.

Greta Garbo: Then why is it hurting us... and painfully so?

Aaron: Because it loves us.

Paul Muni *(jumps up)*: Nonsense! It's all made up! Where's the proof?!

Aaron: The proof is in this book.

> Aaron walks quickly to his briefcase resting on the windowsill. He takes out a book and raises it high above his head.

Aaron: I translated it into English. In this book, the man who discovered the spiritual laws that govern our world tells us how we, humanity, can survive.

Chaplin: The future is dim, isn't it?

Aaron: Very much so, Mr. Chaplin.

Chaplin: And you want us to...

Aaron: Mr. Chaplin, if not now, then in a few years, or a few decades, Hollywood will understand that it must make movies only about that. *(Shaking the book)* Only about that!

Silence.

Chaplin: Could you leave this book here, with us?

Aaron: Of course! I printed many copies of it in England. I will publish it here, too.

Chaplin: What are you missing in my Charlie character, Mr. Goldberg?

Aaron: Just one thing: We need Charlie to tell everyone that we won't find anything inside our egos except depression and loneliness, and that we will never be happy if we don't learn to love one another, to give to one another. I'm not a filmmaker, so I don't know how to express this visually, but Nature *wants* us to be happy! And your Charlie, he is so wonderful, he will live on for generations, and if only you could add that purpose to him, if only he could say this to people...

Chaplin: Thank you, Aaron, I will think about it.

Vivien Leigh: So, one can find a way out of loneliness?

Aaron: If we create unity throughout the world, what loneliness can we speak of?

Greta Garbo: It sounds beautiful.

Rachmaninov: I would really like to believe it.

Aaron: Well, my ten minutes are up. *(He takes out his wallet)*

Chaplin *(stops him)*: You know, Mr. Goldberg, I won't get rich off your money. Better you use it to publish your books. Moreover, don't let our smiles and accord fool you. We are actors, aren't we, my darling? *(Looking at Greta Garbo)*

Greta Garbo nods.
Vivien Leigh sadly lowers her eyes.
Fleming raises his hand in indignation.

Chaplin: Still, we learned something from your speech. We were touched by your confidence. I watched my friends and noticed that their eyes were

HOLLYWOOD
HOT SHOTS
L 0436
363
A HOLE IN ONE
Featuring
PURE & SIMPLE
EXCLUSIVE SALES AGENTS
Novelty Records Distributors
1016 NO. HIGHLAND AVE.
HOLLYWOOD
IN HOLLYWOOD
NOT LICENSED FOR RADIO BROADCAST

twinkling. It's not every day that someone can reach down and touch their stony hearts. You know what? I have a business proposition for you: Let's meet again to talk about this at length – not for ten minutes. I promise that I will bring to that meeting the cream of the Hollywood crop. *(His eyes meet those of Clark Gable)* If they don't agree to come, I'll pay them and then they will surely come! *(Clark Gable nods)*

Rachmaninov: I promise I'll be there. Even without your stinking money, Charlie.

Greta Garbo: I will also be there. I am intrigued.

-So will I... And I..., - more voices chime in.

Aaron *(looks at everybody beaming with joy)*: If you could only know how grateful I am to you! If you could only know...

***

Documentary footage.1937-1938.
Hitler's parades.
Messerschmitt factories working day and night.
Hitler and his officers discuss the conquest of Europe. The invasion of Austria, of the Czech Republic.
Pogroms[69] against Jews.
Construction of concentration camps.
USSR, Stalin's ethnic cleansing.
Showcase trials of innocent people.
Firing squads executing the military's top brass.
Demonstrations of workers demanding death to traitors.

***

Moscow. Kremlin.
Rav Ashlag is walking a lengthy Kremlin corridor lined with red carpet and dotted with guards.
He passes all of them uninterrupted.
Bureaucrats carrying piles of documents are going past him without noticing him.
Rav Ashlag opens a door and enters Stalin's office.
Stalin raises his eyes from his book.

---

69 A pogrom is a form of violent riot, a mob attack directed against a particular group, whether ethnic, religious, or other, and characterized by killings and destruction of their homes and properties, businesses, and religious centers.

Stalin *(without a hint of surprise)*: Ashlag? I received your letter. Please have a seat.

Rav Ashlag sits down.

- So, you are writing here... *(Stalin scans the page and points his finger to a line)* here it is: "Russia has sinned gravely and the Creator won't forgive it." (*He raises his eyes to Rav Ashlag)* You also write that we have taken the spiritual laws of equality, love, and brotherhood, torn them away from some spiritual root, and conspired to implement them on the earth, and that we did it not for the sake of some Creator, but for our own sake.

Stalin gives Rav Ashlag a stare that would have rendered most of his ministers unconscious.
Rav Ashlag remains calm.

-You are writing that we will suffer - says Stalin. - Is this true?

Rav Ashlag *(calmly)*: Yes.

Stalin: You write well, but you are wrong. We think that we can correct our people, a little bit at a time, and come to communism on our own, without your Creator. *(He doesn't let Rav Ashlag object)* We will mend them, you will see! I understand that Man is a lying, corrupt, and jealous egoist, as you call him. My best people exemplify it.

Stalin stands up and starts to pace about the room.

- I remember when they were common workers and peasants; they wanted justice.

Stalin packs his smoking pipe with tobacco and lights it.

- As soon as they came to power they started stealing. They want nothing to do with the collective farms. Every nobody wants to be a big shot, and their women want to dress like Parisians. *(He fumes, his face turns red)* They don't give a damn about all your brotherhood and equality. If it were up to them, the rest of the people could starve to death tomorrow.

Suddenly he stops opposite Rav Ashlag.

-You know what? Let's take a walk.

They go out to the Kremlin yard.

Stalin: Perhaps it's true that man is a born egoist, as you are saying, but we will make an altruist out of him, redesign him. Just wait and see, Ashlag, how enlightened our happy communist future is going to be.

> The gates open before them and they leave the Kremlin and walk across the Red Square together.
> Security guards escort them silently.
> Unexpectedly, Stalin pats Rav Ashlag on the back.

- Don't worry, we will correct those who don't want to live in equality.

Rav Ashlag: You won't be able to correct them.

Stalin: Why not?

Rav Ashlag: First, you have to correct yourselves.

Stalin *(with a smirk)*: And what's wrong with me?! Tell me, don't be afraid!

Rav Ashlag: You don't realize that you are evil.

> Stalin stops in the middle of the Red Square.
> Rav Ashlag is standing opposite him.

Stalin: I am evil?

Rav Ashlag: Yes.

Stalin: Evil?!

Rav Ashlag: There is an ideal, Stalin, and you don't recognize it.

Stalin: And you do?

Rav Ashlag: I do.

Stalin: So, what is this ideal then, in your opinion?

Rav Ashlag: The law of absolute and infinite love.

Stalin: That's your ideal?

Rav Ashlag: When you have attained absolute love, you will have attained the Creator. He is that law.

Stalin: Is that so? And I thought He was a bearded grandfather type who spits at us from above.

Rav Ashlag *(without answering him)*: Only then, Stalin, will you be able to bring the world to correction. Only after you make this your ideal, only when He becomes your goal.

Stalin: But you have to wait a long time before arriving at such an ideal, don't you?

Rav Ashlag: You simply have to want it.

Stalin studies Rav Ashlag from head to toe.

-You are an interesting man, he says all of a sudden. – You know that I won't listen to you, and yet you are telling me all this. What do you expect? Are you naïve or just an idiot? Do you really think that we would sit and wait for that animal called Man to aspire to absolute love? No, we can't wait, we'll correct him ourselves, differently, using persuasion, force, and fear.

Stalin turns around and slowly, with his arms folded behind his back, starts towards the Mausoleum.
Rav Ashlag follows him.

Stalin: You shouldn't underestimate fear. It's a potent weapon in the war against egoism.

Rav Ashlag: This is another grave mistake of yours, Stalin. You cannot correct error through terror.

Stalin shoots a sharp glance at Rav Ashlag from the corner of his eye.

Rav Ashlag: You can't coerce people into adopting the law of love; you simply can't. It will result in dreadful bloodshed. A lot of blood has already been spilled everywhere. Just look at who you are killing - your best and brightest generals, scientists. It defies common sense, and this is on the eve of the worst war in human history.

Stalin *(sullenly)*: They are traitors.

Rav Ashlag: They threaten you, nothing more. Your ego cries out: "Don't let them get away alive!" They are robbing you of your glory!

***

Documentary footage.
Freight trains carrying prisoners rolling by.
Public executions of "enemies of the state."
Exhausted workers cutting wood in the frozen forests of Siberia.
Prisoners burying their friends in permafrost.

***

Red Square.

Rav Ashlag: Try to imagine that you are as one body, that you are brothers, and that in killing them you are slowly killing yourself. What would happen then?

Stalin *(stops short)*: Enough! You can stop now, I've understood everything. I'm a practical realist, and you are an idealist and an obscure person. Let me tell it to you straight: You can't make an omelet without breaking eggs. I agree, a lot of innocent blood will be spilled, but a new generation will rise...

Rav Ashlag: Of empty people that believe in nothing, people that will grow up on destruction, blood, and injustice.

Stalin is silent.
His security men feel his tension and begin to move in.
Stalin waves them off with a slight movement of his finger.

Stalin *(harshly)*: I listened to you, now you listen to me. And listen well. *(He looks into Rav Ashlag's eyes unblinkingly)* We don't believe in any laws of some God. Your God is just a Jewish invention. Where is He? I've never seen Him. *(Stalin sneers)* And even if He does exist, your God is bringing us closer to Him by force, isn't He? Your absolute love, just look at the kind of world it has created for us – a world of endless suffering. How much blood has already been spilled, how much more is yet to be spilled? Answer me! It's an interesting question, isn't it?

Rav Ashlag tries to answer, but Stalin stops him abruptly.

Stalin: Silence! Don't answer. You've said enough and I understood everything.

He turns and heads back to the Kremlin.
Rav Ashlag follows him.
The guards step aside to let them in.
They stop at the entrance to Stalin's office.

Stalin: So, you can't correct people with force?

Rav Ashlag: It is a terrible mistake to even try.

Stalin: It's an upper law you say?

Rav Ashlag: Only He can do it.

Stalin (*sighs)*: We will try our method anyway. *(He smiles directly at Rav Ashlag's face)* I don't believe a word of what you said. Any other day, I would've ordered you shot as an instigator. But for now, you may live.

He extends a hand to Rav Ashlag.

Stalin: Farewell, Ashlag.

Rav Ashlag: You will spill a lot of blood. *(He is looking into Stalin's eyes, but seems to be talking to himself)* How much more blood must be spilled for people to listen?

Rav Ashlag turns around and walks back toward the exit from the Kremlin.
Stalin follows him with his eyes.
He summons the captain of the guards with a quick gesture.

-Vladimir, take him to the exit, – Stalin says to his bodyguard and disappears behind the door.

Rav Ashlag turns the corner.
He is crossing the Kremlin courtyard.
Captain Vladimir runs to the telephone.

-Hello, Sergei! – he shouts.

The guard at the Kremlin entrance picks up the phone and reports:

-Right away, Comrade General!

He gets in position and opens the gun holster in anticipation of Rav Ashlag.

But Rav Ashlag doesn't come out.

***

Documentary footage of 1939.
The Nazis invade Poland.
The Warsaw ghetto is formed.
Jews bearing the yellow star of David walk the streets with a sense of gloom and fatal resignation.
A troop of Nazis is leading a group of old Jews.
They can hardly walk, and every time they stop, soldiers goad them with the butts of their rifles.

Among the Jews are Rabbi Feldman, Rabbi Zilber, Rabbi Epstein, Shmuel the teacher, and the redheaded coachman.
They are shuffling, exhausted and depressed, deep in thought.
Rabbi Zilber collapses. The rest of them try to lift him, but he can't walk anymore. Two soldiers drag him around the corner. The sound of gunshots.
Solomon's bookstore is burning.
Solomon himself, old and disheveled, is standing nearby, pressing to his chest the only book he managed to salvage – *The Book of Zohar*.
The Nazi troop gathers him into the group of Jews they are leading.
Rabbi Feldman notices the book in Solomon's hands.

Solomon *(whispers excitedly)*: This book contains comments by Rav Yehuda Ashlag himself. (He opens it) Here, you see? It's his handwriting. He was only seven then.

Rabbi Feldman nods his head in torment.

Solomon: What a great man! Oh, how great he is, Yehuda. No one has ever attained his greatness.

The coachman *(walking behind Rabbi Feldman)*: My Moshe saw it clearly. Right away he recognized that a great sage had visited our house. *(To Rabbi Feldman)* He gave my son a book, just like this one, and he managed to read it before he passed away. Rav Ashlag extended his short life. *(With tears in his eyes)* He asked me to come with him. But how could I leave my Moshe behind? His grave is right here, and I thought I would lie right next to him when the time came. *(To Rabbi Feldman)* Tell me, honorable Rabbi, do you think they will let me see my son's grave?

A man is thrown out of a nearby house.
He rolls on the ground and immediately stands up and yells:

-I'm not a Jew!

The officer laughs and whips him across the face with his club.
Blood is running down the man's cheek. It's Yan.

-Tell them! Why don't you tell them who I am! – He is screaming to his comrades and to the cute-looking Polish woman he once rescued who is standing among them.

Everyone is silent.

Yan: You can't let them take me away. They are sending us to certain death. Wanda?!

The girl looks down.

One of his friends: You are not Yan, you are Yankel. You are a Jew, not Polish, and there's nothing we can do about it.

Two Germans pick up Yan and throw him into the crowd of elderly Jews, along with the rabbis, Solomon, the coachman, and the teacher. They are all miserable and silent.

***

Documentary footage of the Warsaw ghetto.
More concentration camps are being built.
Trains packed with prisoners are running nonstop.
None of them knows what lies ahead. Some are still smiling.
Scenes of burning and pillaging of Jewish towns.
Nazis celebrating new year's eve of 1940 in Warsaw.

***

Jaffa. Outside Rav Ashlag's home.
Rav Ashlag trudges toward his house.
A fifteen-year-old boy is waiting for him at the door.

The boy: Are you Rav Ashlag?

Rav Ashlag: Yes.

The boy: My name is Zyama. Rav Baruch sent me. He ordered me to find you and tell you everything.

Rav Ashlag leans down to look at the boy.

Rav Ashlag: Is he dead?

Zyama: No.

Rav Ashlag *(sighs with relief)*: Come inside, Zyama.

***

Poland. Jewish village.
Documentary footage of a pogrom.
Burning houses.

Fascist rioters drag a young woman by the hair into the street. Another group is shooting a crowd of Jews in a yard.
People are running through the street in panic.
Germans, roaring with laughter, are chasing them down on motorcycles.

Zyama's voice: We knew that only old Baruch could save us.

A group of Jews—elderly, young, and women with children—is running toward Baruch's house. Old Baruch, his bushy hair completely white by now, is standing on the doorstep.

Voices: Save us, Baruch! They are burning down our houses!

Baruch *(harshly)*: Stop howling! Get inside, all of you!

The small crowd is pushing and shoving in an effort to enter Baruch's house.
Baruch remains by the door. He is looking into the skies at a cluster of fast- approaching clouds.
He can see a ghostly image of German soldiers, their sleeves rolled up, walking through the burning fields, driving their motorcycles.
Baruch opens his mouth in a wide grimace, full of rotten teeth, and shakes his fist at the sky.

Baruch: And still, I love you!

He slams the door shut.
The frightened Jews huddle together, barely fitting inside Baruch's small house.
They all look at Baruch with hope.
Women are holding their babies tightly to their chests.
Everyone is silent.
No one is crying.

Baruch: So, cursing the Creator, aren't you?! Silence! I have talked to Him just now. Everything is going to be fine.

***

Jaffa. Rav Ashlag's house.
Rav Ashlag and Rivka are listening attentively to Zyama.

Zyama: We were all sitting very quietly. Everyone knew that he was talking to the Creator. And if the Creator had promised something, then... (*Looks at Rivka and Rav Ashlag back and forth and says shyly*) Do you have a little something to eat?

Rivka is rummaging in her pockets and takes out a piece of dry bread.

Rivka *(to Rav Ashlag)*: I was saving it for Rachel, but I forgot to give it to her.

Zyama bites eagerly into the dry bread.

Zyama: I came to you as soon as I could. First I went to Jerusalem, and they told me there that you were in Jaffa. They didn't give us any food on the ship. And speaking of the journey, you wouldn't believe all the miracles that happened to me.

Where was I? Oh, yes, suddenly I see that Baruch is looking straight at me. He walked up to me and told me in a low voice, so that no one could hear...

***

Poland. Jewish village.
Baruch's house.

Baruch: You are going to Jerusalem.

Zyama *(frightened)*: Which Jerusalem?!

Baruch: The capital of the world.

Zyama: To the land of Israel?! How will I get there?

Baruch *(whispering quickly)*: You will get to Jerusalem. The road will be smooth. You will find Rav Ashlag and tell him everything.

Zyama: But I can't, I have a mother and sisters here.

Baruch: Silence! I told you to go and that's that. I will take care of your mother and sisters.

We can hear motorcycles stopping outside the house.
The Nazis are drunk.
They look inside the house through the cracks between the boards.
They see the group of Jews crowded there.
They laugh and try to break down the door.

***

Inside Baruch's house.

Baruch *(to Zyama)*: If you only knew, you little Jew, with whom you are going to meet! *(Suddenly he squints, his eyes are full of tears)* Don't look at me! Don't tell him! No, tell him, tell him Baruch was crying with happiness!

We can hear the Germans talking outside.
Through the cracks, we can see them running toward the house holding jugs of gasoline.

***

Jaffa. Rav Ashlag's house.

Zyama: He said to me – I was repeating these words all the time to memorize them – he said...

***

Jewish village. Baruch's house.
People are howling with fear.
The Nazis are dousing the house with gasoline.

Baruch *(oblivious to the situation, whispers to Zyama)*: Tell him, the High Priest,[70] the greatest of the great, that I, Baruch – a funny bird, a drunkard and a zero - ask for his forgiveness on everything. I leave in happiness for I had the privilege of connecting to a great soul, whom the Creator loves so much. And furthermore, tell him that nothing should stop him. *The Book of Zohar* must reach all those miserable people.

***

Jaffa. Rav Ashlag's house.
Everyone is silent.
Rivka is crying softly.

Zyama: And then there was a miracle. Baruch pushed me up through the chimney onto the roof. I managed to hide in the bushes and I saw everything.

---

70 The High Priest is one who has acquired the quality of love and bestowal to the fullest, who has obtained complete faith and love for the Creator and for all creations.

***

Jewish village.

Baruch's house is burning.

Zyama's voice: They set the house on fire. Oh, how it burned!

***

Jaffa.

Zyama *(suddenly in a low voice)*: And no one inside was screaming.

Rav Ashlag sits up in his chair.

***

Jewish village. The house is ablaze.

The Nazis surround it nervously.

We can hear them speaking in German:

-Are they in there?

-Well, you saw them with your own eyes!

-Why aren't they squealing?!

-To hell with them!

-I don't like this one bit!

Zyama's voice: Neither the women, nor the children, nobody was screaming. The house burned to the ground.

Zyama's face, looking through the bushes, his eyes reflecting the glow of the flames.

Zyama's voice: I saw how those Nazis looked at the house.

***

Jaffa. Rav Ashlag's house.

Zyama *(in triumph)*: They shit their pants!

***

Jewish village. Baruch's house is engulfed in flames.

A wall collapses, then another one, finally the roof caves in.

Zyama's voice: I wanted so much to run away, I could barely stand the fear. But I stayed. My mother and five sisters were in there.

Baruch's house is gone.

Zyama's voice: When the fire died out, I saw the Nazis rummaging through the ashes.

***

Jaffa. Rav Ashlag's house.
The eyes of Zyama.
The eyes of Rav Ashlag.

Zyama *(whispering)*: There was no one there, I swear. When they were gone, I checked it myself. The Nazis left everything and ran away from that house. *(In a barely audible voice)* But there was something else. (*Turns silent*)

Rav Ashlag: What? What did you see?

Zyama *(sighing)*: I saw Rav Baruch and all our Jews, and my mother, and my little sisters. I saw all of them.

Rav Ashlag: Where?

Zyama *(triumphantly)*: I swear, I could see... a flock of white birds rising up above the forest. They were flying here, to the land of Israel, to the south.

Rav Ashlag's eyes widen with surprise.

Zyama's voice: Why do you seem so surprised? Everyone knew old Baruch is a kabbalist and that he could perform miracles. He saved them.

Rav Ashlag stands up and starts walking along the wall.

Rivka's voice: Do you have a place to stay, Zyama?

Zyama: When my mother and sisters come, we will rent a place.

Rivka: Until then, stay with us.

Zyama: Thank you.

Rav Ashlag is standing by the wall looking at Rivka and Zyama.

Rivka *(raising her eyes at him)*: Let him stay with us. We managed to feed nine souls, we will manage with ten. Why are you looking at me like this?

Rav Ashlag: We are going back to Jerusalem. I have to be there. Thank you, my beloved wife.

***

Jerusalem, 1940.
Documentary footage.
Ben-Gurion is carried on the arms of supporters at a demonstration in Tel Aviv. Jabotinsky shakes a fist at a gathering in New York.

***

More footage.
The Warsaw ghetto. Corpses are being tossed into a mass grave.

***

Tel Aviv.
A few pages from the Labor Party newspaper, then pages from the Revisionist Party newspaper.
The dispute between the parties spills onto the streets. Demonstrators fight in the streets of Tel Aviv.

***

Footage from the Warsaw ghetto.
A terrible famine, emaciated faces of children dying in the streets.

***

Jerusalem. Night. Classroom.
Rav Ashlag slams his fist on the table in despair.
His students have never seen him like that before.

Rav Ashlag: The time it takes me to finish my books, prepare them for print, get them published... it takes too long! Meanwhile, every minute is priceless.

Chaim: Maybe we should give out leaflets on the streets?

Shimon: There has to be something better, substantial yet accessible.

Baruch: I've got it! *(Looks around at everybody)* A newspaper!

Rav Ashlag's hand freezes in mid air.
He looks at Baruch swiftly.

Rav Ashlag: A newspaper?! Of course! A newspaper! I can write and publish immediately! Why didn't I think about it earlier?! The question is, where will we get the money?

Chaim *(confidently)*: We will find money, don't worry about that!

***

Night. Rav Ashlag's house.

He is writing vigorously.

Cigarette after cigarette is dying in the ashtray as new lines appear on the paper.

"The future of our starving brothers in Europe depends on our unity."

***

Night. The railway station.

Arab workers are loading bags of cement onto a train car.

Rav Ashlag's students are slowly moving with them, laboring under the heavy bags.

***

Morning.

Rav Ashlag is writing.

His head begins to drop toward the table.

The thin arm of his daughter, Bat Sheva, who is sitting behind him, touches his shoulder.

He wakes up and continues to write.

***

A Jewelry store.

The owner, a Turk, is weighing on the scales a gold necklace with a star of David pendant.

Shimon is standing in front of him, shifting his weight from one foot to another.

The Turk counts the money.

Shimon leaves the store.

Chaim and Baruch are waiting for him outside.

***

Day. Rav Ashlag is writing.
His head falls on the table with a thud.
The door to the room is slightly open.
Rivka is standing over him.
She tries to pry the quill from his fingers, but she can't do it on her own.
Bat Sheva is helping her open one finger at a time.
Rivka kneels down and takes Rav Ashlag's feet out of the basin with the cold water.
He doesn't wake up.

***

Road construction.
Along with Arab laborers, Baruch is laying long iron rods on the road.

***

Rav Ashlag is writing.

***

Los Angeles. Hollywood.
The film set of Charlie Chaplin's "The Great Dictator."
Aaron is standing aside with the telephone in his hand.

Aaron: You're short how much? I am wiring the money over right away! Why didn't you call me earlier? Chaim, tell the rav that we have a group here in Los Angeles. Tell him... *(shakes a book in his hand)* that I've published the book in America!... Yes, I have! Tell him that I love him more than life! Tell him that I am well! Tell him that tonight, Chaplin is bringing together all the producers to his house and I will give them the book as a present. I will tell them about the wisdom! Tell him that there is no greater joy than that! *(Aaron hangs up, his eyes are shining.)*

***

Jerusalem.
A cold printing house with broken windows.
The presses make such a terrible noise that it blankets everything.
Rav Ashlag is standing in front of the printing press.
Baruch is standing next to him.
At a distance, Chaim is warming his hands over a barrel fire.

Shimon prepares the movable type and hands it over to Rav Ashlag, who loads it into a composing stick.
The first page is printed.
Zyama picks it up and brings it over to Rav Ashlag, who examines it meticulously.
He tears the page up and begins to rearrange the type.

Rivka picks up the torn pieces of paper off the floor, puts them on the table, and lays out bread, onions, and olive oil from her basket.

Rav Ashlag is standing by one of the shattered windows and proofs the text of a freshly printed page.

Rav Ashlag's voice: "This paper, *The Nation*, is a creation that was born in pain, through hard and dreadful labor-pangs, from amidst the venom of hatred that had struck the nations... "

***

Documentary footage of the Warsaw ghetto.
An old Jew is stripped to his underwear.
Children are led into freight train cars.

Rav Ashlag: "Even the most advanced nations have locked their doors before us."

***

Documentary footage.
Transport trains deliver Jews to the death camps.

***

Jerusalem.
Pages are coming out of the printing press.
The title of the paper is *The Nation*.

Rav Ashlag's voice: "No miracle will happen unless we unite..."

***

Documentary footage.
Repeated conflicts between rival parties in Israel.
Switzerland in all its glory. People skiing in fancy resorts.

A banquet at Buckingham Palace.
All-you-can-eat contests in Texas.
Children starving to death in the streets of a ghetto.

Rav Ashlag: "We need unity, firm and unbreakable as steel."

***

Printing press.
Hands are putting newspaper pages together.
Piles of newspapers stack up against the wall.
Rav Ashlag is holding a stack of papers in his hands, his face is glowing.
He loses his balance, but Baruch manages to catch him and put him down in a chair.

Suddenly Shimon breaks out in a yemenite dance.
Chaim joins in a hassidic dance, and everyone starts dancing.
Their weary faces light up with joy.

***

Los Angeles. Night.
A Ford sedan is zooming through a night street.
It turns onto a highway by the sea.
Wind rushes in through the open window.

Aaron is smiling broadly as he drives.
His face is lit up by the headlights of oncoming traffic.

***

Chaplin's villa. Night.
Charlie Chaplin is greeting guests.
A row of luxurious cars is pulling up in his driveway.

***

A highway along the seashore.
George Gershwin is playing on the radio.
Aaron exits toward the villas.
The lights of an oncoming car blind him momentarily.

The sound of screeching brakes, followed by the sound of crashing metal.

Aaron's sedan flips over and starts to roll down in slow motion toward the sea.
Books scatter out from its back.
Like birds, they fly up, flapping their white wings, and then dive down after the rolling car, until they disappear into the night.

***

Jerusalem. Rav Ashlag is standing in the middle of a busy intersection.
People, horse-drawn wagons, buses, and cars are moving past him.
People are watching in surprise mixed with curiosity at the orthodox Jew handing out newspapers on the street.
They take the paper and immediately start reading.

Voices of the people reading *(uniting into one)*: "Oh, if each of us felt this peril personally, no one would think about one's factional belonging, for the trouble would mold us all into one dough..."***

Jerusalem.
Rav Ashlag is walking down the busy street personally handing out the newspaper to passersby.
He seemingly bows to everyone in a plea.
People take the paper and open it right away to understand what it's all about.
Rav Ashlag is looking at them with gratitude.

Voices of the reading people: "...We are like a pile of nuts, united into a single body by the sack that envelops and squeezes them. However, such fusion does not make them a single body. The only thing they lack is the natural unity from within..."

A red-haired orthodox Jew sneers in Shimon's face as he slowly tears the paper into small bits.
Shimon grabs him by his lapel, but Chaim and Baruch are quick to intervene and drag him away.
Another Jew, this one secular, takes a paper from Zyama.
He takes a few steps, then crumples it, annoyed, and throws it in the garbage.
Zyama rushes to remove it from the trash and delicately straightens the paper on his knees.

On every corner, people are reading the paper.

An elderly voice: "...to discover and to rekindle the natural love that has dimmed within us... we must understand that people's lives depend on this..."

A young voice: "...on sensing this danger... the eyes of our children are watching us..."

Rav Ashlag is walking along a narrow street.
He stops to catch his breath.
Chaim walks up to him.

Chaim: Rav, I have some bad news.

Rav Ashlag looks at him wearily.

Chaim: Aaron... he died in a car crash in Los Angeles.

Rav Ashlag is silent. He sees a young man reading the paper on the other side of the street. He sees an elderly orthodox Jew leafing through the paper. He sees a wagon driver reading portions aloud, following the lines slowly with his forefinger.
He picks up another pile of newspapers and walks down the street. Shaking with exhaustion, he continues to hand out papers to every person he sees.

***

Late at night Rav Ashlag walks back to his home.
He opens the door and sees Rivka's frightened face.

- Yehuda!

Immediately two British officers grab him on each side.
Rivka tries to reach for him, but two other soldiers stop her.
A British officer gets up from a chair in the living room.

Officer: Mr. Ashlag, you are charged with communist propaganda, forbidden in the territory of Palestine. You are under arrest.

***

Rav Ashlag is being led down the street and shoved into a car. The door slams in his face.

He is looking at Rivka who is standing at the doorstep.
She is not crying. She waves to him.

***

Police station. A whitewashed room.
A seated British officer is briskly writing something.
A few copies of *The Nation* are on his table.
Rav Ashlag is standing in front of him.
The officer raises his head.

The officer: Sign here.

Rav Ashlag signs.

The officer: Do you know what you are signing?

Rav Ashlag: It's not important.

The officer: Do you care to know who insisted on your arrest?

Rav Ashlag: No.

The officer: Very well, you are forbidden to publish your newspaper. Furthermore, you are banned from any political activity. You are free to go... for now.

Rav Ashlag turns around and walks to the door.
From behind comes the officer's voice:

-By the way, I really liked your paper, Mr. Ashlag.

Rav Ashlag stops.

The officer: You wrote here... *(finds the right place in the text and reads out loud)* "...the ties of love that bring together the nation... have atrophied and detached from our hearts; they are long gone. If we do not restore them, we shall perish and bring disaster upon the entire world."

Rav Ashlag is standing at the door looking at the officer.

The officer: Here in Palestine I can feel very strongly how all of us are tied together by a thread. You were betrayed by your own brothers.

Rav Ashlag leaves.

***

The printing house.
Rav Ashlag is standing in the doorway next to the open gate.
The machines are silent.
Movable type is scattered on the floor in disarray.
The last run of newsprint is burning in the yard.
Pieces of charred paper flutter all around Rav Ashlag.
He picks up one of the pieces on which he can still make out the beginning of a phrase: "but should we miss the calling of the hour…"

***

Rav Ashlag's house.
The branches of an old tree cast their shadows on the white ceiling.
The silence is deafening.
Rav Ashlag, pale and still, is lying in bed.
His hand is resting on a book.
A voice comes from behind the closed door:

-It is a heart attack - no doubt about it. And quite serious at that. I will give you another prescription. It calms down the brain. The thing is, my dear, that while his body is paralyzed, his brain is working with amazing intensity.

Documentary footage. June 22nd, 1941.
The Nazis invade the Soviet Union.
The first bombings. Rows of houses on fire.
Crowds of refugees on the roads.
Snapshots of triumphant Germans.

***

Jerusalem. Rav Ashlag's house.
A simple dinner at the Ashlag family.
Everybody is eating in silence.
Rav Ashlag towers above everyone in his tall chair.

A knock on the door disturbs the quiet meal.
Rivka gets up to answer it.
The British officer who released Rav Ashlag is standing at the door.
Rivka blocks his way defiantly.

- He is very sick. – She says tensely. He had a heart attack; he is just beginning to recover. You have no right to arrest a sick person.

- Don't worry, I'm here on a different matter.

Rav Ashlag approaches slowly and stands behind Rivka.
The officer hands him a letter.

-I have a letter for you, Mr. Ashlag. My cousin is a first mate on a British ship. A German sailor had given this to him. He, in turn, received it from an officer in Warsaw. It seems to have been sent six months ago. It was lying in my cousin's place until I recently noticed your name on it.

Rav Ashlag opens the letter immediately. His eyes scan quickly through the first lines:

- "Dear honorable Rav, whose greatness we failed to acknowledge. We are writing to you from the depths of pain and the void of despair."

***

Documentary footage of the Warsaw ghetto appears slowly.
Human skeletons are hobbling in the streets.

- "And not that it's hard for us - it's difficult for everyone now - but we stand guilty before you and before our people. You pleaded with us to hear you, but we were deaf and full of hatred and pride."

The tormented eyes of the emaciated rabbis are now looking straight at us.

- "We chased you away, cursed you. We were blind with rage. And here we are, locked up in the ghetto, homeless and robbed of our human dignity. All our loved ones are here: our children, our relatives, all the Jews of Poland. And all this is happening because of this group of proud criminals... us. You were right. The responsibility for what will surely befall our people lies squarely on us. It is a feeling that's impossible to bear."

Rav Ashlag is still standing in the doorway.
Across from him, the British officer is silent.
Rav Ashlag is absorbed in the letter, oblivious to everything around him.

HALT!
SPERRGEBIET!
STOP
STREFA ZAKAZANA

Documentary footage appears again.

Corpses are shoveled en masse off the streets of the ghetto and onto wooden carts.

-"We know all too well that we are not leaving this place alive. If only we'd have listened to you then! If only..."

Suddenly, the face of Rabbi Feldman appears.

He is calm, but looks extremely tired.

- "Rabbi Feldman died yesterday. He asked to give you his great love and admiration."

Rabbi Feldman smiles.

-Shmuel, the teacher, was killed for trying to protect a ten- year-old boy who was being beaten in front of everyone."

Shmuel, the teacher, beams at Rav Ashlag.

His eternal nemesis is now smiling at him.

-"Rabbi Zilber died of exhaustion."

Rabbi Zilber hardly lifts his head.

-"The redheaded coachman had told us about the time you met. He was shot trying to escape the ghetto on his way to visit his son's grave."

The coachman is waving to Rav Ashlag.

-"Grief is embracing everything. It appears that the ghetto is going to be annihilated soon."

***

Rav Ashlag remains motionless.

Rivka approaches him and takes a quick peek at the letter.

Her eyes well up with tears.

Her glance stops on the last few lines:

-"Don't stop your attempts to open our eyes, great Rav Ashlag. Bring us to unity, make us love one another. Maybe then the Creator will embrace us, your brothers, who didn't heed your warning."

***

Poland. Documentary footage.
The destruction of the Warsaw ghetto.
Transport train cars pull up close to the ghetto wall.
Nazi soldiers shove people up the ramps.

***

Rav Ashlag's hand holding the letter drops down.

-Are they all gone? – Rivka asks.

-No, - she hears Rav Ashlag's voice in response.

-Did you know it would come to that?

Suddenly she sees that his hand is trembling.

-You did all you could, – she says hastily.

She looks into her husband's eyes and sees the anguish growing in them.
She quickly continues:

-I remember how you demanded they leave. I remember! You warned them!

-Yes, - he says quietly.

-You explained everything to them!

-Not everything. I failed to explain it to them. You see, they stayed.

-You cannot blame yourself for that, Yehuda! (*she is trying to look into his eyes, but he avoids her*) You had a heart attack! You have me, your family, your students, and the rest of the world! The world that will hear you still... Yehuda?!

He is silent.
All this time, the British officer is standing there.
He doesn't speak a word of Yiddish.[71] But he is waiting patiently.
The children quietly look out from the dining room.
Rivka strokes her husband's hand.

-Calm down, Yehuda, calm down, - she whispers.

His hand stops trembling.

71 Yiddish—a language spoken by *Ashkenazi* Jews of Eastern Europe. It is a fusion of German dialects with Hebrew, Aramaic, Slavic languages, and traces of Romance languages.

-Excuse me, Mr. Ashlag, - the officer finally breaks the silence. – I have to go, but before I leave could I purchase some of your books and articles on Kabbalah?

Rav Ashlag lifts his eyes to him, but doesn't quite hear him.

-But of course! – Rivka exclaims. She turns to her husband: You see! – Please come in, - she leads the officer to the bookshelves. – You have everything here – books, articles. They're very cheap!

The officer picks up the book that Aaron published and leafs through it for a few minutes before saying:

- I'll take everything! Everything you have.

***

Jerusalem. Night. Classroom.
Rav Ashlag is wrapped in a wool blanket.
He is still weak, but nonetheless leading the lesson.

Rav Ashlag: There is a parable about a group of friends wandering through the desert, hungry and thirsty.

***

Nazi footage.
People are being thrown into the streets, shoved and beaten.
They are forced onto transport trains.

Rav Ashlag's voice: And behold, one of them has found a settlement full of food and water. He remembers his unfortunate brothers and begins to call on them and blow the horn, hoping that his desperate, hungry friends will hear his voice and come to that bountiful place.

Rav Ashlag winces in pain.
He wraps the blanket tighter and turns his head to the window.
He is met by the hollowed eyes of the ghetto children.

Rav Ashlag's voice: ...We were lost in a terrible desert along with the whole of humanity, and now we have found a great treasure trove.

Rav Ashlag's hand glides along the open book.

Rav Ashlag's voice: This book is a treasure the world is yet to discover. *The Book of Zohar* will satisfy our souls with a life-giving nectar and peace.

Rav Ashlag closes his eyes.

Zyama's voice: Our kin are being slaughtered out there, and we are talking about books. Nobody will ever understand us.

The students all turn to look at him.
Rav Ashlag is looking at him, too.

Rav Ashlag: This book holds the salvation of the entire human race, Zyama *(speaking slowly and calmly)*. The solution lies neither in political decisions nor in stronger armies or heroic feats. It is here in this book. *(His hand is resting on the book)* In it is the light of love. You open it and if your intentions are pure, you draw this love into this world. And it begins to flow outward through you and change everything.

Zyama *(crying)*: I believe you, but it's difficult… because I know I will never see my mother and sisters again.

Rav Ashlag: Your body feels the hardship. I understand you, Zyama. It can't feel the bodies of your loved ones and it hurts. But try to break through to the soul and then you will feel a different world. The souls are immortal. They are happy because they are inseparable from each other and from the Creator. *The Book of Zohar* writes about it. The time has come to reveal this to everyone.

Zyama: I know you will do it; old Baruch told me that.

***

Rav Ashlag's room.
He is writing.
Rows of medications line the table.
The Book of Zohar lies open in front of him.
A ray of light shoots up from the pages of the book, meets the ceiling, and draws bright concentric circles on it.

Rav Ashlag's voice: Know this, our flesh and blood brothers, that the essence of the wisdom of Kabbalah is the knowledge of how love descends from the heavenly heights down to our lowly existence.

Rav Ashlag follows the ray of light up to the ceiling.
He sees himself walking the empty streets of Warsaw.
He is looking through broken windows at snowstorms made of feathers from torn pillows.
A child's boot is resting sideways on a doorstep.

A prayer book lying torn in the mud.
He can feel everything that's happening there.

Rav Ashlag's voice: And we shall seek every means to save ourselves. And we will find only one.

Rav Ashlag is walking through the dreadful war footage.
He sees it all.

Rav Ashlag's voice: *The Book of Zohar* contains all of life's laws, all the happiness destined for this world.

***

Jerusalem. Room.
Rav Ashlag writes and then reads aloud what he wrote:

- "I can restrain myself no more. I have decided to open before you *The Book of Zohar*, to remove the locks that have guarded it for centuries so that by studying it you may draw the light into this world... the centuries-old mystery of *The Zohar* has now been unlocked."

The door opens and Rivka comes into the room.
She is anxious.

Rivka: The Nazis are bombing Jaffa.

Rav Ashlag: We are going to Jaffa.

Rivka: Didn't you hear what I said? The Nazis are bombing Jaffa and Tel Aviv.

Rav Ashlag: No, it is you who didn't hear what I said – pack our things, we are going to Jaffa.

***

Jaffa. Explosions can be heard.
A few of the houses are burning.
Bombs are going off at sea, raising high columns of water.
When the water settles, we see Rav Ashlag wading in the shallow water and then beginning to swim.
His strokes are powerful and within moments he's already in the open sea.
Rivka is standing on the shore, sheltering her eyes from the glare of the sun, looking intently at her husband.

Suddenly she sees a black dot on the horizon.
The dot grows bigger until it becomes a plane.
Rivka starts screaming, she is running up and down the beach, waving her hands.

Rav Ashlag is gaining speed.
He is slicing through the waves like a torpedo.
Looking up, he sees a war plane at the top point of a wingover, its wings adorned with black crosses.

The plane is preparing to attack the lonely man in the water.

Rivka *(screams)*: Yehuda-a-a!

Rav Ashlag rolls on his back.
He is floating in the water, his arms outstretched.
The Messerschmitt is about to dive.

Rivka *(screams)*: Yehuda-a! No-o-o-o!

Rav Ashlag calmly looks up at the approaching plane.
He can see the pilot.

The pilot is tightening his grip on the stick.
He takes aim.
Rav Ashlag's head is in the crosshairs.
Rav Ashlag's eyes are looking directly at him.

The pilot's eyes.
The eyes of Rav Ashlag.
The pilot's eyes again…

Suddenly the plane makes a sharp turn and begins to climb, its engine roaring. It gradually retreats into the horizon.

Rav Ashlag is floating in the water, his arms wide open.

Rivka is sitting on the sand, exhausted from screaming.

The plane disappears.
Silence falls.
We can hear only the waves crashing on the shore, then falling back into the sea.

erkorps, Gruppe 4 (Berlin-Kurmark) Berlin W 35, Großadm
Prinz Heinrichstr.1
G l e i t f l i e g e r - A u s w e i s:B
Name: Stoy NOFF
Geb.Datum: 12.März 1913
zurzeit: Luftwaffensportverein Jagdfliegerschule Werneu
hat am 22.Januar 1939 nach Ablegen
5 Flüge auf dem Gelände
theoretischen

Rav Ashlag is swimming back with steady strokes.
He emerges from the water onto the sandy beach.
Rivka covers him with a towel and looks into his eyes.
He quickly dresses and walks away, as if she's not there.
She hurries after him.

Rav Ashlag: We can go back home. They won't come back.

***

Jerusalem. Night. Rav Ashlag's house.
Light comes out of the window in Rav Ashlag's room.
We can see Rav Ashlag's profile, writing.

Rivka is standing outside his room holding a tray with a cup of coffee and a piece of rye bread.
She knocks on the door gently.
No reply.
She listens and hears what sounds like a muffled rocket explosion.
She quickly puts the tray on the floor and runs out of the house.

She is standing in front of the house and looks at the lit window.
The light that emanates from it rises upward, tracing a radiant path into the night sky.

Inside the room we can see Rav Ashlag pacing.

***

Room. Rav Ashlag leans over the book.
He reads a few lines from *The Zohar*.
Then he straightens up and approaches the window.
From the window he darts toward the wall.
From the wall back to the window, and again he sits down.
Once more, he reads a line or two.
Gets up and then repeats a peculiar pattern over and over throughout the night…

***

Classroom. Rav Ashlag's students are sitting opposite him as he reads:

"You have chosen me to bring the light into this empty world and You have placed guards on the path to You."

***

A flash of light.
A mountain side with a deep ravine running through it.
Rav Ashlag enters the dark crevice.
Faint light shines in the distance.
He takes just a few steps when a black silhouette crosses his path.
It blocks his way, a mere hundred steps from Rav Ashlag.
We cannot see the face of the figure.

-"And you said, -*(we hear the voice of Rav Ashlag)* - "Go!" And I went."

The man in black[72] starts to run toward Rav Ashlag.

-"And you said: 'If you can endure them, you will reveal the light to the world. And if you fail, a raven's wing shall obscure the world.'"

Rav Ashlag is standing still.
The black man is quickly closing in.

***

Classroom.
The students are looking at Rav Ashlag.
He is silent, but we can hear the sound of his voice:

-It's all within you. The black man is your thoughts about yourself. The white man is your thoughts about others. They have to collide.

The dark crevice.
The black man crashes into Rav Ashlag.

-Hold on to the white!

Rav Ashlag's body shudders from the blow.

-And you shall pass through!

He screams.

***

72 A man in black: Huge egoistic desires that appear a moment before the attainment of superior spiritual degrees. The struggle with them is the last test before entering the White City.

Jerusalem. Classroom.
Everybody is looking at Rav Ashlag.

-Hold o-o-o-o-on t-i-gh-t! – He screams.

Over and over again, the black lump thrusts itself into Rav Ashlag.

Rav Ashlag's voice:

-Hold o-o-o-o-on!

The classroom.

-Hold o-o-o-o-on!- Everybody echoes him.

***

The black figure knocks Rav Ashlag off his feet.
But he jumps to his feet at once.
The black shape bounces back and retreats.
He stops. He lowers his head and the head turns into a dark shell.

Rav Ashlag's scream:

-Hold o-o-on tight!

***

Jerusalem. Classroom.

Rav Ashlag: Don't let go!

All together: Don't let go!

Rav Ashlag's hands are fiercely clutching the table.
His knuckles are white.

***

Inside the crevice.
The black shell is hurtling toward Rav Ashlag, a trail of fire at its tail.
The distance between them rapidly diminishes.

***

Jerusalem. Classroom.
Rav Ashlag speaks up suddenly in a serene voice:

-To attack means to attack oneself. If we can come right now to a single unified intention - to one single thought to love as He loves, to give as He gives, fully, leaving nothing to ourselves – we will prevail. We must engage in one simple act – to hold this thought within us. Hold it!

***

The black shell explodes into Rav Ashlag, knocking him up into the air, and he flies back.
He lands on his feet.
He is shaken, but he doesn't fall.

The black man ricochets against the wall and disintegrates into ten black shadows.
A moment later, they dissolve in the air.

The light appears once again in Rav Ashlag's eyes and he is walking toward it.

***

Jerusalem.
Rav Ashlag's house.
A long table loaded with food and a large bottle of vodka stands diagonally across the living room.
Rav Ashlag is sitting in the middle of the table.
His students surround him.
The room is full of guests.

We can hear somebody's whisper: Where did they get so much food?

Someone else's whisper comes in response: I heard they sold everything they had.

Whisper *(mockingly)*: What did they have?

In reply: They had a 17th century *Book of Zohar*.

Whisper *(surprised)*: And he sold it?!

Rav Ashlag: Tonight, I have finished the first volume of the commentary on *The Book of Zohar*. *(Looking around)* The Creator has allowed me to do it. And it could mean only one thing – that the light is finally beginning to descend into this world, for the first time in many centuries.

Rav Ashlag stands up and raises his glass filled with wine to the rim.

Rav Ashlag: Before us are one hundred and twenty five degrees of the great book of light, which we can only ascend together! *LeChaim*![73]

All: Le*Chaim*!

Rav Ashlag: Today we celebrate the great holiday of victory! *Purim*![74]

Somebody coughs from the far end of the table.

Rav Ashlag: You wish to point out that I am wrong, and that today is not *Purim*?

The voice: Honorable Rav Ashlag, *Purim* is on the fourteenth of *Adar*, and today is the twenty-seventh of *Shvat*.[75]

Rav Ashlag: We are starting it early, honorable Rabbi Druker. *LeChaim*!

Rav Ashlag sips from his glass.

Rav Druker's voice: Honorable Rav Ashlag, tonight you have completed the first volume. *(He clears his throat)* Hmm... and tonight the Nazis surrendered in Stalingrad. Is this a coincidence?

Rav Ashlag: Only a coincidence, Rabbi Druker. *LeChaim*!

All: *LeChaim*! *LeChaim* to Baal HaSulam.[76]

Shimon: Can we call you Baal HaSulam from now on?

***

Documentary footage.

Military campaigns in Europe.

Successive German retreats.

Assassination attempts on Hitler.

The Americans open a second front.

Documentary footage.

The smoking crematoriums at Auschwitz-Birkenau.

---

73 *LeChaim* – A traditional toast in Hebrew meaning "to life."

74 *Purim* – A Jewish holiday signifying the aversion of an attempt to obliterate the Jews by Haman, the Persian advisor to king Xerxes. In spirituality, it is a sensation of complete freedom from the ego, one's final correction.

75 *Adar* is the sixth month in the Hebrew calendar. *Shvat* is the fifth month.

76 Baal HaSulam (Owner of the Ladder) is Rav Yehuda Ashlag's epithet, after his *Sulam* (Ladder) commentary on *The Book of Zohar*.

Exhausted, pallid-looking Jews behind barbed wire with neither hope nor life in their eyes.
Dim light falling on long rows of black barracks.
Soldiers in watchtowers; guards on patrol.

The shadow of a man in a high fur hat moving along the barbed wire fence.
Baal HaSulam is walking inside the camp.
Two patrol guards with a dog are walking toward him.
The dog starts to growl, then bark violently.
The guards, however, notice nothing.

***

Jerusalem. Classroom.

Baal HaSulam: Rabbi yochanan said, "when you see a generation upon which troubles come down like raging rivers, expect the Messiah."

Zyama: Where is he? If that's true, surely he must be here already!

Baal HaSulam: How do you imagine the Messiah, Zyama?

Zyama: He is the one man that can unite us all, otherwise, what kind of Messiah is he?

Baal HaSulam: Do you think the Messiah is a human being?

Zyama: How can it be otherwise?

Baal HaSulam: perhaps it's some kind of force?

Zyama: A force?

Baal HaSulam: Yes, a force. A force that pulls you out of this egoistic world.

Zyama: So it's not a human being?

Baal HaSulam: And what if it's a state of justice that will be established after all this suffering? Can't a country be the Messiah?

Zyama: But there is no such country.

Baal HaSulam: Such a state will be formed. It will rise eventually... but is it worth so many victims?

Zyama: No.

Baal HaSulam: No?

Zyama: I'm thinking about my mother and my sisters, about all those who were killed. I can't help it.

Baal HaSulam: Do you hate the Creator?

Zyama *(after a pause)*: Honestly? Sometimes I do.

Shimon *(jumping from his chair)*: You miserable fool!

Baal HaSulam *(interrupting him)*: No, it's alright.

Shimon: What's alright?! How can your student, our friend, say that he hates the Creator?!

Rav Ashlag: Anything toward the Creator is better than indifference.

Zyama: Even if I hate Him?

Baal HaSulam: You are already in a dialogue with Him. You are blaming Him, which means you understand that everything comes from Him, both happiness and troubles. The Messiah is the force that can reveal to you the one and only truth - that what we call trouble cannot come from the Creator. All that comes from Him is love and benevolence, and all the rest comes from you, from your petty ego. And you have to deal with it, as do all of us.

***

Suddenly, the classroom disappears.
The end of the ravine approaches.
The light is finally here.
Suddenly a black shadow[77] scuttles in front of the light, then another one, and another, and many more. The shadows converge on Baal HaSulam.

***

Jerusalem. Classroom.

Baal HaSulam *(screams hoarsely)*: Hold o-o-o-on!

All: Hold o-o-o-on!

Baal HaSulam: Hold o-o-o-on!

All: Hold o-o-o-on!

77 Black shadows are man's last self-centered desires. They make a final effort to move the person away from obtaining spirituality, aiming to cause one to want this revelation even more. Subsequently, it transpires that these shadows are actions of the Creator, who repels a person while simultaneously drawing the person toward Him.

***

Inside the crevice.
A strike to his face brings Rav Ashlag down to the ground.
He puts up his hand to block a barrage of blows, but is then hit again.
The shadows descend on him.
The white spot ahead becomes blurred.

-Hold o-o-o-n! – His voice gets weaker

Suddenly one of the shadows is yanked back, then another, and another.
A certain force lifts Baal HaSulam from the ground and he finds himself embraced by Baruch and Chaim.
Shimon and Zyama are also running toward them.

Suddenly a huge stone tears off the top of the hill and lands in their way.

***

Documentary footage.
Battles in Berlin.
The last days of the war.

***

Jerusalem. Rav Ashlag's home.
A loud festive meal.
Rav Ashlag's students frolic in a hassidic dance.

Rav Druker *(clears his throat over the din of music and singing)*: Ehmm-hmm... could I ask you something, honorable Rav Ashlag?

Rav Ashlag: Please, Rabbi Druker.

Rav Druker: You have finished another volume tonight, honorable Rav Ashlag. *(The noise subsides, everyone is listening)* And tonight, they say this terrible war is over.*(Pause)* Is it a coincidence?

Rav Ashlag: You've asked me that before, Rabbi Druker, and I've answered.

Rav Druker: I waited for the exact moment you finished writing, the instant you have placed the last period. I even asked your daughter Bat Sheva to mark the exact time. It happened to be the exact same time that Nazi Germany signed the protocol of capitulation. Ehmm... coincidence?

All eyes are fixed on Rav Ashlag.
Everyone is waiting.
Rav Ashlag looks around.

Rav Ashlag: Coincidence, Rabbi Druker, merely a coincidence. But let us drink to the conclusion of another volume… and to the end of the war, and let's always remember that there is none else besides Him. *LeChaim*!

All: *LeChaim*!

***

Berlin. Hitler's bunker. Chaos.
Officers are running in the corridors.
Some are burning documents right on the floor.
One officer is lying face down in a pool of blood.
A drunk SS officer is shouting obscenities while pressing himself against the wall.

Baal HaSulam is walking along the corridor.
Nobody pays attention to him.
He walks past the security guards, opens a heavy door, and enters a big hall.

From behind, we see a man slumped on a chair.
Only his pale hand is clearly visible, hanging feebly above the carpet.
Baal HaSulam approaches the man.
It's Hitler.
Baal HaSulam looks down at him.
Hitler raises his hand.
His lips whisper something, but no sound is coming out.
His eyes are weary, lifeless.
Suddenly he starts screaming soundlessly at Baal HaSulam, foam shooting out of his mouth.
Still, no sound.

***

Documentary footage. The war is over.
A victory parade in the Red Square.

Soldiers and officers are marching in toe in front of the tribune where Stalin and his government watch on.
People dropping Nazi flags on the wet pavement.
Americans welcome their heroes.
The French hug theirs.

Little children wearing the infamous striped prisoners' uniform come out of Auschwitz.
They show off their numbers, tattooed on their little forearms.
Military delegations are touring the camp.

***

Israel.
Baal HaSulam walks along a lengthy corridor.
He opens a door and enters an office containing a single table and three chairs.
Ben-Gurion rises from his table to greet him.
He is short and as lively as always.

Ben-Gurion: Rav Ashlag, have no doubt, I still remember our conversation, I often think about it.

Baal HaSulam: We are on the eve of founding our state, which is why I asked to meet with you.

Ben-Gurion *(sits, offers him the chair across from him)*: The *kibbutz*[78] is a prototype of our future state.

Baal HaSulam: You will have to make only one adjustment.

Ben-Gurion: You talked of unity; a *kibbutz* is unity. You talked about equality; that is the foundation of a *kibbutz*. You spoke of love, and they are living according to the principle, "love your friend as yourself."

***

Documentary footage of the first *kibbutzim*.
People are beaming with enthusiasm.

---

78 A *kibbutz* (Hebrew: "gathering," "clustering"; plural: Kibbutzim) is a collective community in Israel. Kibbutzim began as utopian communities, a combination of socialism and Zionism. Today, most kibbutzim have been privatized and have given up many of the socialistic properties of their lifestyles.

***

Ben-Gurion's office.

Baal HaSulam: The *kibbutzim* won't last! Egoists cannot build Heaven on Earth.

Ben-Gurion: But we suffered so much that it's only natural for us to become equal.

Baal HaSulam: Dear Mr. Ben-Gurion, you need to add just one thing to the concept of the *kibbutz* – the upper force. Then everything will be alright.

Ben-Gurion: After this war, you'll never be able to get them to make such an amendment. They will send you and your upper force to hell. They've lost their loved ones, their relatives, children, parents. What are you talking about?! What upper force are you talking about?!

Baal HaSulam: I know them, I am ready to explain, to clarify... to teach the wisdom of Kabbalah. They will understand everything.

Ben-Gurion: You are naïve.

Baal HaSulam: It's not me who is naïve.

Ben-Gurion: Still, we shall build here a Jewish state.

Baal HaSulam: For the whole world.

Ben-Gurion: For Jews, whom the whole world persecutes.

Baal HaSulam: For Jews to bring the knowledge about the supreme law of love to the whole world.

Ben-Gurion: That's what you call the Creator.

Baal HaSulam: This *is* the Creator.

Ben-Gurion *(pauses, looks at Rav Ashlag)*: Someone's on his way to see me now. He is an old friend of mine who went through the hell of the holocaust. You can't imagine what they did to him. He used to be so full of life, so fiery, but no more... dear Rav Ashlag, please don't burden him with your supreme law of love. People who went through these horrors, they are all very angry. They will tear you to pieces, limb from limb.

Baal HaSulam: In three years time, when you become the head of the people's council, and later the prime minister, you will have to bear the full responsibility.

Ben-Gurion: So, you already know when the state is going to be established?

Baal HaSulam: Try to listen – this state can exist on spiritual laws, and only on spiritual laws!

A firm knock on the door.

Ben-Gurion: It's him. Punctual as always. *(To Rav Ashlag)* I warned you. *(Louder, to the door)* Come in.

The door opens and a frighteningly skinny man walks in.
He is very quiet, hunched over, his eyes are weary, his smile – forced.
He greets Ben-Gurion, they hug.
Ben-Gurion helps him to sit down.
The man slowly turns his head to Baal HaSulam.

Ben-Gurion: please meet Rav Ashlag, a great idealist.

The man looks fixedly at Rav Ashlag and suddenly starts to stand up. His weak legs betray him, his head is trembling, but he manages to say:

-Yehu-u-uda!

Baal HaSulam: Yankele...

Yankel: Yehudale...

Baal HaSulam takes a step in his direction and Yankele falls into his arms, hanging on to him. His tears flow freely.

Yankele *(weeping)*: My beloved Yehuda, if you only knew how many times I remembered you there, how many times I begged for you to come to me, to explain my life to me. If you only knew, my beloved brother!

Ben-Gurion is watching the scene in disbelief.

Ben-Gurion: It seems... that you two know each other...

Baal HaSulam: We've known each other for a very long time.

Ben-Gurion's office.
An hour later.
Yankele is sitting in a chair.

He is holding Baal HaSulam's hands in his.
Ben-Gurion is sitting next to them.

Yankele: ...and afterwards came the ghetto and all that horror around it. Then there was Auschwitz, where I was loading the bodies of my brothers and sisters into the ovens, and then came my own death.

Ben-Gurion: Surely, you didn't die.

Yankele: No, I did.

Ben-Gurion: In a manner of speaking?

Yankele: You are talking to a dead person now.

Ben-Gurion: Come then, we will bring you back to life! *(He pats Yankele on the shoulder)* There is much to be done, my friend!

Yankele pays no attention to him.
He is looking at Baal HaSulam.

Yankele: Let me tell you when I knew that I was long dead. It was after my second attempt to escape. They beat me up and threw me naked into a holding cell. It had a cement floor and barely enough room to stand. I asked for death, but death didn't come. Many times I lost and regained consciousness, every time only to come back to the same nightmare and the wish for death. I can't remember how much time had passed. I woke up in this terrible, cold death chamber when suddenly I felt warmth. It was as if someone had thrown a warm blanket over me. I will never forget this sensation. I thought I was losing my mind. You know me, I was always a logical person and never believed anything I couldn't touch with my own hands. And here I was... I started to look around me for its cause.

Baal HaSulam is looking at him calmly.
Yankele grasps his hand firmly.

Yankele: And I found it. I could feel a tiny beam of light penetrating my cell through a small opening high up.

Ben-Gurion: You said it happened at night.

Yankele: It was night. But the light was shining from afar.

Ben-Gurion: Yankele...

Yankele *(raising his hand, stopping him, talking to Rav Ashlag)*: But that's not important. What was important is that I felt. I felt... love. *(Nods)* Yes, yes, this feeling stirred waves of emotions in me. How can I explain it? How can I describe this feeling of endless love, absolute perfection, complete safety and infinite happiness? What I felt in the cell was real! I can remember each moment perfectly. I understood only one thing – that it came from that almost imperceptible illumination that shone through my window. Never, never, ever have I felt anything like it. *(He searches for words)* I felt that I was alive! *(Hastily, fearing that he will be interrupted and won't manage to say something)* And I kept thinking that it was worth it... that it was well worth going through all the suffering in the world just to experience something like that, if only once.

Silence in the room.

No one wants to disturb it.

Ben-Gurion: And what happened then?

Yankele: Then, everything disappeared.

Ben-Gurion: And you were back in your cell, in the same life.

Yankele *(to Rav Ashlag)*: I immediately thought of you. You were always there, but now I began to talk to you, as if you were really there, next to me.

Baal HaSulam: It's a very rare thing what you felt, but it happens. Certain people experience this after great, inhuman, suffering. In return for the suffering the Creator allows them to taste the initial degree of the spiritual world.

Ben-Gurion: And for that a person needs to go through this hell?

Baal HaSulam: No, you don't. You don't! All you have to do is choose the path of light instead of the path of suffering. And this is exactly what I am proposing to you now. And you won't listen to me. You can reach a state of eternal bliss without being in torment first. It can happen now, in this lifetime. But you won't hear me!

Ben-Gurion: I?

Baal HaSulam: You are the head of the future State of Israel. Trust me, choose the path of light and everything will turn out differently.

Ben-Gurion: But it sounds so illusory.

Baal HaSulam: This is the only law you have to honor. You must rise above the same logic that brought the world to where it is now, rise above all the self-centered calculations the world was making before the war. Where are they now? Transcend all that seems unreal today and say, "I will build a state based on spiritual laws." Israel cannot be like the rest of the world. We can't merely exist here, aimlessly. Israel is the state of the Creator.

Ben-Gurion: And what's behind these words?

Baal HaSulam: Only one thing: To live by the law, "love your friend as yourself." Not for the sake of having a good life, but for the purpose of revealing the Creator and for that purpose only!

Ben-Gurion: And you know how to live according to this law?

Baal HaSulam: I do.

Ben-Gurion grows silent for a moment, then stands up and extends a hand to Baal HaSulam.

Ben-Gurion: Thank you, Rav Ashlag. I have a lot more to do today. *(To Yankele)* Please stay. I would like you to head the *kibbutzim* project.

Baal HaSulam gets up and walks to the door.

Yankele *(to Ben-Gurion)*: I'll be right back.

He goes out after Baal HaSulam.

***

A narrow corridor.
Yankele is facing Baal HaSulam closely.

Yankele: It won't come back anymore, this feeling, will it?

Ball hasulam: No. Such a feeling is given to a person only once. After that, it's up to him to decide.

Yankele: Do you want me to come with you?

Baal HaSulam: In such cases, you don't ask, you either leave or stay.

Yankele: I think I could help you if I handle the *kibbutzim*. I'll have to build up my strength first. Then I'll come.

Baal HaSulam: Very well.

Yankele: Are you angry with me?

Baal HaSulam: There is no coercion in spirituality, Yankele. A person follows his heart. Your heart is still in this world, despite all that has happened. You can't ignore it. But you have the beginning of a spiritual bud in you. You do. You will come.

Yankele: Yes, I will come.

Baal HaSulam hugs him, turns around, and walks down the corridor toward the exit.
Yankele follows him with his gaze for a long time.

***

Documentary footage.
The U.N. Assembly debates the establishing of The State of Israel.

***

Israel. Tel-Aviv.
People listening intently to their radios.
The U.N. Assembly votes on the ratification of The State of Israel.
People on the street congregate around public radio sets.
Tense anticipation.
The U.N. decides in favor of the establishing of The State of Israel.
A surge of exultation on the streets.
Tears of joy on people's faces.
Celebrations and festivities begin throughout Israel.

***

Baal HaSulam is holding a large sharp nail.
He proceeds to carve on the handle of his kiddush knife: "The State of Israel."
He straightens and admires the knife in front of him, showing it to his children and his students, who are sitting at the table.
He uses the knife to cut the bread.

***

Ben-Gurion, surrounded by friends and bodyguards, is walking down a corridor. Baal HaSulam approaches him. Ben-Gurion throws up his arms.

Ben-Gurion: I can't, I can't see you today, honorable Rav Ashlag.

Baal HaSulam tries to come closer to him, but two young security guards push him against the wall.
Suddenly, and with surprising agility, Baal HaSulam confidently pushes them aside and advances toward Ben-Gurion.
The guards are standing pressed against the wall, unable to move.

Ben-Gurion: It's utopian, can't you see it?!

Baal HaSulam: It's utopian to try to create the State of Israel *without* a spiritual foundation.

Ben-Gurion: We will introduce obligatory studies of the Torah in the schools and we will make the Sabbath[79] a day of rest.

Baal HaSulam: I'm not talking about that. I am talking about the purpose of the creation of the state.

Ben-Gurion: The purpose is for it to serve as a home for the Jews.

Baal HaSulam: The purpose is for it to be the house of the Creator.

Ben-Gurion: I don't have time to argue with you.

Baal HaSulam: More blood will be shed.

Ben-Gurion: Rav Ashlag, we are declaring the independence of the Jewish state on the 14th of May. Period.

Ben-Gurion walks on.
His puzzled guards are released from the strange grip of the wall and hurry after him. They look back at Baal HaSulam, who remains in the corridor, alone.

***

Night. Classroom.
Rav Ashlag is surrounded by his students.

Baal HaSulam: on May 14th, the sovereign State of Israel is going to be declared.

---

79 Sabbath (Saturday) – the seventh day of the week, counting from the beginning of the creation. In the spiritual work of a person, Sabbath is a sensation of ascent, freedom from egoism, a feeling of love.

ISRAEL IS BORN
U.S. RECOGNIZES JEWISH STATE
Proclamation by Head Of Government
gyptian Air Force Spitfires
omb Tel Aviv; One Shot Down
Special Assembly Adjourns
2 Villages Taken In Road Battle

***

Documentary footage. May 14, 1948.
Ben-Gurion stands on a stage inside a crowded hall at the Tel Aviv Museum. He raises his gavel and pauses for a moment before banging it on the podium.

Ben-Gurion: We hereby declare the establishment of a Jewish state in the land of Israel, to be known as The State of Israel. Forever.

***

Tears of happiness on people's faces.
The streets are alive with flags, dancing, music, and laughter.
The young state is celebrating its birth.
The day turns into evening, evening into night.

***

Baal HaSulam's classroom.

Baal HaSulam: But war is going to break out that very same night.

***

The night of May 14, 1948.
Suddenly the joy is interrupted by artillery fire.
Shells exploding. Panic.
The start of Israel's War of Independence.

***

Classroom.

Baal HaSulam: It's written in *The Zohar*: "At that time the sons of Ishmael will awaken the nations of the world to assemble on Jerusalem... and they will make a pact between them to destroy Israel... and they will come from seven sides... and it will be an hour of miseries for Jacob..." *(he is silent)*

Zyama: Is that it? It doesn't say any more?

Baal HaSulam: "However, they will not crush the house of Jacob but he will be saved from it."

Zyama: So they won't beat us?

Baal HaSulam: Not in this war.

***

> Documentary footage of the war.
> Explosions go off in the night.

Radio announcer's voice: Our young state has been viciously attacked by seven nations who made a criminal pact among them.

The voice of Ben-Gurion: Nothing will break us! *(The sound is full of static)* Every person capable of bearing arms...

It is overlaid with other voices: Where are your arms!?

A voice shouting from a radio transmitter: They are surrounding you, Itzik, behind you, behind you!

***

Baal HaSulam's voice: There will be a severe shortage of weapons in the early days of the conflict. But a week later, Russia and the Czech republic will begin shipping guns and ammunition.

***

> Documentary footage.
> Ships loaded with arms are approaching the shores of Israel.
> Now the weapons are being unloaded into boats.
> We can already see soldiers with rifles in their hands running across the battlefield.
> They dive into trenches. Some of them fall, shot by enemy bullets.

***

> Jerusalem. Rav Ashlag's classroom.
> His students surround him like bodyguards, devouring his every word in silence.

Rav Ashlag: The turning point will come after twenty-one days of fighting. After ten days of heavy fighting, we will capture the cities of ramla and lod and unite them with Jerusalem.

Zyama: You are almost done writing the book of light that will bring redemption to the world...

Baal HaSulam: First, will come darkness. It is unavoidable. The brighter the light, the more darkness it reveals. The world will discover pharaoh. But will people want to flee his rule?

***

Documentary footage of the end of the war.

Armored vehicles enter Jerusalem.

The Israelis breach the Egyptian fortifications in sinai.

An Israeli flag is hoisted up a pole.

The peace agreement is signed.

Baal HaSulam's voice: If you don't listen to me today, 50 years from now you will have a state weary of wars, its people robbed of ideals, sharing but a single dream – to escape this place as quickly as they can.

***

A conference hall full of people.

Rav Ashlag is standing on a stage, facing the audience.

A voice from the audience: What nonsense! Who invited him here?!

Another voice from the audience: We are celebrating victory, not defeat!

Baal HaSulam: The purpose of the state's creation is not to make a country for Jews.

Boos from the audience.

Baal HaSulam *(overpowering the whistles)*: The purpose is to build a state that will live according to the upper spiritual law.

Voices: Where was your spiritual law when we were burning in Auschwitz?

Loud voices, booing and whistling.

Baal HaSulam *(ignoring the cacophony)*: The Jews have to come to this first here, in this land, and then bring the rest of humanity to it.

More whistling and jeering:

-Get him off the stage!

-The world does not exist! There exists only the sovereign State of Israel!

-We will build a society of equals, a paradise for Jews, on our own, without any upper forces!

The audience is applauding wildly.
Baal HaSulam is waiting for the applause to subside.
The audience calms down.
Baal HaSulam is looking over the audience.

Baal HaSulam: You will not build a paradise here! Nobody needs such a state, neither you nor the world. The Creator does not dwell in it.

Whistles and shouts.
Suddenly, Baal HaSulam stops speaking and everybody quiets down.
He looks far into the distance above the heads of the people.
A few of the people in the first rows turn around trying to see where he is looking.

A surprised voice from the audience: Well, why have you stopped talking all of a sudden?

***

A flash of light.
Baal HaSulam walks out of the ravine into the light.
Baruch and Chaim appear after him.

Baal HaSulam whispers: Jerusalem.

Baruch and Chaim are beaming.
Behind them, Shimon and Zyama appear from the darkness of the ravine.

Suddenly, they bump against an invisible wall.
Zyama cries and immediately lashes against the wall. Blood drips from his hands.
Shimon hugs him, restraining him.
They silently watch their friends walking toward the White City.

Shimon's voice: Go! We will hold you in our thoughts! Just get there!

Zyama is weeping silently, pressing himself against Shimon.

Shimon: Keep your thoughts on them! On our great brothers!

Baal HaSulam is leading the way toward the wide open gates of the White City.

A voice from the audience: Hey?!

That yelp brings Baal HaSulam back into the hall.

***

The conference hall.

Baal HaSulam *(standing in front of the frozen audience, speaking very, very softly)*: Please understand me, listen to me. All you need is to wish... wish to unite with that law... that source of life! Hold this goal in front of you and you will see how the entire world wishes to see us flourish because we will be drawing the light into this lowly of all worlds. The light will enter the kingdom of darkness, the realm of the ego, and will change everything and everybody in an instant. And everyone will see in this light that the world is united, that we are all one family tied in the exalted bonds of...

Silence. Everyone is looking at Baal HaSulam.
He is focused on a point up ahead.

...Love.

***

A flash of light.
Baal HaSulam, Baruch, and Chaim are approaching the wide-open gates of the White City.
Shimon and Zyama are leaning against the invisible glass wall.
They are unable to move forward.
Baal HaSulam enters the White City.
His students linger for moment and then follow him.

-They are inside! – Shimon's excited voice is heard.

Baal HaSulam, Baruch, and Chaim are walking through the city.
Beautiful people are smiling at them.
People from all races, all nationalities.

Baruch: It is not a dream.

Baal HaSulam's voice: This is the Jerusalem of the heart.

Chaim: Lord! How great You are! How much love You have!

Suddenly Shimon no longer senses the barrier in front of him.
He can hardly believe it.
Carefully, he extends his hand forward.
It "goes through."

-Let's walk together, Zyama. *(He struggles to remain calm and keep his intention)* The main thing is – not a single thought about yourself! Come on!

They step through the barrier together.
They walk toward the city gates, restraining themselves from running.
They don't look back, only forward.
Suddenly shrieks and howls interrupt this idyll.

***

The conference hall, packed with people.
Baal HaSulam is facing the raging crowd.

Screams: Get off!!

Someone hurls a tomato at him.
He doesn't attempt to dodge it.
The tomato flies an inch from his face and splatters on the wall behind him.
The crowd roars… and disappears.

***

A flash of light.
They are walking through the White City, smiling and content.
Baal HaSulam is leading his students.

Baruch whispers: My god, the love!

Zyama whispers: My god, the love!

Suddenly dark shadows dart in front of them and disappear.

Baal HaSulam's voice: Hold o-o-o-n!

Another dark silhouette appears.
Zyama's dark double is rushing at him.

Baal HaSulam's voice: Not one thought about yourselves!

The double dissolves in mid-air.

-And when people's eyes open, – says Baal HaSulam. - They will discover that they've been living as if in a dream. And they will yearn to live according to the law of love.

***

Conference hall.
Baal HaSulam is saying these words in front of the restless crowd.
The crowd howls in return.
Baal HaSulam raises his hand and the shouting subsides.

Baal HaSulam *(calmly)*: I will speak now and you will listen.

The crowd quiets down as if hypnotized.
Everyone is looking at Baal HaSulam.
Someone tries to open his mouth to scream, but his jaws just twitch uncontrollably.
Another man opens and closes his mouth like a fish out of water.
Not a sound is coming out.

Baal HaSulam: The law of the state will be the love of others because that's the only condition for the revelation of the Creator.

Portraits of people, frozen in place, listening in silence to Rav Ashlag.

Baal HaSulam: The State of Israel will assume this law and will become the focal point of the world.[80]

Ben-Gurion is listening, holding his head in his hands.

Baal HaSulam starts to pace up and down the stage.
Everyone's eyes are fixed on him.

Baal HaSulam: These are the principles of the future society *(stops)*: The whole world is one family. The whole world is one people, living according to the law of the Creator.

---

80 In Kabbalah, The State of Israel is a state that lives by spiritual laws. "Israel" is not a name of a physical state, but rather the goal to which all of its citizens aspire—*Yashar El* (straight to God).

Portraits of people looking at Rav Ashlag.

Baal HaSulam: The world can't survive any other way in the nuclear age. The Creator built it this way. He has given people the technology, and they created the atomic and hydrogen bombs. If you don't hear me now, we will face a third and a fourth world war and the bombs will do their job. And the few that will survive the carnage will have no other choice but to take upon themselves the law of unity.

Baal HaSulam stops in the middle of the stage.
He says very clearly:

-"A person or a nation will receive according to the need. The rest will go to benefit their fellow people." *(Pause)* And if all the nations of the world accept this law, wars will be a thing of the past, for they will serve no purpose. The great crisis that is upon us will be averted, and even nature will not avenge us with floods and other disasters. Nothing but peace and harmonious balance shall be our lot – and only because each person will love his neighbor. That is all. It is all so simple. Think about it. But we have very little time.

***

Baal HaSulam turns around and leaves the hall.
Everyone follows him with their eyes.
He leaves the building and the windows to the street open to let dozens of curious heads out.
Only when he has covered some distance can we hear the renewed roar of indignant voices and screams coming from inside the hall.

He is walking down the street.
We can hear a few people trying to catch up with him, but he doesn't turn around.
It's Ben-Gurion and his two young bodyguards.

Ben-Gurion: Rav Ashlag!

Baal HaSulam stops.

Ben-Gurion: Do you believe in this?

Baal HaSulam: I can see it.

Ben-Gurion: As prophet Isaiah says, "And the wolf shall dwell with the lamb, and the leopard shall lie down with the kid; and the calf and the young lion and the fatling together; and a little child shall lead them."

Baal HaSulam: There are neither leopards, nor lions, nor calves. The little child is not a boy at all, but your desire - David - to live in accordance with the law of love and justice, in order to make the whole world as one heart. This is the meaning of this quote.

Ben-Gurion: I can't imagine what your life must be like; you're an outcast, people think you are a madman.

Baal HaSulam: I am living Him. My life is much easier than yours.

Ben-Gurion is struggling to find the right words.

Ben-Gurion: You know, I didn't want to tell you before your speech, but Yankele was killed. The first battle. They told me that he just stood up and walked in the middle of the firefight. Well, farewell, Rav Ashlag. Thank you for being so... full of light.

Ben-Gurion turns around and leaves. His young bodyguards follow him.
Rav Ashlag is standing silent in the middle of the street.

***

Night. Baal HaSulam is writing slowly.
He is wrapped in his warm blanket, but his hand is shaking and his eyes keep shutting in exhaustion.

Baal HaSulam: Baruch?!

Baruch walks in from a dark corner in the room.

Baruch: I'm here, Father.

Baal HaSulam: I have eight lines left to write. He doesn't let me finish them.

Baruch: Father, let me help you to your bed.

Baal HaSulam: No, if I lie down, there's a good chance I won't get up again.

Baruch: Then dictate them to me; I will write them down.

Baruch takes the pen and looks at his father.
Baal HaSulam closes his eyes.

Baal HaSulam: I will come out to the people… I will blow the horn… and I will tell them… *(gasps)*: "My beloved ones… *(can hardly breathe)* here it is, that great book… *(his state deteriorates by the second)* I received the power… to reveal it… to you… why do you not… hear me…"

Suddenly, Baal HaSulam falls silent.

Baruch: Father!

Baal HaSulam closes his eyes and slips down from the chair onto the floor.
Baruch leans over him.
Baal HaSulam can't move, his body is paralyzed.

-Father! Father! – Baruch screams. - Mother?!

***

Baal HaSulam is lying in his bed.
The doctor is standing next to him.
Rivka and Baruch are at his side.

Doctor: I won't sugarcoat it, Rav Ashlag, and I am telling you this on purpose so that you understand the severity of the situation. You went through two major heart attacks in a row. A normal human heart would not take it. No work for you, you hear me, absolutely nothing! No worrying, no exertion. *(He turns to Rivka and Baruch)* He must stay in bed and think of nothing.

Rivka: That's impossible.

Doctor: Well, then he will die.

Baruch: He hasn't finished his commentary on *The Book of Zohar*.

Doctor: And what does that mean?

Baruch: It means he cannot die.

Doctor *(angrily)*: Mark my words!

The doctor irately gathers his instruments and leaves the room.

***

Jerusalem. Old printing house.
Baruch is setting the type.
Baal HaSulam is sitting next to him, wrapped in his blanket.
He speaks with his eyes closed:

It is said in *The Book of Zohar*: "He who attains the law of love will fear neither the upper ones nor the lower ones. He will suffer neither disease nor afflictions, for he is connected to him and learns from him every day. He is learning the great love."

***

The *Purim* festival.
Baal HaSulam is sitting by the festive table.
The house of the Ashlags hasn't seen such joy for a long time.
A violinist starts playing a cheerful melody.
Rav Ashlag's students cavort in funny masks.
Children in costumes are dancing, grandchildren are shouting with joy.
Baruch is dancing in front of Rav Ashlag, carefully balancing volumes of *The Zohar* with the *Sulam* commentary on his head.
The books go from hand to hand.

Rivka's face suddenly shows some concern.
She sees Baal HaSulam slowly getting up from his chair and making a few moves on the dance floor.
Immediately, the violin stops playing.

Everyone is looking at him with alarm and admiration.
Baal HaSulam's eyes find Rivka's.
He smiles at her.
Everyone hails him with delight.
The music explodes again.

Baal HaSulam slowly walks around the room.
The faces of his students, Baruch, and Rivka are spinning around.
Suddenly an orthodox Jew runs into the room.
He is out of breath.
He immediately sees Baal HaSulam and walks up to him.

The Jew: Rav Ashlag, I just received a telegram from Russia. I don't study Kabbalah, and my rabbi strongly objects to you, but I don't know what to do! My relatives are there, my children are there.

***

Moscow. Stalin's summer house.
Stalin is walking in our direction along a lengthy corridor.

The Jew's voice: Stalin has issued a secret order – to send all the Jews to concentration camps, already built in Siberia, and execute the most prominent ones.

Stalin shakes his finger at someone and proceeds to lock all the doors.
He turns around and surveys his quarters.
His boot steps in the blood red carpet.

***

Jerusalem. The Ashlags' home. *Purim*.

Baal HaSulam *(to the Jew)*: And you want me to...

The Jew: Stop him! I was told that if there is one man on the face of the earth who can do it, it's you.

Baal HaSulam: You hope for a miracle?

The Jew: I have no one else to turn to. You are my only hope.

Baal HaSulam *(pause)*: There are no miracles in this world.

The Jew: So nothing can be done?

Baal HaSulam: Now that it touches you, now you are screaming!

The Jew: But my children are there!

Baal HaSulam: Millions were killed there, and you were silent.

The Jew: I brought you my troubles, my pain, and you...

Baal HaSulam: There is none else but the Creator. You should turn to Him. *(Looks around at everyone)* We are in the middle of a holiday, friends! Think about the world at large and not about your own little worlds! This is the holiday of the world liberating itself from the reign of egoism. Let's rejoice! This is the celebration of our victory over evil! *(Addressing the Jew)* Join us.

The music starts again.
Everyone resumes their dancing.
Only the orthodox Jew is standing motionless in the middle of the room.
He is weeping.
He turns around and leaves, slamming the door.

***

Moscow. Stalin's country house.
Stalin, his eyes bulging, is crawling on the carpet.
His hand extends to grab the doorknob but it misses and drops down feebly.

***

Jerusalem.
Baal HaSulam is sitting at the head of the table.
The music stops.
Everyone turns to him.
Rivka looks at his face.
Nearby, Baruch is bowing his head.
His students come closer and sit at his feet.
Baal HaSulam smiles at them.

***

A flash of light.
Baal HaSulam is sitting at the gates of the White City.

-How perfectly You have set it all up - he sighs. - Such joy to feel You, to be next to You! What great delight!

The gates of the city are wide open.
Gentle music is coming from inside mixed with laughter.

Baal HaSulam smiles.

-See, everything is as You wanted. People came. They are together. They are happy and free! They feel good with You!

***

The film ends.

Fade to black.

***

Suddenly, the film starts again.
Modern day interview excerpts roll up.

***

Moscow. Park.
We see a man with short hair.
Oleg Demidov.

-I had served nine years by that time in camps, in Siberia. I had a good reputation in the criminal world. I was certain that this was my life and this was my destiny. I even stopped worrying. I told myself – there is no other law. Man is but a wolf to another man. And one winter, it got so bad, I didn't know what to do with myself. Vodka didn't help, I got sick and tired of drugs – they didn't work either. And one night when they brought the new ones into the camp, I was talking to one of them next to a barrack and he was telling me: "Have you heard anything about Baal HaSulam?" No, I told him. – "Try finding his book and read it; it might help. There's a good Russian translation by Michael Laitman; find it." I asked my people and they found the book, in Novosibirsk, they brought it to me. It was a little shabby book in a simple white paper cover. I lay down to read it ... and was lost. That was the first time I met the most important person in my life – Baal HaSulam, Rav Yehuda Ashlag. He revealed the light to me. He saved me. He came into the world to help all of us and I am praying for him every minute of my life.

***

New York. Manhattan. Broadway.
Seth Bogner is standing amidst a busy street.

-I am a millionaire. I never had any problems with money. I had different problems that didn't allow me to live. Seems like I have everything, but in fact I feel like I have nothing. It lasted until I discovered this great man. When I say his name, I feel my heart wrenching. He is more than a father, he is closer than the closest ones. He is everything, kindness, love, safety – everything... the great teacher – Baal HaSulam. You can trust him absolutely. He will guide you to happiness. You, all of us, the whole world – to bliss. Baal HaSulam. I can talk about him forever.

***

Ankara. A busy street. People are bustling.

A young guy is sitting on a bench, he wears a short beard.

This is Mutlu.

-I am a Muslim. All my family are religious Muslims. I was living in Turkey until I was 22, then two years in England, then I moved to Australia. I remember crying when I was reading Baal HaSulam's book. This is it, the thing I was searching for all my life! The meaning of birth, of living a complete and meaningful life – every second of it, revelation of the great and bright world. It's all him, Baal HaSulam, the most precious man of all.

***

Bulgaria. Sofia.

Empty orthodox church. The candles burn.

The priest Ivan Milonov.

-I graduated from the spiritual academy in Sofia, I became a priest, and I knew everything about Christianity. I also read heaps of books on other religions, faiths, and spiritual teachings, until I found a little book. It was the book of Baal HaSulam. It had everything I had been looking for. It contained so much light that I remember myself almost losing my breath with admiration. I immediately started translating it into Bulgarian in order to bring this miracle to my people, to show them – look what a treasure I've discovered!

Baal HaSulam is the greatest, most sacred name. He told us how all of us can live in this world, all of us together, people of every religion and every nationality. All we have to do is just hear him!

***

Brussels. Café.

A middle-aged man is sitting at one of the tables outside.

He has a very kind face.

Tharsi.

-I am a film producer. I am Belgian, not a Jew. One night I was browsing the internet and came across the name, Baal HaSulam. I started to read. I lost track of time. The night passed and there was morning, daytime. I kept on reading. I read everything there was in English. Then I started listening to the lessons of Baal HaSulam's follower, Rav Laitman. He never made even a small deviation from the text. His motto was to study according to the sources. This is the source of life that I've found–the books of Baal HaSulam. It's the light that was brought into this world. The book, *The Last Generation*, is the instruction for receiving this light. What else do we and our insane world need? Just to take it for ourselves, that's it.

I personally have just one wish–to shoot a big film about Baal HaSulam so that every person in the world will know that name!

***

Jerusalem.
A man is standing across from a small two-storey house.
It's Michael Laitman.

-I'm a student of Rav Baruch Ashlag, who was the firstborn son of Baal HaSulam. The way he talked about his father was different from how we usually talk about our parents, respectfully, with love, remembering them all the time. No. He talked about his father as though describing a miracle that manifested in the world. The seven miracles of the world are nothing compared to this miracle. Next to us there lived a person who talked with the Creator the same way I'm talking to you now. He lived in the future world and described it to us. It's the world of the light, absolute love, the world of happiness that is prepared for everyone. Open his books, if only just to try them, and you will sense the light in them.

This is the light that cleanses us, the light that will end all the troubles in the world.

Further Reading

To help you determine which book you would like to read next, we have divided the books into six categories—Beginners, Intermediate, Advanced, Good for All, Textbooks, and For Children. The first three categories are divided by the level of prior knowledge readers are required to have in order to easily relate to the book. The Beginners Category requires no prior knowledge. The Intermediate Category requires reading one or two beginners' books first; and the Advanced level requires one or two books of each of the previous categories. The fourth category, Good for All, includes books you can always enjoy, whether you are a complete novice or well versed in Kabbalah.

The fifth category—Textbooks—includes translations of authentic source materials from earlier Kabbalists, such as the Ari, Rav Yehuda Ashlag (Baal HaSulam) and his son and successor, Rav Baruch Ashlag (the Rabash). As its name implies, the sixth category—For Children—includes books that are suitable for children ages 3 and above. Those are not Kabbalah books per se, but are rather inspired by the teaching and convey the Kabbalistic message of love and unity.

Additional material that has not yet been published can be found at www.Kabbalah.info. All materials on this site, including e-versions of published books, can be downloaded free of charge directly from the store at www.kabbalahbooks.info.

BEGINNERS

The Spiritual Roots of the Holy Land

The Spiritual Roots of the Holy Land takes you on a wondrous journey through the land of Israel. As you take in the breathtaking pictures of the holy land, another layer of the age-old country is revealed–its spiritual roots, the ebb and flow of forces that have shaped the curvy landscape that is sacred to billions of people around the world. At the end of the book, you'll find roadmaps of Israel, to help you locate each place you visit, whether in mind or in body, and more detasils on the forefathers who have made this land the focal point of an entire planet.

Self-Interest vs. Altruism in the Global Era: How society can turn self-interests into mutual benefit

Self-Interest vs. Altruism in the Global Era presents a new perspective on the world's challenges, regarding them as necessary consequences of humanity's growing egotism, rather than a series of errors. In that spirit, the book suggests ways to *use* our egos for society's benefit, rather than trying to suppress them.

The earlier chapters offer a novel understanding of Creation in general, and of humanity's existence on this planet, in particular. Then, we are offered a birds-eye view of history as a record of humankind's growing egotism. The final chapters address our current social and political challenges, and explain how we can use our egos to resolve them, rather than letting them ruin our collective home, as we have done so many times before.

A Guide to the Hidden Wisdom of Kabbalah

A Guide to the Hidden Wisdom of Kabbalah is a light and reader-friendly guide to beginners in Kabbalah, covering everything from the history of Kabbalah to how this wisdom can help resolve the world crisis.

The book is set up in three parts: Part 1 covers the history, facts, and fallacies about Kabbalah, and introduces its key concepts. Part 2 tells you all about the spiritual worlds and other neat stuff like the meaning of letters and the power of music. Part 3 covers the implementation of Kabbalah at a time of world crisis.

Kabbalah Revealed: A Guide to a More Peaceful Life

This is the most clearly written, reader-friendly guide to making sense of the surrounding world. Each of its six chapters focuses on a different aspect of the wisdom of Kabbalah, illuminating its teachings and explaining them using various examples from our day-to-day lives.

The first three chapters in Kabbalah Revealed explain why the world is in a state of crisis, how our growing desires promote progress as well as alienation, and why the biggest deterrent to achieving positive change is rooted in our own spirits. Chapters Four through Six offer a prescription for positive change. In these chapters, we learn how we can use our spirits to build a personally peaceful life in harmony with all of Creation.

Wondrous Wisdom

This book offers an initial course on Kabbalah. Like all the books presented here, Wondrous Wisdom is based solely on authentic teachings passed down from Kabbalist teacher to student over thousands of years. At the heart of the book is a sequence of lessons revealing the nature of Kabbalah's wisdom and explaining how to attain it. For every person questioning "Who am I really?" and "Why am I on this planet?" this book is a must.

Awakening to Kabbalah: The Guiding Light of Spiritual Fulfillment

A distinctive, personal, and awe-filled introduction to an ancient wisdom tradition. In this book, Rav Laitman offers a deeper understanding of the fundamental teachings of Kabbalah, and how you can use its wisdom to clarify your relationship with others and the world around you.

Using language both scientific and poetic, he probes the most profound questions of spirituality and existence. This provocative, unique guide will inspire and invigorate you to see beyond the world as it is and the limitations of your everyday life, become closer to the Creator, and reach new depths of the soul.

Kabbalah, Science, and the Meaning of Life

Science explains the mechanisms that sustain life; Kabbalah explains why life exists. In *Kabbalah, Science, and the Meaning of Life*, Rav Laitman combines science and spirituality in a captivating dialogue that reveals life's meaning.

For thousands of years Kabbalists have been writing that the world is a single entity divided into separate beings. Today the cutting-edge science of quantum physics states a very similar idea: that at the most fundamental level of matter, we are all literally one.

Science proves that reality is affected by the observer who examines it; and so does Kabbalah. But Kabbalah makes an even bolder statement: even the Creator, the Maker of reality, is within the observer. In other words, God is inside of us; He doesn't exist anywhere else. When we pass away, so does He.

These earthshaking concepts and more are eloquently introduced so that even readers new to Kabbalah or science will easily understand them. Therefore, if you're just a little curious about why you are here, what life means, and what you can do to enjoy it more, this book is for you.

From Chaos to Harmony

Many researchers and scientists agree that the ego is the reason behind the perilous state our world is in today. Laitman's groundbreaking book not only demonstrates that egoism has been the basis for all suffering throughout human history, but also shows how we can turn our plight to pleasure.

The book contains a clear analysis of the human soul and its problems, and provides a "roadmap" of what we need to do to once again be happy. *From Chaos to Harmony* explains how we can rise to a new level of existence on personal, social, national, and international levels.

Kabbalah for Beginners

Kabbalah for Beginners is a book for all those seeking answers to life's essential questions. We all want to know why we are here, why there is pain, and how we can make life more enjoyable. The four parts of this book provide us with reliable answers to these questions, as well as clear explanations of the gist of Kabbalah and its practical implementations.

Part One discusses the discovery of the wisdom of Kabbalah, and how it was developed, and finally concealed until our time. Part Two introduces the gist of the wisdom of Kabbalah, using ten easy drawings to help us understand the structure of the spiritual worlds, and how they relate to our world. Part Three reveals Kabbalistic concepts that are largely unknown to the public, and Part Four elaborates on practical means you and I can take, to make our lives better and more enjoyable for us and for our children.

INTERMEDIATE

The Kabbalah Experience

The depth of the wisdom revealed in the questions and answers within this book will inspire readers to reflect and contemplate. This is not a book to race through, but rather one that should be read thoughtfully and carefully. With this approach, readers will begin to experience a growing sense of enlightenment while simply absorbing the answers to the questions every Kabbalah student asks along the way.

The Kabbalah Experience is a guide from the past to the future, revealing situations that all students of Kabbalah will experience at some point along their journeys. For those who cherish every moment in life, this book offers unparalleled insights into the timeless wisdom of Kabbalah.

The Path of Kabbalah

This unique book combines beginners" material with more advanced concepts and teachings. If you have read a book or two of Laitman's, you will find this book very easy to relate to.

While touching upon basic concepts such as perception of reality and Freedom of Choice, *The Path of Kabbalah* goes deeper and expands beyond the scope of beginners' books. The structure of the worlds, for example, is explained in greater detail here than in the "pure" beginners' books. Also described is the spiritual root of mundane matters such as the Hebrew calendar and the holidays.

ADVANCED

The Science of Kabbalah

Kabbalist and scientist Rav Michael Laitman, PhD, designed this book to introduce readers to the special language and terminology of the authentic wisdom of Kabbalah. Here, Rav Laitman reveals authentic Kabbalah in a manner both rational and mature. Readers are gradually led to understand the logical design of the Universe and the life that exists in it.

The Science of Kabbalah, a revolutionary work unmatched in its clarity, depth, and appeal to the intellect, will enable readers to approach the more technical works of Baal HaSulam (Rabbi Yehuda Ashlag), such as *The Study of the Ten Sefirot* and *The Book of Zohar*. Readers of this book will enjoy the satisfying answers to the riddles of life that only authentic Kabbalah provides. Travel through the pages and prepare for an astonishing journey into the Upper Worlds.

Introduction to the Book of Zohar

This volume, along with *The Science of Kabbalah*, is a required preparation for those who wish to understand the hidden message of *The Book of Zohar*. Among the many helpful topics dealt with in this text is an introduction to the "language of roots and branches," without which the stories in *The Zohar* are mere fable and legend. *Introduction to the Book of Zohar* will provide readers with the necessary tools to understand authentic Kabbalah as it was originally meant to be–as a means to attain the Upper Worlds.

The Book of Zohar: annotations to the Ashlag commentary

The Book of Zohar (*The Book of Radiance*) is an age-old source of wisdom and the basis for all Kabbalistic literature. Since its appearance nearly 2,000 years ago, it has been the primary, and often only, source used by Kabbalists.

For centuries, Kabbalah was hidden from the public, which was deemed not yet ready to receive it. However, our generation has been designated by Kabbalists as the first generation that *is* ready to grasp the concepts in *The Zohar*. Now we can put these principles into practice in our lives.

Written in a unique and metaphorical language, *The Book of Zohar* enriches our understanding of reality and widens our worldview. Although the text deals with one subject only–how to relate to the Creator–it approaches it from different angles. This allows each of us to find the particular phrase or word that will carry us into the depths of this profound and timeless wisdom.

GOOD FOR ALL

The Point in the Heart: A Source of Delight for My Soul

The Point in the Heart; a Source of Delight for My Soul is a unique collection of excerpts from a man whose wisdom has earned him devoted students in North America and the world over. Michael Laitman is a scientist, a Kabbalist, and a great thinker who presents ancient wisdom in a compelling style.

This book does not profess to teach Kabbalah, but rather gently introduces ideas from the teaching. *The Point in the Heart* is a window to a new perception. As the author himself testifies to the wisdom of Kabbalah, "It is a science of emotion, a science of pleasure. You are welcome to open and to taste."

Attaining the Worlds Beyond

From the introduction to *Attaining the Worlds Beyond:* ... Not feeling well on the Jewish New Year's Eve of September 1991, my teacher called me to his bedside and handed me his notebook, saying, 'Take it and learn from it.' The following morning, he perished in my arms, leaving me and many of his other disciples without guidance in this world.

"He used to say, 'I want to teach you to turn to the Creator, rather than to me, because He is the only strength, the only Source of all that exists, the only one who can really help you, and He awaits your prayers for help. When you seek help in your search for freedom from the bondage of this world, help in elevating yourself above this world, help in finding the self, and help in determining your purpose in life, you must turn to the Creator, who sends you all those aspirations in order to compel you to turn to Him.'"

Attaining the Worlds Beyond holds within it the content of that notebook, as well as other inspiring texts. This book reaches out to all those seekers who want to find a logical, reliable way to understand the world's phenomena. This fascinating introduction to the wisdom of Kabbalah will enlighten the mind, invigorate the heart, and move readers to the depths of their souls.

Bail Yourself Out

In *Bail Yourself Out: how you can emerge strong from the world crisis*, Laitman introduces several extraordinary concepts that weave into a complete solution: 1) The crisis is essentially not financial, but *psychological*: People have stopped trusting each other, and where there is no trust there is no trade, but only war, isolation, and pain. 2) This mistrust is a result of a *natural process* that's been evolving for millennia and is culminating today. 3) To resolve the crisis, we must first *understand* the process that created the alienation. 4) The first, and most important, step to understanding the crisis is to *inform* people about this natural process through books, such as *Bail Yourself Out*, TV, cinema, and any other means of communication. 5) With this information, we will "*revamp*" our relationships and build them on trust, collaboration, and most importantly, care. This mending process will guarantee that we and our families will prosper in a world of plenty.

Basic Concepts in Kabbalah

This is a book to help readers cultivate an *approach to the concepts* of Kabbalah, to spiritual objects, and to spiritual terms. By reading and re-reading in this book, one develops internal observations, senses, and approaches that did not previously exist within. These newly acquired observations are like sensors that "feel" the space around us that is hidden from our ordinary senses.

Hence, *Basic Concepts in Kabbalah* is intended to foster the contemplation of spiritual terms. Once we are integrated with these terms, we can begin to see, with our inner vision, the unveiling of the spiritual structure that surrounds us, almost as if a mist has been lifted.

This book is not aimed at the study of facts. Instead, it is a book for those who wish to awaken the deepest and subtlest sensations they can possess.

Children of Tomorrow: Guidelines for Raising Happy Children in the 21st **Century**

Children of Tomorrow is a new beginning for you and your children. Imagine being able to hit the reboot button and get it right this time. No hassle, no stress, and best of all–no guessing.

The big revelation is that raising kids is all about games and play, relating to them as small grownups, and making all major decisions together. You will be surprised to discover how teaching kids about positive things like friendship and caring for others automatically spills into other areas of our lives through the day.

Open any page and you will find thought-provoking quotes about every aspect of children's lives: parent-children relations, friendships and conflicts, and a clear picture of how schools should be designed and function. This book offers a fresh perspective on how to raise our children, with the goal being the happiness of all children everywhere.

The Wise Heart: Tales and allegories by three contemporary sages

"Our inner work is to tune our hearts and our senses to perceive the spiritual world," says Michael Laitman in the poem Spiritual Wave. *The Wise Heart* is a lovingly crafted anthology comprised of tales and allegories by Kabbalist Dr. Michael Laitman, his mentor, Rav Baruch Ashlag (Rabash), and Rabash's father and mentor, Rav Yehuda Ashlag, author of the acclaimed *Sulam* (Ladder) commentary on *The Book of Zohar*.

Kabbalah students and enthusiasts in Kabbalah often wonder what the spiritual world actually feels like to a Kabbalist. The allegories in this delicate compilation provide a glimpse into those feelings.

The poems herein are excerpts from letters and lessons given by these three spiritual giants to their students through the years. They offer surprising and often amusing depictions of human nature, with a loving and tender touch that is truly unique to Kabbalists. Indeed, *The Wise Heart* is a gift of wisdom and delight for any wisdom seeking heart.

TEXTBOOKS

Shamati (I Heard)

Rav Michael Laitman's words on the book: Among all the texts and notes that were used by my teacher, Rav Baruch Shalom Halevi Ashlag (the Rabash), there was one special notebook he always carried. This notebook contained the transcripts of his conversations with his father, Rav Yehuda Leib Halevi Ashlag (Baal HaSulam), author of the *Sulam* (Ladder) commentary on *The Book of Zohar*, *The Study of the Ten Sefirot* (a commentary on the texts of the Kabbalist, Ari), and of many other works on Kabbalah.

Not feeling well on the Jewish New Year's Eve of September 1991, the Rabash summoned me to his bedside and handed me a notebook, whose cover contained only one word, *Shamati* (I Heard). As he handed the notebook, he said, "Take it and learn from it." The following morning, my teacher perished in my arms, leaving me and many of his other disciples without guidance in this world.

Committed to Rabash's legacy to disseminate the wisdom of Kabbalah, I published the notebook just as it was written, thus retaining the text's transforming powers. Among all the books of Kabbalah, *Shamati* is a unique and compelling creation.

Kabbalah for the Student

Kabbalah for the Student offers authentic texts by Rav Yehuda Ashlag, author of the *Sulam* (Ladder) commentary on *The Book of Zohar*, his son and successor, Rav Baruch Ashlag, as well as other great Kabbalists. It also offers illustrations that accurately depict the evolution of the Upper Worlds as Kabbalists experience them. The book also contains several explanatory essays that help us understand the texts within.

In *Kabbalah for the Student*, Rav Michael Laitman, PhD, Rav Baruch Ashlag's personal assistant and prime student, compiled all the texts a Kabbalah student would need in order to attain the spiritual worlds. In his daily lessons, Rav Laitman bases his teaching on these inspiring texts, thus helping novices and veterans alike to better understand the spiritual path we undertake on our fascinating journey to the Higher Realms.

Rabash—the Social Writings

Rav Baruch Shalom HaLevi Ashlag (Rabash) played a remarkable role in the history of Kabbalah. He provided us with the necessary final link connecting the wisdom of Kabbalah to our human experience. His father and teacher was the great Kabbalist, Rav Yehuda Leib HaLevi Ashlag, known as Baal HaSulam for his *Sulam* (Ladder) commentary on *The Book of Zohar*. Yet, if not for the essays of Rabash, his father's efforts to disclose the wisdom of Kabbalah to all would have been in vain. Without those essays, few would be able to achieve the spiritual attainment that Baal HaSulam so desperately wanted us to obtain.

The writings in this book aren't just for reading. They are more like an experiential user's guide. It is very important to work with them in order to see what they truly contain. The reader should try to put them into practice by living out the emotions Rabash so masterfully describes. He always advised his students to summarize the articles, to work with the texts, and those who attempt it discover that it always yields new insights. Thus, readers are advised to work with the texts, summarize them, translate them, and implement them in the group. Those who do so will discover the power in the writings of Rabash.

Gems of Wisdom: words of the great Kabbalists from all generations

Through the millennia, Kabbalists have bequeathed us with numerous writings. In their compositions, they have laid out a structured method that can lead, step by step, unto a world of eternity and wholeness.

Gems of wisdom is a collection of selected excerpts from the writings of the greatest Kabbalists from all generations, with particular emphasis on the writings of Rav Yehuda Leib HaLevi Ashlag (Baal HaSulam), author of the *Sulam* (Ladder) commentary of *The Book of Zohar*.

The sections have been arranged by topics, to provide the broadest view possible on each topic. This book is a useful guide to any person desiring spiritual advancement.

Let There Be Light: selected excerpts from The Book of Zohar

The Zohar contains all the secrets of creation, but until recently the wisdom of Kabbalah was locked under a thousand locks. Thanks to the swork of Rav Yehuda Ashlag (1884-1954), the last of the great Kabbalists, *The Zohar* is revealed today in order to propel humanity to its next degree. Ashlag's *Sulam* (Ladder) commentary has made *The Zohar* accessible to all.

Let There Be Light contains selected excerpts from the series *Zohar for All*, a refined edition of *The Book of Zohar* with the *Sulam* commentary. Each piece was carefully chosen for its beauty and depth as well as its capacity to draw the reader into *The Zohar* and get the most out of the reading experience.

More importantly, as *The Zohar* speaks of nothing but the intricate web that connects all souls, diving into its words attracts the special force that exists in that state of oneness, where we are all connected. *The Zohar* is the bridge that connects us to that source of energy and vitality that permeates all of reality.

FOR CHILDREN

Together Forever: The story about the magician who didn't want to be alone

On the surface, *Together Forever* is a children's story. But like all good children's stories, it transcends boundaries of age, culture, and upbringing.

In *Together Forever*, the author tells us that if we are patient and endure the trials we encounter along our life's path, we will become stronger, braver, and wiser. Instead of growing weaker, we will learn to create our own magic and our own wonders as only a magician can.

In this warm, tender tale, Michael Laitman shares with children and parents alike some of the gems and charms of the spiritual world. The wisdom of Kabbalah is filled with spellbinding stories. *Together Forever* is yet another gift from this ageless source of wisdom, whose lessons make our lives richer, easier, and far more fulfilling.

Miracles Can Happen: Tales for children, but not only...

"Miracles Can Happen," "Princes Peony," and "Mary and the Paints" are only three of ten beautiful stories for children ages 3-10. Written especially for children, these short tales convey a single message of love, unity, and care for all beings. The unique illustrations were carefully crafted to contribute to the overall message of the book, and a child who's heard or read any story in this collection is guaranteed to go to sleep smiling.

The Baobab that Opened Its Heart: and Other Nature Tales for Children

The Baobab that Opened Its Heart is a collection of stories for children, but not just for them. The stories in this collection were written with the love of Nature, of people, and specifically with children in mind. They all share the desire to tell nature's tale of unity, connectedness, and love.

Kabbalah teaches that love is nature's guiding force, the reason for creation. The stories in this book convey it in the unique way that Kabbalah engenders in its students. The variety of authors and diversity of styles allows each reader to find the story that they like most.

About Bnei Baruch

Bnei Baruch is an international group of Kabbalists who share the wisdom of Kabbalah with the entire world. The study materials (in over 30 languages) are authentic Kabbalah texts that were passed down from generation to generation.

HISTORY AND ORIGIN

In 1991, following the passing of his teacher, Rav Baruch Shalom HaLevi Ashlag (The Rabash), Michael Laitman, Professor of Ontology and the Theory of Knowledge, PhD in Philosophy and Kabbalah, and MSc in Medical Bio-Cybernetics, established a Kabbalah study group called "Bnei Baruch." He called it Bnei Baruch (Sons of Baruch) to commemorate his mentor, whose side he never left in the final twelve years of his life, from 1979 to 1991. Dr. Laitman had been Ashlag's prime student and personal assistant, and is recognized as the successor to Rabash's teaching method.

The Rabash was the firstborn son and successor of Rav Yehuda Leib HaLevi Ashlag, the greatest Kabbalist of the 20th century. Rav Ashlag authored the most authoritative and comprehensive commentary on *The Book of Zohar*, titled *The Sulam* (Ladder) *Commentary*. He was the first to reveal the complete method for spiritual ascent, and thus was known as Baal HaSulam (Owner of the Ladder).

Bnei Baruch bases its entire study method on the path paved by these two great spiritual leaders.

THE STUDY METHOD

The unique study method developed by Baal HaSulam and his son, the Rabash, is taught and applied on a daily basis by Bnei Baruch. This method relies on authentic Kabbalah sources such as *The Book of Zohar*, by Rabbi Shimon Bar-Yochai, *The Tree of Life*, by the Ari, and *The Study of the Ten Sefirot*, by Baal HaSulam.

While the study relies on authentic Kabbalah sources, it is carried out in simple language and uses a scientific, contemporary approach. The unique combination of an academic study method and personal experiences broadens the students' perspective and awards them a new perception of the reality they live in. Those on the spiritual path are thus given the necessary tools to study themselves and their surrounding reality.

Bnei Baruch is a diverse movement of tens of thousands of students worldwide. Students can choose their own paths and intensity of their studies according to their unique conditions and abilities.

THE MESSAGE

The essence of the message disseminated by Bnei Baruch is universal: unity of the people, unity of nations and love of man.

For millennia, Kabbalists have been teaching that love of man should be the foundation of all human relations. This love prevailed in the days of Abraham, Moses, and the group of Kabbalists that they established. If we make room for these seasoned, yet contemporary values, we will discover that we possess the power to put differences aside and unite.

The wisdom of Kabbalah, hidden for millennia, has been waiting for the time when we would be sufficiently developed and ready to implement its message. Now, it is emerging as a solution that can unite diverse factions everywhere, enabling us, as individuals and as a society, to meet today's challenges.

ACTIVITIES

Bnei Baruch was established on the premise that "only by expansion of the wisdom of Kabbalah to the public can we be awarded complete redemption" (Baal HaSulam). Therefore, Bnei Baruch offers a variety of ways for people to explore and discover the purpose of their lives, providing careful guidance for beginners and advanced students alike.

Internet

Bnei Baruch's international website, www.kab.info, presents the authentic wisdom of Kabbalah using essays, books, and original texts. It is by far the most expansive source of authentic Kabbalah material on the Internet, containing a unique, extensive library for readers to thoroughly explore the wisdom of Kabbalah. Additionally, the media archive, www.kabbalahmedia.info, contains thousands of media items, downloadable books, and a vast reservoir of texts, video and audio files in many languages.

Bnei Baruch's online Kabbalah Education Center offers free Kabbalah courses for beginners, initiating students into this profound body of knowledge in the comfort of their own homes.

Dr. Laitman's daily lessons are also aired live on www.kab.tv, along with complementary texts and diagrams.

All these services are provided free of charge.

Television

In Israel, Bnei Baruch established its own channel, no. 66 on both cable and satellite, which broadcasts 24/7 Kabbalah TV. The channel is also aired on the Internet at www.kab.tv. All broadcasts on the channel are free of charge. Programs are adapted for all levels, from complete beginners to the most advanced.

Conferences

Twice a year, students gather for a weekend of study and socializing at conferences in various locations in the U.S., as well as an annual convention in Israel. These gatherings provide a great setting for meeting like-minded people, for bonding, and for expanding one's understanding of the wisdom.

Kabbalah Books

Bnei Baruch publishes authentic books, written by Baal HaSulam, his son, the Rabash, as well as books by Dr. Michael Laitman. The books of Rav Ashlag and Rabash are essential for complete understanding of the teachings of authentic Kabbalah, explained in Laitman's lessons.

Dr. Laitman writes his books in a clear, contemporary style based on the key concepts of Baal HaSulam. These books are a vital link between today's readers and the original texts. All the books are available for sale, as well as for free download.

Paper

Kabbalah Today is a free paper produced and disseminated by Bnei Baruch in many languages, including English, Hebrew, Spanish, and Russian. It is apolitical, non-commercial, and written in a clear, contemporary style. The purpose of *Kabbalah Today* is to expose the vast knowledge hidden in the wisdom of Kabbalah at no cost and in a clear, engaging style for readers everywhere.

Kabbalah Lessons

As Kabbalists have been doing for centuries, Laitman gives a daily lesson. The lessons are given in Hebrew and are simultaneously interpreted into seven languages—English, Russian, Spanish, French, German, Italian, and Turkish—by skilled and experienced interpreters. As with everything else, the live broadcast is free of charge.

FUNDING

Bnei Baruch is a non-profit organization for teaching and sharing the wisdom of Kabbalah. To maintain its independence and purity of intentions, Bnei Baruch is not supported, funded, or otherwise tied to any government or political organization.

Since the bulk of its activity is provided free of charge, the prime sources of funding for the group's activities are donations and tithing—contributed by students on a voluntary basis—and Dr. Laitman's books, which are sold at cost.

HOW TO CONTACT BNEI BARUCH

1057 Steeles Avenue West, Suite 532
Toronto, ON, M2R 3X1
Canada

Bnei Baruch USA,
2009 85th street, #51,
Brooklyn, New York, 11214
USA

E-mail: info@Kabbalah.info
Web site: www.Kabbalah.info

Toll free in USA and Canada:
1-866-LAITMAN
Fax: 1-905 886 9697